Praise for *New York Times* bestselling author
MICHELLE SAGARA
and The Chronicles of Elantra series

"No one provides an emotional payoff like Michelle Sagara. Combine that with a fast-paced police procedural, deadly magics, five very different races and a wickedly dry sense of humor—well, it doesn't get any better than this."
—Bestselling author Tanya Huff on The Chronicles of Elantra series

"Intense, fast-paced, intriguing, compelling and hard to put down...unforgettable."
—*In the Library Reviews* on *Cast in Shadow*

"Readers will embrace this compelling, strong-willed heroine with her often sarcastic voice."
—*Publishers Weekly* on *Cast in Courtlight*

"The impressively detailed setting and the book's spirited heroine are sure to charm romance readers, as well as fantasy fans who like some mystery with their magic."
—*Publishers Weekly* on *Cast in Secret*

"Along with the exquisitely detailed world building, Sagara's character development is mesmerizing. She expertly breathes life into a stubborn yet evolving heroine. A true master of her craft!"
—*RT Book Reviews* (4 ½ stars) on *Cast in Fury*

"Each visit to this amazing world, with its richness of place and character, is one to relish."
—*RT Book Reviews* (4 ½ stars) on *Cast in Silence*

"Another satisfying addition to an already vivid and entertaining fantasy series."
—*Publishers Weekly* on *Cast in Chaos*

"If you are searching for a rich and rewarding fantasy read different from the usual fantasy fare, then you can't go wrong with *Cast in Ruin* and The Chonicles of Elantra series. Heartily recommended."
—*SciFiGuy* on *Cast in Ruin*

"Sagara does an amazing job continuing to flesh out her large cast of characters, but keeps the unsinkable Kaylin at the center."
—*RT Book Reviews* (4 ½ stars) on *Cast in Peril*

The Chronicles of Elantra
by
New York Times bestselling author

Michelle Sagara

CAST IN SHADOW
CAST IN COURTLIGHT
CAST IN SECRET
CAST IN FURY
CAST IN SILENCE
CAST IN CHAOS
CAST IN RUIN
CAST IN PERIL

And
"Cast in Moonlight"
found in
HARVEST MOON
an anthology with Mercedes Lackey and Cameron Haley

MICHELLE SAGARA

CAST IN SORROW

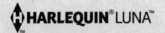

Recycling programs
for this product may
not exist in your area.

CAST IN SORROW

ISBN-13: 978-0-373-80356-9

Printed in U.S.A.

www.Harlequin.com

CHAPTER 1

To say that Private Kaylin Neya was out of her element was to master the art of understatement. Fish out of water had nothing on the groundhawk whose entire life had been lived within the boundaries of Elantra—either on the city streets or in the fiefs at its heart.

This had become obvious the moment she entered the forest, walking between Severn and Teela and surrounded— literally—by Barrani. Or as she walked through forest, at any rate, because this far across the known map, it was *all* forest. Never an aficionado of fine art, she'd nonetheless seen paintings, and the occasional diorama of ancient forests, and she had known what to expect: tall, majestic trees, shade-dappled forest floors and shafts of brilliant, solid sunlight illuminating strategic patches of charming undergrowth, with the occasional frail animal thrown in for good measure. In the paintings, there were no Barrani, no dragons, and no angry

Leontines; there were no drug dealers, no muggers, no frauds, and no rapists. The artists evoked a sense of peaceful idyll.

Hah.

Painters should have been Court diplomats—men and women who'd mastered the art of telling pretentious lies with more or less straight faces. For one, they left out the bugs. On some level, Kaylin didn't blame them—if she'd had the choice, she'd've left them out, too. Unfortunately, she didn't. The insects didn't appear to bother the Barrani. She was glad—in an entirely petty way—that they occasionally bit Severn, because it made their choice of dinner snacks racial, rather than purely personal. He didn't appear to take offense as much.

Then again, he had other things on his mind, chief among them, not tripping over inconveniently placed tree roots and landing on his face. His left eye had, over the course of two days, developed a purple-black tinge. He'd taken one wound to his upper left thigh, and two broad gashes across his left rib cage, one of which had exposed bone. He'd allowed her to heal the wounds by a few days' worth, no more.

This was a greater liberty than any of the injured Barrani allowed her, and she was tired enough not to push the point. The Barrani version of gratitude for the gift of healing involved knives—or worse—in dark alleys.

Avoiding Barrani, however, was not an option.

The Lord of the West March and what remained of his soldiers formed up at the front—and the rear—of the delegation. To either side, what was left of the party that had set out from the High Halls walked in single file. Kaylin wasn't given the option of choosing her position in that delegation: she was wearing a very fine, obviously magical, green dress, and the *dress* demanded respect, even if the wearer didn't.

Travel, some idiot in her office had said, *is fun.*

Kaylin, surrounded by somber, tense—and deeply blue-eyed Barrani—had a few words to say about *that*. Teela made clear she could say them with her mouth shut. So Kaylin, navigating forest, footpaths, and a plague of blood-drinking, buzzing insects, began to make a list. It was, in her mind, titled Things Not to Do if You Want to Have Fun During Your Involuntary Leave of (Probably Unpaid) Absence.

First on the list: avoid making deals for crucial information with a fieflord. Even if the Halls of Law were desperate for that information. The particular fieflord in question, Lord Nightshade, didn't seem to have any trouble navigating the forest, and the insects avoided him. He wore a tiara with an emerald at its peak, and robes that looked ridiculously fine in comparison to the practical Barrani armor that almost everyone else was wearing. She added a corollary to the first point: do not agree to attend a religious rite in the West March without first ascertaining that the fieflord in question did not also plan to attend.

Second on the list: do not travel with the Barrani High Court. It had seemed both convenient and smart to accept their offer of transportation; after all, the Barrani knew where they were going. Kaylin didn't. Her knowledge of Elantran streets was second to none—or close—but the West March wasn't *in* Elantra. At the time, because she'd had no idea how to *reach* the West March, getting there on her own had seemed impossible.

Impossible couldn't be worse than this. She slapped her arm and squashed an insect. The chill in the air, as she smeared insect body across the sleeve of her incredibly important ceremonial dress, could have frozen moving water.

If the imaginary person for whom the list was being created had had no choice in either of the first two, she emphatically underlined point three: if you see a strange dress in a closet that only appeared *after* you'd entered the room of your inn, *ignore it*. Under no circumstances was such a dress to be worn. Unless you were Barrani, and maybe not even then. Yes, the dress was a lovely shade of green. Yes, it was comfortable. Yes, it was suitable for the Barrani High Court—and it didn't require the help of two strong people to put on. It was even practical; the skirts were wide enough that Kaylin could run—at full stride—while wearing it.

Unfortunately, the Barrani didn't respect or revere it because it was practical. They revered it because it was the manifestation of the will of the heart of the green. Some poor sucker, shoehorned into the dress, was meant to serve in a primary role in the recitation of the regalia—the very rite that a smart person would have gone out of their way to avoid attending if they were paying attention to point one.

Fourth on the list—although technically, it might be better placed between points two and three: avoid Barrani inns. The Barrani version of an inn was known as a Hallionne. Or the Hallionne, in plural. As inns went they were creepy, in part because they were alive and sentient—and mind-reading. Best not to forget the mind-reading part. They reminded Kaylin of nothing so much as the Towers or Castles in the fiefs, and no one with two brain cells to rub together voluntarily lived in either. She felt a twinge of guilt at this because she counted Tara, the Tower of Tiamaris, as a friend. But it had been a long two days—it was a very minor twinge.

Because the Hallionne were sentient, they were able to do things that normal inns couldn't—like, say, choose the rooms in which their guests stayed. Want a different room? Too damn bad. You could stay in the room the Hallionne chose for you—or you could sleep under the trees, where the forest version of Ferals would eat your liver for a midnight snack. The Hallionne also had a pretty broad idea of physical shape and changed it apparently at whim.

The small dragon perched on her shoulder tilted his head, and after a pause, squawked in her ear.

Point five, which might also be point zero: do not take large, strange eggs home with you. They hatched into delicate, small dragons. Not that the actual dragons of Kaylin's acquaintance thought so—but honestly, the little guy had miniature dragon breath. Except he didn't spew flame; he spewed… clouds. That could melt steel without heating it first. That could kill Ferals. That could bypass the usual magical wards placed on doors.

Squawk.

Or maybe point five should be: do not have a dragon for a roommate. Because dragons for roommates attracted assassins the way Kaylin was currently attracting insects—and if you were planning on killing a dragon, you'd need enough magical conflagration to destroy a city block.

Or two.

And that much magic had certainly been enough to destroy the only home Kaylin had ever truly owned. Or rented. On the other hand, if your life goal was to live in the Palace, dragon roommates who just happened to be the only living female of the species were definitely the way to go.

The small dragon squawked again.

"All right, all right. Scratch that. Unhatched eggs are good." Especially since the act of hatching seemed responsible for the fact that Kaylin—and Bellusdeo, the maligned dragon roommate in question—were still alive. That was not the usual outcome when an Arcane bomb exploded in your face.

He squawked.

"They're bad?"

"Lord Kaylin," Severn said. She glanced at him. "Is there some difficulty?" His words were both High Barrani and stiff as boards. They reminded her, immediately, that she was surrounded by Barrani Lords who were just as stiff, but probably less friendly. You could get some warmth out of most boards by burning them; at this point, Kaylin wasn't so certain the same could be said of the High Court, or at least its present members.

Only Nightshade looked amused.

Amusing Nightshade was not high on her list of things to do, although it didn't quite make the list of things not to do she was composing.

Let's see. Six? Six: if a Hallionne offered to let you stay in his special, safe space, and the space looked like a haunted graveyard, *don't do it.*

She was aware, as she stubbed her toe for the thousandth time, that she was being more than a little unfair. But the imitation graveyard had been a bedroom, of sorts. In the heart of the Hallionne, his brothers slept.

Small and squawky dragon sidekick had breathed on their tombstones, which had caused them to wake. The waking had been disturbing. The brothers themselves, disturbing as well but in a different way—they'd adopted the forms of Barrani Lords, but the minute they'd opened their collective mouths it was clear they had very, very little in common with the Hallionne's most frequent guests.

Seven: if the Hallionne offers to let you take the portal paths through the outlands to the West March, say no. Loudly. Leontine optional. In theory, the portal paths were risky. Theory and practice aligned, but not in the ways she'd been told to expect.

In theory, the outlands existed as a kind of potential space. They were gray and formless in their natural state. An entire group—such as, say, the group that set out from the High Halls what felt like months ago—could pass through the arch of the portal intent on reaching the same destination, but only two people were guaranteed to do so.

One of them was Kaylin Neya, wearer of the dress that deserved respect.

The other was Lord Nightshade, wearer of the emerald tiara. Like Kaylin's dress, the tiara was given to someone chosen to participate directly in the recitation of the regalia. Unlike Kaylin, Nightshade seemed to approve.

She'd been surprised to enter the outlands to find the bowers of normal, if tall, trees. So had the Consort. The Consort. Kaylin wanted to add an eighth item to her growing list: *don't piss off the Consort.* But in this case, she couldn't. Kaylin understood why the Consort was angry. She also understood that given the same possible outcomes, Kaylin would stand by the choice she'd made.

She glanced at the Consort as she thought it; the Consort was dressed in white armor, a gift from the Lord of the West March. She carried a naked blade, and her hair was swept off the back of her neck. She was, on the other hand, the only Barrani to confine her hair. As if aware of Kaylin's attention, the Consort glanced at her. Her eyes were blue. They were not as dark a blue as almost everyone else's.

Teela's were certainly darker.

"Honestly, kitling," the Barrani Hawk said, frowning. "I can *hear* you thinking."

On most days, the Barrani who worked in the Halls of Law looked both arrogant and bored. At thirteen years of age, Kaylin had found the arrogance irritating. The boredom, she understood. Today, she missed it.

"Teela—"

"If I hear one more word about the insects, I swear I will bite you myself." She spoke in quiet Elantran for the first time in two days.

The rush of gratitude Kaylin felt at the sound of her mother tongue should have embarrassed her. Clearly, from Teela's expression, it embarrassed one of them. "Do *not,*" Teela continued in the same Elantran, her brows furrowing, "start to worry about me."

"But—"

"I mean it."

"Can I talk about something else instead?"

"I'm certain to regret it," was Teela's brusque reply.

As it wasn't a no, Kaylin said, "Why do so many Barrani try to divest themselves of their names?"

"Do they?"

"Illien in Barren. The walking dead in Nightshade."

"Two small examples do not constitute a multitude."

"Well, no. But I think that's what Iberrienne was trying to do."

Teela shook her head. "I think you're wrong."

Kaylin wasn't so certain. Eighth on her list, then: do not speak the True Name of a Barrani Lord who you don't intend to kill immediately afterward. She hadn't planned it. But she had seen Ynpharion's True Name, and she had seen the substantial shadows it both cast and fed. The shadow had taken the form of his name, and the shape. It was as if he had two names, identical in form, but entirely different in substance.

She didn't understand how. But she was certain that the shadow name—for want of anything else to call it—had given the Barrani Lord the ability to transform himself into the Ferals that hunted in the less safe parts of the West March and its environs. It was as a Feral that he had first approached Kaylin.

It was as a Feral that he would have killed her, too. But her dragon sidekick had conferred a type of invisibility on her. Or on himself. That invisibility had given her the time to observe, and the time to plan—even if the plan was half-assed and desperate.

She knew the True Names of both Lord Nightshade and

the Lord of the West March. She understood that in theory, this gave her power over them. But she now understood that theory was its usual pathetic mess. Neither Nightshade nor the Lord of the West March had ever fought against her knowledge. They accepted the threat she might one day pose. They did not feel threatened by her *now*.

They had, she understood, gifted her with the knowledge of their names.

But Lord Ynpharion had not. She'd spoken his name, strengthening its existence, in an attempt to burn away the shadows that clung to it. She'd succeeded. But there had been no way to ask his permission because before she had invoked his name, he wouldn't have given it. He fought her.

He fought, and he lost. This was a new and painful experience for Kaylin, and it was not one she was anxious to repeat.

Ynpharion walked to one side of the Lord of the West March, in what should have been a position of honor. To the naked eye, he was as proud, as focused, as unflappable as any other Barrani present.

But Kaylin saw beneath that surface. She saw his self-loathing, his disgust, and his fury—most of it aimed squarely at her. The only reason he kept it to himself was his fear of exposure. Kaylin held his name.

No one but Ynpharion knew it. If he exposed the truth, it might justify murderous action—but it would justify, as well, eternal contempt. He had not lost volition to a Lord of the High Court; he was in thrall to a *mortal*. If the truth remained hidden, nothing would justify an attempt to harm the woman in the green dress; it would be—according to Teela—an act very close to treason. Kaylin, being that woman, was to serve as harmoniste for the recitation.

If Ynpharion attacked her now, his chance of success was slight. So were his chances of survival. Death would put an end to the humiliation, but Ynpharion was not young. He knew that Kaylin, mortal, would survive a bare handful of years. He was not enslaved for the rest of eternity—just the pathetic span of the years remaining her.

A handful of years against the eternal contempt of the High Court. He had chosen, for the moment, to endure. But his rage was a constant battery.

She could have lived with the rage, the loathing, the disgust. It was the fear she found hard. He was afraid—of Kaylin. He was afraid of a mortal. The fear fed into his self-loathing. It was a downward spiral of ugliness.

She wasn't spared his descent.

Kaylin had no trouble finding hidden depths of self-loathing and disgust on bad days. She didn't really need to bear the brunt of Ynpharion's, as well. At the midpoint of day two she'd given serious consideration to walking him off the nearest cliff. Sadly, the forest path didn't seem to lead to a conveniently high cliff.

The only refuge Kaylin had found was in silent complaint. And, damn it, pain. The soft, supple shoes she'd taken from Hallionne Sylvanne were proof against normal wear, but they didn't provide much protection when foot connected at the toe with gnarled roots.

Teela caught her before she could fall. "Lord of the West March," she said, above Kaylin's head.

He turned, glanced at Kaylin, and nodded. "We will call a brief halt."

The two mortals were not the only people present to benefit from the break. Lord Evarrim joined them. He barely acknowledged Kaylin's existence. That was normal. He didn't spare a glance for the small dragon perched like a bad shawl around her neck, which wasn't. His lower jaw sported some of the same bruising that Severn's eye did, but it was less obvious on the Barrani face.

On the other hand, he was Barrani; any obvious injury was unsettling.

Evarrim was no longer wearing the tiara that Kaylin had once considered so pretentious. Nor was he dressed in Court robes; he wore an unadorned chain shirt and plate greaves. "Cousin," he said.

Teela's eyes narrowed.

"Are you determined to remain for the recitation?"

Even the insects fell silent.

"I am determined, *cousin,* to escort the Consort and the harmoniste to the green."

Evarrim was apparently immune to the glacial cold of Teela's voice. It was impressive; most of the office—or at least the mortal parts—would have been under their desks or scurrying for a convenient just-remembered meeting. "And not the Teller? Interesting."

The Teller was Nightshade.

Kaylin's gaze bounced between the two Barrani. Teela's eyes were a shade darker; Evarrim's were as close to green as they'd been all day. The bastard was enjoying himself. "Your concern is noted," she finally replied. "It is irrelevant, but noted."

He rose. "Very well. The Consort and the Lord of the West March have expressed a similar concern; they are, of course, more guarded." He bowed, stiffly. He actually walked stiffly. But he walked away.

"Teela—"

"Don't even think it." Teela rose, as well. She didn't march into the forest, but she left Kaylin and Severn alone with their lunch, hovering ten yards away, sword in hand.

"What was that about?" Kaylin asked—quietly. Teela was

far enough away that whispers shouldn't carry, but they might; Barrani hearing was in all ways superior to human hearing.

He exhaled. "What did Teela tell you?"

Kaylin grimaced. "What makes you think she told me anything?"

"You're fidgeting."

Kaylin shot a guilty glance at Teela's back. "She hasn't told me much that we don't already know. We know the recitation involves True Words; it's like the story Sanabalis told the Leontines. We know that the story isn't chosen by the Lord of the West March, the Teller, or the lowly harmoniste; the heart of the green decides."

"Did she explain what the heart of the green *is?*" When Kaylin failed to answer, he asked, more pointedly, "Did you ask?"

Teela had been talking about the death of her mother. So no, Kaylin hadn't really asked.

She feinted. "It has something to do with the Hallionne. I'm not sure the Barrani understand it fully." She removed the small dragon's wing when he stretched and covered half her face. "The recitation of the regalia has an effect—a lasting effect—on those who listen to the telling. It's the biggest reason the Barrani make the pilgrimage to this insect-plagued, weed-covered, Feral-infested—" She stopped as Teela glanced over her shoulder, and lowered her voice again. "The Barrani who've passed the test of name in the High Halls are expected to travel to the West March and listen to the recitation.

"There, if they're lucky, they're empowered. Somehow. Don't give me that look. I wasn't making lists. I don't know how the effect is measured. But…the ceremony has an effect."

"On all participants?" He gave the dress a pointed look.

She frowned. "I'm not sure. I'd guess no. But on some."

Severn nodded.

"Some ambitious moron on the High Council came up with a great idea. It was during one of the Draco-Barrani wars." She frowned. "I'm guessing not all adults are affected by the regalia in an obvious way. Maybe someone thought adults were less malleable. But anyway, one of the nameless High Lords suggested that if the regalia had subtle effects on the adults, it might have stronger, more useful effects on children. Those children would then be like a super-next generation, and they might make a difference in the wars.

"The High Lord of the time liked the idea.

"So twelve children were chosen. Teela was one of the twelve. Or maybe there were thirteen—they speak of twelve lost, and Teela's not lost. The children were considered gifted; smarter, faster, that kind of thing. They all came from significant families." She glanced past Teela, and caught a brief glimpse of Nightshade. "The children were brought to the West March.

"The denizens of the West March were *not* happy. Because they weren't happy, they didn't offer the visitors from the High Halls the hospitality of their homes; the children—and the Lords they traveled with—were placed in the Hallionne of the West March."

"The Hallionne that's considered unsafe by the rest of the Hallionne."

Kaylin nodded. "It wasn't considered unsafe at the time— but staying in the Hallionne was the equivalent of being told by family that they don't have room for you and you should go to the nearest Inn."

"The Barrani of the West March didn't want the children exposed to the regalia?"

"No. But most of the Barrani of the West March aren't Lords of the High Court, so they didn't have a voice. They couldn't prevent the children from appearing at the recitation—but they tried anyway. They died."

"During the recitation?"

Kaylin nodded, remembering the cadence of Teela's voice. Teela, who never really talked about anything except drinking and work. One of those Barrani had been her mother. "The children listened to the recitation. It was—it was a complicated tale. I think Teela said that a harmoniste and a Teller had been chosen by the heart of the green, and both collapsed the moment it was done. It was considered auspicious; most of the recitations have neither. Just the Lord of the West March."

"A harmoniste and Teller have been chosen for the upcoming recitation."

"I'm the harmoniste. Believe that I noticed."

"What happened?"

Kaylin shrugged. "The children changed. It wasn't obvious during the telling; it became obvious after. They'd returned to the Hallionne before it became clear how dangerous they were. They didn't apparently feel much loyalty toward the Barrani; I think most of the Lords responsible for their journey died in the Hallionne at their hands."

"How did Teela survive unchanged?"

"That would be the question." She hesitated again. "The Ferals that almost killed us—"

"Don't call them Ferals around the Barrani; it annoys them."

"They haven't come up with a better name. Fine. The Not Ferals that almost killed us are related, somehow, to the lost children the Barrani said were dead. When we were fighting in the forest before we reached Hallionne Bertolle, one of our attackers called Teela by name.

"And she answered. She called him by the name he used to use before he—before. Nightshade recognized the name: Terrano." She hesitated again. She glanced around the smallish clearing; Nightshade wasn't visible. "Severn, I think Nightshade wanted me to attend the regalia because of the lost children."

"Was one of them his?"

Kaylin blinked.

The thought had honestly never occurred to her. Nightshade wasn't married. He had no consort. But when the children had been taken to the West March—the same West March she was approaching—Nightshade had been a Lord of the High Court, and not Outcaste. She literally had no idea what his life had been like before the fiefs. He might have had a consort, a wife, of his own. Barrani loyalty was always situational; if Nightshade was made Outcaste, what were the odds that a wife of any position would choose to accompany him into the dismal exile of the fiefs?

"I…I don't know. I have no idea if Nightshade has—or had—children." And she wasn't going to ask. But the thought was arresting and disturbing, and she tried, mostly successfully, to push it aside. "I don't think the lost children want Teela dead. I think they want her to—finally—join them. It's like they think she was left behind, or held back."

"And Evarrim is aware of this."

"Evarrim is a—"

Severn cleared his throat, and Kaylin took the hint. "The whole High Court is probably aware of it by now. Terrano wasn't exactly subtle. I'd guess most, if not all, of the High Court is worried."

"They don't trust Teela."

Kaylin rose. "They're Barrani; they don't trust anyone." The small dragon sneezed in her ear. "I think," she added, glaring at the small dragon, "we're moving again."

The forests of the West March, or its environs, weren't exactly light-filled to begin with. The trees were too tall. But when evening began to set in, Kaylin missed the light. Moonlight was barely visible from where she was standing—and she'd chosen the spot because from here she could see at least one of the moons.

She stayed in range of Teela. She kept Severn more or less in line of sight. But what she wanted—what she missed about a city that was in theory vastly more crowded and consistently noisy—was a bit of privacy. There were no doors in the forest, and no small, enclosed space she could call her own.

But she didn't have that in Elantra anymore, either. The attempt to assassinate Bellusdeo had not only destroyed her flat, it had destroyed a large chunk of the building itself.

The small dragon snapped at something large and chitinous that was crawling up her arm; the damn bug didn't even crunch. "Do *not* breathe on it," she said when he opened his little jaws.

The small dragon snapped its jaws shut and whiffled.

"Kitling."

She looked up from a furious attempt to kill a buzzing, flying bloodsucker. The tone of Teela's voice made insect blood loss a triviality. She walked away from the only obvious—to mortal vision—moonlight, making a beeline for Teela.

Teela was not the only Barrani to draw weapon; the entire clearing had fallen silent.

Kaylin listened. She heard nothing.

Even the insects were quiet for one long, drawn breath. Severn unwound his weapon chain—and to her surprise, that made almost no noise, either.

The Consort lifted her chin. "From the north," she said. The Barrani turned.

In the forest, night was spreading across the ground.

CHAPTER 2

The Lord of the West March spoke three short phrases that Kaylin did not understand. Light flared in the forest, spreading across flattened undergrowth and fallen branches until it hit a wall of darkness it couldn't penetrate.

The Consort was right: the wall of darkness existed only to the north of the group; to the west, east, and south the summoned light faded naturally. As Kaylin reached Teela's side, the small dragon dug claws into her shoulders, throwing his wings wide. He almost dislodged the precariously embedded stick that kept most of her hair out of her eyes. Reaching up, she fixed this. She couldn't afford to be half-blind. She also tried to remove him; in response he batted her hands away with his head.

And a hiss.

His wings, however, were rigidly spread. They were, Kaylin suddenly realized, covering half her face—and her left eye.

She stopped trying to remove him, and instead turned to look at the moving, black wall through his wing.

"We have Ferals," she said.

The Lord of the West March was less prone to be annoyed by her inaccurate description. "Where?"

"In the wall." When he failed to answer, she added, "I see the darkness moving in as a wall. The light doesn't breech it."

"Lord Evarrim? Lady?"

"I see the…wall…that Lord Kaylin describes. I cannot see anything moving in it."

"Lord Severn?"

Severn held a blade in each hand; he came to stand beside Kaylin, and then took one step forward. He didn't set the chain spinning. "I see the shadow. I don't see what it contains."

Neither could Kaylin—with her right eye. But the translucent wing that covered the left eye clearly showed forest Ferals. She frowned. "There are three," she said. She spoke softly, squinting. "I can't be certain, but I think there are two Barrani behind the Ferals."

"Do you recognize them?"

This was not a reasonable question to ask of a mortal, even a human Hawk. "No. Neither are Iberrienne, if that's what you're asking. I think one is female. They're not obviously armed," she added, aware that this didn't mean they were harmless.

"An'Teela?"

For a long moment, Teela stared into the moving wall; the Barrani shifted formation, drawing into a tighter front line that faced north. "I see the shadow," she finally said. "Lord Evarrim, can you bring it down?"

Evarrim replied tersely, "I have been making that attempt." His tone made clear that it wasn't wise to emphasize his failure.

The darkness wasn't a flood; it was slow, but inexorable,

and as it moved, it swallowed the edge of the light, changing the shape of safety in the clearing. The Ferals seemed content to move beneath its cover; they didn't snarl, growl, or speak; they didn't charge. Kaylin glanced at Ynpharion. He was instantly aware of her, but for the first time since the Lord of the West March had led this wilderness trek, his loathing and fury were directed at something other than Kaylin.

She didn't ask him what he could see. At the moment, she knew. He saw the moving darkness, and he wanted to obliterate anything that was hidden within its folds. She readjusted the small dragon. Living masks were awkward.

"Is the darkness transforming the trees?" The Lord of the West March asked.

Kaylin frowned. "No, I don't think so."

"Does the light continue?"

That was what was wrong. "Yes. It does. It's why I can see them at all."

She heard a shout and turned; the other Barrani held their ground. "Incoming from the west."

The Lord of the West March glanced once at his sister. "Call them back," he told her softly.

The Consort's eyes widened, their color darkening. She looked as if she wanted to argue but in the end, she did as he asked. Her commands, Kaylin understood. "Lord Kaylin, stand beside me. Under no circumstances are you to now run—or fight—on your own." She lifted her chin, frowning. "Where is Lord Calarnenne?"

Kaylin froze. Nightshade was not standing within the boundaries of the Lord of the West March's light. When he'd chosen to leave, she didn't know—but she knew where he now was, because she could see him clearly. He had crossed the threshold of moving darkness, to the west of the farthest Feral, and he was now making a silent approach, using the cover of standing trees, toward one of the two Barrani who walked behind those Ferals.

As if, she thought, he had seen them. Maybe he had. Maybe the tiara that graced his brow at the whim of the heart of the green allowed it. She was only grateful that wasn't the case with Teela.

Nightshade, don't.

He failed to answer. Inasmuch as he could, he had shut her out entirely. And she knew what it would cost to force him to listen, or worse, obey.

You could not. He sounded amused. *It is true that names are cages, Kaylin. But understanding the shape of the cage does not immediately give you the key.*

They're not who they were.

No. But Terrano approached your Teela; he had no desire to kill her. Something *remains.*

"Lord Kaylin?"

"He's beyond the darkness," was her flat reply.

Teela's brows joined a moment over the bridge of her nose. She did not put her momentary disgust into words. Instead, she turned to the Lord of the West March. "If you will allow it, cousin, I will distract them while you retreat with the Consort."

He shook his head. "There are three to the west, at a greater distance. Your ability with sword has always been impressive, but I am unwilling to sacrifice you in a staying action; we have lost too many already."

"I am the only person present who might survive it."

"Yes. That is problematic in its own right. What the fief-lord chooses to do makes no material difference to his position; he is already Outcaste. We are ready."

The light in the clearing grew harsher, brighter, before he had finished. Arrows flew in a volley; some struck the Ferals. None touched the Barrani behind them, although two splintered before they could. The darkness wavered, thinning under the renewed light.

"Follow the Lady, Lord Kaylin, if you cannot see the path itself. Step on nothing outside of its boundaries." He drew sword. The Consort grabbed Kaylin's arm.

"I'm the only person who can see—"

"Not for much longer," the Consort said, voice the same texture as the edge of the sword she carried. "My brother is waking the heart of the forest, and we do not wish to be standing here when it fully responds."

The Ferals snarled and leaped; one growled what sounded like a Barrani battle cry. The small dragon squawked; Kaylin said, "Go if you can help them." He dug in instead, as the Lady began to run, still attached to Kaylin's arm.

At their backs, the call of a horn shattered the silence.

Barrani words followed, some of them wedged between the growls and snarls.

If there was a path beneath the Consort's feet, Kaylin couldn't see it, but she didn't doubt it was there. The Consort never hesitated; she didn't stumble, she didn't call a halt. The Barrani didn't require it; what she saw, they saw. The only person to break small branches or crush undergrowth or stub her toes was Kaylin.

Severn saw as Kaylin did: a bunch of trees and small plants in a nighttime sky. He was not as important as Kaylin's dress; no one grabbed his arm, no one dragged him, and no one treated him as if he was likely to get distracted and wander off.

But he sheathed his weapons for the run; the Barrani, with the single exception of the Consort, did not. The small dragon had folded his wings at the start of the run, but he perched on her shoulder, rather than draping himself across both, as he usually did. None of them looked back; none of them mentioned the Lord of the West March or those who might have stayed by his side.

Nor did they mention Nightshade; they probably hoped he'd be killed.

Kaylin was good at running. But the years in which she'd learned to run in pursuit of a criminal rather than in terror from one made this flight hard. She knew they had the numbers to stand and fight—and they'd just taken a greater part of that number on a run through moonlit forest, leaving one of the few Barrani High Lords she actually liked to stand on his own.

As incentive, it wasn't.

Even her certain sense that she wasn't a match for any of the five she'd personally spotted didn't make it better.

It is not easier for the Consort, a disembodied voice said. Nightshade's. *But she understands her duty and her responsibility. If the Lord of the West March is lost, he will be replaced. If the Consort is lost, the replacement will be difficult, and it is all but guaranteed to be a long time coming. There will be any number of Lords willing to make the attempt to fill her role—but very few will succeed, and if they fail, they are also lost to us.*

She grimaced as the top side of her feet hit the underside of a raised branch and sent her staggering. Her weight didn't unbalance the Consort, but it was close.

And if she is lost, he continued, *there will almost certainly be a succession war. You have never seen one.*

Her death won't kill the High Lord.

No. But she has not yet had children. If she perishes here, she will not. Any Barrani who can touch the lake of life will therefore be mother to the High Lord to come. I understand that politics have never been of import in your life, but you are a Lord of the High Court and you must come to understand at least the obvious basics.

A branch slapped her in the face, which caused the small dragon to hiss in fury. "Sorry," she muttered. "I'm not used to carrying a passenger."

Where are you? Kaylin all but demanded.

I am at the side of the Lord of the West March. He has not fallen, and, Kaylin, he will not. You are only a few miles from the edge of his domain, and in his domain, he has strength that not even the High Lord in the High Halls possesses.

"Nightshade," she said, in out-of-breath Elantran, "is fighting beside your brother now. They're both alive."

The Consort didn't reply. She didn't appear to have heard. But she gave the arm she was using as a rope line a brief squeeze—and then increased the pace. This had one advantage: it gave Kaylin very little time to think.

There was no obvious moment at which the forest transformed. It didn't fall away; it didn't immediately open up into an obvious clearing. The path the Barrani followed remained invisible to Kaylin; it didn't widen or flatten enough for carriages or wagons to use. Which made Kaylin wonder exactly how the carriages the High Court had abandoned would have made it here in the first place.

In spite of this, she knew when they'd arrived. Something about the forest changed; it took her a moment to realize what. She could hear birds. It was still night, but the differing shades of gray were clearer. The Barrani party slowed to a walk. They did not, in any other way, relax.

Nor did the Consort let go of Kaylin's arm; her fingers were now tingling, the Consort's grip was so tight. "Let me do the speaking," she said. To Kaylin's surprise, she spoke in very quiet Elantran.

It was a warning, of sorts. There was no one in sight— present company excepted—to speak to. Severn approached the Consort but stopped ten yards back. The rest of the Barrani remained armed; Severn chose to leave both hands loose by his side. It was hard to tell if he was paler, or if the run had exhausted him, but if it had, he failed to acknowledge it.

He waited.

Birds sang. From within the group, birds apparently answered. Kaylin felt less relieved about the sound than she had moments ago. The arrows that studded the path in rapid succession didn't help. Or it didn't help her; the Barrani surrounded her and didn't even blink; clearly this was the Barrani version of a gate check. Two of the Lords of the High Court lifted bows of their own; after a moment two arrows arched into the air, landing with audible thunks in the trees high above where the Consort stood.

The Consort raised an arm; moonlight touched her fingers and her hands, silvering her skin in a way Kaylin found disturbing. It wasn't magic—it wasn't the magic that caused Kaylin's skin to ache until it felt raw. But it wasn't natural; the moonlight touched nothing else here. Kaylin couldn't see the moon for the trees. Arrows flew again. Three, this time.

Kaylin took a step back, or tried; the Consort had not released her arm. She opened—and closed—her mouth. The Consort's eyes were midnight-blue. They were standing in the home of the Lord of the West March, the seat of his power. This was supposed to be *safe* ground. But Kaylin knew the Barrani, and there was no mistaking that eye color as the rest of the Consort's skin began, like her raised hand, to shine.

Silver had never seemed so wrong. Pale skin had never seemed so threatening. It was *not* a color Kaylin associated with life. She was afraid. She was afraid for the Consort. The fear of her hatred, her anger, and her endless disapproval was swallowed by it.

Kaylin, what is wrong?

She didn't have the words for it.

Kaylin!

Look, she told him, whispering although no one else in the world could hear. *Look through my eyes.* She felt his presence for a moment.

Tell me what's happened. Quickly, Kaylin.

She didn't use words; she didn't have to use them. He saw what she had seen. *Tell me I don't have to worry,* she thought.

You will not believe it. Not when we speak like this.

The Consort moved her hand, opening her palm and turning it up toward the sky. Three arrows flew. To Kaylin's surprise, they didn't hit anything; they were struck—in almost perfect unison, by three arrows traveling in the opposite direction. The Consort watched the arrows fall, her chin slowly lowering as she did.

Her hair was bound, like Kaylin's; unlike Kaylin's, the run hadn't dislodged any of it. Teela approached—without any signal from the Consort—and released the Consort's hair. It fell down her back in a cascade of silver as Teela once again retreated. The Consort's lips lost color.

Ask the Lord of the West March—ask him what's wrong—ask him what I should do.

Do nothing unless she releases you. She has taken the risk. Respect it.

It would be a helluvalot easier to respect it if I understood it.

He laughed. He laughed, but the laughter died abruptly as the first of the birds came to land in the Consort's upturned palm.

Except it wasn't a bird. It had the shape, but none of the movement; although it had what looked like wings, they never flapped; they were rigid and extended, a dark plane of shadow, and as the creature alighted in the Consort's open palm, she saw that it had claws. But it had no face, no head; the whole of its body appeared to be…wings. Those wings wrapped themselves around the Consort's hand, obscuring both it and the light it shed.

She grimaced. She didn't lose color—in Kaylin's opinion there was none left to lose. What she lost was illumination. Some of the disturbing light was leeched out of her exposed skin. No one drew audible breath in the clearing; no one but the Consort. Her breath was even, steady, voiceless.

Kaylin wanted to scream. She opened her mouth and the small dragon bit her ear. She turned to glare at him, which was a relief; he met her furrowed brow with wide, opal eyes. Opal, shining eyes. He also yawned, exposing almost solid teeth.

For a long moment, the shadow remained perched in the Consort's palm, and then it began to sink, vanishing into her skin as if absorbed. Light faded, then. The Consort's grip on Kaylin's arm loosened. As if that were permission, Kaylin pulled her numb arm free and slid an arm around the Consort's shoulders. She didn't ask any of the questions she desperately wanted to ask. Instead, she let the Consort lean heavily against her.

"Lord Evarrim," the Consort said. "Lord Haverel."

Both men bowed in silence; they asked no questions. The archers who had fired the first three arrows failed to materialize; the path failed to widen; the West March—if that didn't refer to this entire godsforsaken forest—continued pretty much as it had begun.

No, Nightshade said, voice soft and tinged with something unfamiliar. *It is not. Be cautious. You are almost upon the green.*

Nightshade, what was *that?*

A messenger, he replied. Unless she forced the issue, he wasn't going to tell her more. She suspected he didn't actually have the answer, and felt his keen amusement. *You are learning,* he said.

The two lords so named stepped forward. "Lady?" Lord Haverel bowed. His glance strayed briefly to Kaylin—who apparently had the ignorant effrontery to *touch* the Lady while trying to bear the greater part of her weight.

"The way is clear," she said. "Gather. We will continue to—" Her blue eyes rounded as the second bird appeared and began its gliding descent; it was joined, seconds later, by a third, a fourth, a fifth.

Kaylin didn't need to speak to Nightshade to know this was bad. She wasn't certain what this disturbing ceremony was supposed to be or do. "Lady—"

The Consort lifted an arm, lifting chin and exposing the long, white line of her throat. She pulled herself free of Kaylin, planting her feet as the two lords—Evarrim and Haverel—stepped aside. As the sleek, black forms continued to glide above her in a slowly decreasing circle, she lifted both of her arms, exposing her palms.

Both arms raised, she looked as if she were inviting embrace—but her expression was fixed; her arms were shaking. "If I falter," she said, to Kaylin's surprise, "you have permission to heal me." She spoke in formal High Barrani, her words surprisingly distinct. Kaylin waited for the disturbing glow to once again grace the Consort's pale skin. It didn't.

"You can't do this," she said, in Elantran. In High Barrani it would have sounded too much like a command. In her mother tongue, it sounded like the plea it was.

"They cannot be allowed to fly," was her soft response.

"They clearly flew *here*."

"They will not stop here, if they are given no harbor." The Consort closed her eyes. Two of the shadows alighted almost delicately, their stiff wings folding around her open hands, encasing them. Like the first such creature, they had claws, and like the first, they seemed to sink into her hands, into her skin. But this time her hands, the length of her arms, became a shade of very unhealthy gray-green as they vanished. Her shaking arms fell, as if they weighed too much to be lifted. But they stopped at the height of her heart, palms open again, and waiting.

Kaylin had seen corpses that color in Red's morgue. The Consort trembled for one immobile moment before she steadied herself and opened her eyes. Her eyes were Barrani-blue. Her arms were trembling, but she held them before her, palms once again empty and open.

Kaylin, however, had had enough. She took one look at the gathered Barrani; they were silent, blue-eyed, witnesses. None of them spoke. None of them moved.

Do not interfere—

Shut up.

The Consort was taller than Kaylin. Everyone in this party was. But her arms weren't raised above her head, where their reach would be impossible to match. Kaylin extended her own arms, and laid her hands above the Consort's, their backs resting against the Consort's icy palms. She heard one sharp, drawn breath. It was Teela's. No one spoke.

The shadows descended, gliding along a decreasing circular path as if following a funnel no one else could see. Kaylin wasn't Barrani; she flinched when they landed. But when they did, she lifted her hands from the Consort's, drawing them away from the Lady and toward herself. She moved slowly and deliberately, as if the creatures in her hands were alive and might spook.

But she did not want them touching the Consort when they began to fold their wings.

They gripped the edges of her palms with their claws; the claws sank, like small, sharp blades, into her skin. They were cold. They were cold enough they almost felt hot. Wings

folded in perfect unison, engulfing her hands. She resisted the
urge to shake them off—mostly because she knew it wouldn't
work. She wasn't the Consort. A steady, quiet stream of Leontine left her lips, with a few choice Aerian words thrown
in for good measure.

Her arms began to burn.

The small dragon, forgotten until now, rose; his claws
gripped her shoulder. He hissed, squawking and spitting; he
didn't draw breath. The shadows turned toward him as his
wings rose, batting her cheek and nose.

If her skin had melted, it wouldn't have surprised her. She
felt almost as if it should, the heat was so intense. Through
the interior of sleeves that were more hole than material, she
could see the marks on her arms: they were gold-white in
color, and bright enough that she had to squint to make out
their individual shapes. The light was not the subtle light that
had imbued the Consort—but then again, Kaylin had none
of the Consort's restraint, none of her perfect, regal dignity.

The dragon continued to squawk, which was both a comfort and a distraction; the claws of the shadows cut deeper—
but there was, to Kaylin's eye, no resulting blood. Nor did
the creatures sink into her hands and vanish, as they'd done
with the Consort.

Instead, to her dismay, they seemed to grow more solid,
not less, as the seconds passed. They were black, their wings
developing texture, height, distinguishing characteristics. The
light of her marks didn't seem to dim—but they didn't vanish,
either. The shadows weren't somehow eating them.

She thought they might become some echo of the small
dragon, because they seemed to be listening to him, mes-
merized by his squeaky, birdlike voice. He turned to look at
Kaylin, hissed loudly in annoyance, and then turned back to
his audience. They mirrored the motion. Kaylin's hands were

numb. Her arms were shaking. Shadows had no weight and little substance; what was now sitting in her palms was no longer entirely shadow.

Nor were they like the shadows cast by a gliding bird. The wings lengthened, brightened, and took on color; the indistinct, smooth surfaces of their shadow form cracked, giving way to—to *feathers*. As those wings snapped out, shards of shadow fell away, shaken off as if they were bits of shell.

Kaylin grunted. Two pairs of eyes turned to look at her; those eyes now rested above very, *very* prominent beaks. They inhaled and the golden feathers across their breasts rose; she could see white down beneath them. She had never seen birds this large. They didn't really look like birds—they looked like predators. They were far too large for her hands, far too heavy; she struggled with their growing weight because she didn't want to piss them off by dropping them.

As if aware of this—and the possible loss of dignity—they released her hands, leaping to the ground to one side of Kaylin and the Consort. When one of the Barrani Lords moved, they rose, their wings high in warning. That they didn't knock either Kaylin or the Consort off their feet was a miracle.

A deliberate miracle. One of the birds turned to face them. "Lady," it said.

Kaylin offered the Consort an arm—and her shoulder. The Consort was willing to let Kaylin absorb most of her weight, but her eyes—her eyes were a shade of gold, ringed in pale blue. They looked like the sun at the height of a cloudless sky. Kaylin had almost never seen that color in Barrani eyes before.

From the forest beyond them, Barrani approached. They were armed with bows, and they wore a different style of armor—if it was armor at all. But their hair was the ebony of Barrani hair, and it fell unimpeded down their backs. They moved slowly, and their eyes, as they approached, were the same gold as the Consort's.

"The Lord of the West March requires aid. We go now," the bird on the left said. His voice was clear, resonant; it had none of the squawk she expected of birds.

The Lady closed her eyes. Opened them rapidly, as if afraid that what she'd seen would vanish. The birds lifted wings again, and this time, the wings continued in a flurry of motion that took them into the night air.

The Barrani of the West March were silent as they watched the two birds take flight; silent as they watched them wing their way to the east, where the Lord of the West March was fighting. Only when they'd passed beyond sight—well beyond Kaylin's—did they break away.

It was clear there were complicated rituals of approach. Kaylin shouldn't have been surprised. Everything the Barrani did was complicated. But it was also clear that they'd dumped most of those rituals the minute they'd seen the birds emerge from the shadows. The gold of their eyes had given way to an emerald-green that Teela's eyes rarely reached. They were happy.

"Lady," the man in the lead said. He bowed. It was a low, complicated bow.

She felt the Consort tense—but the Consort was exhausted. There wasn't a lot of strength left for tension. "Lord Barian. This is Lord Kaylin of the High Halls; she has made the pilgrimage to the green, as all our adult kin must."

To Kaylin's surprise, he turned to her. "I am the Warden of the West March," he told her, and he offered a bow that was almost identical to the one he'd offered the Consort. The rest of the tension left the Consort's body then. Kaylin grunted as she took the rest of the Consort's weight. Barrani, while tall and slender, were not exactly weightless.

"We are in your debt, harmoniste." He held out his arms.

Kaylin's closed automatically around the Consort, and a black brow rose. So did the corners of his mouth.

"The history of the West March and the High Halls has not always been peaceful, but she is the Lady; she will come to no harm while my kin reside in the greenhome."

"She's already come to harm," Kaylin replied. She spoke in less formal Barrani.

The Warden's smile faded. "You are mortal. Rumor traveled that a mortal had been chosen by the green; it was only barely given credence. There are those who will not be pleased, Lord Kaylin. I would have been one of them. But I am grateful now that I came in person to greet the Lady, for if I had not I would not have seen…what we have witnessed this night.

"The Lady is welcome in the greenhome. She is welcome in its heart. And you, Lord Kaylin, have my welcome and my gratitude. I am in your debt."

"The Barrani hate debt," she replied.

He surprised her. He laughed. But he held out his arms again. "I will bear your burden with honor and dignity; you may travel as witness, Lord Kaylin."

Kaylin knew she couldn't carry the Consort. But she was fairly certain Teela could. "Teela?"

Every Barrani from the West March—there appeared to be eight—stiffened at the sound of the Barrani Hawk's name, and their eyes instantly lost most of the emerald-green the sight of the giant birds had placed there.

CHAPTER 3

There were good career reasons why Kaylin had never been considered a diplomat. Since she had no desire to *be* one, it had never mattered much. There were also good career reasons why Kaylin was not the on-duty Hawk at investigations that involved the upper echelons of the Human Caste Court.

But not even Kaylin could miss the sudden chill in unfamiliar Barrani eyes. She gave the Consort a tiny shake; the Consort did not respond. More than a tiny shake was impossible, given the sharp intake of breath the tiny one had caused.

Lord Barian said, "Lord Kaylin."

Teela proved that there were reasons why she was also seldom the on-duty Hawk in delicate investigations, besides the usual racial ones; the Human Caste Court didn't like being questioned by arrogant immortals. She stepped forward, moving without haste and with her characteristic, arrogant grace.

The two Hawks now bracketed the Lady.

Lord Barian's eyes narrowed. "An'Teela," he said.

"I am Lord," Teela replied. "The customs of the West March differ from those of the High Court, but surely not so greatly. Or perhaps you neglect the title as a subtle way of claiming kinship, cousin?"

Severn joined them.

The West March Barrani couldn't have failed to notice that he was mortal. They'd noticed everything else. But…Severn unsheathed his weapon blades for the first time since they'd stopped running, and as Kaylin watched the Warden's eyes darken, she lifted her chin. It was either that or cringe.

Evarrim came to stand beside Teela; Teela failed to notice him at all. Instead, she exhaled. "Kitling." She turned to the Consort, and slid arms around the back of her neck and her knees. Kaylin supported some of her weight as Teela shifted her grip. She wouldn't drop or desert the Lady while she lived.

When Teela carried the whole of the Consort's weight, she turned to face Lord Barian.

"The heart of the green has never denied me," she told him. It had the feel of a ritual phrase, but also the defiance of an insult. She glanced at Kaylin, frowned, and added, "If you have forgotten your promise to Lord Sanabalis, I have not."

"Promise? What—" Oh. "I should have stayed home, Teela," she said, in Aerian. "The Exchequer can't be worth this." But she reached up to grasp the links of the heavy gold chain she wore around her neck; the links were skin-warm. She pulled the chain out, revealing the amulet that Sanabalis had given her. She wouldn't have taken it at all, but he'd made clear that she wasn't going if she didn't. And that she was to wear it prominently at all times while she was a guest in the West March.

Arrows left their quivers and bows were pulled. The Barrani of the West March clearly didn't live in a city—or an Empire— ruled by a Dragon, but they knew what the amulet meant.

"I really hope you're not enjoying this," Kaylin said out of the corner of her mouth.

"How uncharitable," Teela replied. Her eyes were the same blue as Barian's, but her lips were now curved in a hard, tight smile. Lifting her voice, she switched to High Barrani. "I introduce Lord Severn. He has passed the Tower's test, and the test of name; he is a Lord of the High Court, and he has come to affirm his claim in the heart of the green."

"Impossible."

"Yes, in theory. But the harmoniste, as you've noted, is mortal; she is a Lord of the High Court, and she wears the blood of the green. Unless you wish to claim her robe to be a clever and nefarious counterfeit, the choice is no longer in your hands. And, Warden, I think not even you would be so arrogant."

"It is not Lord Kaylin's inclusion that is under discussion. She is, of course, welcome."

Teela smiled. "And Lord Calarnenne?"

"There is no Lord Calarnenne."

"That, Warden," a familiar voice said, "is harsh."

Teela didn't move. Neither did Severn. Kaylin had to turn to look over her shoulder. Nightshade approached the silent Barrani, at the side of the Lord of the West March. The tiara across his brow was unmistakable; the emerald at its peak was glowing. On his forearm sat one of the two eagles; the other accompanied the Lord of the West March.

The Lord of the West March didn't comment. Instead, he approached Kaylin. Bird on arm, he offered her a perfect bow—a bow she couldn't duplicate, no matter how many hours she spent taking lessons under Diarmat's foot. *"Kyuthe,"* he said. "Kaylin. An'Teela. You carry my heart in your arms."

"I know," she replied. Her voice lost its hard edge. "Even

were she not, she is the Lady. I will allow no harm to come to her while I still draw breath."

He nodded as if no other answer was possible, but he did not attempt to take Teela's burden from her; nor did he command her to deliver the Lady into Lord Barian's arms. Instead, he spoke a single word Kaylin couldn't catch before he touched the Consort's brow. She didn't wake.

Lord Barian clearly considered the Lord of the West March above suspicion. "She intercepted three," he said gravely.

"Three." His lids fell, the sweep of dark lashes like bruises against his skin.

"There were five, Lord. The harmoniste intercepted two before they could reach the Lady."

"Yes," was the soft, tired reply. He opened his eyes; they were blue. "I am aware of her intercession. She is mortal, Barian—and impulsive in ways the young are. And for the moment, I am grateful for that impulse. Remember the results of it," he added, in a slightly stronger voice, "and forgive her lack of familiarity with our customs."

"The other mortal—"

"He is hers," the Lord of the West March replied. "Lord Kaylin will not allow him to be driven off; she will certainly object to his execution. Lord An'Teela did not lie; Lord Severn survived the test of name." He glanced at the blades in Severn's hands, and his eyes darkened; for a moment Kaylin thought he would say more.

The eagle on his arm said, "He is to be granted passage and hospitality while either remain."

Lord Barian bowed.

"Come, Kaylin, An'Teela. We will repair to my domicile."

Kaylin wasn't certain what to expect. The first Hallionne she'd encountered had been a tree. A huge, ancient tree, true—

but nothing about it had screamed building. Yet its interior was large enough to house the entire Barrani contingent, plus the two mortals who were caught up in the pilgrimage. Easily.

It occurred to her as she walked by the side of the Lord of the West March that the entire West March might be the same: any one of these trees could be buildings as grand, mysterious and architecturally impossible. There wasn't a pressing need for something as mundane as a passable road if you had a building provided for all of your equally mundane needs.

But the High Halls had drives. Palatial drives. And the Lords of the High Court spent money in the city, given the way the Merchants' guild fawned all over them. The Hallionne were, to all intents and purposes, like the Towers or Castles in the fiefs—and as far as Kaylin knew, there was only one Tower in each fief.

"We are at the outskirts of the green," the Lord of the West March told her. "The Hallionne of the West March has not been habitable for centuries. It is not there that you—or any member of the Consort's entourage—will stay. But no; there are few roads that lead to the West March, and we did not travel by any of them. My people do not require paths of heavy stone to smooth their way." His answer reminded her that he had, as Nightshade had, offered her his True Name. If she wasn't careful, he could hear her thoughts.

"The carriages?"

"There is a road," he replied. "It is not easily traversed by your kind because they cannot easily find it." His smile was almost gentle. Kaylin tried not to take offense when she realized he was treating her as a child; in strict years, she was. "Understand that An'Teela is an unusual member of the High Court. By birth, she belongs to two worlds."

"Like you?"

"Very like. She is of the West March and she is of the High Court. There are very few who have her lineage."

"But she's not trusted by either."

"She is trusted—inasmuch as any Barrani Lord—in the High Court. But her history makes her position in the Court of the Vale unusual."

"You—you have your own court here?"

His brows rose, and his smile deepened. His eyes were a shade of emerald-green; she'd amused him. "Yes," he said, "and there is very little in my life that does, at the moment. I consider it a gift. The West March has its court, the Court of the Vale; it always did. You will find that any gathering of significance does.

"You are aware that my title is Lord of the West March. Are you aware that the High Lord is also called the Lord of the Green?"

She nodded.

"This, then, is the green. My brother is the leader of our people—but in theory, the leader of the Human Caste Court is the leader of yours."

"That's a pretty tenuous theory," Kaylin replied. "I've never met him, and even if I had, I don't serve him."

"No?"

"I serve the Halls of Law. My ruler is the Eternal Emperor." She spoke quietly, but was reminded that the Barrani had excellent hearing when they all fell silent. Part of her was irritated. What she'd said was true. It was fact. Finding fact offensive was pointless.

On the other hand, fact was hundreds of miles away, and offense was up close and personal. She made a mental note not to mention dragons—any dragons—while in the West March. Then again, she probably didn't have to. Teela had made her take Sanabalis's amulet out, and the Barrani generally knew what it signified: she belonged to a dragon.

As she fingered the heavy chain, the Lord of the West March frowned. "It is best not to draw attention to what you bear." It wasn't the first time she'd visited a Barrani court wearing a sign that said Property of Dragon Lord. In fact, it wasn't the first time she'd worn *this* sign. In the High Halls, it had seemed less dangerous.

"I wasn't allowed to leave until I'd promised to wear it." But Sanabalis was also hundreds of miles away.

"It is *never* wise to break an oath given to dragons," the Lord of the West March told her.

"It's probably stupid to give them the oath in the first place," she conceded, falling into her mother tongue. "But we weren't going to get the information we needed unless I promised to make the pilgrimage to the West March. And I couldn't make *that* promise without also taking the amulet."

"Lord Sanabalis did not feel that my ring would guarantee your safety?"

"It's probably stupid," she said, after a long pause, "for me to open my mouth at all."

He laughed. "It is not in our nature to trust others to protect what is valuable to us. Even were it, that trust would not cross this particular racial divide. I had heard rumor that some Imperial overtures had been made."

"Yes. But I don't think that's going to happen again in this generation."

"No. The High Court was unamused by the presence of the Emperor upon their land."

"He was a little angry."

"Dragons do not generally breathe fire in the middle of the city when they are merely annoyed."

"I didn't say he was annoyed—I said he was angry. You

can't blame him. One of the High Lords had just attempted to assassinate the only known female dragon."

"As a Lord of the High Court, Lord Kaylin, it is best not to spread that sentiment."

Kaylin, tired and unexpectedly angry herself, said, "She was living with me at the time. Every item of value I owned was destroyed during that attempt."

The small dragon squawked.

"Almost every item. I understand why Iberrienne tried to kill her. But I'm not willing to pretend that was a good thing. Even if my home hadn't been ripped to pieces by an Arcane bomb, I still wouldn't. I'm an *Imperial Hawk*."

"Yes, Lord Kaylin, you are. What I now wonder is what else you might be." He glanced at the Warden of the West March; Lord Barian was no longer walking. He, and the men who had arrived by his side, had spread out in a line ten yards from Teela, the Lord of the West March, and Kaylin. "Ah. We've arrived."

They had; there was a small stream, too slender to be called a river—and far too shallow—and the Barrani began to line up at its far edge as the Warden of the West March signaled a halt. "A word of advice, Lord Kaylin. The would-be assassin is Outcaste. Do not use his name in polite company."

And what am I supposed to call him?

Outcaste, Nightshade replied, amused.

Outcaste what? Outcaste number twelve or ninety?

The context will make it clear. The Lord of the West March has claimed you as kin. He will guide you, as you allow. He is not his father; he is not his brother. He is like—very like—his sister. He will indulge you where it is safe to do so. Do not make the mistake of believing his indulgence to be a social norm. It is not.

She wanted, very badly, to fall over and sleep. Had she been at home, she probably wouldn't have made it out of her clothing first. Severn joined her and slid an arm around her shoulder. He didn't speak. He didn't need to speak. She accepted what he offered, leaning against his shoulder; letting him carry some part of her weight.

From there, she could watch.

She could watch as the bed of this modest stream began to widen, to stretch away from the Barrani on all sides. The stream itself could be crossed with a simple leap—or a running leap, in Kaylin's case; the river it had become was far too wide.

While thinking that, she saw the Lord of the West March take a step forward, into the moving current.

His foot never hit water. It hit air instead, and that air obligingly became a bridge. It didn't rise out of the water. That would have been too simple. No, it appeared in broad strokes, as if painted in place by an insanely fast, insanely good artist. It was brighter than the rest of the landscape; brighter than the moonlight should have made it, and it appeared, to her eye, to be made of glass.

Given that most of the Barrani were wearing armor, this was not comforting.

The Lord of the West March then turned to Teela. "An'Teela." He did not offer her an arm; she couldn't take it and continue to bear her burden. But she inclined her chin and preceded him. If material composition of the bridge concerned her, it didn't show. She climbed what appeared to be slope without stairs until she stood at the midpoint of the bridge; there she paused to look out at the currents of the river.

Kaylin, following, stopped beside her. "Teela?"

The Barrani Hawk looked down her perfect nose. "Home," she said, wearily. She turned then, and walked down the incline that led, at last, to the city at the heart of the West March.

The Barrani did not appear to favor stone—at least not underfoot. Elantra had roads. Even in the fiefs, where the roads were broken and undermined by weeds and water runoff.

But the Barrani of the West March had lawns instead of roads. Grass gave way to stairs, many of which went down, rather than up; it gave way to doors and to trees. There were flowers, as well, but the flowers didn't seem to grow in specific, boxed beds; they seemed artless and wild—but for all that, they didn't get in the way of the High Court, or anyone else who walked the green.

The trees that had been the only constant during the overland trek were everywhere, but they grew in more ordered rows; they were at least as tall as the trees on the other side of the bridge. But there were no fallen branches, no hollow, standing trunks; here, the trees were like lampposts, without the lights.

In fact, the trees seemed to mark what passed for road here; they formed explicit boundaries in rows, opening up or ending, as if they were the walls of a maze. Mazes were the province of the monied. Warrens—like mazes made of buildings—were the province of the wretched, but Kaylin had no sense that she'd find slums in the West March.

The Lord of the West March glanced at her, the corners of his eyes and lips crinkling. She'd amused him again.

"It is seldom indeed that I see my own home from the vantage of a visitor entirely new to it. It is…engaging. We will follow this road, as you call it, and turn to the right; the trees—the type of trees—are indicators."

"Of what?"

"Ah, forgive me. They would, in your parlance, be street names, I believe."

It wasn't a short walk. Kaylin, who had always known that Teela was physically strong, was more than impressed when they at last reached the home of the Lord of the West March. If stone wasn't favored as a general building material, it wasn't absent here. The building reminded Kaylin very much of the

High Halls in Elantra—at least from the outside. The stairs that fronted it were flat and wide, the columns that held the roof almost the height of the trees that stood to the right and left of the building.

They were carved in the likeness of warriors, and words were engraved across the rounded base of each; Kaylin couldn't read most of them, although she was certain they must be High Barrani. Then again, she couldn't read most examples of High Barrani carved or written centuries ago; she was assured that the language was the same—but the style of the writing made the entire thing look like a mess of loops and crosses. It was aesthetic, but not practical.

She could make out individual letters at the beginnings of words.

"Can you read these?" she asked Severn. He had sheathed his swords when Nightshade and the Lord of the West March arrived.

"Not all of it, no. That one means *weapon* or *sword,* depending on the context."

"Thanks. I was kind of hoping to feel less stupid."

"Then you don't want to be left behind," he replied, grinning. "The Lord of the West March is opening his home to the High Court. We want to be there before he's finished."

"He's not likely to close the doors in our face—for one, I don't think there are any." But she moved as she spoke.

"I suspect the ring you're wearing would grant you entrance, regardless. It won't, however, speak for me."

She hesitated. "I couldn't help but notice that the Barrani here don't like your weapon much."

"It's not the weapon," he replied as he cleared the stairs. "It's the wielder. I suffer from mortality."

"It's a curse," she agreed. "How much trouble are they going to cause?"

"I'm uncertain. The weapon was damaged in our melee with Iberrienne. There are only two places in which it might be repaired. The West March is the least hostile."

"I don't want to know where the other place is."

He chuckled. "No, you really don't."

She did, of course. But she'd already said too much. The hardest thing about Barrani Courts was the amount of silence they demanded.

Learn, Kaylin. Learn quickly. When you last attended Court, you were considered an oddity, a distasteful necessity in a city infested with them. In the West March, that is not the case. The Emperor's shadow does not reach the green—but the shadows of three wars mark it. When the Consort wakes, you will be called to give your report of the events that occurred when you went missing in the Outlands. The fact that the Hallionne Orbaranne is standing—and whole—is the only point in your favor.

Dress, remember?

Ah. You mistake me. There is not a Barrani here who will attempt to dispose of you while you wear that dress. But the moment the telling is done—if you survive it—you will not be wearing the dress.

She froze. *You won't be wearing the crown, either.*

No.

And you're Outcaste.

I believe I am aware of that. I understood the risk, Kaylin. It is my opinion that I will be in far less danger than you yourself will be. The Barrani are not Dragons; Outcaste is a political statement. It is only relevant if the Outcaste in question has no power—but it is rare indeed that those without power are made Outcaste. Think of what you will tell the Court of the Vale when they bid you to speak. Think of how you will handle their accusations.

They haven't accused me of anything.

Not yet. But if you falter, they will. It is the nature of Courts.

It's the nature of carrion creatures, she snapped.

He chuckled. But he entered the hall without comment from anyone, and Kaylin scurried after Teela and the Consort.

The interior of the building—the parts that were visible in a straight walk from the door to a large suite of rooms—was distinctly different from the High Halls. There was far less stone here, and the wood was warm and bright; the floors were pale, but hard, the frames and lintels of doors carved out of the same wood. There were small trees, small fonts, and—as Teela stepped through a wide set of open doors—a large, circular courtyard.

In the center of the courtyard was a fountain.

Kaylin stopped walking. The Barrani at her back didn't run into her, but they did move pointedly to either side. Teela, however, stopped. The Lord of the West March, sensitive to his sister, returned from the head of the procession. Kaylin was aware of them both, but she couldn't take her eyes off the fountain—and she wasn't even certain why.

Fountains weren't exactly common in Elantra, although they weren't unknown. Where they existed in crowded, well-traveled, public areas, they accumulated dirt, dead leaves, small sticks, and an assortment of pebbles. They also generally sported small children who were likely to get their ears boxed in the immediate future.

The water here was clean. It was clear as new glass. It reminded Kaylin of the height of summer, not because there was anything about it that suggested seasons, but because it promised blessed relief from the heat. The only noise in the courtyard was the fall of water and the slight weight of footsteps. Barrani didn't have thunderous, heavy steps unless they were making a point.

"What do you see?" The Lord of the West March asked.

"Water." As answers went, it defined inadequate—it was

a *fountain*. Of course it had water. She was aware of the basin into which the water fell; the fountain was not the heavy, worn stone she was accustomed to seeing. A layer of what she assumed was gold-leaf gilded the basin, and writing, again in gold, the base into which it was set.

"I see the bridge," she said, after a long pause. "And mist or fog."

The Lord of the West March nodded, eyes narrowed. "An'Teela?"

"I see a fountain," she replied. "Water is, apparently, falling from a small rift in the air above the basin."

"You don't see a bridge." Kaylin's voice was both flat and resigned.

"No, kitling."

"And I shouldn't, either."

"It is not a test," the Lord of the West March said with a tight smile. "There is no correct answer."

Kaylin glanced at Severn.

I see what Teela sees.

Damn it. The small dragon squawked and pushed himself off her shoulder.

"Kitling," Teela said sharply. "Remember what happened the last time your pet was near water."

The Lord of the West March lifted a hand—in Teela's direction. "What does he intend?"

Kaylin, however, reached for the small, winged rodent. She caught his legs and pulled him down as gently as she could; he wasn't amused and let it be known. He sounded like an enraged chicken.

"His previous interference," Teela said, "forced the Lady to wake Hallionne Kariastos."

Brows rose over green-blue eyes. "Is he as he seems?"

"A familiar?" Teela shrugged. "If he is, legend proves unreliable in its particulars. But it is clear that Kariastos understood him in some small measure, and he proved himself useful on the forest paths."

He'd done more than that, but Kaylin didn't argue. "What," she whispered, "is the problem?"

The small dragon nipped her hand. He was still annoyed, but not so much that he tried to take a chunk out of her. A cat would have, by this point; he was trying to lift the wings over which her palm was cupped. He chose to squawk instead. She heard his voice, and mentally adjusted her description. He sounded like a crow.

She couldn't make out words; she wondered if Teela was right. Hallionne Bertolle had seemed to understand him, and he'd certainly said something more complicated than "hungry" or "sleepy" or "get lost." Maybe she wasn't listening the right way—but she wasn't an ancient, sentient building. She wasn't even immortal.

The small dragon caught her hand in his jaws. He continued to squawk while doing it, but the sound was muffled. Sighing, she lifted her head and froze.

The bridge was gone, as was the mist; water fell, but it fell in a sheet, and the sheet had the shape of long, flowing robes. "Teela," Kaylin whispered. "Has the fountain changed?"

"No. Not to me. You no longer see a bridge?"

Kaylin shook her head. "I see the Tha'alaan." Lifting her face, she stepped toward the water elemental on her pedestal.

Kaylin.

She reached out with one hand; the small dragon seemed content to spread his wings without leaping immediately into the air.

You are far from home.

"Tell me about it." She hesitated. Water rose in the shape of a transparent limb and an open hand. Kaylin slowly raised her palm. When the two—flesh and water—connected, she heard the voices of the Tha'alani. Touching the Tha'alaan was always a shock, but never unpleasant; it was like finding an unexpected bonfire on the winter streets of the fief. It promised safety, warmth, and a place to rest. Even if she didn't belong by birth, she felt welcome when someone else opened the door. She was a guest, here, in a place where there were no secrets and little judgment.

"An'Teela, come. If our *kyuthe* wishes to marvel at the fount, I will not deny her, but we have the responsibility of the Lady, and we must see to it."

"I have to go," Kaylin whispered. "Will you be here?"

If I understand your question correctly, yes. I am bound to this place. It is not a harsh binding, she added, when Kaylin inhaled sharply. *But I seldom hear mortal voices.*

"Do you hear any voices at all?"

Only one.

She was certain then that the water spoke of the Lord of the West March. "Do you speak to him?"

He does not hear my voice. Sometimes, I hear his. It is not the voice of my people, but I do not fear it.

"Kitling?"

"Coming. Sorry." She lowered her hand while the small dragon leaped up onto her shoulder and whiffled.

CHAPTER 4

Beyond the fountain was an open arch that led into a cloister. At the end of this cloister was a door. Kaylin's arms started to itch on approach. Magic generally had that effect on her skin— but she'd seen so much magic that hadn't in the past weeks she almost welcomed the familiar sensation. The fountain, which was clearly magical in nature, had had no effect at all.

Neither had the Hallionne, or the cold, gray mist in the outlands.

She had a few dozen questions to ask her magic teacher when she made it back to his classroom.

"Your room, Lord Kaylin, is beyond these doors. Lord Nightshade has similar rooms." Before she could speak, he added, "They are the rooms occupied by the harmoniste and the Teller respectively, when we are fortunate enough to have them chosen."

Severn caught her arm before she could ask the most obvious question.

"You will not find my domicile similar to the Hallionne. The Hallionne—when awake—are not comfortable residences for my kin. They are all awake now," he added. "We have not seen such excitement since the close of the last war. You will have to touch the door ward."

"Do I have to bleed on it?"

His brows rose, and then he chuckled. "I forget my own youth, it is so far behind me. The Hallionne exact a price for their hospitality that the Barrani do not; they also provide security that the Barrani do not. You have spent time in the High Halls; you will find my abode similar in many respects."

"The fountain—"

He shook his head. "There are fountains within the High Halls."

They weren't the same. Kaylin approached the door and laid her palm against the ward engraved on its surface; her arm went instantly numb at the shock of it. The door ward did not, however, set off alarms in any other way, which made it less painful than the wards in the Imperial Library.

The Lord of the West March nodded and the door rolled open. It was not a small door; the Norannir could comfortably fit through its frame. Kaylin felt dwarfed, but expected as much; the Barrani built everything to make visitors feel small and unworthy.

She felt Nightshade's amusement and noted that he didn't likewise have to touch the door.

No, Lord Kaylin. This is not the first time I have visited the West March, you may recall.

"Lord Severn, your quarters are not within this wing, but if you will accompany us, I would speak with you."

Severn inclined his head. He was watchful, but cautious. She wondered if he'd sleep at all as a guest in these halls. On the other hand, she was fairly certain that no other hall would be open to him.

★ ★ ★

The Lady's room was at the end of a hall so wide and vaulted it looked like the nave in one of the great cathedrals. The doors at the end of that hall were closed, but they suited the hall; they were taller and grander—or at least their arches were—than the exterior doors. She turned to look over her shoulder and was surprised to see that most of the Barrani had departed; to where, she wasn't certain.

This allowed her to relax, inasmuch as one ever did in Barrani Halls. She understood why the Barrani disliked the Hallionne, but she missed them. The Hallionne were tasked with preventing harm from coming to their guests, and they took their responsibilities seriously. Given that most of the harm that could befall their guests came from their other guests, it worked out well for Kaylin. She wasn't stupid enough to take on the Barrani in all-out melee, and she wasn't clever enough to slip poison into their food or drink.

She also wasn't clever enough to avoid them.

When the doors to the Consort's chamber were open, the Lord of the West March led Teela toward yet another set of more modest doors on the far end of a more modest hall. There was a small fountain on the left wall, and three slender trees, like artistic pillars, on the right; there were no visible guards.

The doors were warded. Kaylin, whose arm was still numb, was happy she wouldn't have to open them. Instead, she scurried to catch up with Teela and helped her by turning down the bedcovers. Teela very gently set the Consort down as Kaylin fussed with pillows; there were far too many of them.

"Do not," the Lord of the West March said, "attempt to heal the Lady."

Kaylin hadn't even considered it, given the way Barrani reacted to healing—although the Consort had given her explicit, public permission. "I wasn't going to. I just… I don't like her color. Can I remove the armor, or do you expect her to sleep in it?"

The Lord of the West March glanced at Teela. "If you do not consider it demeaning," he finally said, "you may tend to the Lady; she will not wake."

Teela's eyes were markedly bluer, but she said nothing; she wasn't exactly a stranger to armor and its care. "Honestly," she said, as she began to undo buckles, "I cannot take you anywhere, kitling. You will note, for future reference, that I do not even remove my *own* clothing when I bathe in the High Halls."

"That's probably why you don't live in them," Kaylin shot back.

Teela's eyes widened. She laughed, and they also changed color. "Maybe," she said, in Elantran. "When the Lord of the West March forbids healing, he does so for a reason."

"I healed him."

"Indeed, which is why I mention healing at all." She rose and tendered the Lord of the West March an enviably perfect bow. "It is unusual for the Consort to absorb three," she told him gravely.

"How unusual?" Kaylin asked. She'd been truthful: she did not think the Lady's color was healthy.

"It has never, to my knowledge, happened before."

"What usually happens when the—the black bird things fly? Teela, what are they?"

"Before today? They were considered the nightmares of the Hallionne."

"And now?"

"You saw the eagles."

Kaylin nodded as if this made sense.

"The eagles were—long ago—considered the heralds of the Hallionne. They kept the Lord of the West March, and his Warden, apprised of any difficulties within their impressive range. There is a reason the West March has never fallen."

"But…"

Teela sighed. "I will allow one."

"The Hallionne is lost. Bertolle said as much, I think."

"Indeed. He did. But the heralds are here, kitling. And they are here because you chose to interfere. No one of us understands how or why—but you've known the Barrani for much of your life. How many of us like to loudly proclaim our own ignorance?" Before Kaylin could reply, she added, "Exactly." Folding her arms, she continued. "The substantiation of the nightmares began several hundred years ago."

"The shadow birds."

"Yes. They are not impervious to physical harm, but it was discovered that they seek a target when they appear. They are not easily detected before they do so; nor can they be entirely contained within the Hallionne. The Hallionne," she added, "is off-limits."

"I'm not an idiot, Teela."

"Of course not. The Consort—and to a much lesser extent, the Lord of the West March—has an affinity for these nightmares."

"She has an affinity for the Hallionne in general."

"And your point is?"

Kaylin was hungry, tired, and worried. None of which mattered. "The Lady woke the Hallionne."

"If I recall correctly, she woke the Hallionne to prevent the possible damage or destruction of your little pet."

The small dragon hissed.

"Fine. It doesn't matter why—she *could* wake the Hallionne."

"It is the responsibility, in times of war, of the leader of the war band."

"This isn't a time of war. She woke the Hallionne. Nightshade helped."

"An'Teela, is this true?" the Lord of the West March said, which showed that he was paying attention to every word.

Teela exhaled. "Yes. You will forgive Lord Kaylin; she is unfamiliar with the Hallionne."

"I will, of course, forgive her her ignorance—where it is to be found. I am not entirely certain that she is ignorant in this case. Why do you feel the Lady has an affinity for the Hallionne?" His voice was cooler, and his gaze was all blue.

"I think it's the other way around. I think the Hallionne have an affinity for the Lady," Kaylin replied. "Bertolle and Kariastos appeared genuinely fond of her. Kariastos told me she was dearer than—"

"Enough." The Lord of the West March held out one taut hand. "You will not speak of this again."

Kaylin blinked. She understood that the Barrani considered any affection—or gods forbid—love they personally felt to be an almost unmentionable weakness, but she'd never encountered the inverse.

Teela chuckled, her eyes the safe green that touched none of the Lord of the West March's. "Lirienne, you will frighten her. Think like a Hawk, kitling."

She was. She had no doubt that the Lord of the West March believed her; it was because he believed her that he wanted her to shut up. Which meant the Hallionne did, as she pointed out, have an affinity for the Consort.

"If it makes any difference," she said, "the Hallionne also seemed fond of—or concerned about—Teela." It did make a difference—to Teela. Kaylin decided to shut up.

I fear it is late for that, Nightshade said.

"How do you explain the nightmares? If they come at

random and every Barrani is more or less equal, what does it mean?"

"We do not explain," he replied. "She is the Lady. You think of her as the mother of our race, and that is not entirely wrong—but it is not the way she is viewed by the Lords. We protect her with our lives because without her, there will be no future for our people. But we understand that she is, in subtle ways, in ways that cannot be measured by our kind, different. Exalted, Lord Kaylin. Much is expected of her because of the burden she is capable of bearing."

"Have you ever seen the Lake?"

"No."

"Oh. Was the Lake created by the same ancients that created the Hallionne?"

No one replied. Remembering Teela's comment about Barrani and their possible ignorance, she didn't push the point. Instead, she turned back to the Consort. "I don't like her color," she said again. "And if she doesn't wake by morning, you're going to have to post guards at the doors to keep me out." She flashed a grim smile.

"If she does not wake by morning," the Lord of the West March replied, "I will reconsider the matter."

Kaylin had one question to ask, and she asked it of Teela as they traveled the hallway, although she knew it was probably unwise. "When the Consort talks of Nightshade, she uses the name Calarnenne."

"That was his Court name," Teela replied.

"Yes, but..."

"Did I not tell you I would only allow one *but* today? If you're too lazy to even reframe your concern, don't speak."

"...I hear his name as if it were his True Name."

Teela said, "Yes, and...?" as if Kaylin had just said "water is wet."

"But True Names are dangerous and people don't like it when they're spoken, and I don't want to ask why everyone is using it because I don't want anyone to know that I *know* it."

Teela's dark brows rose as she stared at Kaylin in bemusement. The laughter that followed filled a hall that was otherwise notable for its utter silence, and made Kaylin feel a good six inches shorter.

"I'm glad you're finding mortality so funny."

"Oh, not all mortals, kitling. Just you."

"That makes it so much better. Could you answer the question so I don't feel humiliated for no reason?"

"You don't speak a name. Even when you invoke it, it's not a simple matter of speech. You call it speech. Others don't. It's very like detection of magic. You're highly sensitive to magic; you can see when a spell's been cast. You can read the mage's signature in the shadows of the enchantment.

"Anyone who is capable of detecting magic can. But no two mages see that signature and its effects in the same way."

"It's why multiple mages are called in for difficult cases."

Teela nodded. "And why an appropriate Records trail is so difficult to maintain. When you hear Nightshade's Court name, you are hearing spoken language. Like any other part of High Barrani, there are guidelines that control form and utterance. But you are hearing only that. When you say 'Lord Calarnenne' you are speaking simple words.

"When you speak his name—if you are *ever* unwise enough to do so—you might scream it and none will hear the whole of the truth; it is not just the mouth that utters the name."

"I could see the Dragon Outcaste's name, once."

"And you've never been suicidal enough to attempt to use it."

"I couldn't. I couldn't hold it all in one place for long enough—it's too big."

Teela said nothing for a long moment. "I will need to bathe and change before I join the High Court in the dining hall. I would suggest you bathe, as well; the dress is, of course, without blemish—but your hair looks like it's a nest of weeds."

"Thanks."

"This is your room," Teela said.

"Where's yours?"

"Closer to Corporal Handred's. Don't make that face. The Lord of the West March escorted your Corporal to his rooms; he is guaranteed to have arrived there in safety."

"He's not guaranteed to remain that way."

"No—but then again, neither are the rest of us." Teela smiled lazily. "Things are unlikely to be boring."

"I don't mind a little boredom, Teela."

"That's because you have less than a century worth of life in which to contain it. If you were actually immortal, you'd have a different attitude."

Kaylin snorted. The door to her room was closed and warded. She lifted her left palm and placed it across the ward. What the door ward at the start of the wing had failed to do, this one did: it started to peal, like a series of badly formed, dissonant bells.

"I hate magic," Kaylin said under her breath. She added a few choice Leontine words in the bargain as sword-wielding Barrani appeared around the corner. The small dragon leaped off her shoulders and headed toward them, which was infinitely worse. Kaylin ran after him in a panic. "Don't!" she shouted. "I'm used to this kind of nonsense, and I can survive it. I probably *can't* survive you turning them into puddles!"

"Puddles?" Teela drawled. She had moved—quickly and

silently—to stand by Kaylin's side, but hadn't drawn her own sword.

"You know what I mean."

"I really don't, kitling."

The men who clearly served the Lord of the West March slowed when confronted with a faceful of tiny dragon. Kaylin almost laughed. The small dragon was little and curmudgeonly—but he wasn't harmless. It was too easy to forget that fact.

"Come back here right now."

Fluttering, he spun to face her. He squawked.

She held out a hand, and added, "Please?"

Teela glared at them both as the small dragon landed. She said nothing, which told Kaylin that she disapproved of her handling of her companion, and she didn't trust the guards enough to speak publicly.

The Lord of the West March appeared some fifteen minutes later. The door ward had fallen silent at the arrival of the guards, but the door hadn't magically opened in the meantime, which left Kaylin cooling her heels in the hall, an annoyed Teela to her left.

"I am beginning to understand," he said—in Elantran, which was almost shocking, "why you display such antipathy toward magical convenience." To his men, he said—in the language of the Court, "Lord Kaylin is harmoniste; she does not pose a threat." He glanced at the small dragon. "You vouch for your passenger?"

As the small dragon was once again lounging across her shoulders, Kaylin nodded.

Teela was not amused.

"Please activate the ward again."

She did. Her arm was numb; her hand unfortunately wasn't. The door made a lot of noise, and once again failed to open.

The Lord of the West March frowned. He caught Kaylin's hand before she could drop it, glancing at her fingers. "Try the other hand," he said. "Or transfer my ring to this one."

He noticed her hesitance, but she managed not to let loose with a litany of complaints against door wards and magic in general. Barrani guards tended to take that kind of thing personally. She usually touched door wards with her left hand because she was right-handed, but didn't feel the need to share; all the Barrani who worked in the Halls of Law appeared to be ambidextrous. She chose to move the ring; her hand was now numb.

But when she touched the door ward again, the door opened.

"Yes," the Lord of the West March said to his assembled guard, "she wears my symbol. She is as kin in these halls."

Given the way Barrani generally felt about their kin, this wasn't saying much.

Kaylin was, until Bellusdeo's arrival, used to having some privacy when she walked through her doors. The fact that these doors weren't hers was driven home by the presence of two Barrani attendants. Teela, who insisted on a sweep of the rooms, didn't blink; she did give curt instructions—to Kaylin.

"They are here to see to your needs," she told Kaylin when they departed to prepare the bath. "If harm befalls you while you are in their care, they—and their families—will suffer for it. If you send them away, they will also suffer, although the penalties will be less extreme."

"Why will they suffer if I send them away?" Kaylin asked. She felt as if she'd stepped onto a bridge and discovered it was actually a tightrope.

"If you send them away, their service will be considered

inadequate. It will reflect poorly upon the hospitality of the Lord of the West March."

"I don't have attendants in the High Halls," Kaylin pointed out.

"You do. But they are responsible to *me,* and I am familiar enough with your idiosyncrasies that I do not choose to censure them. You are not in my domain now. What you do here will affect those who have been chosen—no doubt personally—by Lord Lirienne. You will therefore allow them to assist you. You will treat them as servants who are worthy of consideration and respect—but you will not find them intimidating. If you must feel self-conscious about their presence, do *not* share. Understood?"

Kaylin nodded.

"We will dine. After dinner, it is likely that the Lord of the West March will call a council meeting. You are a Lord of the High Court; you are not a Lord of the West March. There is some overlap, but it is not one hundred percent. I expect you to be called to that meeting, although I consider it unwise."

"Can I refuse to go?"

"I have considered the matter with some care. The Lady is not yet awake—and, kitling, I am at least as concerned as you are. Believe that Lord Lirienne is likewise worried. If she were present, I would feel less conflicted—but she won't be. It is my hope that the council will be delayed until she is awake. The Warden of the West March is unlikely to fulfill that hope."

Kaylin waited until she was certain Teela had finished. "That wasn't a yes or a no."

Teela smiled grimly. "Exactly. The ring you wear grants you a measure of freedom; it also constrains you. Any insult you offer, you offer in the name of the Lord of the West March. Lirienne is, in case you have not carefully followed our history, the direct descendent of the High Lord who caused so much damage to the green. As such, his position is precarious. He is, however, also his mother's son. He is held in cautious regard.

"He cannot therefore afford political difficulty."

"Teela, I'm *already* a political difficulty. I'm mortal, and I'm wearing this dress." She reached for the heavy gold chain around her neck, adding, "And a Dragon's symbol."

"You understand. You have impressed the Warden."

"Then why are your eyes blue?"

"Kitling, honestly, I am thinking of demanding that you live in the High Halls for a few of your mortal months. This is not a question you should be capable of asking, at this point."

"I'm beginning to think I've done Diarmat an injustice," Kaylin said.

"Oh?"

"I can safely loath him when he condescends me. Which is pretty much every time he draws breath."

Teela laughed, her eyes shading to green. "Bathe."

Barrani baths were pretty much small, warm pools. Kaylin's idea of a bath—in her old apartment—generally involved a lot of cold water in a rush. But she had some experience with baths like this one; she'd spent time with Teela in the High Halls. It wasn't that she hated the Barrani. She wasn't usually smart enough to fear them, except when their eyes went midnight-blue—and *any* sane person did that.

They just made her feel self-conscious. They were probably centuries old, but they looked like women—and men—in the prime of a perfect youth. They had no obvious blemishes. They didn't get fat—or thin. They weren't short or gangly. They never had pimples.

During a normal day at the office, none of this mattered. Most of the crimes the Halls of Law dealt with involved other people. Other mortals. They were crimes the Barrani consid-

ered so trivial it was a wonder any Barrani served the Halls
of Law at all.

They'd been part of the department before Kaylin's arrival;
she wasn't certain how they'd come to serve Marcus. But Marcus was Leontine; the Leontines could go one-on-one with
Barrani and expect to come out even. In a frenzy, they could
expect to come out on top, in Kaylin's opinion.

Humans? Not so much.

So she was being served by people who were taller, smarter,
stronger, and infinitely more graceful. She was being served
by people who probably knew more languages than Kaylin
had fingers. She was being waited on—perfectly—by people
who, in their youth, probably considered humans to be annoying or endearing *pets*.

And yes, she felt guilty about it.

So she found their perfect silence oppressive. She found
it uncomfortable. Teela's instructions made it clear that this
was Kaylin's problem—not theirs. The small dragon seemed
to agree—but he didn't apparently care for the silence, either,
given the squawking that started up when Kaylin slid quickly
into the bath.

The Barrani might have waited on humans day in, day out.
They did not, however, wait on small, translucent dragons.
When he first set up squawking—at them, apparently—they
stiffened, turning immediately to face him as he hovered in
front of their faces.

"If you are going to keep that up," Kaylin said, glaring up
the five feet that separated them, "I'm packing you in a small
crate and sending you back home."

Squawk.

"I mean it. They are here to help me bathe and dress. They
are not here to drown me. They aren't here to drown you,
either. Cut it out."

The attendants exchanged a glance.

The small dragon landed on Kaylin's shoulder and bit her ear. She pulled him off and held him out in front of her face. "I've had a pretty crappy day, and I *do not need this* right now!" Her hands stiffened as she finally noticed the marks on her arms. They were glowing faintly, more bronze than gold. A very Leontine curse followed; Kaylin lifted herself out of the bath, sloshing water on a floor that, when slippery, probably killed people, or at least people who weren't Barrani.

The small dragon squawked in a quieter way. He looked smug.

Kaylin looked very wet. "The water in this bath," she said, modulating her voice and forcing it into High Barrani, which was *so* not the language she wanted at the moment, "where does it come from?"

The two attendants exchanged another glance. Kaylin did her best not to take it personally, and mostly succeeded. "There is a spring; this hall is built around it. The water for the baths within the personal rooms of the Lord of the West March comes from that spring."

Kaylin frowned. "The fountain in the courtyard—is it connected to the springs in some way, as well?"

"It is."

She turned immediately to the small dragon and dropped into Elantran; while the Barrani in the city could be expected to know Kaylin's mother tongue, the Barrani of the West March might not. She considered Aerian, but her Aerian wasn't as fluent. "It doesn't matter if the water's elemental, idiot. It's *safe*."

The small dragon wasn't having any of it. She had no idea why he reacted so poorly to the water; he hadn't reacted that way to fire, and fire was, in Kaylin's opinion, vastly more dangerous.

Or, given he was a miniature dragon, maybe not. The small amount of dignity she did possess was unlikely to hold up in the face of an argument with a pet—and given the reaction of the servants, they seemed to see it as a pet and not a mythical, sorcerous creature. Wilting because she was hungry, she turned to her attendants. "Could we do this bath the old-fashioned way?"

The Barrani were not, apparently, accustomed to the human version of bathing, since it mostly involved nothing but buckets. It also involved hot water, which was a blessing. They didn't complain; they asked a few brief questions, their tone neutral enough it couldn't be called curt. Kaylin toweled her own hair dry, but allowed the Barrani to set it. They combed it to within an inch of Kaylin's life; she was surprised there was any hair left when they'd finished. She'd picked up an annoying assortment of plant bits on the walk between Orbaranne and the West March; the Barrani obligingly dislodged all of it.

They even brought jewelry. Kaylin politely refused. Her ears weren't pierced; holes were what other people put into you against your will. She already had one necklace. They didn't approve, obviously—but also, silently. If Kaylin hadn't been so certain Teela would rat her out to Sanabalis, she would have left the damn medallion in her room.

And if it is lost?

Losing something significant that belonged to a Dragon was not high on Kaylin's list of acceptably painless suicides. *I'm wearing it, aren't I?*

Yes, you are. You are perhaps unaware that you are the only person in this Hall who could wear it and expect to survive the week?

She hadn't really considered that at all. *It doesn't mean it won't upset people.*

Nightshade was highly amused. *If it upset no one, there would* be little point in it. *You do not belong in any Barrani Court, but you are here; you wear the blood of the green; your companion is of note to even the most powerful among our kin. Word has almost certainly traveled, Kaylin; the Lord of the West March may find his hall rather more crowded than even he anticipated.*

Damn Barrani and their boredom.

You understand.

CHAPTER 5

In the Halls of Law, the mess hall could get crowded. Unless it was deserted, it was never quiet. There were scores in the wood of old tables and benches, some of which commemorated old war stories, and some of which were part of them. Kaylin didn't know everyone who worked in the Halls on a first name basis, but she came close.

She was reminded that Barrani weren't human when she entered the dining hall. Instead of one long table, it boasted three, but each of the three was immaculate. If the tables were wooden, she couldn't tell; they were covered in pale cloth. The cloth itself was of no fixed color; hues changed as she walked. There were chairs, not benches; instead of candles, there were globes of what looked like hanging water.

Kaylin knew people did this with glass—but glass didn't ripple and surge like a liquid. She found it disturbing.

It was far less disturbing than the silence that enveloped a relatively quiet hall as she entered. Nightshade hadn't been wrong; the hall was crowded. The tables were longer than any single table she'd seen, and wider than most of the ones in the mess hall. The chairs were filled. A sharp, rising panic made her dare a sweep of the room to find Teela or Severn; she found Severn first.

"Lord Kaylin."

At the head of the middle table—a table that was slightly taller than the two that bracketed it—stood the Lord of the West March. He didn't rise; he hadn't apparently taken his seat. Which meant, in Dragon etiquette terms, that no one could start to eat. Because she was late.

Being late had never filled her with so much horror.

A glimmer of a smile touched the eyes of the Lord of the West March; he'd clearly chosen to be amused. This set the tone for the rest of the meal—or it should have. For elegant, graceful, stately people, the ones gathered here watched like eagles. Or vultures.

Not vultures, surely, a voice that was not Nightshade's said.

Her eyes rounded and she had the grace to flush.

Walk, Kaylin. Do not scurry, but do not dally. As you suspect, all eyes—or ears—are upon you. You have a place of honor in this hall while you wear the blood of the green; your place after you have served your purpose will be decided by your behavior before the recitation.

She knew his True Name.

Yes.

Nightshade could—and did—intrude on her thoughts as he pleased; the Lord of the West March had never done so. It hadn't even occurred to her that he could until he spoke.

This deepened his amusement.

You are unaccustomed to power, kyuthe. *It is an advantage—to me. But you are not in the friendly and tolerant environs of the High Halls now.*

She didn't stumble by dint of will. His smile deepened; his

eyes were a shade of green that was tinged with blue, but not saturated by it. She didn't need to tell him that the High Halls did not define either *friendly* or *tolerant* in her books, but she had a feeling that if she survived this, it would. At least where Barrani were concerned.

The small dragon raised his head and brought it to the level of her cheek. His wings remained folded, although today they couldn't do much damage to her hair; she was fairly certain she would never again be able to take it down. Men and women turned in their seats as his head swiveled from side to side.

The servants had almost entirely ignored his existence.

They did not. They were aware of him.

Will they make reports to whoever they work for?

Most assuredly. They are mine. They report to me.

You probably know everything I know already, she said, not bothering to hide the defensive note creeping into her thoughts.

No. I understand what a name means to you. You believe that the interest shown you is unwarranted; you assign it to the blood of the green. Were all else equal, you would be correct. Keep walking.

She did. But she kept her gaze firmly on the Lord of the West March; she glanced once, briefly, at Severn, but looked away.

All else is not equal. You are Chosen; you bear the marks. It is the only reason the blood of the green has not started a minor—and brief—interracial war. You carry a creature on your shoulder that is capable of killing the transformed. My kin do not know what role you played in the liberation of Orbaranne, but they suspect the truth.

The…truth.

That it was not by my hand alone that she was saved.

She had reached the head of the table; the Lord of the West March held out a hand. She slid her right hand into his and he led her to the seat she was meant to occupy; it was to the right of his, across from Nightshade.

All of these things make you a threat. But you spoke to the night-mares of the Hallionne, and woke his dreams. The Barrani of the High Halls, saving only the Consort, lend this little weight in comparison to the rest of the things I have pointed out—but to the West March, it is your single, saving grace. Do not hide it; do nothing—at all—to lessen its impact.

She sat. Her mouth was dry. She was certain that dying animals felt this way when the shadows of vultures passed over them. Before—and after—the bath, she'd been hungry; she was not hungry now. Now, anxiety shoved hunger to one side. The marks on her arms, legs and back were normally hidden; the marks that had, over the course of the year, crept up the back of her neck, were not. Nor was the rune that squatted high in the middle of her forehead.

She'd gotten used to the dress over the past couple of weeks. It was both comfortable and practical; even the long, draping sleeves had more in common with Barrani hair than mortal cloth: they caught on nothing. She could, with a perfectly straight face, make an argument for the dress as a uniform in the Halls—that's how practical it was.

But the attention the dress now received made it alien and uncomfortable again.

The small dragon nudged her cheek, rubbing his snout against newly clean skin. He warbled.

If she were being honest, it wasn't the dress. It wasn't the marks of the Chosen; not even the new one, which, unless she spent time in front of a mirror, she couldn't see. It was the weight of expectation. It was the certain sense that she'd just punched in above her pay grade, and now had to act as if she worked here.

She'd spent a lot of time in her fourteenth year seething with outrage because no one took her seriously; she could remember it, and it embarrassed her to think about it now. But she'd never understood—even when under Diarmat's blistering condescension—how much *safety* there was in that. When no one took you seriously, there wasn't a lot you could do to screw things up. Nothing you said or did really counted; people expected you to fall flat on your butt.

She'd wanted to be taken seriously. She'd yearned to be treated as an equal. Evanton had once said, *Be careful what you wish for,* the wizened little bastard. She had a heaping plateful of what she'd wished for, and swallowing even a mouthful was proving difficult.

And why was that?

She remembered eating in the mess hall for the first time. She'd been so proud. That had lasted right up until someone told her that she was the official mascot. She hadn't reacted well. But—and she realized this now—she'd had the luxury of her very poor reaction. She expected people to look down on her. She looked for signs of it in everything. She bristled with anger at her certainty that everyone was.

She needed some of that anger now, but it was gone.

She was certain everyone at this table looked down on her; Severn was seated at the table to the left, near the foot of the table; Teela had chosen the seat to his right. She couldn't see them unless she swiveled in her chair, and she knew better.

Where had her anger gone? What had it even been? Oh. Right. She'd been enraged that the Hawks thought they could judge her when they'd had such *easy* lives. They hadn't grown up in the shadow of Castle Nightshade. They'd had food, and a place to live, and families that were mostly still alive. They thought she was stupid and naive; they thought she was hapless and ignorant.

She'd wanted to see *them* survive Nightshade, and then they could sneer at her.

Looking around the table—which she could politely do—

she realized that she'd lost that anger. Somehow, when she wasn't looking, it had frayed, and she'd done nothing to stitch it back together to keep it going. She was no longer certain that the people around her had had easy lives. Yes, they lived forever if left to their own devices, and yes, they were, to a man, stunningly gorgeous and graceful.

But given the chance, Kaylin would live none of their lives. True, she daydreamed about being born Aerian. But Barrani or Dragon? Never. War and death defined the Immortals; they lost eternity to it. If they had friends, they didn't claim them in public; friendship, affection, even love appeared to be the ugly stepchildren of their races.

"Lord Kaylin," someone said, and she blinked. It was Lord Barian, the Warden of the West March. His eyes were blue. The eyes of everyone at this table, with the exception of Nightshade, were now blue. She had a sinking suspicion she'd missed something.

No, Kaylin. But you must pay attention now, the Lord of the West March said.

What's his title?

You may address him as either Warden or Lord Barian. Neither will give offense.

"Lord Barian." She inclined her head. Her hair felt like a helmet.

"You have joined the High Court only recently."

"Yes."

"I am curious. To become Lord of that Court, one must take the test of name; when one does not possess such a name, how is one tested?"

She found the embers of her anger then. "You have no doubt journeyed to the High Halls to take that test yourself, Lord Barian."

Careful, kyuthe.

Lord Barian met, and held, her gaze. He did not answer.

"The Barrani seldom speak of the particulars of their test. They don't announce its results. Either they survive, or they do not. I am not, as I'm certain you're aware, Barrani. My test did not involve any customary ritual; I was given no preparation. Nor was I told not to speak of the experience." Or at least, not all of it. "But I assume the Lords of the Court hold their silence with cause.

"If you have seen the Tower, you know what waits there. To become a Lord of the Court, in the case of the two mortals who bear the title, all that matters is survival."

"Will you speak of what you saw?" Another Barrani, farther down the table, said. The woman spoke softly, but clearly, and as silence seemed to have descended on both of the other tables, the room's acoustics easily carried her words.

Kaylin glanced at the Lord of the West March; he watched her, his eyes slightly narrowed. She looked to Nightshade, whose eyes were emerald; they were probably the only green eyes in the building at the moment.

"Yes."

If she'd thought the room quiet before, she discovered how wrong she was.

"Mortal memory is not, as you're all well aware, reliable. It's not perfect. Elements of what I witnessed have faded. If any who have seen what I saw wish to correct me, I will take no offense." She thought she heard Teela snort. "I wasn't raised in the High Halls. I was a visitor there, but the building is immense. I was searching for the courtyard, and I found the Tower instead.

"There was a word on the Tower wall. I could see it. The Barrani who had passed the Tower's test could see it; the others couldn't."

"You...could see the word."

She nodded. "And I understood that it was both an invitation and a command."

Nightshade said, "It was an invitation. None can be commanded—not even by the Tower—to take that test. But those who choose to abide untested will never gain a place in the High Lord's Court."

Is this your story, or mine?

It depends. If you ask your Corporal, he will assuredly claim that I had some greater hand in its writing.

"I chose to enter the Tower. Lord Severn chose to accompany me."

"The Tower allowed this?" The woman's eyes rounded slightly.

"Yes."

"At the base of the Tower—and arriving at that base was not a simple matter of descending stairs—was a hall that was much rougher hewn than any of the halls I'd seen in the High Halls. At the end of that hall was a cavern." She fell silent for a long moment, considering her possible words with care.

"The Hallionne were built for a reason," she finally said. "The Towers in the fiefs of Elantra were built for a reason. The High Halls exist—in the heart of an Empire ruled by a Dragon—" she paused to allow ice to seep into the silence, but did so without apologies; it was true "—for a reason. I met that reason. The test of name is purely a test of resolve, and if you fail your name is lost to the Lake of Life; it is lost until the moment that the creature in the cavernous basement is destroyed.

"What he takes, he holds. I—" She stopped.

The woman who had spoken seemed paler now. "How?"

"Pardon?"

"How does he take what he holds?"

"I don't know. I'm sorry."

"Do they suffer?"

Kaylin wasn't certain how to answer the question, it was asked with such intensity. Honesty, with the Barrani, wasn't always the best policy; it was less risky than slitting your own throat, but not always in a good way. No one came to her rescue; no one gave her advice on what—or more germane, what *not*—to say.

"Yes," she said. "They know where they are. They know they're trapped."

Humans—mortals, really—had pretty clear concepts about souls, not that they always agreed with each other. Kaylin had never been clear on the Barrani life and afterlife. Had the trapped people been mortal, it would have been clearer, for a value of clear that left nothing but bitter, helpless rage in its wake.

The woman fell silent for a long moment. "Thank you, Lord Kaylin."

Kaylin shook her head. She almost reverted to Elantran, but she didn't recognize this woman as one of the party that had traveled with the Consort, and she wasn't certain she'd be understood. "I hated it," she said, voice low. "I couldn't understand, at first, why the test existed at all.

"But I understood it during the *Leofswuld*. No one who intends to rule the High Halls—and the Barrani, even if at a distance—can be vulnerable to the forces trapped beneath it." This was not entirely truthful, but the theory was absolutely sound. "The High Halls houses something ancient and monstrous at its core; it's meant to stand as a wall against that darkness. Those who have faced it and walk away can hold fast. If someone untested took the seat, what's leashed there would be free."

"And you consider that a significant danger."

Kaylin was nonplussed. "I do."

"To our people or your own?"

"Both." The hands that rested in her lap began to ball into fists. "I understand bitterness at the loss. Believe that I understand it. But no one is forced to take that test."

"Are they not?" was the cool reply. The woman glanced across the table, and her gaze fell squarely upon the Warden of the West March.

"No."

Teela cleared her throat; it was audible because no one else spoke. Kaylin dared one look at Lord Barian, and regretted it.

"Perhaps," the Barrani woman continued, "mortal customs are different. Or perhaps your knowledge of the Barrani is inexact. You were not required to take that test—indeed, I imagine that there are those present who would have argued strenuously against such an attempt. But for my kin, there are positions and privileges which accrue only to those who have taken that test and emerged."

"My knowledge of the Barrani people is, as you suggest, inexact. My knowledge of my own people isn't. There are positions within society which I'm unqualified to hold. I'll never be part of the Human Caste Court, and I'll never be wealthy. I was born in the fiefs, and spent all of my childhood there." She did not look at Nightshade, because she was angry. Had she wondered where her anger had gone?

"But I choose the work I do now. If I had been told that my job depended on taking this test—and had I been informed that pass or fail was a simple matter of survival—I would have two choices." She emphasized that last word. "I could have taken the test, in the hopes of keeping my job, or I could have found a different job."

"And if someone was more than qualified for greater duties, but did not, for the same reasons, choose to undertake such a risk?"

"Then he'd have to find a different job. I understand that you feel there's not much choice in that. But—it's a choice, even if it's a bad one." She hesitated, and then said, "The Lady has what we would consider an extremely important job. Mortals don't have True Names; we don't require a Lady of our own. But not everyone can see the Lake of Life. Not everyone who does see it can hold their own name in abeyance; the desire to join what is there proves too strong."

Kaylin, how do you know this?

She didn't answer the Lord of the West March; she concentrated on the Barrani woman.

"Someone who can't pass the test of name won't survive the duties of Consort. If the Consort fails, a search will begin for someone new. But every single one of those women will be tested. I imagine the search won't even extend to those who haven't passed the test, because—" Her brain caught up with her mouth, and she shut up.

"And if someone was found who could touch the words, but had not taken the test?"

"The words would kill her if she weren't strong enough to face what is caged in the High Halls. I'm sorry."

Can I assume that most of the people in the West March don't take the test of name?

Yes. That would be a safe assumption.

And that you're ruling as Lord of the West March precisely because you have?

A glimmer of amusement touched Lord Lirienne's inner voice. *Indeed.*

And last, that the Warden is qualified in all other ways to be Lord, except this one?

Very good.

Is she his wife?

He laughed, although his expression was all graven sobriety. *No. She is his mother.*

Kaylin felt a moment of discomfort as she readjusted her frame of reference. But...none of the Barrani ever looked like a mother, to Kaylin. She couldn't, when it came right down to it, imagine that they could be. She'd never been asked to attend a Barrani birth and wondered idly if they carved their babies out of stone and hauled them to the High Halls only when they felt they could protect their artistry. Birth—of either the Dragons or the Barrani—was not one of the things covered in racial integration classes.

Is there a reason that he's never taken the test of name?

You will have to ask him, although I do not advise it.

What exactly does the Warden of the West March do?

Centuries past, he replied softly, *he spoke with, and tended to, the Hallionne. Lord Barian's father, and his grandfather before him, absorbed the nightmares of the Hallionne. It is Lord Barian's duty now.*

Your sister is not Lord Barian.

No.

Then why did she—

Do you not understand? She knows the burden borne by the West March, and she knows why they must bear it. She is fully capable of doing what the sons of the West March have done.

And anyone else?

No, Kaylin. It is why they die.

And it's why they can't afford to lose him.

Perhaps. But the dreams of the West March fly above this citadel. While they last, they will speak with the Warden.

And not with you.

He did not reply.

* * *

If dinner had ended there, Kaylin would have considered it a win.

The blue-eyed mother of the Warden fell silent. Not to be undone, another Barrani spoke. He was, again, unfamiliar. "I cannot imagine how novel it would be to have a mortal living in the West March. Tell me, Lord Kaylin, how does your experience in the High Halls differ?"

"I'm not a Lord of the Court of the Vale," she replied evenly. She had pretty much lost her appetite. That wouldn't stop her from eating.

"No, of course not."

Now this? This was exactly what she expected from the Barrani. It was, if she was being truthful, what she expected from the Human Caste Court and the moneyed class of her own species.

"There's no convenient—and impartial—test of fitness," Kaylin replied evenly. "Although I'm certain just being a citizen of the West March is qualification enough."

His smile, which was lovely and grating at the same time, froze on his perfect face.

Lord Barian surprised her. He rose. He instantly had the attention of the room, which confirmed Kaylin's sour suspicion that the pathetic mortal was the evening's entertainment. "Enough, Avanel. Lord Kaylin is an honored guest. She has touched the dreams of the Hallionne, which is test enough for the Warden's seat. It is an act of singular grace—and in gratitude, we bid her welcome."

It was a welcome already extended by the reigning Lord of the West March; he did not, in any way, demur. But he watched the Warden; the Warden's glance stopped, briefly, at his, as he surveyed the gathered dignitaries of both Courts.

Avanel didn't apologize. Nor did Kaylin expect an apology;

she imagined that the humiliation of being forced to do so would make her an enemy for life. Dinner was served; wine was offered. A silence broken by the muted syllables of distant conversation ensued, like an armistice.

The next jab at the mere mortal wasn't aimed at Kaylin; the Warden's word appeared to be law. No, the next question came one table over, where Severn was seated.

"Lord Severn."

She turned to see who was speaking and caught the back of a head. The voice was male; the clothing marked the wearer as West March. More than that, she couldn't tell, and she turned back to her food.

"Lord Tanniase."

"It has been some time since a mortal has chosen to visit the West March."

Severn appeared to be eating; he wasn't doing a lot of speaking.

"In fact, I believe the last time one visited, he was not a member of the High Court. His circumstances were, however, highly unusual. Perhaps you recall them?"

"Mortal memory is imperfect, Lord Tanniase."

"Yet you remember me."

Severn failed to reply.

"Perhaps you interact with many of our distant kin in your fabled city. The journey to the West March is not one to be undertaken lightly, yet you chose to make it."

"I did. I believe my sponsor of the time obtained all requisite permissions, and the Hallionne did not refuse me their hospitality."

"The Hallionne do not decide."

"No. I believe the Lord of the West March did."

"In exchange for the warmth of our welcome, you killed a man and took an heirloom with you when you departed."

Kaylin concentrated on her food, which was hard. She wanted to push her chair back from the table, get up, and move to stand by Severn's chair. But he wouldn't appreciate it, and neither would anyone else in the room. She'd never appreciated the visceral nature of Leontine culture quite so much.

"Your memory is harsher than mine," Severn replied. "I was given the heirloom in question because I defeated a Barrani Lord in single combat. I appreciate the concern you feel on behalf of your kin, but believe it misplaced in this case; the weapon was not, and would never have become, yours."

Eat, Kaylin. If you are concerned for Lord Severn, your concern is misplaced.

Is it true? Did he come here to kill a Barrani Lord?

He came, and a man died. Had he, as implied, attempted to steal the weapon he now carries, it would have destroyed him. While he lives, he wields it. It was damaged in the outlands, and there are craftsmen here who might see to its repair. They may well refuse, he added. *But I think it unlikely. He is mortal. The weapon will return to our kin in a brief handful of years.*

Why did you give him permission to travel here? When?

I am not at liberty to tell you if you do not already know. He is, in many ways, yours—but he is a man, not a child. He does not require your permission; nor does he require your knowledge.

"Perhaps we will test your knowledge of our artifacts," Lord Tanniase replied. His voice implied eyes of midnight-blue.

"You propose a challenge?" Severn's voice was softer. Colder. *Who brought him here?*

The Lord of the West March failed to answer.

To Kaylin's lasting surprise, Lord Evarrim spoke. "Lord Tanniase."

"Lord Evarrim."

"I would, of course, enjoy the spectacle of a Lord of any Barrani Court issuing a challenge to one merely mortal; I am certain it would afford us all some amusement. But the outlands appear to be held against us, and the legion of the transformed occupy the forests. The recitation will occur, regardless; if you wish to lower yourself to such a challenge, it might be advantageous to do so when the recitation is complete."

"Are you implying that I might lose such a challenge?"

Lord Evarrim did not reply.

Kaylin couldn't tell whether or not Evarrim's comment was a not-so-subtle goad, but she knew Severn was in no shape to accept such a challenge. He could be in perfect health, and it would still be dicey—enough that Kaylin would bet real money against him.

She ate. The food might have been sawdust. She didn't touch the wine, but remembered enough to use the right utensils. The entire meal reminded her of the entrance exam she had undergone in order to join the Hawks as more than their official mascot. It was worse because she'd wanted to be a Hawk so badly. Passing this exam, on the other hand? The only possible work advantage was that it might prove she was fit for the delicate investigations that involved Barrani—and that meant more time with Barrani.

She was enormously grateful when the ordeal ended. Lord Tanniase had not challenged Severn to a duel. She had been asked no more questions about the High Court, the High Halls, or her unenviable lifespan. She had not, that she was aware of, embarrassed her race or her profession.

But when the Lord of the West March rose, signaling an end to dinner, the Warden rose, as well.

"Lord Kaylin," he said, bowing.

She froze. She was accustomed to being the butt of several jokes; she was even accustomed to condescension. Respect, when it was offered, made her ill at ease; she was certain some game was being played, and she didn't want to become a game piece on whatever board the Barrani had chosen.

But she returned the bow with a nod, stiffening her knees as she remembered the protocols of theoretical equals. "Lord Barian."

"I would converse with you about matters concerning the West March," he said. "If your time is not already spoken for, and you are willing to do so, I extend the hospitality of my humble halls for the evening."

She glanced automatically at the Lord of the West March; his eyes were a cautious blue, but not an angry one. He offered her no guidance. She wanted to say no; she'd had enough testing for one evening. But she wanted to offer no offense, either—not by accident. His intervention had prevented the dinner from descending into mortal-baiting; she owed him.

He noted her hesitation; it wasn't brief.

"I extend my offer of hospitality to Lord Severn; he is, if I am a judge of mortal character, your man."

"I would be honored," she said.

He nodded. It became instantly clear to whom; four men rose and joined him. As did his mother.

Will you at least tell me her name?

Amusement. *She is Avonelle.*

Kaylin wondered why all Barrani names sounded so similar. *Is she Lord Avonelle?*

She is not a Lord of the High Court, as her questions tonight made clear.

Will I seem too obsequious if I call her Lord Avonelle?

No. You have chosen to grace her son with a title that you are not, by etiquette, required to use; extending the same courtesy to his mother would not seem obsequious.

She caught the hidden currents behind that thought and grimaced. Even for the Lord of the West March, fawning respect from mortals was not considered pandering; it was considered inevitable. The Barrani Hawks didn't expect it. But with the single exception of Teela, none of them had a place in the High Court.

Tanniase?

He is a Lord. I understand that you absent yourself from both the Court and its unfortunate politics, but you must learn who comprises that Court. It is relevant, even in the West March. It cannot be irrelevant when the High Halls stand at the heart of your city.

She made a mental note to ask Teela for this information when she had the leisure time to memorize it. She was unlikely to forget Tanniase, however.

CHAPTER 6

Before she departed for the Warden's so-called humble halls, she excused herself. She didn't offer to change, since she was afraid to insult the dress; she did want to let her hair down—literally—because it was so tightly bound it made her scalp hurt.

Severn also excused himself to change; he wasn't wearing clothing that was demonstrably more valuable to everyone present than he himself was. This left Teela serving as her unofficial escort.

"I guess they didn't call a council meeting," Kaylin said as Teela led her to the rooms she'd have had a hard time finding.

"As you surmise. I consider the Warden's offer of hospitality to be at least as dangerous, but there was no politic way to refuse his offer. I'm surprised you realized that."

"I wasn't worried about being politic," Kaylin replied. "He stuck up for me; I owed him one."

"I have warned you in the past about naïveté and optimism, haven't I?"

"Every other day. And no, that's not an exaggeration. Do you think the Warden is playing some kind of game?"

"Yes. It may not be a game of which you will disapprove. Do not needlessly antagonize him."

"Or his mother?"

"I fear it is late for that. Avonelle is the Guardian of the green; she has held that title for centuries. The Warden, in theory, has more power, but theory is always tenuous. Understand that Lord Barian was not her only son; he is merely the only one to survive."

"Did the rest fail the test of name?"

"No. She lost one son in the last war; the other made the journey to the High Halls and failed to return. Barrani mothers are not mortal mothers; mortals feel that immortality, such as it is, is the continuance of their line. The Barrani do not age; we assume that we will exist for all of eternity. We might therefore bear a child every few centuries, if we so choose."

"I saw her at the table, Teela. I know what I saw."

"Yes. It is rumored—and it is only rumor—that she had ambitions for her youngest son; it was he who chose to take the test of name. His brother has not made the same choice; he is the last of her sons. His line is the line of Wardens, through his mother; if he is lost in the same way, it spells an end to the Wardens of her blood unless she bears another son."

"Is it like the position of Consort?"

"No. But there are some similarities."

"Can anyone become Lord of the West March?"

"It is a hereditary title—but yes; the green does not privilege the politics of either Court. The Lord rules, but the Warden serves. It is therefore the position of Warden that the green husbands."

"Teela—what is the green?"

Teela smiled. "I do not know. Perhaps if I knew, I would understand why I alone, of the twelve gathered here, was spared." She hesitated, and then added, "Avonelle was my mother's sister."

The Consort had not wakened; nor had she moved in her sleep. She was a color that Kaylin associated with death. "Is she—is she breathing?" she asked.

Lord Lirienne inclined his head, his expression grave.

"Should I try to wake her?"

"I am not my sister." It was stated as if it were a reply.

Kaylin understood that this man was the Lord of the West March; that he had power and rank; that he was immortal. But she couldn't find the fear that would have forced her to be cautious. "Can I pretend I asked that question again?" She spoke Elantran.

He raised a brow. "To wake her, you will attempt to heal her."

"Not necessarily. I can't heal her if there's nothing physically wrong with her."

"And how would you determine that?" When Kaylin failed to answer, he said, "I will keep watch tonight. If there is any deterioration, I will summon you." He placed his palm over his sister's hand.

Avonelle was not waiting when Kaylin returned to the Warden and his men. Severn was. He glanced at her and she shook her head once. She didn't feel a great desire to discuss the Consort's health in front of total strangers.

The Warden's home was not, by any stretch of the imagination, humble—at least not as mortals understood it. It was as tall and imposing as the building that housed the Lord of the West March; it was not, however, built the same way.

The home of Lord Lirienne boasted a large amount of stone;

it contained the central courtyard with its fountains, and also played home to a theoretically natural source of hot water. The home of the Warden reminded Kaylin of the Hallionne Sylvanne, at least from the outside.

The door was a large tree.

Many of the homes in Elantra were made of wood—but that wood had pretty much stopped growing, on account of being cut down. The doors that led to those homes also boasted things like hinges. And handles. Here, she stared with some dismay at the bark of a very wide tree, glancing nervously at the small dragon.

"I don't have to bleed on this door, do I?"

Severn winced, and she realized she'd fallen straight into her mother tongue in the presence of the Warden of the West March. He didn't wince.

"No, blood isn't necessary," he replied, in Elantran. "You visited the Hallionne Sylvanne on your journey here."

"I did."

"My hall is not sentient. What peace exists within it, I preserve. The door is warded."

Why had she thought this was a good idea? "I have a little problem with door wards."

"How so?"

"Sometimes they object to my presence. It's not all door wards," she added, as he looked down his nose. "But—the ones in the Imperial Palace, and at least one in Lord Lirienne's home—" She grimaced. "It's harder to explain than to demonstrate."

"It will not harm you?"

"No. Not directly."

"Does it harm the ward?"

She should be so lucky. "It hasn't harmed any of the wards so far." She lifted her left hand, and placed the palm firmly against the midsection of the trunk. It was a guess; there didn't seem to be much in the way of obvious markings.

But the small dragon considered it all boring; he didn't hiss, leap up, or bite her hand.

The door opened, in a manner of speaking; the tree dilated, the bark folding back in wrinkles, as if it were cloth. Usually Kaylin would be grateful for the lack of fuss; today, it was slightly humiliating.

"It appears that my wards do not consider you a danger to my home," Lord Barian said. If he was amused, he kept it to himself. He entered and turned to offer her an arm; he nodded at Severn, and the four men Kaylin assumed were his guard stepped back to allow Severn entry.

The interior of the Warden's home matched the exterior in many ways; the halls were as tall as the High Halls, but they weren't made of stone—or at least the supporting beams weren't; they were trees. They grew, evenly spaced; their branches formed the bower of a ceiling. Through the gaps in wood, Kaylin thought she could see stars, but she had a feeling that rain, when it fell, didn't penetrate the branches the way light did.

He caught the direction of her gaze, because she had to tilt her head and expose her throat to see it. "Does it worry you?"

She shook her head. "This is what I imagined the dwellings in the West March would look like."

"Why? The High Halls are marvels of architecture, and they are all of stone."

"The High Halls are in the heart of a city. There are roads and neatly tended lawns and spaces in the inner city where very little that isn't weeds grow. The West March is in the heart of a forest. I could walk for days—maybe weeks—and not meet or hear another living person." She hesitated, and then added, "I thought forests would feel like this: grand and ancient and hushed."

"They did not meet your expectations?"

"There were a lot of bugs and a lot of the transformed. I didn't really get a sense of peace."

He smiled. "There is peace here, at the moment. Come. If you wish sight of stars, we might speak in the bowers above."

This was not a place for the old or the exhausted. The bowers above involved a walk around the central pillar in the hall—a tree which was fitted with a narrow, spiraling staircase. It was as tall as the Hawklord's tower, but the stairs were all filigree from the looks of them; Kaylin could see the ground beneath her feet. The Barrani didn't feel a great need for something as practical as rails, either.

But the stairs did exit onto a platform that seemed to be part of the tree. A bench girded the trunk; it, like the branches, was not shaved of bark. There was something about it that felt natural, rather than unfinished.

The branches here rose; they offered an unimpeded view of the West March—at this height, it appeared to be mostly trees—and the night sky.

"This dwelling is considered rustic," he said softly. "But it is the seat of the Warden; it has been my home for all but a few decades."

"Were the rest spent in the High Halls?"

"Yes. In the shadow of a Dragon, surrounded by a sea of mortals and the specter of failure."

She glanced from the sky to the Warden; no trace of humor touched his expression.

"I hated your city. I hated the noise, the smell, the lack of peace; it is *never* silent unless one is encased in the stone of the High Halls."

"You found them suffocating," Kaylin guessed.

He nodded. "I do not hear the voice of the green when I am in your city."

"Can you hear it now?"

He did smile then. Kaylin had been cautioned not to trust the Barrani; at times, it was hard.

"Ah. Can you see them?"

She squinted obligingly into the night sky. She could see treetops, the occasional glimpse of a building's roof, and a lot of stars. She was about to remind the Warden of the marked inferiority of mortal vision when she caught a glimpse of wings.

She glanced at his face; the entirety of the deck was bathed in a gentle luminescence. His eyes, as he watched the eagles, were green. They were the color of the dress she wore. His eyes rounded as the eagles approached; he stood and walked to the edge of the platform. It had rails—but they were decorative, and they were short.

Severn was a shadow on this deck. He had not spoken, and hadn't moved, since they'd arrived. When she cast a worried glance in his direction, she was surprised; she'd expected him to be wary and watchful. He was the latter, but his eyes were on the approaching eagles, his lips turned up in a half smile that seemed almost unconscious.

When they were close, the Warden held out one arm. "Lord Kaylin, if you would do the same, they will both land."

She held out one arm looking so dubious that Severn chuckled. "I don't have arm guards. I have a dress I'm sure it's an act of treason to damage, and given the Barrani, it won't matter if the eagles cause that damage. I'm wearing it. It'll be my fault."

The first of the eagles landed on the raised arm of the Warden.

The second landed on Kaylin's left forearm. As it alighted,

the marks on her arms began to glow. If she'd had suspicions that these weren't real birds, it was confirmed; this one weighed no more than the small dragon.

The small dragon, however, sat up. He warbled.

"Well met," the eagle said—to the small dragon. The Warden turned at the sound of his voice. The eagle on his arm said, "And well met, Barian. It has been long indeed since we have spoken."

"Too long," the Warden replied. He lifted his free hand and gently stroked the bird's head, as if it were the head of a newborn babe. "What does the recitation hold for us?"

The eagle surprised them both. He answered. But he answered in a language that, while tantalizingly familiar in its parts, failed in all ways to cohere. Kaylin turned to Lord Barian. "Did you understand a word of that?"

He laughed. It was a shock of sound, coming as it did from a Barrani. "Perhaps one. I am fond of the sound of it; they spoke it often in my childhood."

"Your language is confining," the eagle on Kaylin's arm said. "But you are a confined people, huddling in your singular shapes; you are easily broken."

She frowned. It wasn't the first time she'd heard this. "The Warden calls you the dreams of the Hallionne."

"He does."

"But you came from the shadows he called the nightmares of the Hallionne."

"Did we?"

"Yes. What landed in my hands a few hours ago were shadows. But you emerged from them when—"

"Yes?"

"When the marks on my arms started to glow." It sounded lame even to Kaylin, and she'd said it.

"Are we, brother?" her bird said to the bird on the Warden's arm. "Are we dreams or nightmares?"

"They are the same," the other bird replied. "Dream. Nightmare. They are things done beneath the surface of the world."

"So…you don't feel any different than you did when you landed?"

They regarded each other for a long moment, and then turned their beady eyes—and she'd seldom seen eyes that fit that description so perfectly—on Kaylin. "Did we land?"

"More or less the same way you landed just now, but with less feathers."

They regarded each other again, and Kaylin snorted. What had been a suspicion was hardening into certainty as they spoke. "When I visited Hallionne Bertolle, his brothers woke. I don't know if Bertolle has dreams; I don't know what the Hallionne of the West March is called. No one speaks his— or her—name."

"No one who dwells in this small enclave has ever spoken his name," the bird replied. "Bertolle's brothers have woken from the long sleep?"

"They had a little help," Kaylin said, with sudden misgivings. She was certain she'd have bruised shins if Teela had come with them. "Were they not supposed to wake?"

But the birds now had words for each other, and as they conversed in their odd, melodious language, she turned to Lord Barian, who was staring at her. "What it is that you truly do in the city of Elantra?" His eyes were blue—but they weren't the shade that meant anger or suspicion.

"I'm a Private. I serve the Halls of Law in that capacity. I hope one day to be Corporal."

"Truly? You bear those marks, you can speak to the sleeping lost brethren of the Hallionne Bertolle, and you can wake the dreams of Hallionne Alsanis, yet you work as a Private?

I recall very little about the Halls of Law; it is an institution that is irrelevant to the Barrani."

"It's not. For crimes Barrani commit against each other, the laws of exception can be invoked by the party deemed to be the injured party. But for crimes committed against other races, the Barrani are under the purview of the Imperial Hawks."

"And if not the Hawks, the Wolves?"

Kaylin shrugged. "The Emperor."

"It has long been a marvel to me that he shelters behind the ranks of his mortals."

She shook her head, determined not to be offended, although it was hard. "We're not there for his protection, of course. We're there for the protection of the rest of the city. If the Emperor so chooses he can burn down half the city— but most of the people who die in the resultant fire won't be criminals. We do what his fire can't. Is Alsanis the name of the Hallionne that was lost?"

"Yes. Does An'Teela still serve the Imperial Hawks?"

"She does. Neither of us are here as Hawks; we're outside of our jurisdiction."

"Do you consider her a friend?"

"Yes."

"Do you know her history?"

"I can't possibly claim to know all of it, but I know what happened in the West March when she was young enough to be considered a child—and I know that she eventually came back, and she wore a variant of the same dress I'm wearing now. I know how her mother died. I know where. And I know that it's considered an act of high treason to attempt to do now what was attempted then." She tried to dampen the heat in her voice, and slid back into High Barrani. You could insult someone in High Barrani, but you had to work harder to do it.

"I did not come here to discuss Teela."

"No."

"Why did you ask me here?"

"We asked," the eagles said in unison.

"The Consort touched the nightmares of the Hallionne, and she has not yet awakened. Lord Lirienne," she continued, choosing to forego the title that seemed to vex Lord Barian's mother, "said that the Warden absorbs those nightmares, except when the Lady is present."

"I would accept them, regardless, but it is proof that she is present. Lord Lirienne took two war bands and left the West March in haste, at the urging of the Hallionne Orbaranne. We did not know if either he, or the party that set out from the city, survived."

"How did he know to leave?"

"You will have to ask him. I do not speak with any of the Hallionne except Alsanis—and even that speech is limited. I touch the edges of his dreaming, and his nightmare, no more. My grandfather spoke to the Hallionne frequently. After the disaster in the green, he could still communicate with Alsanis; it became more difficult with the passage of time.

"They're not trapped in the Hallionne," Kaylin said. She meant the transformed. The lost children. He knew.

"They were," he replied. "The Hallionne's defenses are strong; what occurs within its walls occurs at the heart of his power. The Hallionne were not, and have never been, what we are; they have a breadth of experience that we could not survive. The children are called lost for a reason; they are no longer Barrani in any meaningful way."

"Are they the nightmares of the Hallionne?"

"No."

"Nightmares first, lost children later." She hesitated and then said, "They remember who—and what—they were."

"Demonstrably; they would not be so great a danger to us otherwise."

"Dreams of Alsanis," Kaylin said quietly to the two eagles, "how do I wake you? When you landed in my hands, did you sense me at all?"

They glanced at each other. "Yes. You wear the blood of the green, and beneath its folds, you bear the marks of the Chosen."

"Can you read them?"

They turned to stare at each other, and then once again, at Kaylin. "Can you not?" one finally asked.

It was embarrassing to admit her failure to the large birds, but ignorance wasn't a crime. "No."

"But—"

Severn joined her, sliding an arm around her upper back. "Have you spoken with others who bear similar marks?" he asked.

"Yes. Not often. We are not Chosen. The Hallionne are not Chosen. They could not be and do what must be done; they do not travel."

Neither did Kaylin, if she had any choice in the matter. She kept this to herself.

"Were the others able to read the marks?"

"How could they not? The marks were of them."

"I didn't choose the marks," Kaylin said quietly.

"Then how do you bear their weight?"

"They chose me."

"How can you do what must be done if you cannot read what is written?"

"The marks didn't come with instructions," Kaylin said, voice flat.

Severn, however, said, "Can you tell her what they say? Can you tell her what task they're meant to accomplish?"

They glanced at each other again. "We are not Chosen," they finally said—in unison. They said more, but it was unintelligible; it was clearly language, and just as clearly beyond her grasp.

She lifted a hand. "Can you teach me the language you speak?"

They considered each other again. "It is vexing," the one on Barian's arm said, "but we do not believe it can be taught to such a small mind. You cannot speak it."

"But the marks would not be given to one who is mute," the other eagle said.

"Demonstrably they were," Kaylin said. She was annoyed; no one liked to be talked about in the third person when they were in the literal middle of a discussion. "Wait."

Severn knew that tone of voice.

"Can the lost children speak the language?"

There was a long pause. "Yes," the eagle on Barian's arm said, the single word spoken in sorrow. "Yes, now they can."

"Did the Hallionne teach them?"

The eagles fell silent. Kaylin reached out and grabbed the leg of the bird on her arm before it could fly; Barian's eagle was already gone.

"I won't ask more," she said softly. "But I need to understand what you are."

"We are the dreams Alsanis," the eagle replied gravely. "What we see and know, he sees and knows—but he can no longer discern what is fixed in place."

She rushed onward. "The Wardens take the nightmares of Alsanis."

"They do. It is to the Wardens that we come, when we are conscious."

"Do the nightmares end?"

"End?"

"When we—when mortals—have dreams or nightmares, they end when we wake. Sometimes they drive us in terror from sleep, they feel so real. Will the Consort wake from the nightmares of Alsanis?"

"Barian," the eagle said, "does she speak truth?"

"She speaks truth as mortals perceive it, although mortals are capable of lying."

"What would be the point in lying now?" Kaylin said, in frustrated Elantran. "Nightmares *aren't* reality. Lying about them won't change either the nightmares or real life."

"The nightmares of Alsanis are not the nightmares of mortals," was Barian's reply.

"I'm beginning to understand that. Most mortal nightmares don't fly through the air, land on a person, and get absorbed. *Will* the Consort wake?"

The eagle said, "Take me with you, Chosen. Take me to her."

"That's not an answer."

"The Barrani do not sleep."

"Yes, but she's sleeping now."

"Take me with you," the eagle said again. To the small dragon, he spoke unintelligibly; the small dragon squawked. "Barian, it would be best if you accompany the Chosen."

"I have offered her the hospitality of the Warden's perch," he replied.

"Can I just say one thing? I'm not Barrani, and mortals *do* need sleep."

"The marks you bear should protect you," the eagle replied.

Kaylin looked down the long spiraling stairs. Sleep wasn't in the cards. She released the eagle's leg.

"My apologies, Lord Kaylin," Lord Barian said. His eyes were the more familiar shade of blue, at least where Barrani were concerned. "I did not intend this."

She said nothing for about twenty steps. "Lord Lirienne said that the Wardens of the West March die prematurely because of the burden of the nightmares. Is he wrong?"

"He is not." Barian's words were stiff.

"Five nightmares came out of the trees on the edge of the West March. Is that normal? Is that what usually happens?"

"No, Lord Kaylin."

"Call me Kaylin, or just skip the name. I don't particularly care for the title 'Lord.'"

Silence. It was broken by Lord Barian, and only after another twenty steps had gone by. "It is a title you earned."

"Yes, but it's only important to Barrani, and none of the Barrani Hawks use it. It doesn't change my job description. It doesn't change my duties. And it sounds pretentious."

He laughed. She actually liked the sound of his laughter. At any other time, she might have joined him.

"If five such nightmares are unusual, and they arrived at the exact same time as the Consort, did it not occur to you to intervene or give her warning?"

"You must have known," he replied. "You intervened."

"Yes—but you might have done the same. You're the Warden. I'm a *Private* in service to the Imperial Hawks."

"And yet you did intervene. Why?"

"Because she's the Consort and whatever the black birds were they were clearly causing a lot of pain!" She struggled to hold on to her temper, but every step of descent increased her anxiety. Anxiety was a product of fear, and Kaylin had never handled fear well.

"And it was your responsibility as Lord of the Court to come to her aid."

"No!" She exhaled. "Yes." She slowed and tried to walk in a more measured, less stomping, way. "Tell me how the nightmares affect you."

"Do you generally speak about your mortal nightmares?"

"Only if I'm feeling spiteful and want to bore the guys in the office."

"Lord Severn?"

"She means it literally. She does speak from time to time of her nightmares; it is not uncommon in mortal cultures." Severn spoke in High Barrani. "If the Consort fails to wake—and Kaylin is beginning to realize that this is now likely—it is Lord Kaylin who will attempt to wake her."

"How?"

"How did Lord Kaylin touch the dreams of the Hallionne?" he replied, his voice the essence of the calm Kaylin lacked. "She does not ask for the information to imply any weakness upon the part of the Wardens; no more does the Consort accept the burden of those nightmares as criticism. But Lord Kaylin is awake; the Consort is not.

"The Lady was forced by circumstance to fully wake Bertolle; she was forced, only a few days later, to wake Kariastos. Were it not for the Consort, it is my belief—my mortal belief—that the Hallionne Orbaranne would now be lost. The Consort's ability to speak to the green has been tested without pause since she left the High Halls. It is possible that the absorption of these nightmares, without the prior wakenings, would not have unduly taxed her; we will never know.

"What we now know is that she sleeps. What Lord Kaylin asks, she asks because any information might provide prior warning."

"Prior warning?"

"Lord Kaylin is a healer," Severn said.

CHAPTER 7

In general, Barrani were more likely to be impressed if Kaylin was introduced as a rabid, three-headed dog. Kaylin stumbled, and righted herself on the side of the tree. She glanced at Barian, whose eyes were predictably darker in shade.

"Barrani do not require sleep," he said. "In that, you are correct. Frequently, when in the sleeping Hallionne, my kin will do so; it passes time. Sleep is therefore not a foreign concept. We are not often visited by either dream or nightmare in the mortal sense; I believe, in cases where sanity is not in question, sleep *is* required for mortals to experience either state."

"You have nightmares when you're awake?"

"In a fashion. We do not seek the nightmares of the Hallionne for the simple experience—although there are those among my kin who might for the novelty of it. The Wardens absorb the nightmares of the Hallionne in part because they are, and have been for centuries, our only contact with Alsanis."

Kaylin concentrated on the descent, her hand hugging bark,

her forehead growing permanent furrows. "Why are the Wardens the keepers of the Hallionne?"

"If you mean to ask why the other Hallionne have no visible keepers, I commend you on your observation. The answer is twofold. I will give you the common and accepted variant. The Warden tends the green. The heart of the West March is the heart of the green; it is where the ancient stories are remade and renewed. Ancients once lived in the West March; the forests and the environs were their creation.

"It is said that the Ancients who created our race chose to dwell here." He fell silent until the descent ended, once again, with solid floor. Kaylin, by dint of lessons with Diarmat, had learned to wait; she didn't press him for the second explanation.

"The Lord of the West March has said little about the battle surrounding the Hallionne Orbaranne. What I know is this: many of the men and women who set out into the forest at Orbaranne's urgent request were lost. Those who returned spoke of the transformed, and a forest infested with the particular danger they posed.

"They thought the unthinkable, when they arrived within range of Orbaranne: that the Hallionne had fallen."

Kaylin said nothing. She knew, better than anyone, how close that had come to being the truth.

"I have also been told that the danger passed, and only when it had—and miles of forested land had been utterly leveled—did you exit the Hallionne at the side of the Lord of the West March. You did not enter it by his side."

"No."

He paused again, falling silent as the Barrani often did when they were sifting through their perfect memories. "You spoke of the brothers of the Hallionne Bertolle."

She nodded.

"They were, at one point, kin to the being that ascended. They were, in a loose sense, his family. They remained with the Hallionne, asleep in the heart of his domain. Did you likewise see Orbaranne's kin?"

She shook her head. "Orbaranne didn't have brothers—not the way Bertolle once did."

"Did you speak with the Hallionne Orbaranne?"

She hesitated. He marked it. But she finally said, "Yes. We waited together for the Lord of the West March. I think she knew he was coming; I certainly didn't."

"Did anything about Orbaranne strike you as unusual?"

"I'm not Barrani. I don't generally enter the Hallionne, and as far as I can tell, the Barrani don't really *like* them. But now that you ask, yes. Orbaranne seemed almost human, to me. I've been inside other buildings that have personalities and voices. Most of them can appear human, but they're really not." He led and she followed, thinking. "The transformed tried to destroy Orbaranne."

"Yes."

"Iberrienne kidnapped hundreds of humans in order to do so." She hesitated again. "When they failed, she kept the humans within the Hallionne. She said they wouldn't be able to remain for long—but they were her guests."

"And guests are the reason for the Hallionne's existence."

Kaylin nodded, her frown deepening. "Is it possible that she was mortal, when she chose to become Hallionne?"

"That is a question only the Ancients—or the Hallionne herself—could answer. Did you note anything else about Orbaranne?"

Had she? Kaylin remembered the last glimpse she'd had of the Hallionne.

Hallionne were buildings, like Tara was a building. They could hear what anyone within their walls was thinking—

and their walls could be immense; the outer dimensions didn't confine the interior at all. Within their realms they were like small, distinct gods; they could change the furniture under your butt if you thought it was uncomfortable. They could re-create—down to the smallest of details—an apartment you'd lived in for most of your adult life, even if you couldn't remember them as clearly yourself.

So it wasn't a surprise that Orbaranne could re-create the festival gates of Elantra. It wasn't a surprise that she could map out the streets and the buildings—in varying states of repair— that girded them. But she couldn't create the *people*.

And for a brief time, she didn't have to. She had guests— she'd called them guests—in the form of over a hundred humans who had been taken, marked, and dramatically altered by Barrani. They couldn't leave; Orbaranne knew that. But she couldn't keep them, either. While they were willing to stay, she provided them the comforts of the best parts of home.

Which was the duty of a Hallionne.

But it wasn't why. Kaylin knew. She'd seen the expression on Orbaranne's Avatar. Orbaranne was *happy*. She had company.

"I think—I think the Hallionne get lonely," she finally said. She expected Barian to say something dismissive; if Teela were here, she certainly would have.

But he said, with a pained half smile, "Yes. Even Alsanis. We would visit, as very small children. My earliest clear memories are of Alsanis. He was always bemused by infants, and there were so few. He expected us to be able to assume adult form instantly, and at will."

"Alsanis was like Bertolle?"

"I do not know Bertolle. I have never spoken with him. But I believe you would find them similar. The hospitality of the Hallionne was not, of course, required by the denizens of the West March; we did not go to his halls for protection or escape. We paid our respects. We listened to his stories. Ah, no, not the regalia—but stories of a bygone age, in which nothing in the universe was solid or fixed.

"Imagine a world in shape and form like the Hallionne: ever-changing, always responsive, always both ancient and new. The second duty of the Wardens, and the duty that is only rarely referenced, is that: we were his distant, lost kin. We kept him company. It is a small thing; to most of my kin, who see the Hallionne as fortresses in times of war, it is insignificant.

"Children are lonely. Children crave affection and company. Yes, Lord Kaylin, even Barrani children. But it does not, and cannot, define them. They do not speak of it; it is a weakness. But if it is a weakness, it is one I believe the Hallionne share, and in just the same fashion. It does not define them, nor does it define their duties; it is a yearning."

He had led her to the entrance of the hall, and offered her an arm. "Lord Severn, will you wait or will you return to the halls of the Lord of the West March?"

"I will accept your counsel in this," Severn replied, which almost shocked Kaylin. The small dragon was seated, rather than supine, and he turned his tiny head and clucked at Severn. He didn't appear to be angry.

"I have offered you the hospitality, and therefore the protection, of my home. It is a protection that does not extend beyond my halls, but none of those who serve me will act against you, except at need."

"Lord Kaylin—"

"Will go, with the dreams of Alsanis, to the Lady's side. She may well go beyond, to a place where neither you, nor I, may follow. I leave the decision in your hands. But I offer this: I will protect her with my life. I play no games. I little care for the politics of the High Court in this single instance.

While Lord Kaylin is within the West March, I will offer her the full protection of my line."

"No one will harm me while I'm in this dress," Kaylin said.

"You are almost entirely correct," Lord Barian replied gravely.

"It's considered almost treason to hurt this dress."

"Ah, no. That is your interpretation, and it is not entirely correct. It is considered treason in the West March to act against either the harmoniste or the Teller. It is considered treason," he continued, "to subject children to the regalia. I invite you to consider why."

"Because it was tried, and it was an unmitigated disaster."

"Indeed. We are a practical people, Lord Kaylin. I understand that you consider our manners complicated to an extreme, but there are reasons for the laws we hand down."

Kaylin was exhausted, but she was good at working through exhaustion; if she hadn't been, her work at the Guild of Midwives would have killed her. The thought of the midwives and their infrequent emergencies made her throat tighten. She'd had time to inform them that she'd be traveling outside of the city for at least six weeks. She'd also seen the look on Marya's face as she received the news.

Marya wasn't above using guilt as a lever when things were desperate—and things could get desperate, as the midwives guild itself was not a high-powered guild with golden pockets. But if Kaylin didn't pay dues to practice under the auspices of the guild—and she didn't, as she couldn't afford them—she didn't charge for her services. Being called at all hours of the day or night seemed a small price to pay for the opportunity to save the lives of women and their newborns.

She was aware that the midwives guild *did* charge for some of the services she provided, but she'd made absolutely clear that there was to be a sliding scale—with zero on the poor end of the scale. Deadly emergencies weren't particularly snob-bish; they came to people in all walks in life. The people who couldn't afford her services were Kaylin's chief concern.

On the other hand, her presence in the guild had done much to increase the money coming in. She considered charg-ing a fee, but she was beyond lousy at negotiating on her own behalf: she would have to put a price on her services, and to do that she would have to evaluate them objectively. There were doctors in Elantra, some of whom Kaylin privately con-sidered to be quacks, but none of them had Kaylin's talent.

None of them had Kaylin's marks.

The marks had been the indirect cause of deaths across the city. Deaths of children who had the misfortune to be about the same age as Kaylin had been at the time, and who had also had the misfortune to be poor and unprotected. She hadn't killed them. But if these marks hadn't existed on her skin, they wouldn't have died.

Doing volunteer work at the midwives guild was an act of atonement. She couldn't go back in time to prevent deaths from happening—no matter how desperately those deaths scarred her. Death was death. But she *could* be there at the start of a life; she could be there to stop death from arriving. The marks themselves implied a power that she had never fully un-derstood, but she'd come to understand one thing well: she could heal. She couldn't bring the dead back to life, for which she was grateful; if she could, she would have had to move out of the city—in secret—change her name, and go into hid-ing. The requests from the bereaved would never, ever stop.

If her ability was an open secret in the upper echelons of the Halls of Law, it wasn't taken completely seriously by those on the ground floor; most of the old guard saw her as the angry thirteen-year-old she'd been when she'd first walked through the doors. They'd never seen her power at work, and couldn't believe that it wasn't somehow an exaggeration. And she'd learned—over time—to appreciate that.

The Barrani had never doubted her ability.

But only the Barrani had seen her use it to kill. Even Marcus had only seen the end result, not the death itself. The Barrani considered murder to be an extreme form of politics, rather than a gross miscarriage of justice. Flamboyant murders—such as those that involved the Arcane arts—were considered variations on a theme. If you *could* kill, the implements didn't matter. The information about methods used was useful as a counter, no more.

It was really hard to outrage the Barrani when it came to big things; they'd seen it all. Healing, which would be considered a blessing by most, was an act of aggression and intrusion; squashing a bloodsucking insect was clearly so outrageous that an entire war band could fall completely silent while staring daggers at any part of her body that wasn't covered in dress.

She was reminded of the fact that the Barrani could be outraged—coldly—by the most unpredictable things when the Lord of the West March appeared at the head of eight armed and armored men shortly after she arrived at his hall with the Warden in tow. The eagles chose to land before the doors were slammed in their faces.

"Warden," the Lord of the West March said, in a tone that implied the difference in their respective ranks.

"Lord Lirienne," the Warden replied, in a tone that negated that difference. Kaylin desperately wished that Severn—injured and recovering—had not chosen to remain behind. If he wasn't at home among the Barrani, it didn't show, but Severn had never been self-conscious.

"Lord Kaylin."

"I'm—I'm sorry to bother you. I know it's late."

One of his brows rose; the corner of his lip twitched. In

Barrani, this was indicative—in this situation—of riotous laughter. At her expense, of course. She glanced at the Warden, and saw a similar, if more pained, expression on his face. She didn't enjoy the humiliation of being the object of hilarity, but was old enough now to appreciate the way it cut the tension between the two men.

"This was Lord Kaylin's request?" the Lord of the West March said, his tone softening.

She willed him to say yes; it wasn't as if the Barrani considered lying a crime. Given the length of time it took to respond, she thought he'd considered it. "It was not entirely her request, no."

The eagles, silent until this moment, turned the intensity of their focus upon the Lord of the West March; they might have been puppies, given his reaction. "We asked. If we have transgressed, forgive us. We had hoped to have more time."

"You will not remain among us."

"No. We do not know how long we have, but the pull to oblivion is strong. The Chosen said that the Lady absorbed three of the nightmares, and has since remained asleep. Has she awoken in the Chosen's absence?"

"No."

"We would like to see her."

All of the Barrani in the hall except the Lord of the West March tensed.

For no reason she could think of, Kaylin said, "I'll be with them the entire time." This would not have brought much comfort to most of the people she shared an office with.

"With your permission, I will also remain," the Warden said. It sounded like a genuine offer, not a demand.

"It will be a very crowded room," Lord Lirienne replied.

"Lord Kaylin is your *kyuthe*, Lord Lirienne. I have not asked the circumstances that drew her to your attention; I am sure there is a story behind it, when we have the leisure to indulge in them. I know, however, what drew her to mine: she touched the nightmares of Alsanis, and the eagles woke. We have argued long about the fate of Alsanis—but the dreams speak with his voice; they see."

"I have never argued that Alsanis is dead," Lord Lirienne replied. "Nor has the High Lord."

"You have argued that he is altered beyond all recognition. The Hallionne has not opened its doors since the day of the betrayal; were he so transformed that he did not prize the safety of his guests—"

"His guests are not confined to the Hallionne," Kaylin said, in anxious High Barrani.

Lord Barian stiffened and turned to face her after glancing briefly at the Lord of the West March. What he saw confirmed Kaylin's words.

"If you're speaking of the children who were lost."

"We are. You cannot comprehend Alsanis's sorrow," he told her softly. "Although he was Hallionne, the children confined within his walls killed all but a handful of the Barrani Lords who had traveled with him. He could not protect his guests; the minds of the lost children were too chaotic, too unordered. They thought all things simultaneously—and none. He offered what warning he could; he closed whole wings in an attempt to contain the lost.

"And he closed his doors entirely to the Wardens, and my line. Only through the dreams of Alsanis could we speak to him at all. He chose to sacrifice himself in order to prevent further deaths; he could not offer hospitality in safety to any."

"Except the lost children."

"He did not consider it hospitality—but he could not immediately destroy them. He tried," he added softly. "They were anathema to the green."

"They didn't leave through the front doors," Kaylin told him softly. "They left through the portal paths. When they attacked Orbaranne—and they were involved, I'd bet my eyes on it—the brunt of their attack was on the portal paths."

"They fielded a large force on normal roads, as well—but I concur. They did not slip out through the literal front doors."

She turned to the silent eagles. "Did Alsanis grant them permission to leave?"

"They did not leave," the eagle on her arm replied gravely.

"They did—"

"They are not as you are. They did not leave the Hallionne." He turned to the eagle that now rested upon the Warden's arm, and they conferred in their lilting and entirely unintelligible language.

"Are they at war with Alsanis now?"

"No."

"Are they at home?"

"Yes."

The Lord of the West March raised one hand. "That is enough, Lord Kaylin. If you have come to offer aid to the Consort, we must not tarry."

Not a word was spoken as they traversed the great halls, not even by the eagles. They might have been part of a funeral procession, given their expressions. What the eagles meant to Lord Barian, they clearly did not mean to Lord Lirienne, but the almost open suspicion with which they'd been greeted at the doors had been set aside.

No, kyuthe, *it has not. Avonelle's questions this eve were an open act of hostility available only because you are both mortal and foreign. Had Lord Barian's brother succeeded in his test, it is likely he would now be Lord of the West March.*

But—but that's a hereditary title.

Heredity, like any other custom, is subject to the demands of power. If I could not hold the West March against her son, I would not deserve to rule it. Her son failed.

She frowned. *You liked him,* she said, in some surprise.

It is not relevant. Had he become a Lord of the High Court, one of the two of us would not have survived.

Lord Barian didn't take the test.

No. His brother's failure was vindication for his cowardice.

Kaylin frowned. *I don't think he's a coward.*

No?

No. I think he feels responsible for the West March. He can fulfill those responsibilities as Warden. He can't, if he's dead.

He is not like his brother; he looks inward, rather than out.

I don't think the green cares.

"The green does care," the eagle on her arm said.

Lord Barian's brows rose slightly; Lord Lirienne's expression did not change at all.

This is why you don't care for the dreams of Alsanis. Kaylin grimaced.

The Lord of the West March laughed. *It is one reason among many. At the moment, I am enraged by their existence.*

To Kaylin's surprise, this was true. He made no attempt to hide the depth of his fury; it opened up in front of her like a door.

I do not know what Barian told you, he continued when she failed to find words, *but my sister cannot be woken. We have tried. Lord Nightshade and Lord Evarrim have been by her side since dinner. She does not respond to touch, to sound, or to the enchantments it is safe to cast. Barian allowed her to take the burden of his responsibility upon herself. If she fails to wake, I will kill him. I will not kill him quickly. I may be moved to allow his mother to live.*

Kaylin glanced at Lord Barian. Swallowing, she said, *I'll wake her.*

You are so certain you are capable of it?
She wasn't, and he knew it.

To her surprise, Lord Evarrim and Nightshade were still in attendance when they at last arrived. The Consort lay between them; they stood watch. Evarrim noted Kaylin's presence with a grim nod that all but screamed distaste; Nightshade offered her the nod that passes between equals. Neither man spoke, but as she approached the Consort, they stepped back to give her both room and their silent permission.

Evarrim seemed ill-pleased by the presence of both Barian and the eagle that rested, weightless, on her arm. As it was clear that the bird was there with the Lord of the West March's permission, he said nothing.

Lord Barian seemed entirely unconcerned that an Outcaste wore the Teller's crown.

Kaylin knew the Consort's skin shouldn't be the color it was. Barrani skin was generally flawless and pale—but this had a sallow, green tinge that looked worse than unhealthy. She stopped herself from checking for a pulse, and then realized it didn't matter. The only person present she would have spared her sudden fear already knew what she was feeling.

She knelt by the Consort's side, and very carefully touched her hand. It was cold. Morgue cold. "Lord Barian," she said, in High Barrani, "if you have anything of import to tell me about the nightmares of the Hallionne, now is the time."

"I can tell you less about the nightmares than our companions can," he replied. "They are one."

She resisted the urge to snap something rude in Leontine.

"He is not wrong," the eagle on her arm said. She released the Consort's hand and attempted to remove the bird; his weightless claws tightened. "Do not be foolish. We have accompanied you for a reason, Chosen. If you set us aside, how will you speak to the nightmares?"

"Probably the same way I'm speaking to you," she replied. "But less politely."

The bird spoke to its companion; their voices rose.

The Barrani found their discussion fascinating. Kaylin, hand once again touching the still iciness of the Consort's, found it annoying. She closed her eyes and counted to ten; she made it to four, and not for the usual reason.

In the silence of watchful Barrani, in the darkness behind closed lids, she could hear the eagles speak, and the language that sounded so painfully familiar took on the tones and the range of sound she associated with song. There was a distinctive cadence to the words, a stretching and thinning of syllables that speech didn't normally contain.

Music—even wordless music—had a feel to it. It evoked emotion. There was a simple harmony to the speech of these creatures, although she couldn't quite place how—they seemed to take turns, to be singing different parts, and their voices were distinct. They didn't overlap. But there was no point in expecting dreams in the shape of eagles to actually make sense.

"Lady." Kaylin's voice was rough and tuneless in comparison.

The Consort didn't answer—no surprise there.

Kaylin inhaled, exhaled, and then reached out with the power that she used to heal the injured. If there was nothing wrong with the Consort physically, there would be nothing *to* heal.

The dreams of Alsanis continued their song, and as Kaylin listened, she understood why it sounded so familiar; she had heard something similar before—but never in voices like these. The Consort had sung something with the same feel, the same tone, when she had been forced to wake the Hallionne

Bertolle. There was a yearning, a desire, and an emptiness to the song of the dreams of Alsanis that reminded Kaylin very much of the Consort's song of awakening.

She started to tell the eagles that the Consort wasn't a Hallionne and couldn't be woken that way, but stopped. She had no idea whether or not that was true, anymore, because something about the Consort was subtly different from the other Barrani she had healed. She almost forgot to breathe, the panic was so sharp.

But it was hard to hold on to it; the song of the dreams of Alsanis was too insistent, too urgent; there was a warmth—a heat—to the urgency. She felt it pass through the Consort's hand into her own. As it did, she heard a second song.

If the first song was the conversation of the dreams, the second was the construction of the nightmares. It should have been cacophony. It wasn't. Somehow, the two disparate songs overlapped and blended; they were distinct, but they were—as the eagles had said—part of a single piece.

Kaylin's arms began to burn. So did the back of her neck, her legs, and a small spot in the center of her forehead. She knew the marks that adorned over half her body were now glowing. *Lady,* she thought, squeezing the Consort's hand. *Wake.*

There was nothing wrong with her body. There was nothing to heal. But Kaylin knew, as she listened, that the Consort wouldn't wake without intervention. Barrani didn't require sleep, but even Barrani could starve to death.

The small dragon bit her ear hard enough, she was certain, to draw blood. She let loose a volley of Leontine as she opened her eyes and grabbed for him with her left hand. Her right remained tightly clasped around the Consort's.

"Lord Kaylin, your ear is bleeding."

"I kind of guessed that. I don't suppose you have a cage?"

The small dragon squawked. He batted her face with surprisingly heavy wings as he pushed off her shoulder, roundly berating her in his unintelligible bird-speak.

Except what she heard was cadence. Rhythm. Nothing in his lizard vocal chords evoked music, but she realized that he was trying to sing when both of the eagles fixed their gaze on him. Their voices rose; she was caught instantly by the shift in their song, as if it were current and she was almost drowning.

Her very frustrating companion squawked back. It was a harsh noise; it blended with nothing. If he'd tried to coax notes out of a drum, he'd have had an easier time. As if he could hear the thought, he then turned his attention back to Kaylin, and this time, his voice was softer and almost plaintive, although it wasn't any more musical.

"You want me to sing?" she asked.

He nodded with his whole body, bobbing up and down in place.

"Only because you've never heard me." She glanced once, apprehensively, at the gathered Barrani lords. Singing off-key and out of tune in the West March was not the same as singing with the foundlings in the foundling halls, and that was the only place she readily joined a group song.

But the small dragon landed on her shoulder and nudged her cheek, and she knew he not only meant her to sing, but meant to join her. How much worse could she sound?

"What," Nightshade said sharply, "do you intend to sing?"

"Badly, and probably off-key, whatever it is," she replied. "But not on purpose. The eagles are singing," she added, "and I think small and squeaky wants me to join them."

"The eagles are not singing," the Lord of the West March said.

"But they are," Lord Barian said. The two men's gazes met, and both fell silent.

Kaylin wanted to ask Lord Lirienne what he heard, but the

eagles' voices had grown higher and more urgent, and she turned to listen, closing her eyes and concentrating on a song that was two parts. Two parts, and what seemed like a dozen. There was no room for her voice in the throng.

She made room. She wound her voice—dissonant, unmusical, and uncertain—around the squawking of her small dragon, finding words that spoke to what she heard, even if there were no similar words in the music of the dreams and nightmares of a Hallionne. Feeling self-conscious made her voice even weaker than it usually was, but it wouldn't be the first time she'd made a total fool of herself.

Her arms ached. The burning, she was used to—if one could ever get used to that sense of skin being seared. But they also trembled, as if she'd been carrying way too much for too long. She looked at the small dragon; he was watching her, his squawk gentled to a croon.

She wished she could understand him. For now, it was enough that the eagles seemed to. The only two people caught in this song that couldn't were Kaylin and the Consort herself, because as Kaylin found voice and exposed a ridiculous vanity, she heard the Consort singing.

But the Consort lay unmoving, her eyes and lips closed. Her skin, sallow, was now beaded with perspiration—but so was Kaylin's. It made it hard to keep the grip on her hand. She changed that grip, entwining their fingers and tightening her hold.

She didn't know what the birds hoped to wake, and in the end, that wasn't her problem. What she wanted—what she needed—was to wake the Consort. She needed to make herself heard over the beautiful storm of sound that occurred when dream and nightmare clashed.

The dragon batted her cheek and shook his head.

The marks on her arm were a gold-white glow; she had to

squint to read them. Not only were they on the edge of tear-inducing brightness, they seemed to be moving as she watched.

Gripping the Consort's hand tightly enough she started to lose feeling in her own fingers, Kaylin reached out with her free hand, passing it over the brilliant lines and dots that formed runes on most of her skin. They were warm, but not searing, beneath her callused palm—but they weren't solid. She felt resistance as her hand passed through them. The small dragon was bouncing up and down, although he didn't stop his noisemaking; nor did he vary its rhythm.

Still, she understood that he meant her to do what she was trying—and failing—to do: take them in hand. Lift them.

No, she thought. Not them. One. Just one. In the past, she had lost marks before: to the trapped spirit of a dead dragon, to the Devourer, to the small dragon hatchling. But the marks had lifted *themselves* off her skin; she hadn't chosen. She hadn't had to choose.

She had no idea why they were hers; someone immortal, someone older, wiser, and more knowledgeable—someone like the Arkon—should have been chosen instead. She didn't know what they were for. She had no idea why a word was necessary now—but she understood, watching the marks, that it was. And that this time, the hand of the Ancients wasn't going to make the choice for her.

Her hands shook, and not because she was nervous. She closed her eyes.

Eyes closed, she could still see the marks, but the light didn't burn her vision. Her body didn't impede it, either. It wasn't just the marks on her arms that were slowly beginning to rise.

CHAPTER 8

She could see—with her eyes closed—the shape of nightmares. They were clearer and darker than they had been the first time she'd encountered them; there was so much light here, the edges of shadow wings were harsher and sharper. They implied bird—or maybe bat—without any of the other physical traits: they were like the shadows the eagles cast in flight.

She held on to that thought as the voices of the actual eagles filled her awareness, blending in rhythm, if not in actual sound, with the voice of her squawky sidekick. Her ear was throbbing. After this was done, she'd have pointed words with the little dragon.

The shadows filled her vision as they wheeled in the confined space.

Except it wasn't confined; it had no obvious shape, no floor, no roof, no walls; it implied a vast and endless sky—the kind you'd crane your neck to look up at. But it was a sky without color or cloud. She heard the voices of those shadows as clearly as she heard the eagles of Alsanis.

She looked down.

It was a mistake. She could see herself. She wasn't translucent, and she wasn't terribly impressive, but the dress she wore was: it was the essence of green, and green was the color of life in the West March. It was, she thought—and wondered why—the color of blood.

Beneath her feet, the shadows swooped and darted, their flight patterns interwoven with the patterns of feathered wings. They had no obvious beaks, no obvious *faces,* but their song came from somewhere, and it echoed. Given that there was nothing for sound to bounce off, this was impressive.

But no, even that was wrong: there was. The runes that graced over half of her skin had expanded outward in the shape of a sphere, and the sounds of raised voices were caught and returned by each element they touched. The shadows flew through them, rather than around; the flight path of the eagles was therefore far more constrained.

She almost opened her eyes when the small dragon bit her ear—again. It was more a nibble than an actual bite; she turned automatically in his direction and saw, to her surprise, that he was present in this vision. His body was composed of the same translucent flesh, and his eyes were the same black opalescence. But his wings seemed both more amorphous and larger; they were, she realized, very like the wings of the shadows above in shape and size; they passed through her, although his claws did not.

The only thing Kaylin couldn't see was the Consort.

The small dragon warbled and nudged her cheek. Kaylin opened her eyes.

Nothing changed.

She closed her eyes and opened them again, but the odd sky, occupied as it was by runes and birds and their cast shadows, remained firmly fixed in her vision; she turned, and turned again, looking up and down as she did. She was no longer in the Consort's room.

Lirienne.

There was no answer.

Nightshade?

Silence. She inhaled slowly, counting to ten. The small dragon bit her ear. This time it was harder, and his warble was higher. Exhaling, Kaylin nodded, remembering what she had so reluctantly set out to do. She began to sing. She had faint hope that her actual body—she had no doubt she still had one—was silent in the halls of the Lord of the West March. Barrani voices were clear and resonant and she had never heard one sing off-key, not that song was common.

Mortal voices, not so much, and Kaylin's was on the bottom end of that scale.

But this wasn't about the quality of voice. It wasn't even about the words; she could have chosen words at random, the syllables of the eagles made so little sense. It was about harmony. About tone. It was about rhythm. It was about emotion, because even if she couldn't understand a single word, she felt she understood intent.

There was a desolation, a yearning, and an emptiness in this song. No, not emptiness, but an awareness of loss, of all that had been lost and might never come again. It was hard to listen carefully with her eyes open, and as closing her eyes didn't apparently change a damn thing, she gave up trying.

The eagles flew. The shadows flew. Their song soared and plummeted, as if it were the sole expression of everything they were. Maybe it was. She couldn't understand more than the emotion behind the long, winding words—and she probably didn't understand all of that, either. Just enough.

She became aware, as she watched, that her marks were stationary. So was she. While the eagles flew, while the shadows darted, she was as fixed in place as any of the marks. The small dragon's claws curled into her collarbone, and she grimaced; her song banked briefly while she struggled not to swear.

She was mostly prepared when the dragon's wings began to flap; they were silent, their movements suggesting power and grace. Kaylin began to move. Her flight was unwieldy; it had none of the grace or speed of the dreams or nightmares. But the slow, steady climb took her closer to the nearest of the floating marks.

It was larger than she was. She could see every detail of its full shape; on her arm, it was flattened and almost lifeless in comparison. It seemed natural that it shed its brilliant, golden light; it was like sun—but it didn't burn and didn't blind. At least, not yet. It felt almost alive as she reached out to touch it. She couldn't read it; it was too large for that. She couldn't intuit its meaning.

But she had come here to find the Consort.

The marks that adorned her skin were like a miniature world around her. They were individual glyphs, differing in shape and size, in simplicity and complexity. They were very like images that might be called up in Records for her inspection. And she knew, again, that she had to choose one.

She didn't have time to waffle, but to make a decision based on—on *nothing,* really, when so much rode on the outcome, was almost paralyzing. She let her hand fall away. As it did, the rune faded from sight. She nodded to the small dragon and began her awkward flight toward the next one.

Every time she failed to choose a mark, it vanished. When this had happened a dozen times, she realized that the marks were returning to her skin. They were still glowing, and frankly, when they were part of her skin, they were warm.

With so few reattached, it was uncomfortable; she had no doubt, when she was done, it would be painful.

But she'd live with the pain if she could wake the Consort.

Hells, she'd live with the pain at this point if she could *find* the Consort. The sky was full of wings and runes and nothing else; the birds circled; the shadows circled. The Consort was nowhere to be seen. Kaylin forced panic to take a backseat again; it was hard because it kept trying to grab the reins and set the course. She inspected rune after rune, wondering if this many of them could truly fit on her skin.

Every so often the small dragon bit her ear to catch her attention; it was always when she had forgotten to keep singing. Had he not been her only viable form of movement, she'd've bit him back.

The sky was slowly becoming an empty space; the flight patterns of the dreams and the nightmares of Alsanis had become less complex with the reabsorption of each word. Kaylin still hadn't found the one she was looking for—and she was terrified that she hadn't because she didn't *know* what she was looking for.

She had never been good with words.

Oh, she could be a smart-ass. Almost a decade with the Hawks would have that effect on anyone. But when it came to important things? She couldn't choose the right words to save her life. She blurted, if she could get them out at all. She tripped over them, even though she knew what she wanted to say. Or at least knew what she wanted to *convey*.

It was simple to know what she felt.

It was hard to make other people understand it. Words were sometimes more of a barrier than a bridge, especially because it was so easy to choose the wrong ones. It was just as easy to hear the wrong ones—to think she understood what the other person was trying to say to her. To hear what the words meant to her, not what they meant coming from someone else's mouth.

She was not the right person to be choosing words.

She stilled, frowning. These weren't Elantran words. Or Leontine or Barrani or Aerian, either. These were True Words. In theory, if she chose the right word, there was no way to misinterpret it. It had no hidden meanings, no barbed cultural contexts, no past associations she could trip over like a clumsy toddler. It would convey the whole of what she meant, not more, not less.

This would have been comforting if she *knew* what she was supposed to *mean*. Or if the cost of failure wouldn't be so high. Without the right word, the Consort wouldn't wake.

And without it, Kaylin thought, as she bypassed four more runes, Kaylin wasn't so certain that she'd find her way back herself. Opening and closing her eyes didn't shift or change the scenery much; she was still here.

She stopped singing. The dragon, predictably, complained. She traversed sky, listening to the songs of eagles and their shadows, on wings that weren't hers and never would be. As she did, she passed more of the floating marks and they vanished in her wake, dwindling and returning to her skin. She heard the sorrow and the loss and the yearning carried by the voices of dreams and nightmares. She understood them in a way that didn't encompass words, they were so much a part of her life.

She'd heard that—and desire—in the Consort's song of wakening, in the lee of the Hallionne Bertolle. She'd even joined the Consort, singing the part Nightshade would have taken had he been there. Desire—the desire she'd heard—wouldn't touch this emptiness. Not in Kaylin's life. She hesitated. This *wasn't* her life, was it? It was the Consort's. The Hallionne's.

But it had been left to Kaylin to choose a word that would somehow respond to it. Kaylin's choice. Kaylin's imperfect choice. She stopped when there were only two runes in the whole of the sky. The eagles and the three shades continued to fly, their path unimpeded by obstacles, their voices soaring and diving as they did.

She didn't understand how to say these words. Any of them. But as she looked at the two that remained, she understood what they meant.

They were almost of a size; their shapes were different. In the first, the long, straight line of the rune was central; the looping adornment to one side of that line was complex; the dots to the other side, and the single stroke at its height, a frame.

The second rune had no central element that she could see; it was a balance of delicate squiggles, dots, slender strokes. Its shape suggested a cohesion that closer approach dispelled.

Both were luminescent gold. Broken into components, they shared several base shapes—but it was the combination that made them so distinct. The combination, she thought, and the essential meaning. It was to the more complicated, delicate rune that she drifted.

She could almost hear it as she approached. It seemed to sing—or at least to hum, as she could make out no distinct syllables—in time and in tune with the dreams and nightmares. It was at the heart of their song; it was isolation, writ large and made strangely compelling. Seeing it, hearing it, she felt that she understood the song in a way that she hadn't before. If she could *speak* it or sing it, she was certain that whoever was listening would know that she did, at last, understand.

It was larger than *I'm lonely.* It was larger than *I'm alone.* Choice and consequence and acceptance and pain were tied into it, part of it. This was loss, the result of loss; the result left when something whole had been shattered, and the pieces imperfectly swept away.

Yet there was no anger in it; no resentment, no desire for vengeance or destruction. It was—it was like a dirge. A funeral dirge. It was a farewell, a goodbye, uttered by the people who remained behind. Behind, Kaylin thought, and alive.

She skirted its edge, and then turned, almost blindly, toward the other word.

She couldn't hear it, from here. She didn't know what it meant. She glanced at the small dragon; he was staring pointedly at the side of her face. His tongue—solid, now, where the rest of his body wasn't—flickered out to touch her cheek, and she realized she was crying. Normally, this would embarrass her. Here, it didn't matter. Tears had no meaning to dreams, to nightmares.

She moved away from the rune; she had not dismissed it and it did not fade as she left; she could feel its light and heat as she rose above it and moved to the only other True Word in this sky.

Unlike the first rune she'd approached, she thought this one was silent. It didn't hum; it didn't have a voice—if *voice* was even the right word. It stood aloof from the song that moved around it, carried by invisible thermals. Kaylin almost dismissed it.

But something about its shape was familiar. Something about the whole of its three-dimensional form felt right. *Right?* she thought, grimacing. *Right for what, exactly?* This would have gotten her zero on any test she'd been forced to write to enter the Hawks; it wouldn't have even gotten part-marks. It may have gotten derision and criticism.

It's not about instinct, she could hear Teela saying—at a remove of too many years. She sometimes wished she knew

Teela's True Name, because Teela's voice occupied so much space on the inside of her head anyway.

You've got decent instincts. Most people do, even mortals. But instinct isn't law. It certainly isn't Imperial Law. You don't get to kick down a door or break through a window because it feels "right." That usually leads to demotion or dismissal, if the Emperor's in a good mood.

So I shouldn't trust my instincts.

Did I say that? Honestly, kitling. You put words in the mouths of everyone around you; we probably don't need to speak at all—you can carry both sides of the conversation. Understand, however, that they'll both be your sides. You need to trust your instincts. And then you need to be intelligent about proving the truth of them to people who don't have the same reaction you do. We call it covering your ass. It's an important component of Hawk work.

Did she understand what this rune signified? No. And staring at it wouldn't give her that understanding. She needed to approach it more closely, and she needed to hear it over the competing songs that filled the air.

What she felt, as she approached, was the warmth of sunlight on a still, cold day. It was the hearth fire in Marcus's house, when the Leontine kits were sprawled in one messy, living fur heap in front of it, and invited her—by more or less tackling her, knocking her over and dragging her—to join them.

Kaylin couldn't imagine living with Marcus's Pridlea; his wives, although she loved them, were terrifying. But from the first night he'd taken her home, she'd felt as if she almost belonged.

"I don't suppose," she asked the small creature who was both her passenger and her only form of locomotion, "that we could take both of them?"

The dragon said nothing. He didn't even warble. When she hesitated, he bit her ear again. She growled. Marcus's kits would have choked with laughter at the sound she considered a growl.

She wanted this word. She wanted what it reminded her of. She realized she had no *single* word to describe it. It didn't matter. She knew that it wasn't home, not exactly, but it was close: welcome, warmth, acceptance. Acceptance of Kaylin, a human, in a home meant for Leontines. Acceptance and a place for her. It wasn't love; it wasn't even the promise of love.

But love could grow in a space like that if it was freely offered and freely accepted.

If she could only choose one word, it would be this one.

Thinking that, she looked over her shoulder. Only one? Was that what she had to do? Her arms ached; her legs ached; the back of her neck was burning. Only the mark on her forehead failed to cause pain, probably because it was singular.

In the absence of clear rules—hells, in the absence of murky ones—there was instinct. There was previous experience. Using the power granted her by the marks allowed her to heal—but healing didn't change the marks themselves.

But freeing the trapped spirit of an ancient, dead Dragon had: one rune had vanished. Interacting with the Devourer had, as well—but she'd lost more.

Yet she'd also gained marks. She couldn't be certain that they hadn't always been there; she felt that they were emerging with time. Only the mark on her forehead was one she had chosen—and she hadn't consciously decided to add it to her skin; she had been in a panic because she didn't want to see it destroyed.

There were no rules.

She turned away from the rune that offered warmth across so many spectrums, and once again faced the one she thought of as mourning. She hadn't examined it as closely because she didn't *want* to return to what it evoked in her. *Mourning* was not the right word. *Grief,* maybe. But even that felt thin.

She reached out and placed a hand around one of the thinnest of the curved lines that comprised the rune that meant almost-home. When she started to move, it came with her. She was surprised that it had no weight, no drag; it wasn't small and it appeared—to her eye—to be very solid. But it didn't fade away; it didn't return to its place on her skin—wherever that was.

Nor did the other rune disappear; it waited.

I don't want to go there. But want or no, she went; the wings were not, in the end, her wings.

There are places no one wants to revisit.

Kaylin was afraid of this word and what it meant, even though she'd seen enough at first glance to get the gist of it. This was not a word she wanted to define anything. The one that she now carried with her, yes. But not this one.

The dragon was singing. The eagles were singing. Their voices had flattened into a single thing; she could no longer hear harmonies or the subtle shifts that indicated multiple voices. Her own voice was silent.

She had been to so many dark places in her life. She had suffered so many losses. She had lost the only home she had known, but had never lost the desire for, the need for, a home. She had lost her family. She had lost the person on whom she had most relied. She had become something she hated, and stayed there for long enough it was still hard, on some days, to look in the damn mirror.

"I don't want to do this," she told the small dragon. But she flew toward the rune anyway. "I mean it."

His squawk was turned to song and not to what often sounded like angry, harping lecture—absent intelligible words.

And she realized that it didn't matter. She couldn't understand the thing if she didn't examine it. She probably couldn't understand the whole of its meaning, regardless; she wasn't an Ancient or an Immortal, or the distant relative of a world-devouring creature. This wasn't, and would never be, her language; her understanding would always be imperfect.

But...the rune itself seemed so personal. It seemed, for just a moment, to be part of her, exposed, writ large. Since closing her eyes made no difference in this space, she gritted her teeth instead. She was angry.

But she'd been angry at herself, on and off, for a long time. Anger didn't control her actions anymore; it just made long, hard days longer and harder. What she'd done in the past, she couldn't change. She could refuse to make the same stupid choices; it wouldn't stop her from making different stupid choices in the future. If she learned something from them—if she survived for long enough to learn something—she could narrow the stupidity options. She was human; she would never narrow them to zero. But no one did. Even the Hawklord made mistakes.

On most days, she pulled herself up off the ground from her figurative face plant, and kept moving, reminding herself that it was normal to make mistakes. Everyone had to fail sometimes. On some days, no.

And she could see failure in this rune. Failure. Loss. Grief.

But she couldn't see rage, self-loathing, the desire to lash out and break everything in sight. She couldn't see what she'd felt when she discovered the death of the two children she had known and loved best.

No, that wasn't quite right. She could. She just couldn't see *all* of what she'd felt. She couldn't see her own sense of betrayal at Severn's hand. She couldn't see her certain sense that if it were not for *her,* both girls would still be alive. There was no self-loathing.

There was loss. Isolation. A hint of choice—but it was a choice that would be made, again and again, a defining choice. It was…it was like responsibility. No, that wasn't quite it. It was duty. It was defining duty. It was as strong as her sense of duty to the Hawks.

Yes, she hated the bureaucrats. She hated the stupid regulations that seemed to serve no purpose, unless one *wanted* criminals to get away. She hated parts of Elani street, her regular beat. But she loved the work. She loved the sense of purpose it gave her life.

Would she still love it so much if every Hawk she knew and worked with now were dead and gone? Would she feel the same sense of purpose if she were the only one left to do the work? Would she still do the work? Could she?

Loss. Grief. Shades of things Kaylin could understand if she rearranged parts of life on the inside of her head.

She turned to the small dragon. "We're taking them both."

His eyes widened, although given their size in the rest of his face, it was hard to tell. She reached out for the rune, and gripped it firmly in her right hand, the left being occupied. She wasn't certain what to expect, but it was warm to the touch; as warm as the first rune had been.

Only when it was firmly in hand did the singing suddenly stop.

The silence was intimidating because it was so complete. She turned to look at the eagles; they were hovering in place; even the path of their flight, interwoven as it had been with the shadows, had disappeared. They were facing Kaylin. Since the shadows had no faces, it was harder to tell what they were looking at, if they looked at anything at all.

Barian had called them the nightmares of Alsanis.

She stood suspended in the air, her hands on two runes—not one. Nothing besides movement and sound had changed; the runes were still visible, and much larger than they had been on her skin. She'd hoped that the choosing of the words was the end of her responsibilities. When a mark had lifted itself off her skin in the dusty back rooms of the Arkon's personal collection, the Dragon spirit trapped there had flown free.

Clearly dead Dragons and Imperial libraries had nothing in common with empty, gray sky, although Kaylin personally thought they had a lot in common with nightmares. The two words did not collapse or merge; they stayed pretty much where they were.

But the eagles didn't. The shadows didn't. The sky didn't fall away from Kaylin's feet; they did. They suddenly folded wings and dropped in a dead man's dive. Kaylin kept her hands on the runes and glanced at the small dragon.

He warbled.

"I don't like it."

As was often the case, what she liked—or didn't—made no difference. Her companion hissed and folded the wings that had allowed her to move freely—if slowly—in what was nominally sky. Weight returned. Given weight and nothing to wedge it between or hang it from, so did falling.

She tightened her grip on the words she had chosen, but they didn't hold her up; they came with her. After a few seconds of panic, and the realization that she couldn't streamline her own dive while attached to the words, she accepted the fact that she could do nothing but go along for the ride.

She just hoped that the landing wouldn't be fatal, and that it would bring her closer to the absent Consort.

CHAPTER 9

She fell for what felt like an hour before she saw the first sign of actual geography. As landscape went, it wasn't promising: it looked like a small, dark pit. From this vantage, she couldn't see bottom.

As she approached the pit, she realized that *small* was the wrong word. It was huge. She thought it the size of a city block, and revised that as she fell; it was the size of a city. A large city. When she finally reached its upper edge, she wasn't surprised she couldn't see bottom; she could no longer see the whole of its shape.

Turning—which was difficult—she saw the sky recede as she continued to fall. The small dragon dug claws into the skin below her collarbone, and she cursed him in Leontine.

The Leontine bounced back in an echoing, strangled kitten sound—the usual result of the combination of human throat and the deeper Leontine curses. She chose a few of the less throaty words instead, and then, for good measure, switched to Aerian. It was the Aerian that caught her attention, probably because she mangled the pronunciation less. The echo was not attenuated. It wasn't stretched. It was almost exact, and it continued as she dropped.

She spoke in her mother tongue and listened to herself, growing quieter as syllables bounced off walls so distant they should never have reached them at all.

She then switched to Barrani. All languages had useful words, but it was hard to swear in High Barrani. Kaylin had always believed that High Barrani was the language of Imperial Law because it was the most stilted, pretentious, and boring of the Elantran tongues.

High Barrani returned to her in her own voice, but instead of a diminishing echo, she heard a resonance to the sound, an amplification. The runes in her hands—hands that were gripping tightly enough her fingers were beginning to tingle—shook. She stopped speaking; the trembling, however, continued.

She *hated* working in the dark. Figurative dark, literal dark—she was hemmed in by her own ignorance. There'd been solutions to that, in the Halls of Law. She'd worked. She'd learned. She'd studied—at least she'd studied the important stuff. Here, she had nothing to go on. Everything was a risk. Every decision had to be made on air and instinct and hope. She was afraid of the consequences because she couldn't even begin to predict them.

And…it didn't matter. She could fall forever—seriously, that's what it felt like—or she could take risks and pray that the only person who suffered when she did was herself.

She returned to High Barrani. She was unsettled enough that random words rolled off her tongue first; she shook her head, and when she spoke again, she began to recite the Imperial Laws. She was rusty, she knew; only the important ones were word-for-word clear: the ones that defined murder, kidnapping, theft, and extortion. She chose those because they were the ones around which she'd based her life.

They'd given her purpose. They'd given her wings. They'd given her family. Hope. Yes, her work regularly brought her into contact with the people most likely to break those laws, but she balanced the constant exposure to the least law-abiding citizens with her work at the midwives' guild and the Foundling Hall. The worst and the best.

That job had brought her here.

"Go left," she told the small dragon.

This time, he didn't warble; he huffed. She had the distinct impression he would have said "about time, idiot" if he'd actually been able to speak in a language she could understand. This was why Kaylin did not own cats. On the other hand, at least the small dragon listened; he spread his extended, diaphanous wings and she drifted toward the left wall. It was not close; it took a long time.

She wondered if time was passing for the Consort; she wondered if her own body had collapsed in the Consort's room.

Taking a deeper breath, she let go of that thought and returned to Imperial Law. It wasn't as dry as it should have been because it had meaning to her. She thought of the first murder investigation Teela and Tain had allowed her to tag along on. And of the first investigation she'd attended as an actual Hawk and not an unofficial mascot. Or an official one.

She'd never understood why the Barrani had chosen to take the Imperial Oath to the Halls of Law; she'd never understood why they served. They'd said they were bored. But... they were *good* at what they did. She'd learned a lot from Teela, and most of it was within regulations.

When she reached the far wall, her hands were vibrating because the runes themselves were shaking. It was as if the component parts wanted to fly free of each other, and that was *so* not happening right now. Not yet.

The small dragon dug claws into collarbone again. She bit back the urge to tell him to shut up or be helpful, because it was his wings that were moving them both. She forgot frustration as they at last approached surface.

It wasn't a wall. Or rather, it wasn't the side of a pit. It looked like—like a carved likeness of the flattened streets of a very, very bizarre city. Parts of that city were laid open, as if they'd been sheared; rooms were exposed—or what she assumed were rooms.

And what had she expected? The Consort had fallen unconscious because of the nightmares of Alsanis—and Alsanis was a *building*. A sentient building. She looked right, left, up, down—the vista, the flattened, exposed likeness of something that she'd be afraid to police—stretched out for as far as the eye could see. Everything was cast in shadow; it was not, as she'd thought at first glimpse, of black stone or rock.

Nor was it completely without light. Here and there, she caught flickers of something that might have been candle or lamp; she caught movement, but only out of the corner of her eye. It reminded her of cockroaches. She *hated* cockroaches.

The buildings themselves were not uniform. And, as she drew closer still, she realized they *weren't* squashed and flattened. But they had been. They seemed to gain dimension, stories unfolding where her flight brought her close. She could see what might have been streets, but they were dark hatches that grew even less distinct as the buildings themselves emerged following the trail of her flight path.

The runes in her hands, had they been alive, would be agitated and panicked; they'd probably be screaming. She wondered if those screams would be laden with fear or joy, which was an odd thought.

She nudged the small dragon, and he banked to the right; buildings rose out of their flatness, the flickering lights becoming the heart of windows and arches. Stone, she thought, and then reconsidered. This was some part of the Hallionne, if *nightmare* was a word that could be literally applied. The rules of normal architecture didn't mean anything here.

She had no idea what she was doing, but seeing a city unfold as she passed above it made her feel almost at home. It wasn't Elantra—but it wasn't an endless forest full of insects and talking Ferals, either.

On the other hand, it didn't seem populated. Small twitches at the corner of her eyes didn't become people of any stripe when she looked. It was a ghost city, a deserted town, absent the usual decay and dilapidation. She nudged the dragon, and he banked to the right, slowing as he straightened out their gliding path.

She saw why: the building that began its ascent as she approached did not stop unfolding; to avoid running smack into its side, the small dragon would have had to ascend just as quickly. She shouted because he didn't even *try*.

"Up! Up!"

He flew straight, the little winged rat. She had the horrible certainty she was about to discover just what these buildings were made of—by splatting against the wall. But beneath a roof with a spire that could impale Dragons in flight form, a balcony opened up. It was longer and wider than Kaylin's entire apartment. *Former* apartment. The wall it jutted from was rounded, and it had no doors; instead, it had an arch that was open to air, as if it were a cloister. The dragon flew straight above balcony rails and beneath that arch, tucking his wings so they'd fit. He also wrapped his tail around her neck.

When they'd cleared the arch, he folded his wings entirely, and she fell a good six feet to the ground. Six feet wasn't usually a problem. Six feet when both hands were occupied wasn't the usual.

She sprained her ankle. At least, it felt like a sprain because it hurt like blazing fire, but she could stand and it more or less supported her weight. "This is *stupid*," she said in Leontine. "I'm not even physically *here* and I have to hobble through this maze with a bum ankle?" She did not, by dint of full hands, punch the wall. Or kick it.

It wasn't a maze, though. It *was* a cloister. Arches cascaded beyond the arch she'd entered; to her right was wall, to her left a shadowed courtyard. The air was still and dry; there was no sound but her breathing. Even the dragon was silent, although he batted her face with one wing. It wasn't an improvement over ear-biting.

As she walked, simple stone walls gave way to small fountains, small statues; the open courtyard continued. She'd never been in a courtyard this large; she was certain it was at least four city blocks in length, and it showed no signs of ending. What she wanted from a city, she decided, was stable architecture and buildings that made sense. Who made a courtyard this bloody high off the ground?

She stopped, turned, and walked toward the open space to her left to look down. She couldn't see bottom. The small dragon whiffled, but he didn't bat the side of her face. "I'm *not* jumping unless we run into Ferals or a really, really ugly dead end. Got it?"

He exhaled—air, not cloud—and flopped across her shoulders, rolling an eye in her direction before he closed it.

"*Now* you're clocking out? Are you kidding?"

He failed to answer.

She started in on a very Leontine reply, but something caught her eye; it was bright, gleaming. She turned to her right; there was a statue against the wall, between the right-hand pillars of two arches. It didn't vanish when she looked at it. She realized that the gleam she saw was the reflection of the two words she was dragging along at her sides as if they were recalcitrant foundlings on an outing.

The statue was made, not of stone or marble, but…glass. It was glass. It stood on a pedestal of white marble. If it had been standing on the floor, it would still have been taller than Kaylin; Barrani were. It looked like a blown-glass representation of a ghost. A male ghost. Its features were delicate, the glass taking the form of ears, chin, perfect cheekbones. Probably perfect skin. Kaylin didn't really believe in ghosts, but none of the stories she'd heard indicated bad complexions, and anyway, he was Barrani.

She stood, bracketed by the two words, watching the light play off transparent surface as if it were a window. A very beautiful window in a nonexistent frame. She peered through his chest, which was at eye level, given the pedestal. She did not see stone; she saw—thought she saw—night.

She wasn't surprised when the window moved his arms. She should have been, but the minute she'd hit balcony, she'd given up on anything making sense. The statue reached out to touch the rune that meant grief and loss. His hand passed through what was, to Kaylin, appreciably solid.

She began to walk again, the statue, the ghost, trailing behind her, his open, empty eyes upon the words she carried. And why wouldn't they be? They were the only obvious source of light.

He was not the only statue. Immediately ahead, between the pillars of two arches, stood another, also male. His face was broader, the cheeks wider, the chin more chiseled; he was otherwise tall and slender, although she thought him taller than the first. He wore a thin tiara across his brow, although it, too, was made of glass.

She stopped in front of him, watching the first ghost—she couldn't quite think of them as Barrani, although it was clear that's what they were meant to be. He, too, reached for the rune that spoke of grief and loss, stepping off his pedestal to do so. He didn't seem to see the first ghost; nor did the first ghost see him. But his hand passed through the rune, as well, and a ripple of expression moved across his face like a liquid wave.

She would have let them take the runes, because there was something about them that was *not* Barrani. They seemed younger to her, and drawn only to grief. The second rune might not have existed at all. But she knew the words weren't meant for them, because as she passed beneath the second such arch, she came to stand in front of a third glass statue.

Unlike the first two, this one was female; the slight swell of breasts and the delicate curve of hips would have given it away, but she also wore a Court dress—a Barrani Court dress— that hung in folds. She wore two rings, two glass rings, and a bracelet that looked almost martial; her hair fell from forehead to knees, unbraided. She was slightly shorter than the second ghost, and of a height with the first; she looked far haughtier than either of the first two. She didn't attempt to touch the rune, but her chin dropped as she looked at it.

She wouldn't reach for it, either, Kaylin thought, because she knew she could never touch it. But she, too, stepped from her pedestal, and she followed as Kaylin continued to walk.

She wasn't surprised to see that there were eleven such statues by the time she reached the T junction at the end of the murderously long, open gallery. The rune had become heavier as she walked; she was practically dragging it, by the end. Two of the glass Barrani were women, nine were men.

Kaylin was annoyed. Not at the rune. Not at the ghosts. Not even at Alsanis.

No, she was annoyed at the High Court. Because they spoke of twelve lost children. *Twelve.* There were *eleven.* She had no doubt, in this amalgam of dream, nightmare, and Hallionne, that these ghosts were the ghosts of the eleven who had been so badly damaged by the ceremony in the green. They had been taken to Alsanis after the end of the recitation, when forbidden blood had been spilled during the telling, as if Alsanis was a jail. They had been sent to the West March by ambitious parents—and they had been sacrificed to that ambition.

But they numbered *eleven,* damn it. Teela wasn't here. Teela *wasn't lost.* Teela had come to the green wearing the dress that Kaylin now wore, and Teela had served as harmoniste. She had come of age. She was a Lord of the High Court.

Teela had lost her mother. So had Kaylin. Kaylin had lost her home. Teela, in theory, hadn't. But what home had she come back to? The West March didn't want her. That was so clear even a non-Barrani like Kaylin couldn't miss it. That left the High Court. No wonder Teela spent as little time there as possible.

Well, the *Hawks* wanted her.

The small dragon squawked.

"We *do,*" Kaylin said. She inhaled. "Pretend I'm talking to myself. I need to get this out of my system before I see Teela again. If she thinks I'm worried about her, if she thinks I feel sorry for her, she'll break both my arms. Without breaking a sweat."

He nodded.

"Right or left?"

He batted her face with a wing. She considered plucking him off her shoulder and dropping him, but paused. "No, you're right," she told him. "That was a stupid question." And she turned to the right because it was her right hand gripping the rune that had drawn every statue off its pedestal.

There were no other statues against the walls—and there were two walls here. If she'd chosen to go left, the gallery was open—but right led into an enclosed hall. It was an odd enclosure, because as she looked up she could see stars. Moons. The moons looked familiar. She thought there were clouds, thin and stretched, across their faces, but it was hard to tell; the pillars sported arches, even if they didn't have ceiling, and the arches got in the way.

But Kaylin walked, dragging a rune that seemed to gain weight with each step, and a rune that seemed so light she could forget it was in her hand. She didn't; she didn't want to let it go yet.

She only knew she was heading in the right direction when she heard singing, because it *was* singing. She would know that voice anywhere: it was the Consort's. The Consort's voice was not the only voice she heard, and sadly, she'd recognize the other five anywhere, as well: the dreams and the nightmares; the eagles and their shadows.

She glanced at the eleven ghosts; they trailed like shadows—reflecting light—behind her. She wondered if they were responsible for the weight of the word in her hand, but they hadn't been able to touch it. Then again, did she expect anything that happened here to make sense?

She cursed. Leontine again. Her ankle hurt, the rune weighed a ton, and she wanted to reach the Consort before she finished singing, because she knew—the way she did in a dream that was about to go very, very wrong—that the song was almost done.

She couldn't run. Her ankle wasn't broken, but the word had become an anchor. She dragged it down the hall, sweating all over a very fine, very magical dress. She wanted to curse, but saved her breath. The small dragon stopped playing shawl; he rose and stretched, digging claws into various parts of her collarbone and neck as he readjusted his position. The urge to curse grew stronger.

He spread his wings, but managed to do so without batting her in the face—which meant, of course, every other wing-slap was deliberate. She could see him lift and stretch his slender, translucent neck; he inhaled.

"Now is *so* not the time," she told him.

As usual, he ignored her. He opened his jaws, with their disturbingly solid teeth, and joined the eagles in song. Kaylin didn't have the breath to start singing again; she didn't try. But the runes were warmer and brighter as she struggled with the weight of the one on the right. They served as lamps, but there was no flicker in the light they cast. The fact that they were behind her and she cast no shadow should have disturbed her more.

It didn't; she was frowning instead at the door she was inching toward. She hadn't seen a single door so far; it figured that the first one she'd find stood between her and the Consort.

The door did not obligingly roll open when she reached it. Of course not. That would be too easy. Her arms were shaking; if she had to drag the word on the right another foot, she'd collapse from exhaustion.

To make matters so much worse, the door—a door that was at least two stories in height, and made of either stone or pocked iron—was warded. Exactly how was she supposed to touch a door ward when both of her hands were full?

She looked at the small dragon.

Hiss, squawk, hiss. His wings rose, and he whacked her in the face. "Look, I *understand* that we have to get through the

This is for Mr. Liebgott, Ms. Gann, Ms. Evans,
Maggie Fehlberg, teachers all.

My teachers. They probably deserved better than I gave them, but they encouraged my love of reading, and when it blossomed—at an early age—into childish attempts to write books (I thought that books were individually drawn and bound, which of course makes no sense), they encouraged that just as fondly.

This book wouldn't exist without them.

door—but it's warded. *You* open it! Just—just bite it, like you did with the tree!"

He hissed again, raising his head and stretching his neck. He inhaled.

Kaylin said, *"No!"*

Small, transparent creatures should never be able to look so smug. She dragged the two words until she was flush against the closed door, grinding her teeth. She didn't want the dragon to breathe on the door—and why, she didn't know. Everything about this space implied dream, which could terrify but couldn't exactly kill.

Except for her ankle. This wouldn't be the first time she'd twisted it; she was familiar with sprains; this was not dream pain. Dream pain usually ripped your heart out and left you screaming in fear or rage, or weeping helplessly. It didn't give you a bum ankle.

But this dream would kill the Consort. She couldn't treat it like any other dream she didn't want to be in. She'd seen what the small dragon's breath could do; she wasn't willing to risk damaging the Consort.

And you're willing to damage yourself, idiot? No one is paying you enough for this.

She pressed her forehead into the ward. And of course, given the day—and the weeks leading up to it—alarms began to blare. At least her forehead didn't go numb and her hair didn't catch fire—not even when the door did. She jerked her head back. She couldn't leap away unless she surrendered the words she'd carried all the way here, and she knew it wasn't the time yet.

It would have been easier if the fire hadn't been so damn hot. It was almost white; the edges were gold and orange and too damn close to her face; her eyes watered. The small dragon, however, stayed where he was, neck elongated, chin tilted forward; she glanced at him, saw fire reflected in his eyes.

She glanced back and saw the eleven ghosts; they were white with reflected light, and very slightly transparent. They reminded her, for no reason she could think of, of the small creature clinging a little too tightly to her shoulder.

Kaylin had to admit that it was a pretty impressive way to open a door. Most doors didn't dissolve into ash. The ash clung to her dress. It probably dusted her face, as well, but she couldn't see her face; it certainly settled on the small dragon's wings; he shook them out, which probably didn't help Kaylin any. As the air cleared, she looked through the frame of what had once been a door.

It opened into a very, very large room—but it was a room built in a shape that Kaylin had never seen before; it had so many almost triangular corners recessed into the walls it seemed to be *all* corners. The floor was tiled, or appeared to be tiled, in a way that suggested flagstones and courtyard, and indeed, it was open to air.

Or it was open to sky—but the sky held no moon; it held sun, sunlight, azure, no hint of cloud. And in the center of this spiky, oddly shaped courtyard stood the Consort.

The Lady was pale; she wore robes as white as she now was; as white as the fall of her hair. Her arms were raised, but they were trembling like a junkie's; they had always been slender but now—now they looked emaciated. She stood before a fountain; water fell from air into a basin of ivory and gold. It was a trickle, a drip. The Consort's voice could be described the same way.

On the basin, perched two eagles; the shadows flew above. Kaylin walked, cursing, dragging the rune that seemed determined to scratch the hell out of the stones beneath her feet.

But with the runes, in Kaylin's wake, the ghosts entered the courtyard. As they did, the Consort, voice wavering, lowered her arms and turned. Her eyes widened as she saw Kaylin, and their color—clear tens of yards away—was gold. Kaylin almost never saw that color in a Barrani face: it meant surprise, and it faded into a more natural green as she watched.

The runes did not magically transform any part of this room. They did not become smaller or lighter; they didn't fly away. Kaylin dragged them, heading in a straight line toward the Consort and the fountain. She wasn't certain what she found more disturbing: the fountain or the Consort's fragility. No, that was a lie; she was worried about the Consort. The presence of water, here, would have to wait.

The Consort nodded encouragement—but she didn't move. It was almost as if she couldn't. Kaylin, ankle throbbing, could. As she did, she noticed that the glass statues, the ghosts, began to separate. The first of the statues, the slender man, walked toward one of the triangular corners. His feet left a trail in the stone, which should have been impossible as his steps didn't actually *reach* the floor.

But when he came to the corner, he rose, stepping onto a pedestal of nothing but air. Only then did he look back at the others, and he smiled at them. It was meant, Kaylin thought, to be encouraging, to give them strength; it cut her. She had *never* seen a similar expression on the face of any Barrani she had ever met.

She spun then, Consort almost forgotten; all ten were now departing, walking—as he had done—to different empty corners and taking their positions upon equally invisible pedestals. They weren't still; they didn't become statues in the same way; they looked for each other, sometimes wildly and sometimes casually, as if they couldn't bear to look weak. That, at least, was familiar.

Each of the corners filled this way; only when they were filled did the glass ghosts look into the center of the courtyard, and their gazes fell on the Consort. Kaylin reached her as she lowered shaking arms, and at the last, Kaylin let go of the runes, held out her arms, and caught the Lady as she collapsed.

The eagles fell silent; the shadows fell silent, although they continued to glide.

Kaylin wasn't Teela; she couldn't carry the Consort far—but she could now carry her to the edge of the fountain; the water had ceased to fall. The last drop of water hit the surface of the rippling pool beneath it; Kaylin could see reflected light in the basin.

The light grew. It grew, and it rose; the Consort whimpered, lifting her hands; she had no voice left. But Kaylin shook her head. "It's all right," she said, although it wasn't. She turned to look at the runes she had left at the edge of the fountain. They were glowing, but they had done that since the moment she'd touched the Consort and closed her eyes, entering a dream and a nightmare.

She was afraid to let go of the Consort. She was afraid that if she did the Lady would slip away; the dream would swallow her. She would go where Kaylin couldn't follow.

Lirienne.

No answer. Kaylin set the Consort on her feet and kept one arm around her back, beneath her arms. She stumbled; she'd forgotten her ankle. She didn't fall. The runes weren't that far away.

The Consort whispered something; Kaylin couldn't hear it. It sounded like Barrani, but spoken with a throat so dry only a rasp was left. Kaylin shook her head. She had no idea what the words were supposed to do, and this was the first time she was being asked to decide. To choose the words. To choose their destination.

CHAPTER 10

Kaylin hesitated, but only because supporting the Consort and dragging the heaviest of the runes at the same time was impossible. The small dragon squawked.

"If you can't be helpful, shut up. Not you," she added in panic as the Consort lifted her head.

Kaylin grabbed the rune that had remained weightless; that, she could do. It fit her hand like one of her own fingers, although it didn't vanish at the contact. The Consort's eyes widened, shifting from green to a familiar blue. But she reached out, as Kaylin had, and she touched it, as well. Her eyes widened farther, and took on the oddest sheen of gold. Kaylin noticed that the Consort's hand didn't pass through the rune, the way the others had. She was as real as Kaylin in this place.

Supporting most of the Consort's weight, Kaylin turned to the fountain. The surface of the water in the basin was rippling, and the ripples grew stronger. Light was no longer reflected in it because the water wasn't still enough. She almost asked the Consort where the rune should go or be. Almost. But she understood that somehow, it was her decision to make, wrong or right.

The first word she'd chosen was easy to move; it came with her as if it weighed nothing. She was afraid to let it go, because if that feeling of acceptance, of belonging was somehow a part of her, it was a part she'd worked for. A part she wanted. But she understood that its meaning didn't and couldn't exist in isolation, and she offered it to the only open space it might fit: the fountain, with its rippling water.

The Consort watched, eyes darkening. In the Barrani, fear, anger, and loathing were all expressed with shades of darker blue.

The water rose as the rune began to sink. Given how little it weighed, Kaylin had thought it might float, but she didn't watch it disappear; instead, she turned to the weightier word and saw that the Consort still gripped one long, curved line in white fingers. Kaylin's were about the same color. "Hold on to it," she said, her voice low. "I can't lift it with one hand."

She could barely lift it with two. The Consort understood what she intended. The Barrani Lord was shaking with exhaustion, her eyes ringed in circles that Barrani skin almost never saw, but she planted her feet against the floor, straightening as she did. She put a second hand on the same curved line, and as Kaylin struggled with the weight of the complex word, she strained to help her lift it.

Together they pushed it over the edge of the fountain's basin, scraping gold and ivory; it teetered for a moment on the rim, and the whole of the fountain shook as the rune's weight balanced there.

If Kaylin needed any proof that dreams—at least the dreams of a building—made no sense, she had it; where the weightless rune had sunk into water that was theoretically too shallow, the one she could barely move began to rise. Kaylin's fingers were numb and tingling as she let the word go and turned to the Consort. She slid an arm around her as the Consort began to sway.

Together, they watched the rune rise. It seemed to absorb the sunlight that shone from a near cloudless sky, brightening until they had to squint to see it at all. When it was four yards above them, the shadows took to the air directly above it, the featherless wings moving in time. They began to circle the rune, and as they did, they began to speak.

So did the eagles, although the eagles didn't join their flight pattern.

The rune stretched, thinned, elongated. The light it had absorbed was so brilliant a white, Kaylin lifted a hand to her eyes. She'd tried closing them, but it still made no difference; she might as well have had no eyelids.

She lowered her hand in a hurry when the water shattered.

Shards flew. Kaylin didn't have time to duck; unlike the Consort, she tried anyway. Three glittering pieces of what could only be ice struck her; two hit her arms, piercing skin exposed by the patterned holes in her sleeves.

The third struck her in the chest, just beneath the hollow of her throat. There was no convenient hole in the green, perfect fabric—or there hadn't been. The shard wasn't large, and it wasn't long; she'd taken more serious injuries in the drill yard on a bad day. But it *was* cold; she felt a brief, sharp pain followed by a spreading numbness as the world stopped moving.

No, she thought, not the world—just everything in it. The eagles. The shadows. The Consort. Shards of ice—ice that glittered like broken glass—continued their outward trajectory. She watched, knowing suddenly where they were flying: to the statues that stood on nonexistent pedestals in the spokes of the courtyard.

The statues moved, as Kaylin had, lifting arms to protect their faces. Nothing made sense; Kaylin held her breath as flying ice met standing glass. She wasn't certain what to expect. Where the Barrani ghosts were struck, their entire forms rippled and shivered, as if they were water into which a small object had been violently thrown. The rippling didn't stop; it was disturbing. Worse. The rippling spread, changing their haughty, Barrani expressions, distorting the lines of their faces in a way that implied emotion was the result of external force.

She turned back to the Consort, who hadn't moved at all. The eagles had. If Kaylin hadn't spent too damn long in pointless memory exercises in the Halls, she might not have noticed. Time hadn't stopped—it had slowed. It had slowed for everyone but Kaylin. Reaching up, she grabbed the ice that had lodged in her chest and attempted to pull it out. Her hand went instantly numb; she couldn't even move her fingers.

She stopped trying.

No sign of the two words she'd brought to this chamber remained.

Instead, in the center of what had once been a basin, standing exactly where water would have fallen, was a statue; it was a thing of ice, a sculpture just under six feet in height. Its feet were bare, and its arms; a simple summer shift fell from its straight shoulders, trailing down front and back in a drape that implied heavy silk.

Hair fell in the same way, but Barrani hair always did that. Kaylin lifted her face to meet the clear eyes of the twelfth statue, the twelfth Barrani ghost.

It was Teela.

But she wasn't the Teela Kaylin knew, not exactly. Kaylin knew she'd never seen Barrani children. The eleven ghosts hadn't looked particularly young to Kaylin, either; they looked like Barrani to her.

But Teela did look younger. She didn't look like a child, but she didn't—quite—look like the adult she was now, either; she was caught in the middle somewhere, the way teenaged mortals were. She didn't look gawky or skinny; she looked slender, not quite finished, her chin slightly softer, her expression—well, she *had* one. These colorless, ice eyes were wider, her lips were parted, her hands extended, palms cupped before her as if she were carrying something, offering it, pleading. It made Kaylin distinctly uncomfortable, but she couldn't look away. And because she didn't, she wasn't aware that the other statues, still distorted by whatever had struck them, had started to move. Not until they approached the basin.

The nightmares spoke; the eagles spoke.

The statues were silent until they reached the basin that had become a pedestal. There, they lifted their arms in unison and looked up at Teela, as if reaching for her.

As one, they opened their mouths. And as one, they began to scream.

The Consort staggered as movement returned to the room. She flinched at the sound of Barrani screams because they *were* Barrani voices.

The runes were gone. The water, gone, as well.

Kaylin and the Consort, however, were still trapped in a stone courtyard in the nightmare of a Hallionne; Kaylin couldn't think of this as a dream. She turned to the Consort, trying to quash growing panic. "I'm sorry."

The Consort's voice was thin and rough. "For what? There are very few apologies I will now accept from you."

"I thought—" Kaylin swallowed. She had to lift her voice; even standing as she was right beside the Consort's ear, everything else in the room was making so much damn noise she had to struggle to be heard. "I thought, if I brought the words to you, they'd—"

"Yes?"

"I thought you'd wake up."

"I am not asleep," the Consort replied. *Her* voice was calm and quiet.

"How do we get out of here?"

"The same way we entered," the Consort replied. She raised one hand; it was an imperious gesture. The nightmare shadows wheeled and turned toward her, breaking their flight pattern.

Kaylin's jaw would have hit floor if it hadn't been attached to the rest of her face.

The Consort smiled. Her eyes were still blue, but it was the blue you might see at the heart of an emerald; it suggested the essence of green. She whispered a word. *Alsanis.*

The eagles turned their heads toward her. They spoke; she replied. Kaylin couldn't understand a word. The Consort said, without lowering her arm, "The dreams of Alsanis. Lord Kaylin, what did you do to wake them?"

"I don't know." But she lifted her arms, as well, opening her palms. The Consort lowered hers; she spoke to the shadows. The shadows did not reply with words, but they came, and they landed on Kaylin's arms. The marks on her skin began their slow burn.

This time when she closed her eyes, the courtyard vanished. She opened them again in a panic, and met the Consort's gaze. "I will not leave, Lord Kaylin."

"It's not the leaving I'm worried about," Kaylin lied.

The Consort frowned; Kaylin closed her eyes again. Her skin was uncomfortably hot; her legs ached, and the back of her neck felt as if it had been rubbed raw. But her arms didn't hurt. They felt blessedly cool.

She'd forgotten the small dragon. He hadn't forgotten her.

"If you don't stop biting me, I'll bite you back."

Squawk.

Her arms felt heavy; she struggled to keep them raised. She wasn't going to win.

Squawk.

"Yes, we understand."

She opened her eyes. She was carrying two eagles. She could see tendrils of shadow drifting away from wings as the eagles pushed themselves into the air. One more.

One. Kaylin raised her arms again, and she caught the final shadow. And it was a shadow; it weighed nothing, and implied the flight of a bird she couldn't see overhead. She called the bird, and the bird emerged, cracking shadow as if it were shell.

This fifth eagle, this final bird, turned its head toward the Consort, tilting it to one side. His voice was rich and resonant, his words unintelligible.

"Close your eyes, Lord Kaylin," the Consort said.

Kaylin was tired enough to obey.

"You don't understand dreams of Alsanis."

"No. But it feels like I should, which makes me feel stupid. More stupid," she added. "I can't pin it down. It has the vowels and consonants of High Barrani, but it feels more fluid." She hesitated. "When I was brought to the High Halls for the first time, I was asked to heal your brother."

"Yes. I remember."

"He was willing to *be* healed, and I understand why most Barrani aren't, because I healed him. But—"

"You wonder if the cost to either of us will be the same."

Kaylin nodded. "I couldn't wake him unless—"

"He chose to withdraw into himself, to survive. What you saw was a reflection of that. What you see here is not entirely a reflection of me."

Kaylin frowned. She was certain her face was going to get stuck that way. "I don't see how it's a reflection of you at all."

The small dragon squawked.

She felt the Consort take her hand. "Keep your eyes closed, Private Neya." She had switched into spoken Elantran. The musicality of her voice made Kaylin's mother tongue seem rich and textured and nuanced. "What did you see?"

"Eleven ghosts," Kaylin replied. And she realized, as she did, that she could no longer hear raised Barrani voices. She couldn't hear the eagles, either.

"Ghosts."

"It's what I called them. They first appeared as glass statues, but they followed me. I came to find you," Kaylin added, "because you wouldn't wake up."

"I imagine the Lord of the West March has been concerned."

Barrani understatement.

"These ghosts—"

"I'm certain they're meant to be the lost children. I don't understand why they were made of glass—but I'm certain." She hesitated. "What did you see?"

"Nothing as clear as that. The Hallionne is...not dead."

"What—what did you see at the end? When I—when we—put the words into the fountain?"

She heard—of all unexpected things—laughter. "Fountain? You saw a fountain?"

Kaylin felt herself reddening. "It was like the fountain in Lord Lirienne's courtyard. Sort of. But it was—it was almost out of water. You were—it looked like you were singing to it." And as the words left her mouth, she froze. Because it *did* remind her of that fountain. And because she had touched the water in the real world and she knew that it wasn't ordinary, city water. "What did you see?"

"Water," the Consort replied. "But not as you saw it. Water, land, a vessel. I stood in one of our ancient boats. It was damaged and sinking."

"Are you there now?"

"No, Lord Kaylin. Neither of us is there now."

"And I don't need to know your name. I don't need to call you."

"No. I am not my brother. I feel that I can trust you—but I have learned not to trust my own instincts where the living are concerned. And it is not necessary now."

"Did you—did you see Teela?"

Silence. Kaylin felt cool—blessedly cool—palms against the sides of her face. "Do not speak of that, Kaylin. Do not speak of that to anyone but me."

"And the eleven ghosts?"

"I did not see them, either. It is…safer to speak of them; they are already lost. An'Teela is not."

"I should never have come to the West March. If I hadn't, Teela wouldn't be here."

"I understand why you feel that way," the Consort said softly. "But I see the dreams of Alsanis, and they see us. I won't pretend to understand what it means, but it has been so long. My mother could speak with Alsanis; the eagles once flew to the heart of the High Halls to converse with her. I was a child then, and I listened; it was not considered wise to interrupt my mother. Now they speak with me." Her voice dipped at the end.

"Would you have—would you have woken if I'd minded my own business?"

The Consort laughed again; it was a clear, high sound, and it had no edges. Kaylin leaned into it, and into the hands that still cupped her face. It was so easy to see Barrani women as young: they always looked youthful. But she realized that the

Consort was far older than her mother had been when she died, and she took comfort from that; she wasn't sure why.

"No."

"What did the words *do?*"

"Do you not know? No, of course you don't. You chose two. Why?"

"Because I couldn't just choose one."

"Why those two?"

"Could you read them?"

"In a fashion, and only here."

"I can't—you know I can't—read the words on my skin. I don't even feel like they're mine. But I had to choose, this time."

"You chose well, I think. Were I to choose, I'm not sure I would have made the same choice—but I am not Chosen. One of the two words was heavy; it was hard for you to carry, hard for you to bring here. The other weighed nothing. It is my belief that the heavier word speaks to the heart of Alsanis. It tells him that you understand some essential part of his plight. You are not Alsanis; you will never be Alsanis. At best, you might, in happier times, have been a guest."

"He has no guests now."

"He has the lost children."

"They are not guests. They might have been, once—but they have far outstayed even the most generous definition of hospitality."

"The other word?"

"It, too, speaks to Alsanis—both words did. He could barely hear my voice. But yours—through the words—was clear. It is hope, Kaylin." She had slid from Elantran into Barrani, and Kaylin had followed the seamless transition so easily she couldn't recall when the switch had happened. "I do not know if it is his hope or yours, but I believe he found hope in it.

"It is scant hope," she added softly. "And perhaps it will cause pain; hope oft does when it remains forever beyond our reach. But the hope, he drew into the depths, and the pain, he cast out. Come. I hear my brother, and he is *not* best pleased."

"Can we just leave?"

"While you are in the West March, you will never entirely leave this place. I am sorry. I did not intend to embroil you in the affairs of the heart of the green."

"But you—"

"Yes. But I am Consort, and I have seen the Lake of Life; it is my gift and my duty to touch the words that wait therein. And, Lord Kaylin, in ignorance, you have also done the same, and you survived.

"Many of my kin did not. Lord of the West March, have you chosen to convene a council meeting in my chambers?"

Kaylin's eyes flew open. She was curled in a crouch beside the Consort's bed, her hand—knuckles white—around the Consort's. She was aware of the glares aimed squarely at the back of her neck, and worked to separate their hands, although the Consort's tightened briefly before she let go.

Kaylin stood and met the Consort's blue eyes. She looked far healthier in real life than she had looked at the end of the not-quite-dream, but she still looked pale and exhausted. Her eyes, however, darkened as she looked at Kaylin.

Kaylin looked down.

There was a small jagged *hole* in the dress. In size and shape it matched a shard of ice. Kaylin froze, her eyes widening in panic.

"Yes," a voice said, and she looked up. There were now three eagles on the other side of the bed. The one in the middle was doing the talking. "Everything comes to an end, Chosen."

Could it come to an end when I'm not wearing it?

"Endings and beginnings are often intertwined."

As answers went, this one sucked. It had that street-corner dispensed-wisdom tone. Which would be fine, but she was the first mortal to wear this dress, and of course it would take damage while she was doing it. That it hadn't so far was some sort of miracle, and Kaylin did not want to come to the end of miracles while still wearing it. She was almost afraid to turn around.

"Lord Kaylin."

Kaylin blinked as the Consort held out an imperious arm. Kaylin realized that the Consort, at least, was still lying in bed. She immediately bent to offer an arm to help the Consort to her feet. It gave her something to do, other than panic, but it also made her feel almost ashamed of herself; she was hiding behind the Consort, who was physically far frailer at the moment than she was.

She was grateful anyway, because she turned, supporting the Consort's weight, to face the room at large.

The Lord of the West March was at the side of the Warden. Nightshade was standing to the Warden's left, Evarrim to Lirienne's right. Behind them, stood Barrani in the livery of the Lord of the West March; they had not drawn swords, but their eyes were the color of midnight as they met Kaylin's.

No one spoke. They looked at Kaylin, looked at her dress— and at the hole that wasn't actually *all* that big—and said nothing. They said it really loudly.

"Warden," the Consort said, nodding regally. "You have my gratitude."

He looked genuinely surprised; the blue of his eyes was ringed by a slender, but visible gold.

"You brought the Chosen to my side. I do not think I would have escaped the nightmares of Alsanis, otherwise. Brother," she continued, using the familiar term in a particularly emphatic way, "the nightmares have never been this strong or this cold; nor has he sent five, if indeed the nightmares are sent at all, before now. The Warden could not have known; the nightmares and the dreams of Alsanis have never been under his control."

The Lord of the West March didn't retreat into plausible denial. "I am heartened to know," he told his sister, "that you retain some of the optimism of youth. I have not accused the Warden of deliberate malfeasance. Intent, or its lack, control, or its lack, are irrelevant. You are awake."

"Yes. I will take a light meal in my outer chamber; this is not the room in which I would choose to greet guests." She turned to Kaylin and raised a brow. Kaylin took the hint and accompanied her to the doors, which opened before she reached them. Kaylin would have rushed to get out of her way, as well, given her expression. She didn't entirely understand the Consort, but she understood her expression: she was in charge, at the moment, and she was Not Pleased.

Kaylin didn't have the option the doors had, being attached at the arm. Then again, the doors didn't need the Consort's regal disdain as a shield, either.

The outer chamber was pretty much a hall. It wasn't a *small* hall, either, but the Barrani never did anything modest. There was a long table, visible through a broad, slender arch that didn't look as though it could actually support the weight of the ceiling above it. Before the arch, there was a wide, sparsely furnished room, with a small font in the corner farthest from the bedroom door; natural light—during the day, which this wasn't—would probably fill the room. Kaylin glanced at the Consort; the Consort looked straight ahead.

Dining room, then.

Although her guests were all men of power and import, the

Consort headed straight for the exceptionally tall chair at the head of the table. Her hand tightened once on Kaylin's arm before she slid into the seat. "Unless you enjoy stilted conversation and the suspicion that causes it, you may take your leave."

"The dress—"

"I know. I would like to tell you it is the least of your worries, but that is unlikely to bring you much comfort. You are *not* in the Hallionne, Kaylin. Your role as harmoniste makes attempts on your life unlikely—but that is not now my concern." She glanced, once, at the small tear in the dress. "I mean you no harm, but I am not certain I am…safe." She looked pointedly at Kaylin's shoulder.

Or rather, at the small dragon that was draped across it.

"I will not tell you to avoid An'Teela. I feel the opposite is almost necessary—but you are in the most danger while you are with her. Take your companion with you wherever you go." She looked down the table as the rest of the guests entered the chamber. She didn't rise to greet them.

Kaylin hesitated, but the truth was, her ankle was throbbing— so much for imaginary injuries—and she was exhausted. As usual, she was hungry, but a table full of political, angry Barrani wasn't much of an inducement to stay. She offered the Consort the most perfect bow a groundhawk with a bum ankle could muster, and then backed out of the room—also an awkward maneuver, given the ankle.

For her part, the Consort accepted the obeisance as if it was her indisputable due.

Kaylin.

Great. She could hear two voices on the inside of her head. She wondered idly if they could hear each other.

Nightshade was amused. *No.*

Lirienne didn't answer.

When I was in the Hallionne, she told them both—she hoped it was both—*I couldn't speak to either of you. I couldn't reach you.*

No. It was Nightshade who answered, but that made sense—she had never tried to speak to the Lord of the West March the same way.

You could reach me when I was in the void. You could reach me when I was in the High Halls, healing— She broke off, not that it would make much difference.

Yes.

Why was this different? Did I—did I disappear?

No. To the eyes of all observers, you remained in the room.

Does this happen often?

No, Kaylin. I do not think it could happen anywhere but the green. When you leave, find your Corporal. If you encounter difficulty, call upon the eagles of Alsanis; I believe they will hear your voice.

What can they do?

He laughed, or at least, she felt laughter.

Kaylin. A different speaker. Lirienne. *I am—we are—in your debt.*

If it's all the same to you, I'd like to skip the debt part.

He also laughed. If her ankle hadn't been throbbing quite so badly, she might have smiled. *You would, I think, respect Lord Barian. Because you are not Barrani, I feel it necessary to remind you that trust is unwise. It is likely that we will convene a meeting of the Council of the West March on the morrow.*

Can I—

No. You are the harmoniste, and given the appearance of the eagles, Lord Barian will request your presence even if I do not. You have seen most of Court, if you have not interacted with all of them; they were in the hall at dinner. There is very little you can do to disguise the damage to the dress, and it will cause distress. You may be called upon to explain it; resist.

Who's going to ask?

I will.

But you just said—

Yes. Do not answer when I demand the truth.

So I'm supposed to say nothing?

You are, Nightshade said, *to do no such thing. You are to answer, but you are to avoid the truth in any of your replies. Lie. Or misdirect. The Lord of the West March will allow obvious silence or obvious rebellion; you are mortal.*

Can he hear this?

I can, Lord Lirienne replied. *Because you desire it. I will speak with the Consort.*

You haven't, yet?

No; she has made clear that she is not to be questioned, and she never does so without cause. She took pains to prevent anyone present from interacting with you personally, and she dismissed you in a way that allowed none of us to follow.

But Kaylin, kyuthe, *be cautious. I know it is not in your nature— but try.*

When she reached the end of the hall, she found Severn. She wasn't even surprised to see him; she was mostly grateful. He was human. He was still bruised, his eye in particular; his hair had been singed, and although it was clean it was uneven. She didn't ask him how he'd known to meet her. She did grimace when his gaze fell to her injured ankle.

"Am I hobbling?"

"You're favoring your other foot," was his diplomatic reply. "The Consort is awake?"

"She is now. She's not in a great mood."

"Your ankle?"

"Oh, not that bad a mood. I injured it trying to get her to wake up." When his brows rose, she added, "Long story, and probably boring to anyone who wasn't in it."

"As long and repetitive as your rants about Margot and Elani street?"

"Very funny."

"Heading to your rooms? I know where they are."

The small dragon hissed in that broken way that implied laughter. "Do you know where Teela's staying?"

Severn nodded.

"Can you take me there?"

"Kaylin—"

"I'm worried about her," Kaylin said, lowering her voice instinctively. "I didn't realize what the West March meant to her. She offered to come and I said yes."

"I *insisted* I accompany you," a familiar voice said, in the same Elantran Kaylin and Severn were using.

CHAPTER 11

"Don't make that face. You asked Corporal Handred if he knew where I was staying. You didn't ask him if I was there."

"It's the middle of the night, Teela. It's dark."

"And Barrani require how much sleep? You, on the other hand, look terrible."

"And I know you mean that in the nicest possible way."

"Kitling, what happened to your ankle?"

"I landed badly."

"From what height?"

"Six feet."

"And you did *that?*"

"My hands were full at the time, Teela. I couldn't drop what I was carrying."

"From six feet? You could cut off my hands and I'd stick that landing." Teela's eyes narrowed. "Please tell me the light in this rustic hall is so appalling the hole in that dress is actually a wrinkle."

"Can I compromise and say I didn't put it there?"

"That's not much of a compromise."

"It's the truth."

"Truth is not an excuse."

Kaylin wanted to shriek. Her stomach made noise instead. Teela's eyes slid from blue to their resting blue-green state. "Your rooms."

Kaylin nodded.

"The servants will no doubt be waiting; it is quite late. They will provide food if food is requested."

Kaylin nodded again; it was generally the safe bet when Teela took charge. She glanced at Severn. A look passed between the two Hawks, but Severn didn't disappear. He didn't take the lead, though; Teela had it and didn't look like surrendering it could ever occur to her.

Only when she reached a familiar door—with a ward that made her cringe—did Teela stop.

"I swear," Kaylin said between slightly clenched teeth, "if the door ward sounds the alarm again, I'm going to find an axe."

"That might be more difficult than you imagine. I'd open the door for you, but I believe it's keyed to you."

At least she didn't have to hit it with her forehead. She lifted her left hand and gritted her teeth as she placed her palm against the ward. This time, however, there was no blaring alarms, and no accompanying armored guards. The door swung open, into the hall, and Kaylin entered rooms that were hers while she wore this dress.

They didn't feel like hers. Nothing Barrani really did.

To draw a line under this point, the servants were waiting. Kaylin remembered Teela's pointed words. These servants had their sense of worth and duty tied up in doing their job well.

If Kaylin was obviously uncomfortable—and damn it, she was—she was telling them they were doing it badly.

Inhaling, she drew herself to her full height—which was not impressive in comparison—and said, "I was called from Lord Barian's residence to tend to the Consort by the dreams of Alsanis, and I've only just emerged. I twisted my ankle in a fall, I've spent what feels like hours in the nightmares of a Hallionne and I'm—" Her stomach growled. She flushed. "Hungry." The last word was Elantran.

They waited, and she added, "Please bring refreshments for my guests and me." She wasn't used to sitting rooms that were basically small dining halls, and she had no problem eating while draped across her bed, because if Teela and Tain dropped into her apartment, someone had to sit there.

But she tried. She led the way to the not-so-small sitting room, and chose the largest chair she could find. The servants departed, and Kaylin glared at Teela. "If you think I'm going to usher you to a damn chair, bite me."

Severn, however, sat in the chair closest to Kaylin's. He rested his head against the back of the chair, and as it was low, he was pretty much facing the ceiling. With closed eyes. "You need to talk to Teela," he said. It wasn't a question.

Kaylin didn't answer immediately.

"The Barrani are naturally suspicious. I imagine they don't start that way—but most of the ones who didn't develop suspicion quickly are dead," he continued, eyes still closed. "What Teela faces in the West March isn't the usual, natural suspicion."

Teela sat—on the table, which was situated in front of Kaylin and Severn. It was a low, flat table with edges that curved toward the light in the ceiling. She even crossed her legs.

"I don't think the servants are going to be all that impressed with that," Kaylin pointed out.

"They're not my servants," Teela replied, with a feline smile. "Continue, Corporal."

Severn hadn't even opened his eyes. "You're family, to Kaylin. In a very real way, *kyuthe*. She trusts you."

"I've always told her that was a bad idea."

"Yes. But bad or no, she's grown up under your wing. She trusts you, and I'm willing to do the same. But, Teela—I think the threat they feel is real. The fear behind the suspicion is too solid. You can't normally get the Barrani to agree on anything; the agreement—in the West March—is almost oppressive."

Kaylin turned to glare at the side of Severn's face. The bruised side, damn it. He opened his eyes, lifted his head, and met Teela's gaze. "Warn me, if it comes to that. No matter what's required, Kaylin will never lift a hand against you—not in any serious way."

"And you will?" Teela was amused.

Severn wasn't.

Severn's expression won; the amusement drained from Teela's expression. "If it comes to that, Corporal, I will count on you. What warning I can give, I'll give. But in return?"

Severn inclined his head, his gaze unwavering.

"Be as competent as you are rumored to be."

It took Kaylin a moment to understand what Teela was asking. During that moment, Severn deserted his chair. "I will." He turned to Kaylin, offered a lopsided grin that never reached his eyes, and headed out the door. She rose, as well, and her ankle almost collapsed.

Teela laughed.

"You could find all this less amusing, you know."

"Yes. I could. But it wouldn't change anything, and I prefer to be amused."

To Kaylin's surprise, the small dragon leaped off her shoulders and headed—at high speed—out the door. After Severn.

Teela raised a black brow. "Are you certain that's wise?"

"I didn't tell him to leave."

"You didn't tell him to stay."

"He's a cat, Teela. He goes where he wants." She sank back into her chair. "Why didn't you tell me?"

"If I had to catalog all of the events in my life, kitling, you would be dead of old age before I'd finished."

Kaylin inhaled. "You hear Alsanis."

"Pardon?"

"You can hear Alsanis."

"You're guessing."

"I'm asking."

"You're wrong." Teela rose. "Move over."

"There are sixteen chairs in this room, Teela."

"There are seven. Move over."

Kaylin shuttled to one side, and Teela flopped down beside her. Kaylin closed her eyes and leaned against Teela; she felt, for a moment, that she was in her own apartment, and Teela was lounging on her bed and stealing her pillow. "What did you see?"

"Not what the Consort saw."

"You know this how?"

"She asked me what I saw, and I told her."

"Not wise."

"There's a bunch of not wise in my life today. Being here. Waking the Consort. Talking to you. Severn's worried."

"Yes. I don't, before you whine, find his worry as irritating as yours because he's not worried about me."

"He is—"

"His worry is less insulting; he thinks I'll become far more dangerous than I currently am. You worry that something will break me. What happened to the dress?"

"I'm not sure. No, I know what happened—but I don't understand why. I was *here* the entire time."

"What happened?"

"Ice shattered. Splinters flew. One of them hit me."

"There?"

Kaylin nodded. "It doesn't seem to have pierced skin—there's no blood on the dress."

Teela shook her and Kaylin opened her eyes. "Do not bleed on that dress. I mean it."

"I'm unlikely to make myself bleed, Teela. Tell everyone *else* that." She paused as a thought occurred to her. "Has anyone else bled on this dress?"

"Why do you ask?"

"Something Barian said."

"*Lord* Barian."

"Yes, him. He said there were reasons for all of the laws in the West March."

"There are. There are reasons why it is forbidden to fight—or kill—in the heart of the green."

"It happened before. Before you—"

"Yes. You are not, of course, the first harmoniste; merely the first mortal one. One such man was a Lord of the East. It was before my birth," she added. "But not before my mother's. He was reputed to be cold and proud; a Lord of the High Court. He was not of the West March, and even in the wars, he remained in the East."

"The East is where the High Halls are?"

"Close, yes. After the wars, he came West. He was a political man, and as such, considered the customs of the West March rustic and unnecessary. He was not chosen as either Teller or harmoniste—and at that recitation, there were both. He did not set out from the High Halls, but he joined the pilgrimage when it became clear that this recitation was to be significant.

"The Teller was a man of power and significance in his own right; he traveled with an armed contingent. To challenge him would be costly. The harmoniste, however, was a man newly come to the High Court, and newly come from the test of name. He had very little standing in the Court itself. The Lord therefore chose to challenge the harmoniste." At Kaylin's expression, Teela added, "A genuine challenge, yes. The man could not refuse."

"But—"

"The Lord of the West March did not travel with the pilgrims; nor did the Lord of the High Court. The Lord from the East was therefore one of two who might issue commands to the Hallionne, and the harmoniste was, as I mentioned, considered insignificant. He could not refuse."

Something about the way she said this felt subtly wrong, but Kaylin couldn't put her finger on what.

"He therefore did not refuse. He was not from an insignificant line," she added softly, "so he could not be disposed of in a more convenient way—but the Lord in question felt a lost challenge would serve his purpose." She was smiling again.

"You didn't know this man."

"No. As I said, it was just before my time. But I understood the condescension with which the West March was—and often is—viewed. During the fight itself, the harmoniste was injured. This was not unexpected.

"His robes, however, were cut, and the blood from the wound seeped into the fabric."

Kaylin looked down at her lap with a growing sense of discomfort. "What happened?"

"Fully half of the party that had set out from the High Halls perished."

"But—but from what?"

"The green," Teela replied softly. "I told you—the Lord in question had set out from the East only when word of the significance of the recitation had reached his ears. There are always ambitious Lords; our party was larger when it arrived in Bertolle than it had been when it set out."

It wasn't, now; they had lost many in the attempt to reach Orbaranne through the portal paths.

"He arrived at the edge of the green; he did not make his challenge until he was within the lands ruled by the Lord of the West March. He was not in the heart of the green, but he was upon it."

"The green chooses. The green chose you."

"Teela," Kaylin said, with some frustration, "just what exactly *is* the green?"

The door opened. Teela stretched her legs, stretched her arms, and grinned as the servants entered the room. They carried slender silver trays, which they set upon the table to one side of Teela's feet. Even Kaylin was appalled.

The servants, however, said nothing. They didn't look surprised, shocked, or disgusted. They offered Kaylin sweet water and wine; Teela took the wine. Kaylin waited until the servants had left the room before she turned on Teela.

"I would pay everything I could earn in a *year*," she said, "if *you* had to take etiquette lessons with Diarmat!"

Teela laughed. "Kitling, if you could only see your expression. Don't eat that," she added, as Kaylin picked up what she assumed was some kind of strange fruit. "I know you're not picky, but you won't like it."

"Why not?"

"You will find it very spicy. It's sweet," she added, with a mild frown, "and you have a weakness for sweet food—but there's a subtle spice that clings to the tongue, and you've never been fond of spicy food."

Kaylin set it aside. There was enough food here she could afford to be picky. "What is the green?" She needed to know.

"I have never fully understood it myself. It is not the Hallionne, either separately or in concert, although it works through them; I believe it is part of them, and they are part of the green. They are whole in and of themselves." She hesitated, as if searching for words—which was unusual for Teela. "You're Elantran."

Kaylin nodded.

"You live in the city. But you are not the city."

Kaylin nodded again.

"The Emperor also lives in the city; he claims it, rules it, and hands down its laws. But if he perished, the city would not perish with him."

Given what it would take to actually kill the Emperor, Kaylin wasn't as sure this was true. "The green is—is like a city?"

"Like a sentient city," Teela replied. "It is a place. It has geography. It has laws and rules and customs. We," she added, refilling her glass, "are merely the least of its citizens. We do not make the laws; we merely live—as most of the people in Elantra do—by them. If there is an Emperor, or his equivalent, we—again, like most of Elantra's citizens—will never meet him.

"But cross him, break his laws, and his anger is felt. The green is like the Hallionne, and unlike. I don't believe it hears our thoughts when we are in its domain; nor does it interfere in our lives in immediate, visceral ways. But it can. On that day, it did. Not all of the men who died intended to strip the chosen harmoniste of his role; the anger of the green is not so directed. No one will try to kill you while you wear that dress.

"But, kitling, do not bleed on it."

"I didn't exactly stab myself," Kaylin replied.

Teela fell silent, and not in a good way. She rose, and began to pace. The Barrani Hawk could pace for hours. She could wear ruts in stone. She had, when she chose, a light, graceful step that belied her size. Clearly that wasn't her choice today. "I swear, I will strangle Nightshade myself."

"*After* he's finished the telling."

Teela laughed. "Of course. I know the anger of the green quite well."

"What aren't you telling me?"

"Nothing. Nothing you need to know, kitling."

Kaylin looked down at her hands. "Tell me about the others."

"The others?"

"You're stalling."

Teela chuckled. "You are not my keeper. I am not stalling; I am considering what you usually do with information you shouldn't have."

"Meaning?"

"You run full tilt into the heart of things. You let your fears propel you. You have the caution of a mortal child—what is the word again?"

"Toddler," Kaylin answered reflexively, and found annoyance after the two syllables had left her mouth.

"Toddler. Why do you think I hear Alsanis? Don't frown like that—your face will get stuck that way. Immortal faces don't."

"I saw them, there."

Teela didn't ask who. "Where?"

"I think I was walking through either the dreams or the nightmares of Alsanis. I was trying to find the Consort at the time."

"With full hands."

Kaylin grimaced. "Yes. The full hands aren't important here." She fell silent. "Maybe they are. I was carrying words. I mean—runes. Like the marks on my skin."

"Like?"

"Two of the marks on my skin. I needed to take them with me. I needed to take them to the Consort—don't ask me why. I just did. But—I didn't *find* the Consort immediately; I had to fly through—"

"Fly?"

"Well, the small dragon had to fly, but in the dreaming, his wings were larger. *Any*way, there was a city there, eventually. On the walls of a gigantic pit. We landed in a tall building— that's when I twisted my ankle. The Consort was there, but to get to her we had to walk down the side of a ridiculously long courtyard. I was still carrying the words.

"And I found statues along that wall. They were—they looked like they were—made of glass. They were Barrani, Teela. There were eleven in all: two women, nine men. It's funny," she added. "I had the hardest time telling Barrani apart when I first joined the Hawks. They all looked the same to me. I mean, women looked different from men, but—you were almost the same height, with the same eyes, the same hair, the same general facial characteristics.

"But…the statues, absent of color, didn't. If I saw them again, I would know them."

"You're thinking again. I can hear it."

"Very funny. I saw one of the lost children in the forest on the way to Bertolle."

"And you recognized him, cast in glass."

"No. That's the strange thing. I *didn't* recognize him."

Teela shrugged. "It was dark."

"In both places. The only light in the courtyard was the one I brought with me. The words," she added, "they glowed."

"Very well. Statues." The Barrani Hawk's eyes had lost their green.

"Technically, no."

"If you take much longer to tell me the rest, I'll strangle you myself."

"Didn't you just say—"

"I told you not to bleed on the dress. I don't recall that strangulation causes bleeding."

"The statues moved. They followed me. They tried—they tried to touch one of the words. I thought of them as ghosts," she added. "They always reacted to the same word."

"I am not going to ask you what the word was, because I really will strangle you when you can't answer." Teela folded her arms across her chest as if to stop her hands from acting of their own accord.

"They couldn't touch it; their hands passed through it."

"Yours clearly didn't."

"No. But—every time one of them tried, the word grew heavier. By the end, even you would have found it a strain."

"And that end?"

"I walked into a room. It was behind a warded door. My hands were full; I had to hit it with my head."

A grin tugged the corners of Teela's lips up as she considered this. "It opened?"

"With a lot of noise, and if by 'opened' you mean turned to burning ash."

"Alsanis was never rumored to be this dramatic. Continue."

"The Consort was there. In the center of the room. Which wasn't a room at all—it had no ceiling. The sky on the inside was daylight; the sun was high."

"Did she cast a shadow?"

Had she? Kaylin frowned.

"Did you?"

"I was kind of busy, Teela. Is it important?"

"It's a dream. Or a nightmare. Everything—and nothing—is important."

"The Consort had been singing. She was almost at the end of her song when I arrived; I panicked."

Teela shot Kaylin her best "water is wet" look.

"The weird thing is, she was standing in front of a fountain. The fountain was at the heart of the room. The room was like an eleven-pointed star, in shape; the floors were stone. The ghosts—they all followed me in a line—walked to the eleven corners, and climbed invisible pedestals; they were all facing inward. They were looking at the Consort or the fountain."

"Or you."

That hadn't occurred to Kaylin. "Or me. I had to let go of the words to catch her before she fell. But the words waited."

Teela didn't even tell her that the words weren't sentient. "And then?"

"The Consort touched the words; they were solid, for her. We kind of—kind of pushed them into the fountain."

Teela stared at her.

"There was nowhere else for them to go, Teela, and they had to go somewhere. I'd've given them to the ghosts, but there were eleven ghosts and two words."

"I cannot *believe* Lord Sanabalis considers it wise to teach you magic."

"Whisper that in his ear if it'll get me out of his lessons." She hesitated. She had come to the end of safe story—if mentioning the eleven was safe at all.

Teela, of course, noticed.

"One of the words sank into the water. The weightless one. The other hit water—and rose." She sucked in air, and rose herself. Standing was in all ways less impressive. "The water froze as the rune changed shape, Teela. In the center of the fountain, made of ice, I saw you."

"You have not spoken of this to anyone else?"

"No."

"You're lying."

"It wasn't technically speaking." Kaylin didn't like the color of Teela's eyes; she didn't like the Hawk's sudden stiffness, either. "The eleven came off their pedestals then. They walked to the center of the room, to the lip of the fountain. They lifted their arms—to your image—and, Teela, they screamed."

She wasn't certain what Teela would do. She ate, in silence, although she'd lost all appetite. She was a betting person, but this could go either way; there was a good chance Teela would pivot on heel and leave the room. She had that tight-lipped "keep away" look that would have sent most of the office on whatever errands they could find that took them farther away from her desk.

Kaylin, with eight years of experience in the same office and no reasonable—or farfetched—errands to run, should have said nothing. It was safest. "Teela, what *happened* to the children? What happened to you?"

"Nothing happened to me," was her bitter, bitter reply. Kaylin almost didn't recognize her voice.

"What happened when you served as harmoniste?"

"Nothing." Teela looked over her shoulder to the closed door. "If I had known that you would be involved like this, I would never have allowed you to—"

"We *needed* that information."

"No, kitling, we didn't."

"People were dying—"

"Yes. But we didn't know that at the time, and the truth of the matter is, I don't care about those people." Her eyes narrowed as Kaylin's jaw dropped in outrage that was entirely genuine. "I don't care about them as much as I care about you. Is that better? You don't value yourself. Fine; not all of us labor under your evaluation of yourself."

"You're one to talk."

Teela stared.

Kaylin knew this wasn't smart. She knew it. But she was underslept and overworried and her mouth kind of opened and all the wrong words kept falling out. "You hate it when people worry about you. You hate it when they *care*. You never ask for help, even when you—"

"Need it?" Teela's eyes were now dark blue slits. "What help, exactly, do you think you can offer? You have *no idea* what you're doing. You've no idea what you're facing. You wander around touching things that should never be disturbed, and you don't even realize you're doing it.

"You can barely save *yourself*. Do not insult me by implying that your *concern* can somehow save—" She stopped. Turning, she walked out of the room.

The small dragon returned a short time later, squawking.

"No," she told him, from her glum perch in the chair she now occupied solo. "It didn't go well."

Squawk.

She poked at food. The small dragon landed on the table, skidded across its smooth, flat surface, and smacked into a silver tray. "Don't eat that," Kaylin said. "You won't like it."

He hissed.

"Fine, suit yourself." She pushed herself out of the chair and started to pace. The room was large, but it was still a room, and at the moment, it felt like a cell. She glanced at the small hole in her dress, and then, frowning, at her arms. Ice shards had struck skin—but they'd caused no pain. Instead, they'd stilled the burning of the marks on both arms.

She stopped pacing and looked down at him. His eyes were wide and dark; they were the only thing about him that wasn't translucent, unless you counted his teeth.

"I'm going for a walk." She headed toward the same door that Teela had exited, and he jumped and attached himself to her shoulders. "You don't have to come with me. You can find Severn and keep him out of trouble."

The small dragon bit her ear.

"Listen, buddy, if I wanted pierced ears, I'd've had it done years ago."

Walking through Barrani-owned halls was not as relaxing as a stroll through the city streets. Then again, walking through the city streets often ended up being less relaxing than intended; it was most of the reason Kaylin didn't bother when she wasn't on the job. But she felt caged by expected behavior standards when in the rooms that were theoretically hers.

She felt caged in the halls, period.

The Consort, Teela, and every other person willing to condescend to speak with the merely mortal had made clear that the residence of the Lord of the West March wasn't a safe space, but Teela's little story about blood on the dress made Kaylin bold. That, and it was harder to find a target that was constantly on the move.

She wandered through the halls and found herself in the courtyard. This took less time than she'd feared; this building—at least so far—appeared to be geographically fixed. She could memorize it, as if it were the Imperial Palace, and make an internal map she could follow. At the moment, she wanted air.

Oh, who the hells was she kidding? What she wanted was

water. She wanted the fountain. Men in armor passed her in ones and twos as she walked. They weren't Imperial Palace Guards; they didn't stand at attention all over the bloody place. They did notice her; they didn't stop her or ask her business. She couldn't bring herself to ask them for directions; she might have asked her servants if she'd cleared her head *before* she'd left them behind.

But she did find the exit eventually. The doors weren't guarded—but they weren't closed, either.

She hesitated, and then walked toward them, through them, and beneath the night sky. The moons were high, but not full; the light they cast was subdued. Kaylin's eyes adjusted as she listened to the fall of water into water. Fountain.

From this distance, at this hour, it was exactly as it seemed. There was obviously some enchantment laid on it, because water didn't normally fall from thin air, but the enchantment didn't make the marks on her skin itch, so she didn't class it as magic.

And she didn't classify the water as magic, either, although anyone in their right mind would. She took a seat at the edge of the fountain; she wanted to touch the Tha'alaan, just for a minute. She wanted the feeling of welcome, inclusion, and acceptance—because she wasn't going to get much of that here.

"Lord Kaylin."

She exhaled in frustration, lowering the hand she'd lifted before it made contact with anything wet. She wasn't alone. "Lord Nightshade. How long have you been here?"

"I have only just arrived. The Consort kept us for some time." He emerged into the shadowed light, walking around the curved basin of the fountain. "She did not choose to answer many questions; nor did she choose to ask them. She held court," he added. He was smiling; Kaylin couldn't see the color of his eyes. "She held court almost as if she were her mother. I think she intended to spare you interrogation, where at all possible.

"Lords Barian and Evarrim are not pleased." He glanced at the falling water as if it were of passing interest to him. It wasn't at the moment, and he knew she knew it.

She wanted to touch the water. "Did you attend the recitation where Teela served as harmoniste, or was it after you left the Court?"

He watched her without answering. Kaylin hardly ever found silence comfortable, but she waited this one out. "What did you see in the nightmares of Alsanis?"

She didn't answer. After a pause that was just as long, she said, "I couldn't speak to you when I was there."

"You made the attempt?"

She nodded. "You couldn't see what I saw while I was there, either."

"No. You were unsettled upon your return, if *return* is the word for it. Were it only you, I would be less concerned—but Kaylin, the Consort is disturbed, as well. What did you see? What did you do?"

This was why he had come. She felt the sharp edge of something that was far more than idle curiosity.

She rose. Pacing beneath moonlight felt far more natural than pacing in an enclosed room. "Who did you lose?" Her voice was quiet.

CHAPTER 12

He could have pretended to misunderstand; he was tempted to do exactly that. But it would not get him the information he wanted—and Kaylin realized, with a distant surprise, that he couldn't just pluck it from her thoughts the way he usually did.

No.

He'd tried.

Yes.

She didn't understand why, but at the moment, she was grateful. It didn't bother her that Severn might read her thoughts; he'd always seemed to know what she was thinking—and why. Sometimes he'd understood it before she did, and they were her thoughts.

But...no one—*no one*—had caused her as much pain.

"There were eleven. Eleven Barrani. They weren't children—not by our standards—but they weren't adults, either. Two girls, nine boys. If you don't count Teela."

"You have been speaking with Lord Barian."

She didn't deny it. "I don't know what most of them were called. I don't know their names in the legal sense of the word *name*. The dreams of Alsanis insist that none of the children have left the Hallionne—but I saw Terrano. Teela saw him. You recognized his name."

He said nothing.

"Nightshade, were you there?"

"For the regalia which destroyed the children? No."

"Were you there when Teela returned to the West March?"

"Yes."

"And when she served as harmoniste?"

"Yes."

"Did you understand either recitation?"

His answering smile was thin. "No, Lord Kaylin. I am not entirely certain either of us will understand the recitation in which we are meant to play a large part."

"You think it has something to do with the children."

"They are not children now."

Kaylin watched him. "Do you think they can be saved?"

He watched the water fall. She realized that he wasn't going to answer, because he believed two contradictory things: that they could be saved, and that they couldn't. It wasn't a matter of hope, although he did; the hope was too painful to touch and examine. She shied away from it because it wasn't hers and she had no way of responding to it. He believed that both outcomes were possible; that both were probable. She couldn't tell which he actually wanted.

"What did Teela do?"

"She will not tell you?"

"No. And you knew that."

"I knew you were foolish enough to ask—but An'Teela has long been unusual; there was always the possibility she might answer."

"If blood hadn't been shed during the recitation—if it hadn't fallen on the green—what would have happened?"

"It is a question much discussed," he replied. "We have no answers, of course; it is not an experiment that has been repeated."

"The people of the West March don't trust her."

"No. She is the daughter of the man who ordered the deaths in the heart of the green. She is of the High Court. She survived what none of the others survived. Had she been older, or wiser, she might have parlayed that survival into a formidable base on which to build political power; she did not."

"Why was she spared what the others weren't?"

"I am not the green, Kaylin. I am not of the West March. Teela bears the blood of Wardens in her veins. Her mother was—"

"Barian's aunt."

"Yes."

Kaylin frowned. A thought occurred to her, but she was tired. "Why did they try to kill you?"

"I am Outcaste," he replied.

"The Consort clearly doesn't care."

"No."

"Teela said that it's considered treason to try to kill the harmoniste."

"While he or she wears the blood of the green, yes."

"But not the Teller? Even if the Teller is chosen in the same way?"

"Is he?"

"Well, the green chooses."

"Yes. But the criterion for such a choice is opaque. To my kin it is a random act, a choice that ignores the individual and his power. The robes of the role chosen for me are not significant in the same way; they are not the blood of the green.

But the crown is significant. There have been no attempts to kill the Teller in the past; I believe, given the lack of reaction to the assassination attempt, there will be more in future. The harmoniste, however, is safe.

"We learn from past tragedies."

"The problem with this one, as I see it, is that it isn't."

"A tragedy?"

"In the past. It's not finished. It's not done." She grimaced and sat again. She also fidgeted; Nightshade might have been a statue, he moved so little. "The children are—and are not—trapped in the Hallionne. The Barrani are—and are not—corrupted. Iberrienne was—and was not—Iberrienne, but regardless, he almost certainly came to Elantra to—"

"To find sacrifices."

She stood once more, her hands in fists. She felt no raging fury, though. She accepted that Nightshade was Barrani; he wasn't human. If she were honest, the Exchequer probably had had some idea of what was going on, and he *was* human, and didn't care, either. The Exchequer was unlikely to escape unscathed.

And she hated him more because he, at least, should have known better.

But Nightshade was Nightshade. He was what he was. He had power. He had gold. If you wanted a man in power to pay attention to what *you* wanted, you either had to be a power yourself, or you had to have something he wanted. "I can help you achieve whatever it is you hope to achieve, but I want something in return."

He waited.

"Change the way you rule the fief. What Tiamaris does, you could do. You've never done it. It's probably not as easy as Tiamaris makes it look. But if he can do it, it *can* be done."

He stared at her for a long moment, and then he laughed. It

was bitter laughter, but contained genuine amusement. "You do not even know what I want."

"No." She met, and held, his gaze. "I'll know. When—if—it happens, I'll know. You'll push me. You'll guide where you can. You'll manipulate. You'll do everything in your power to use my power to do whatever it is you want done. I won't fight you, in this. I will do whatever you think needs doing."

"And if I told you to kill An'Teela?"

"Within reason."

"I do not choose to expose it."

Kaylin shrugged. "Suit yourself. I can't pick it out of your thoughts."

"If you wished to assert sovereignty, if you wished to exert power, you could."

"No, *I can't.* I've had one enraged Barrani Lord hammering away at the inside of my skull for days now, looking for weaknesses. If I knew how to forget a name completely, believe that I would. I don't. I have the energy—or the sense of self-preservation—to resist. I have nothing left over—at all—to start playing games with you."

"Kill him."

She'd given it serious thought because she was fairly certain she could. Not in a fair fight, but she could probably force him to stand still long enough to slit his throat. "I can't."

"You won't; they are not the same. In any other case, I would not counsel such a killing; in yours, there is no advantage to his survival. You will not use him."

"I won't use *any* of you." But Ynpharion wasn't like the others.

"No. Not yet. Perhaps not ever. Ynpharion will be called—and questioned—by the Council of the Vale. Listen to him when he answers if you will not force truth from him. You will know when he lies."

She thought of Ynpharion and exhaled sharply. "Ynpharion was a forest Feral when I found him. I don't know if he could shift shapes, but it's my suspicion he could: he could appear to be Barrani, and he could be—whatever it is you call them. But I'm not sure he chose to become what he became. He'd kill Iberrienne slowly if he found him; Iberrienne is the only person he hates more than he hates me.

"He had to have agreed to whatever was done to him; I don't get the impression that he was kidnapped and dragged to Iberrienne kicking and screaming. He allowed whatever happened. He would never allow it again. There's something laid on them, over them—something that changes not only what they can be, but what they want.

"But I swear he'd cut off his own head before he'd serve Iberrienne again in *any* way." She hesitated. "Iberrienne wasn't one of the lost children."

"No."

"But he *was* the one who attempted to destroy Orbaranne." She paced for a bit. "I don't understand where the children are, what they are, or what they want. I don't understand what they attempted to even do with Orbaranne—if we assume they didn't intend to just destroy her.

"And I think we need to know."

"You will find that the Imperial Hawk does not confer either privilege or responsibility in the West March."

"No."

"I will not agree to your conditions, Lord Kaylin; I have no reason to do so. Were I to tell you everything, were you to understand the whole of my part in this tale, it would change nothing. You will do what you do. If I am Nightshade, you are Kaylin Neya. You have my name. If you wish change in the fief, use it. Try." His smile was cutting.

"And if you will not, when you are a Hawk and everything

I do is a crime, ask yourself why. I am one man. Those who suffer under the neglect of my rule are multiple. You spend a life attempting to apprehend those who break Imperial Law; it is your highest duty. You have risked your life—you will no doubt continue to do so—in pursuit of imperfect justice. You *have* the means.

"You are merely squeamish, Kaylin. It is a weakness."

"Yes," she said, facing the water. "But I'm human."

"Are you?" He offered her an unexpected bow, and left her by the side of the water that had fallen without pause throughout their conversation.

She was silent. The small dragon was not. He didn't generally seem to care for Nightshade, but tonight, he had remained flopped across both of her shoulders and the back of her neck, as if the conversation was trivial. Or boring.

"Is he right?" Kaylin asked.

She didn't expect an answer, but the small dragon lifted his delicate head and rubbed it against her cheek.

"Is it just because I'm squeamish?" She lifted her hands; they hovered above the water's rippling surface. She hesitated for one long minute, and then let them fall to her sides. The Tha'alani feared and distrusted Kaylin's people because they felt they were all insane—the outcome of living a life in the isolation of fear, anger, and ignorance.

Tonight she was afraid, angry, and ignorant, and the Tha'alani didn't deserve to be stuck with her thoughts. Or with her.

But she frowned as she looked at the fountain and its base, because it was so familiar. She couldn't change fear or anger tonight. But ignorance? Ignorance could be, as the Arkon said, alleviated. She walked around the fountain's perimeter, pausing to kneel on flat stone to look at the underside of the basin.

She had no light; all she could see was the general shape, and it was pretty much what she'd expect of a normal fountain.

Tomorrow, then. She rose, brushed off her skirt with way more care than she'd brush clothing she actually owned, and headed back to her rooms.

Sleep was a problem.

By the time she'd removed the dress and taken the bath that seemed to be expected, she'd made a list of things she needed to understand. She didn't number the points, because the number shifted; she couldn't be objective.

She needed to understand Iberrienne.

She was certain that the Human Caste Court believed his experiments might pave the way to immortality for the chosen—murderous—few, but people often heard what they wanted to hear. She didn't believe it herself.

But the Arcanum—or at least three of its members—had been involved. She would bet her own money that the other two had no idea of what Iberrienne had intended to do with all of his kidnapped mortals. They thought he intended *something*. They'd aided him, inasmuch as they could. They *knew* about the paths to the outlands. What had they been offered?

They were Barrani. Barrani were less likely to hear what they wanted to hear—or at least less likely to trust it. None of the Barrani expected the full story when they negotiated, not even from their allies. So...they had to have suspicions. The suspicions had been wrong. No matter how Barrani intended to gain power—and they always did—planning the Consort's death was outside the parameters of acceptable risk.

What had Iberrienne showed them?

She could understand how Iberrienne could reach the rest of the Barrani he'd likely ensnared; he was a member of the

High Court. He could walk in—and out—without comment. How did he choose? Was choice even necessary?

Argh.

Iberrienne might have gone entirely undetected if he hadn't tried to level the city block Kaylin lived in with his Arcane bomb. His reaction to Bellusdeo—to a female dragon—implied that he was, at heart, Barrani, no matter how much he'd changed. Unless the Dragons somehow presented a threat to the lost children, and Kaylin couldn't see how that could be true.

She was certain that Iberrienne was involved with the lost children. The transformed. But how? The Hallionne Alsanis was forbidden. But Kaylin had seen with her own eyes that the lost children weren't trapped in the Hallionne. They weren't trapped in the outlands, either. Terrano had approached Teela on the forest path, on land that was technically outside of the green.

And of course, the end point of her worries, and the start of them, which kept her mind running on a narrow, visceral track: Why had the lost boy approached Teela? He had been—he had sounded—delighted to see her. Delighted, surprised. If the lost children had freedom of movement—or enough freedom to somehow contact Iberrienne, couldn't they have contacted Teela on their own?

What did they want from Teela?

Why had Teela been part of the nightmare?

Why had she shattered?

She rolled over, and the small dragon smacked her nose with his tail. He generally slept just above her head on a pillow, the back of her neck being unavailable. She might as well give up on sleep. It wouldn't be the first time she'd gotten almost none. She rose, dragged herself back into the dress that was the best armor—against Barrani—she'd ever wear, and headed out of the darkened room.

She found servants. One man and one woman. They hadn't, from the look of it, been conversing the way she was certain mortal servants would. But they were doing something. Her arms began to itch as she approached them. She was glad, then, that she'd chosen to wear the dress.

She was too tired to care much about tact or appropriate behavior. She wasn't too tired to worry that Teela would be pissed at her. She left the ruder words out, which meant High Barrani as her chosen language of communication. "What are you doing?"

Their eyes were blue. It was a darker shade of blue than the usual; there hadn't been a lot of green in these rooms. The man bowed. "We are securing the room. Mortals sleep."

She really was in a bad mood. Everything made her suspicious. Even the explanation, which on the surface made sense. "No one is going to try to kill me—"

"You do not wear the dress in your sleep, Lord."

She let her arms fall to her side, glancing at the layout of the hall. It was too narrow for sword work; daggers would be fine. But daggers against at least one mage? One Barrani mage? Toss-up.

Teela could—and occasionally did—use magic. She didn't use it often. Kaylin couldn't offhand think of another Barrani Hawk who could. She'd wondered about it at thirteen—and for several years after—because the mages who came to the Halls were pompous men who considered the ability *to* use magic a gift that set them above the rest of the people who had to work for a living.

Teela, however, was the only Lord to work as a Hawk. The rest of the Hawks—according to Teela—hadn't taken the test of name. Kaylin had assumed, when she'd discovered Teela's patrician background, that that was the difference. Maybe it hadn't been. Maybe it was the test of name that somehow conferred that ability.

The test of name seemed to be a bit of a political sore spot for the denizens of the West March. Kaylin couldn't believe that men and women who had survived it would work as servants.

The small dragon was sitting on her left shoulder, watching the servants. Watching Kaylin, as well. He didn't seem to be concerned. Kaylin forced her hands to relax. These were Lirienne's people. She recognized both of them; they hadn't switched between shifts.

But they weren't normally servants. She was now certain of it. She exhaled. "Were you both born in the West March?"

This caused them to exchange a glance, although they kept all expression off their faces. It was the woman who answered. "Yes."

"Have you ever traveled to the High Court?"

"We have both made that pilgrimage. If you mean to ascertain whether or not we are Lords, we are not."

"Actually, what I want to know is whether or not you're normally servants."

The woman's eyes lightened; the man's darkened. "We serve the Lord of the West March," she said. "*Servant* has connotations in the High Halls that it does not in the West March. We are in the service of Lord Lirienne. It is he who decides what form that service takes, and where our specific talents are most needed." She glanced at her companion. His eyes had not gotten any greener.

"You spent more time in Elantra than your friend."

"I spent a great deal of time in Elantra," she replied—in Elantran. "I will not ask you to return to your room, but I must warn you, there is some difficulty in the halls at the moment."

Kaylin glanced at the small dragon; he was staring at the door farthest from where the three stood.

"What difficulty?" she asked, reaching uneasily for the daggers she always carried with her, although they weren't in the usual place.

The drawing of the daggers caused the man's eyes to go all the way to midnight-blue. The woman's were the more traditional "this is bad" color with which Kaylin was most familiar.

"You are not to fight in that dress," he said. "Lord Kaylin." The title was clearly afterthought.

"I'm not going to stand here and do nothing if—"

"When," the woman said, as the itchiness of Kaylin's arms became a burning that spread across her entire skin. "Lord Kaylin, please retreat."

But the back of Kaylin's neck was burning as she turned to look down the small hall. "I don't think that's going to help," she said in Elantran. She added a single Leontine phrase. The small dragon's claws did their usual attempt to burrow. He hissed.

Kaylin didn't even tell him not to breathe, because she could now hear the sounds of fighting in the hall beyond her rooms. She was surprised when he lifted his wings, because he didn't attempt to fly; instead, he spread one until it covered her face.

In theory, his body was translucent, not transparent. In theory.

But this wouldn't be the first time she'd looked at the world through the veil of his wings.

"Lord Kaylin?"

"There's magic here," was her flat reply. The woman spoke to the man. The man didn't speak at all for one held breath. When he did, Kaylin didn't catch the word; it was almost—but

not quite—inaudible. She was certain it was a useful word—
and this was only the second time in her life she'd heard someone Barrani use one.

"Lord Kaylin!" the man shouted.

Kaylin didn't need the warning. Black streaks appeared
on the back wall, growing in number as she watched. They
looked almost like the streaks fingers put on cold windows
in the Halls, but there was something about their shape and
the way they appeared that implied clumsy, hurried writing.

She couldn't tell if what she saw was visible to the Barrani;
she didn't look back to see their reaction. She didn't have to.
The man pushed past her, moving to stand directly in front.
The woman stayed where she was.

Lirienne, what's happening?

No answer, but Kaylin could sense his presence. She was
afraid to push for more than that because she knew he was
fighting.

Nightshade—

We are under attack, he replied. He had no trouble fighting
and talking, at least not this way.

Yes, I guessed that—by what? The Ferals?

The black on the wall—or what she could see of the wall
through Barrani back—had darkened and spread. It no longer looked like writing; it reached ceiling and spread from
the wall to the surface above; she was certain it was doing the
same thing on the floor.

Kaylin, what is happening?

Look.

At the moment, it is not feasible.

*There's a large, black patch on the wall I'm facing, and it's spread-
ing. There's magic here, and it's growing; it is* not *a small spell.*

You are wearing the blood of the green?

Yes. But...I didn't notice that stopping the forest Ferals. I don't think—

Evarrim is down.

She was silent for a full beat; even her thoughts failed. She found them again, quickly. *Where is Teela? Can you see Teela?*

She is with me, the Lord of the West March replied. *We are fighting our way to you now.*

Kaylin shook her head, although he couldn't see it. *I don't think you're going to get here in time.*

What Nightshade found inadvisable, Lirienne now did. He looked. It was an odd sensation; Nightshade's touch was so unobtrusive she was largely unaware of it. Lirienne's was not; she had to fight the instinctive urge to push him back.

He slid away again. Kaylin almost told his servants that he was on his way, but managed to shut her mouth before stupid words escaped them. They'd only wonder how she knew, and the answer was *so* not public information.

She reached out, caught the Barrani man by the shoulder, and pulled him back; he allowed it. "What do you see?"

He ignored the question. To the woman, he said, "We take the front door." He lifted his arms, held them, palms out, in front of him as he continued to back down the hall.

The small dragon squawked.

"Yes," Kaylin told him. "Buy us whatever time you can."

He flew. He flew past the Barrani man who'd inserted himself as a shield between Kaylin and whatever was forming in her apartments. She turned toward the Barrani woman and headed away from the growing darkness. She stopped when she reached the door, and grabbed the woman, in much the same way she'd grabbed her partner.

The woman froze instantly.

"Not a good idea," Kaylin said, her voice muted. It was true—she could hear the sounds of fighting. She could hear—

and this was worse—the guttural roar of an angry beast, and in the depths of that rumble, syllables. But she could feel magic, and it was the wrong magic; it was too strong, too familiar.

Lirienne! Don't come down the hall—my door is trapped!

"Is there any other way out of this apartment?" Kaylin demanded.

The woman didn't even hesitate. She nodded.

"We need to leave. Someone's sketched an Arcane rune on my door, and I think it's going to go off if the Lord of the West March comes anywhere near it." Her legs ached and the back of her neck felt rubbed raw.

"Gaedin," the woman said.

Kaylin looked down the hall. The shadows had spread, inching their way across the floor as if—as if they were the shadows contained in the heart of the fiefs.

He nodded. "We will not have much time," he told her.

The small dragon squawked.

"We're leaving," Kaylin told him. She didn't reach for him, because he was now flapping in front of Gaedin's face. He was facing the back wall.

"Leave him," Kaylin told the Barrani servant as he reached—with some reluctance—for the small dragon's hind legs. "There's nothing here that can hurt him."

He didn't argue. He did take the lead; the woman surrendered it without hesitation. Which was good; he didn't attempt to head into the bedroom or out the arch that was diagonal from it, and those were the only two possible exits Kaylin could see.

Instead, he began to descend through a patch of floor—without lifting it first.

This did not, on the other hand, make Kaylin's skin feel any worse, although considering the exit and the end of the hall, she might not have noticed anyway. There must be stairs, given his movements.

"Lord Kaylin," the woman at her back said, voice low.

Kaylin took a step forward, and fell.

Gaedin was waiting to catch her. Given that her hands weren't full, Kaylin might have been able to land—but her ankle hadn't recovered from the last fall, and she really wasn't looking forward to an all-out sprint if it became necessary.

"Serian?" Gaedin said, voice low.

"Here." The perfect neutrality of the servant's expression had fallen by the wayside. It made Kaylin feel vastly more comfortable. Given the Arcane rune and the creeping shadow, this was stupid, but sometimes she was stupid. "Does this happen frequently where you're involved?" Serian asked Kaylin, in slightly brittle Elantran.

"Define *frequently.*"

Gaedin looked at Kaylin with slightly widened eyes. "I now understand why we were given the roles we were given." He headed down the hall, pausing to cast a spell that meant Kaylin wasn't tripping over her own feet in the dark, since it *was* dark here.

It was also uneven, because the ground seemed to be badly carved rock. Kaylin looked up, and saw no hatch, no trapdoor, and no break in the height of what was clearly tunnel. But she hadn't felt the dislocation—and nausea—that usually accompanied portal transitions.

"You're sensitive to magical energies," Gaedin said. He surprised her; he spoke in reasonable, if accented, Elantran.

"Yes."

"Is there magic here?"

Kaylin frowned. "Yours. Where exactly are we?"

Neither answered.

Squawk. The small dragon alighted on her shoulder. He remained upright and alert, staring ahead into the tunnel. Gaedin's expression made clear that he hadn't expected to see the small dragon again anytime soon.

"He's like a cat," Kaylin explained. "He pretty much goes where he wants; I don't think there's anywhere he can't reach, and no, it doesn't seem to matter if there's magic preventing anyone else from entering. I think he wants us to move."

"He's not the only one," Serian said. "We'll pick up weapons as we go."

If she wondered what weapons could be picked up in a rocky tunnel, the answer was swords. Swords, bracers, and rudimentary armor. They'd been placed in a standing crate in an alcove carved into the rock.

Kaylin.

We're safe. We're not in my rooms anymore, but we're safe. Have you found the Lord of the West March?

We know where he is. It is not possible to join him at the moment.

Who is we?

Corporal Handred is with us.

Frustrated, she looked; she caught a glimpse of Andellen. He was carrying a familiar Barrani Arcanist. *There are Ferals near the Lord of the West March. And, Nightshade? I think someone was trying to open a portal to the outlands. In my rooms.*

Silence. It was the word *outlands* that had caused it. He didn't ask if she was certain; he knew she wasn't. But he also knew that she was. Something about the magic that was spreading across the hall had reminded her—for reasons she couldn't pin down—of the door near the no-man's-land between the fiefs of Nightshade and Tiamaris.

How would that even be possible? she asked.

No answer.

She added it to her list of things that made no sense as she followed the Barrani.

"Why are you hobbling?" Serian finally asked. Her eyes were Barrani blue. Gaedin's hadn't shaded much away from midnight.

"I fell and twisted my ankle. It'll support my weight."

"If you're standing still," Serian replied. She hadn't drifted out of Elantran, but Kaylin thought she understood why. It was always easier to say forbidden things in a language that wasn't your mother tongue.

"How much farther are we going?"

They glanced at each other.

"Are we going to come up somewhere in Lord Lirienne's hall?"

"You might as well tell her," Serian said. "It won't mean much to her anyway."

"We're going to the heart," Gaedin said, in a much grimmer voice than he'd yet used, "of the green."

CHAPTER 13

"How are we going to get to the heart of the green by walking in long caves?"

They both stared at her for that little bit too long.

"Does the Lord of the West March know where we're going?"

"Given the events of this evening, he will." Gaedin started to walk.

Serian, however, knelt in front of Kaylin. "Get on my back. I will disgrace my family for the next century—in the best case—if you don't."

Kaylin climbed on. "How?"

"I'll knock you out and carry you."

"Are you allowed to knock the harmoniste out?"

"I believe intent counts."

"We do not, however, wish to test that theory." Gaedin's voice was clipped. The tunnel branched ten yards ahead; he chose the path to the right, moving at a fast jog. Serian, encumbered by Kaylin, paced him.

"I thought the green would be—I don't know. Grass. Trees."

"You were not wrong. But the routes to the heart of the green are many; some are ancient."

"Tunnels?"

"They weren't carved by my kin," Serian replied. "They were carved by underground rivers. These tunnels are ancient. They existed before we arrived in the West March. They will exist long after we are gone."

"Do they exist beneath all the buildings in the West March?"

"They are seldom carefully explored." The tone of her voice made clear this was all the answer Kaylin's question was going to get; to underline that, she'd switched to High Barrani. "But it is difficult to reach the tunnels, which is why—in emergencies—they are used. There are reputed to be many entrances; there is only one exit."

"And if we're trapped here by the Ferals?"

She shook her head. "The Ferals—as you call them—will find no way to enter these tunnels. There is, however, a danger that we will not be able to leave."

"And that?"

"The judgment of the green."

"The judgment of the green?"

"There is a reason the tunnels are generally considered safe. A risk is always taken when one chooses to enter them."

"Could I find them, if you weren't here?"

"It is our belief that you could not—but you wear the blood of the green. It is possible that the heart of the green would allow it."

"And the small dragon?"

Serian said nothing. The dragon squawked.

★ ★ ★

Kaylin didn't like dark enclosed spaces. She particularly disliked the way those spaces narrowed without warning—and with no guarantee they would widen again. During these stretches, Serian would set her down; Gaedin couldn't move through them quickly, so Kaylin's hobbling had no consequences.

She was afraid to speak to Nightshade, Lirienne or Severn. Even Ynpharion's sullen and unending rage had banked; there was no time for hating on Kaylin when he was fighting for his life. Humiliation at her existence wasn't enough to make him give up.

"Serian," she said, when they had scraped their way through a gap that would have made a small child squeamish. "No one talks about the lost children. Do you know their names?"

Silence.

"Serian?"

"Yes. Only one is spoken."

"Teela."

Serian nodded. She slowed as Gaedin stopped; the tunnel had once again branched.

"If there's only one way out, why does the tunnel branch? This isn't the first time."

"There is only one way out," Gaedin replied. "There is no guarantee that we will reach it. The tunnels are a test."

"Like the test of name."

"Entirely unlike the test of name," was his curt reply. "We are the people of the green. It is expected that we will be able to find our way to its heart."

"And if we can't?"

"We will die here."

"Does every citizen of the green have to take *this* test?"

Silence.

"Is there *any* Barrani culture that doesn't involve tests where failure is death?"

"It would hardly be a test," Serian replied, "if failure had no consequences."

Barrani. "Is there anyone, anywhere, who would tell me the names of the other eleven children?"

Gaedin and Serian exchanged a glance. "There is almost no one you would not offend were you to ask," Serian finally replied. "Do not ask Lord Avonelle. Do not ask Lord Evarrim. Do not—"

"A list of people I *could* ask would be more useful."

"You could, in my opinion, ask An'Teela."

"She won't answer."

"Yes. But she will also refrain from plotting your death."

"She trusts me to get myself killed," Kaylin replied.

"I begin to understand why. The lost children are not mentioned because even mention draws attention. They have no names, Lord Kaylin. Your kind is accustomed to this. You have no names. Your life—and your death—your freedom and the coercion you face from the more powerful, are not a matter of name. Even if you believe in souls, as so many humans do, your souls are not controlled and contested in the same way; at the heart of all your stories is choice, and the folly of choice."

"Serian." Gaedin's voice was weary.

"You are not certain?"

"No." He stepped back.

"Not certain about what?" Kaylin asked, as Serian set her down. The small dragon squawked. "The direction to take?"

They exchanged another glance, which was distinctly more familiar to Kaylin, she'd seen it in the Halls so often.

"You are wearing the blood of the green," Gaedin finally said. "I believe the choice of path must be yours."

"How did you choose so far?"

He didn't answer.

She turned to Serian. "You've done this before. You've both done this before."

"Yes. But the path alters, Lord Kaylin. It is not—it is never—the same. It is taken when the alternatives are more immediately dire."

"And have people been lost here? I mean, people you actually knew?"

Gaedin said nothing. Serian, however, said, "Three. One does not seek the protection of the green for trivialities."

"So—we could just take a wrong turn and never find our way out?"

"Indeed."

"So we could have *already* taken a wrong turn?"

"Yes." Gaedin exhaled and added, "We have not, yet."

"How do you know?"

"I know. This juncture, however, is not clear to me. It is not, before you ask, clear to Serian, either."

And it was supposed to be clear to Kaylin? There wasn't much in the way of signs. There were no distinguishing marks on the floor or walls that gave any clues.

Lord Kaylin, kyuthe, *where are you?*

Apparently? In a maze of tunnels. You're safe?

She felt amusement, anger, and the sharp tang of grief. *No. We are not yet done. You were correct; your rooms were not safe.*

Where are the eagles?

The dreams of Alsanis are with the Consort.

Kaylin froze. *She isn't with you?*

No. She felt his fear, and the deepening of his fury, and she fell silent. She *was* safe. Days would turn safety into a slow death by starvation if they made the wrong choice here, but safety was like that, in the end. There was no certain safety. Kaylin, of all people, should know that.

She couldn't touch the Consort the way she could her brother. She couldn't know—because he didn't—whether or not the Consort was safe.

She did know that Terrano had been willing to allow the Barrani to pass if they left the Consort to him. Did he want to destroy his former people? Did he want something else from the Consort?

And if he did—

"Right," she said. She pushed past Gaedin, her ankle throbbing, her visceral fear greater than pain. The ankle wasn't broken. "Go right."

Give the Barrani this, they didn't question her. Having dumped the responsibility squarely in her lap, they followed. She couldn't tell them what she now feared, in part because she was afraid to name it herself, and in part because she'd have to explain how she knew.

But it was fear in the driver's seat. Fear, and a sense of helplessness. She couldn't find the Consort, she couldn't help her, if she was trapped beneath the ground in a series of stupid and unpredictable tunnels. She didn't doubt what Gaedin and Serian had told her: there was only one right way, only one true path.

Standing and staring in the near dark while waiting, while knowing—and she touched Nightshade, she touched Lirienne, she even borrowed Ynpharion's viewpoint—that there might still *be* time, that there might be something she *could* do was impossible. She couldn't do anything from these tunnels. The possibility of being trapped here with no way out became vastly less terrifying, because by the time they were certain they couldn't leave, it would be way too late.

Speed was of the essence.

Waiting, trying to make the *right* choice just guaranteed

that making the right choice would also be pointless. It would be too late.

She cursed her ankle, and stopped. She couldn't hobble like this, and she couldn't depend on Serian's strength to see her through—not when she had other options. The small dragon squawked.

"I know, I know—I'm going as fast as I can." But she wasn't. She inhaled, exhaled, and then looked at her foot—from the inside. From the same mental space she occupied when she healed anyone else. Her body hadn't been born with a bad ankle; in a few weeks, it would be as good as new. Probably.

But she didn't have to wait a few weeks. She almost never healed herself. Why? Why was that?

It didn't matter. Barrani didn't like to be healed because too much was revealed in the process, but Kaylin *was* herself. What was there to see that she didn't already know?

The glyphs on her arms and legs began to warm, but it wasn't the heated pain that proximity to magic caused, and the heat, instead of scorching, soothed. It sank beneath her skin—maybe because she let it—and traveled down her limbs, settling at last in the ankle she could suddenly feel. She was used to thinking of this as "sight," although she did it with her eyes closed. But she could sense the torn ligaments, the stretched muscles, and the bruising; she knew what parts of the ankle made walking painful, and she knew how to change the shape of those things, channeling warmth and heat and magic into the shape of what it would become with time and rest.

Rest. Hah.

She stepped, firmly, on the ankle. It held her weight without a twinge. Beyond that, she didn't think; she began to move, and the Barrani followed in silence. If Serian had questions about her previous injury, she kept them to herself.

★ ★ ★

Gaedin's light was steady; it illuminated the tunnel in front of Kaylin, and it didn't bobble or waver as he ran. She came to two more junctions; she jogged right at the first and left at the second. It was arbitrary; she didn't feel that one way was the right way, and one wrong. The dragon made the occasional noise, but settled into a more relaxed sprawl on her shoulders. It shouldn't have brought comfort, but it did.

When they exited the tunnels, she'd expected to feel relief. And she did, but it lasted a handful of seconds. As tunnels sometimes did—at least in story—these ended in a large cavern. The height couldn't be seen; the light that had served to make a run through the tunnels safe didn't reach that far.

Serian touched her arm and drew her around. "You have never entered this maze," she said, voice low, breath completely even. "This is where we must be, Lord Kaylin. You've done well."

"It's a cavern," was her flat reply. She'd been jogging along the wall, heading right, and there was no sign of any other tunnels. It was like a giant dead end, unless there were stairs somewhere beyond the periphery of her vision.

Gaedin surprised Kaylin; he chuckled. "It is," he told her, "and it is not. The walls will tell you nothing; it is now the center that we want." He took the lead, drawing the light away and forcing Kaylin to follow; he moved quickly.

Kaylin, after the first stubbed toe, was grateful for his speed.

In the center of the cavern were two things that were immediately obvious. The first was the bottom end of a tree, or what Kaylin assumed was the bottom; there were roots. There were a *lot* of roots. As she'd spent a week stubbing her toes or tripping over smaller versions of the same, she recognized them.

The second was a river. The tree was planted in the river, and the roots, anchored to stone on either side of its current. Water rushed over them, and it seemed to Kaylin, watching, that the river sloped down. She had no desire to jump in to see where it went. Instead, she glanced at her companions, and headed—with care—toward the widest part of the tree she could reach. Reaching involved a fair amount of climbing, but Kaylin was good at that, wide skirts and trailing sleeves notwithstanding.

The small dragon squawked. He batted her face with a wing. This time, Kaylin adjusted the angle of her face and looked through it. She saw a lot of bark. But the bark was faintly luminescent; Gaedin's magical light had nothing to do with the uniform, silver glow. She continued to climb, letting her hands fall away from wing until she'd reached a stable slope; the dragon stretched his wing again when she came to a stop.

This time, she could see a more concentrated silver; it was to her left, and about six feet above where she was standing. The interweave of roots could just reach that light; it would certainly bring her close enough that she might be able to see its source. When she slid, Gaedin caught her and heaved her up, and she navigated footholds in the rough, but sloped root. There was dirt beneath her fingernails and in the creases of her palms; she didn't even want to look at what was on the dress, but of the two—Kaylin or dress—she knew which was more important.

She didn't even swear when she reached the source of the light and saw it was a ward. A door ward.

"I don't have to bleed on this, do I?"
Silence. After a pause, Serian said, "on the tree?"
"On the ward."

The glance that passed between the Barrani might as well have been a shout.

"You don't see a ward here." Kaylin's voice was flat.

"No, Lord Kaylin. Do you recognize the rune?"

"Does it matter? It's a ward."

"In Elantra, the mortal view of wards has been adopted across the whole of your large and crowded city—but they are not the only use of wards, and indeed, not the first."

Kaylin, who had lifted a palm in the usual hesitant way, lowered her hand. "What was the first use?"

"They were meant as containments," Serian replied. "The wards served as warnings to those who might otherwise seek to use magic or to explore what lay beyond the ward itself. They sealed. They imprisoned."

"You said this was where we needed to be."

"Yes. But I also said that not everyone who enters the tunnels survives. These are old, Kaylin; it is beyond our ability to build what was built here. Only those who have encountered the traps and threats of the maze understand their dangers— but they have never emerged to share that knowledge. What do you see?"

"It's a large ward. The center is where I assume my palm is supposed to go—but it's larger than my hand."

"Describe the rune, Chosen. Does it resemble the marks on your arms in any way?"

Did it? "I'm fairly certain it's not one of the marks; it may be the same language. It's more ornate than the door wards I'm used to; the ones I'm used to are very much like the wards in the Lord's hall."

"Yes, they would be."

She reached for Lirienne and found—pain. She pulled back instantly. She reached for Nightshade and found darkness, movement, flitting impressions of hall and stone floor and sword.

She didn't reach for Severn, because it wasn't a word he would recognize, and she didn't want to burden him with her fear. She was afraid.

Gaedin stepped around Kaylin with an ease that implied sloping, rounded trunks caused him no issue with balance. "Allow me, Lord Kaylin."

Serian said nothing.

"You can't even see it," Kaylin said.

"No. But if it is activated by touch, and there is a risk associated with it, I am not wearing the blood of the green." He raised an arm, and she knocked it aside. Serian caught her, because balance was an issue for Kaylin.

Gaedin lifted his arm again, and this time the small dragon launched himself at the Barrani man's face.

"I don't think he thinks it's a good idea." To no one's surprise—or at least not Kaylin's, the small dragon's opinion was, of course, more relevant than hers. Gaedin lowered his arm.

His eyes narrowed, his perfect brow furrowed. He stared at the tree trunk as if he could force it, by dint of glaring, to surrender useful information. Kaylin's arms were itching; she couldn't see any visible magical effects, but he was using familiar magic. He bowed to her and stepped to one side. How he didn't fall off, she didn't know, and she tried not to resent it.

Kaylin raised her hand, grimaced, braced herself as she usually did when touching a door ward, and pressed her palm into the center of the ward.

The world exploded.

It was not the first time that Kaylin had stood at the center of a magical explosion. She had time to throw her arms over her face to protect her eyes as wood chips and bark flew.

None of them hit her arms. None of them hit her at all. She lowered her arms and looked immediately to her left; Gaedin was standing suspended in midair. The root upon which they'd found purchase was gone. So was the large, curving root on which Serian stood. But Serian still stood.

They were encircled by a globe of familiar, golden light. Flying debris hung in the air around them. Kaylin turned back to the ward. To her surprise, it was still suspended in air, glowing a brilliant silver; the tree was damaged. Kaylin was no expert in trees, but the brunt of the explosion had taken out only the section of tree—and its attached roots—directly in front of the activated ward.

The central element of the ward, the star, was gone. The rest of it—the radial points that looked like designed offshoots of that star, remained, as did the framing. Gaedin's magic followed the explosion—but it was slower by far than the ward had been; Kaylin felt it crawling along her skin.

"Gaedin—"

"It is not me," he told his partner. "It is Lord Kaylin."

"Lord Kaylin who claimed to have studied magic for mere mortal months?" She looked skeptical, and Kaylin—who disliked the superiority Barrani often displayed when dealing with mortals perversely liked her better for it.

"It's not me," Kaylin told them both. "It's him." She pointed to the dragon who was rigid on her shoulder.

She followed the direction of his wide-eyed stare. "How important is this tree?"

It was Gaedin who laughed.

"Gaedin. *Kyuthe*," Serian added.

He reined laughter in. His eyes were a midnight-blue so at odds with laughter it made him more disturbing.

Lirienne, can you tell me about this tree?

Silence. She didn't even try to reach Nightshade, because it was pointless; she recognized the silence.

Kaylin grimaced and turned to the two Barrani who had led her to comparative safety. "I hate to tell you this," she said, "but we're not in the West March anymore."

"I can see the ward," Gaedin said.

Serian frowned. The ward was no longer her concern. "Do you know where we are? The cavern looks essentially the same, to my eye."

"It is substantially the same."

"And the tree?"

"It is as you see it."

Kaylin, however, was moving. She wasn't walking, because at the moment, there was nothing to walk *on*. But the bubble that surrounded her began to inch toward a ward that was now suspended against air, and not the bark of a trunk.

"Let Gaedin inspect."

"Gaedin is not as sensitive to magic as I am," Kaylin replied—in Barrani. "And I am not certain he can move of his own volition."

Gaedin said, "She is correct."

"Can you read what's left of the ward?" Kaylin asked him.

"No, Chosen. The center section is missing."

"Yes—it appears to have been the magic behind that explosion." She was frowning now. The bits of bark and wood she was passing beneath and around still hadn't moved. "Gaedin—this debris—are you suspending it?"

"No."

"Am *I*?"

"Not in any detectable way. In my opinion, however, it is either you or your companion. He is a familiar, yes?"

"I don't know what word means in real life. He's certainly

not the familiar of the stories the Barrani used to tell each other." She reached out to touch a piece of bark; the small dragon bit her finger. Hard. Kaylin cursed; he gave her one baleful glare, and then once again oriented himself in the direction of the gaping hole in the side of the tree.

"I don't think it's the dragon, either," she said. "Guys, when was the last time someone disappeared into the tunnels? Do you know?"

"You are not going to like the answer," Serian said.

"Give me the answer anyway."

"Less than ten of your mortal years ago. I believe it was six."

There was nothing in the answer that Kaylin could dislike. "That's good, though—it means the maze has been run and people in it have gotten out. Why did you think I'd be unhappy?"

"One of the two was mortal."

Severn.

Kaylin carefully avoided touching debris—which would have been harder if the dragon weren't in the driver's seat. But she looked at the pieces, at their placement, at their distance from the tree. Her frown deepened. "Gaedin, can you give me more light?"

His reply: illumination. Every piece of debris was sharper, clearer. She could see what she assumed were flight trajectories. She had, with Teela and Red by her side, examined debris in the wake of an Arcane bomb. Pieces of house had embedded themselves in the parts of the walls left standing.

These pieces had traveled out in a sphere seconds after the explosion itself; Kaylin was fairly certain they'd be dotting the cavern's rough wall had they continued their flight. They hadn't. Kaylin, Serian, and Gaedin had experienced the force of the blast; they were alive because the small dragon had intervened.

But pieces of wood, of bark, and even dirt, remained fixed in the air, as if time had frozen. Kaylin could move; nothing else did.

"I think—I think this explosion didn't just happen."

The small dragon squawked.

"We witnessed it," Serian reasonably pointed out.

Kaylin nodded. "We witnessed it. I think we've appeared at the exact moment the tree did explode."

"You don't think the ward was responsible for the explosion itself."

She glanced at the small dragon's profile. "No. I think the ward is responsible for dumping us here. Wherever—or whenever—here is."

"Why?"

"I don't know. The tree looked solid when we approached it." She frowned. "I'm not much of a mage."

Gaedin was extremely politic for a Barrani, and said nothing.

"But when I touched the ward, the center portion of the rune disappeared; the tree—this side of it—exploded, or started to—the pieces haven't moved. So…is it possible that the ward was holding the tree together somehow?"

"It is."

"Door wards don't vanish when touched," she continued. "And *most* of this rune is still here; only the center portion is gone."

"You feel that the ward served two functions."

She nodded. "I don't understand why. Frankly, I don't understand *how*. Either the explosion occurred or it didn't. If it did, how could someone then reverse it and contain it?"

Serian's frown was more subtle than Kaylin's; the color of

her eyes made up for it. "It would make far more sense that the rune caused the explosion."

"And it froze just after it happened?"

"The familiar—"

The familiar rolled his eyes. Kaylin stared at him, and he shrugged his wings. "I'm pretty sure he's only responsible for the shielding on us. Does the shape of the rune look familiar to you?"

Gaedin had been staring at it in silence; he spoke to answer questions, but his gaze didn't leave it. Kaylin was surprised when he began to speak. His voice was sonorous, low, the syllables almost familiar. He wasn't speaking the ancient tongue that Sanabalis had once used to tell a race the story of its birth; he was speaking a variant of High Barrani. She could catch one word in three, but the words she did catch made no sense.

She waited, folding her arms across her chest; those arms shot out when the bubble around the Barrani servant began to flicker. "*Don't* drop him!" she shouted at the small dragon. The small dragon squawked. Kaylin was too far away to make a grab for Gaedin as he lurched in midair.

His eyes widened; she saw gold ring his irises and then he was gone.

Serian said, "that was not a failure on your part."

"What did he *say*?"

"I will not repeat it," she replied. "But I think I understand what has happened. Gaedin is safe. He will probably be deeply chagrined, but I believe we will find him in the heart of the green."

"If we reach it."

"If, indeed, we reach it." Serian began to float toward Kaylin. "He recognized the rune."

"You can't see it."

"I have very, very limited abilities in that regard; magery was not my gift. But if I heard him correctly—" A polite phrase, because if Kaylin had heard him there was no way that the sharper-eared Barrani hadn't. "It is in style and substance similar to runes that exist only in one place."

"The heart of the green."

"Yes."

"Is someone responsible for drawing those runes?"

"If you mean, are they placed there by the Barrani, the answer is no. Not directly. Not even, to my knowledge, indirectly—but as magery was not my gift, there may well be knowledge that was not given to me. But they inform some of the unusual architecture at the heart of the green.

"I think there was enough variance that Gaedin was not entirely certain; he spoke the words of greeting and return, and the rune responded."

"He disappeared."

"I believe he returned, Kaylin. He will be displeased with that return; if we do not follow soon, Lord Lirienne will be likewise discomfited."

"And you won't—"

"No. If Gaedin had realized what the results of that tentative phrase would be, he would not have uttered it. I admit that being your servant has been an unusual challenge; we were both surprised at our deployment. Unless the green chooses to displace me, I will remain by your side."

The dragon had once again turned his stare into the ruin of the tree side. "All right, all right. Take me to it." She wanted roots beneath her feet. She could climb; she could cling to vertical surfaces with a little preparation. Hovering, wingless, over a distant river in the poor light of the cavern, was still disturbing.

Kaylin didn't know a lot about trees.

Her expertise in wood involved chopping it and carrying it in the yards of the Halls of Law. This was not that kind of tree.

"Is this tree somehow planted in the heart of the green?"

The line of Serian's lips thinned. "The tree, as you call it, is indeed planted in the heart of the green."

"What do you mean, as I call it? What does it look like to you?"

"It looks very like the roots of a great and ancient tree. There are no trees within the whole of the West March or beyond it, in the darker forests, that have reached the age of this tree; it is singular in all ways. It is said that it speaks. I have never heard its voice," she added softly.

Kaylin almost touched the tree; her hand stopped before it made contact with the ragged sharp edge of newly broken bark. Gleaming liquid that might be mistaken for sap caught her attention.

"Lord Kaylin?"

"The tree—it's infected. Infested. Something."

Silence. It was bad silence, but at this point there was no way it could be anything else. Serian moved; she seemed to have more control of her movements than Kaylin had. Kaylin glared at the small dragon.

Serian made no attempt to touch anything, but her eyes alighted on the dark, running blackness Kaylin had assumed was sap. She closed her eyes, her lashes a dark, trembling fan against her pale skin. "I believe I understand."

"Explain it to me?" she said, in frustrated Elantran.

"The tree destroyed part of itself."

"What caused it?" Kaylin asked.

"I do not—as you must guess—know. Rumor says that you are a healer. That you became *kyuthe* to the Lord of the West March because of that singular gift. He does not resent you, and he does not fear you—and that was unexpected. The Barrani do not expose themselves to—"

"Healers? No. Believe that I'm aware of just how much they

hate it." She was afraid to touch what she could barely think of as a wound. Even in the darkness, she could see the scintillation of color flowing in the liquid, and if the Barrani of the West March insisted that this black mess wasn't the shadows that plagued the fiefs, Kaylin couldn't see what the difference was.

She examined the tree; very little of the dark infection was visible. If the tree had destroyed some part of itself in an attempt to be rid of it, that said something about the tree. "I've never tried to heal a plant before."

Serian looked mildly offended.

Kaylin hesitated for one long minute, and then placed her hand on the tree's bark, instead of the jagged edge of its wound. She closed her eyes as the marks on her skin began to warm. *It* is *a tree,* she thought, but kept her nervous defiance to herself. Most trees didn't ditch large chunks of themselves in fancy, magic explosions. They certainly couldn't write, and the rune was complicated enough that it hadn't happened by accident.

Most trees didn't *think.*

This one did.

The problem with healing—from Kaylin's perspective— wasn't the exhaustion it left in its wake, although it could certainly have that effect. It wasn't the physical contact, and the sudden knowledge of the limits of another person's body; it wasn't even the sense that, while she healed, there was little separation between her own body and her patient's.

There was just as little separation between thoughts, between identities. She could feel and sense what they could feel and sense.

She didn't know what the tree would offer. And the tree seemed content to offer her nothing. A lot of nothing. A great,

endless darkness. She wasn't even certain that she was connected to the tree at all; she saw a lot of what she assumed
was unlit cavern.

But there was texture to the darkness, and it was a texture
she didn't like. She remembered what she'd done with the
Barrani who had been injured in their skirmishes with the
forest Ferals. They'd been infected—by bite—with the same
transformative shadow, and she'd forced it out. Torn it out.
Which had left injuries that *could* be healed the normal way.

Her arms were burning, but it wasn't the usual heat. It took
her a moment to realize it wasn't her marks—although they
were warm—but the sleeves that covered most of them. It was
the dress, the blood of the green. She felt a moment of sick
fear because she knew she was worth far less than the dress to
the denizens of the West March.

But the dress was somehow *of* the green. And the tree, if
she'd understood anything—and given how little sense things
made, that was questionable—was its heart. She opened her
eyes and saw that the sleeves were…flowing. They were drifting off her arms as if they were liquid.

As if they were blood, Kaylin thought.

She *really* hoped the rest of the dress didn't follow suit, because appearing stark-naked anywhere in the West March was
almost at the top of her list of things Not To Do while on va-
cation. Dying was the first item.

She closed her eyes again, and this time, she whispered into
the silence on the inside of her head. She didn't have the tree's
name. But she had three of her own: the name of her birth,
Elianne. The name she'd chosen when she'd escaped that early
childhood, Kaylin. And the name that she had taken from the
Lake. It was the most significant of the three—if you happened to be immortal.

But Kaylin wasn't. She was a groundhawk. She served the

Halls of Law. She struggled, every day, to believe in justice and that law. Some days, it was harder than others. Some days, it was blessedly easy.

Hello, I'm Kaylin. Kaylin Neya.

There was no answer. Not that she expected words, because usually there weren't any. She touched—was certain she was touching—the tree. She tried to get some sense of its form, of its natural, healthy shape, because that's what bodies knew.

But she touched nothing.

Kaylin is the name I chose for myself. I'm mortal. I can choose the name I answer to. Neya is the short form of my mother's name. Her name was Averneya, but no one ever used it, not even me. I didn't call her by name. I called her Mother.

She had no idea what she was saying, or why.

But for just a moment, one clear, perfect moment, she could *see* her mother's face. She could see it so clearly she lost all ability to form words. She couldn't recall her mother's actual face anymore. She hadn't been able to do it for years. She could remember being held; she could remember some of the songs her mother sometimes sung to her.

Her mother's face was *so clear.* Kaylin forgot the tree. She forgot the healing. She forgot the shadows and the infection and even the Barrani.

She had never seen her mother the way she looked at her now. Had her mother somehow lived, she would still never have seen her like this: she was a young woman. She was— to Kaylin's eye—not much older than Kaylin now was. She had—Kaylin remembered it only now—a long scar, pale and slender, down the right side of her jaw. Her hair was as dark as her daughter's, and her skin was only slightly paler; her eyes were so brown the pupil was lost to them.

Her hands were slender, and her arms; she was underfed.

Her eyes were sunken, her cheeks slightly hollow, their bones high and pronounced. She wore the nondescript, poorly fitted clothing that anyone in the fiefs wore.

But...she was smiling. She was smiling, her lips turned up at the corners, her eyes gentled by expression. She was smiling *at* Kaylin.

They could have been sisters.

Is this what Teela saw when she remembered her mother? A woman, much like herself? A woman who had loved her and who she'd loved in return?

A woman, Kaylin thought, throat thick now, that she could never actually touch again, that she could never grow to know better? She tried to etch this image into her mind, into her memory—her imperfect, mortal memory. Because this woman was alive. She had been alive.

Yes. You remember and you do not remember. You see and you do not see.

Kaylin didn't look away from her mother. She lifted a hand and let it drop. She couldn't touch her mother; her mother was dead. Gone. This was a gift—a strange gift—and she'd always been aware that asking for more was just asking for trouble. Asking for anything usually was.

No, Kaylin, daughter of Averneya, it is not.

No face, no body, appeared to accompany a voice that was so resonant she trembled at each syllable, as if she were caught in it, as if it came from the very center of her body. She turned to look for Serian, and saw no one.

"Serian?"

She is safe, for the moment. You have come to the heart of the green wearing our blood. What do you attempt?

She felt, as the voice filled all conscious thought, ridiculous and small. She had touched a tree. It was as much a tree as the Hallionne were buildings. "I'm trying to—to heal you."

Ah. I am wounded. It is regrettable.

"What hurt you?"

The green, was the softer—the much softer reply.

Kaylin hated confusion, especially when it was hers. "Aren't you the green?"

We are. But we have taken a wound, Kaylin. It has bled, and it has festered since the day it was dealt us; it has not closed.

"Can I heal it?"

She heard—felt—laughter. *We can barely feel your touch. You are not of the green; were you not clothed in some part of ourself, we would not feel you at all. Healing us, as you are, is beyond you.*

She felt completely deflated, but rallied. "If it's beyond me, then why am I here?"

She felt confusion for the first time. Not doubt, nothing as large as that. No, this was sort of like the look adults got on their faces when small toddlers were attempting to speak and their words all came out in repeatable gibberish.

Kaylin attempted not to feel the frustration of the person uttering the repeatable gibberish.

You asked for the judgment of the green.

She turned to look at the small dragon because unlike Serian, he was still with her. He yawned. In the darkness, that companion now spread his wings and held them, rigid, to either side. One of those sides covered Kaylin's eyes.

It wasn't dark here. And she wasn't standing in front of the hollow of a damaged tree.

She was standing on the banks of a river. She lifted her face and the river vanished because the thin membrane of wing didn't follow her eyes. She lowered her face again. The banks of the river were silvered gray—it was night.

She took a hesitant step and realized she could no longer see the bubble that had protected her from the explosion. And gravity. So much of her life since the Devourer had been like this: a waking dream. The problem with Kaylin's dreams was that they could turn, in an instant, with the slightest of gestures or sounds, into full-on nightmare.

And nightmare was here. Across the sand and rock that hedged the river's flow was a dark patch. Even at this distance, it had a consistency that had nothing to do with riverbanks. It also pooled beneath a very ordinary streetlamp. Kaylin frowned and glanced at the small dragon. She began to walk, cautiously and quietly, toward the lamp. She knew she was being stupid—no streetlamp in her own city would be incentive to approach a small, roiling mass of chaos.

As she walked, she continued to speak. Caution replaced frustration. "My companion was born in the heart of a magical storm; he hatched after it had passed. When he's with me, I can sometimes see things I wouldn't normally see."

You are like the Barrani, my distant children. You exist in one place, at one time.

"Yes. You don't."

I am like—and unlike—your Hallionne. My purpose is less circumscribed. But I exist across all planes, and in all places.

"Then the injury—"

Yes. It exists here, in this place.

"Where is this place?"

The green.

"If this were the green, Serian would be here."

She is here. She is not in the here you are in. Chosen, if you desired it, you could see her. You could be where in the here she occupies.

Kaylin had drawn close enough that she could see the hanging lamp clearly. She could see the chaos across which its light fell, but for a moment, the chaos wasn't as important as the light because what lay in the center of the globe was not fire.

It was a word. It was a True Word.

Where the light fell across black and roiling shadow, it fell in strips. It fell in patterns. They were familiar to Kaylin—and they should be. They were very like the marks that adorned over half her skin.

CHAPTER 14

The small dragon was silent. He wasn't draped across her shoulders, either; he looked like he meant business.

"We need to get that word," she told him softly.

He nodded, and lowered his wing. The landscape went dark immediately.

"You're right. It's going to be a pain in the butt. Can you deal with the shadow?"

He failed to hear the question. Fair enough; on bad days in the office, so did Teela. She took it as a definitive *No*. The small dragon lifted his wing again.

The landscape hadn't changed in the interim. She was ten feet from the amorphous boundary of the chaos mass; the lamppost was in its center.

"Why," she said, directing her question to the invisible but encompassing presence in which, she suspected, she walked, "Is there a name here? Why is it trapped like that?" To Kaylin's eyes, it *was* captive. It moved, elements of the whole battering ineffectively against the globe, like a trapped moth.

Or a trapped bird.

The voice, like the small dragon, failed to hear the question. It was the most pressing question Kaylin now had. The word seemed small and almost forlorn, which was ridiculous. But it seemed diminished somehow by its cage.

All such words are caged. And all such words are cages.

Where it cast light in the shape of itself, the shadows were clearest; colors shone and moved beneath the bands of the rune's form. They seemed, in the light, to have a consistent texture—and the chaos in the fiefs didn't. And in the fiefs, wherever it was possible, the shadows spread. They infested land, buildings, and people; the people died.

Here, they touched nothing but lamppost—and ground. They didn't appear to respond to Kaylin's approach, either. Small mercies. She inched closer. The urgency to flee the tunnels, to escape them, to somehow be of use in the battle above, had bled away. She felt she was suspended in time; that time, here, had no meaning.

But the word did.

She thought it belonged, not to a lamppost in the middle of nowhere, but to the Lake of Life. It belonged in the keeping of the Consort. It was a *name*. Kaylin had no idea how to distinguish between True Names and True Words; five minutes ago, she would have said there wasn't any difference.

She didn't believe that now; she couldn't make herself believe it. It was a name, and she couldn't leave it here. "I think," she said, "it's time to breathe."

The dragon said nothing. She was two feet away from the edge of the chaos, and she realized, watching it, that it reminded her of something beside the deadly shadow in the heart of the distant fiefs. It reminded her of Wilson, Hallionne Bertolle's lost brother. It reminded her of the brothers she hadn't tagged with an inappropriate name; they had become almost exactly this in the race through the outlands, creating something that had form and substance in a sea of gray fog and nothing.

That path had kept them together. It had probably saved their lives.

"Or not."

The dress that had caused her so much trouble was now sleeveless. It looked like a summer shift. Everything else about it remained the same, but the marks that had been partially obscured were completely visible. She grimaced. It was the least of her problems now; she'd worry about it later.

She took off one boot and placed it at the edge of the puddle; it was the only thing she could throw that wasn't a weapon, and she didn't have enough of those.

She watched the dark sludge beneath it. She wasn't surprised when it started to move, bubbling beneath the very green leather. She was, however, surprised when it inched away, leaving a gap through which sand and a few rocks became visible. Those and the boot itself.

Said boot hadn't been devoured, and it hadn't—as far as she could see when looking through dragon wing—been transformed. It was still a boot. On the other hand, she thought, as she bent, stretched, and caught it in two fingers, the boots had come with the dress.

She slid her foot back into it, squared her shoulders, and began to walk into the dark mess. Almost everything in her direct experience screamed *retreat;* her feet were steady but her steps were hesitant. They were also small.

Around her feet, iridescent color rippled and surged away. Only where the light of the word—the name—touched it, did it remain solid beneath her feet. She reached the lamp, and discovered once again that height—or more specifically the lack of height—was a disadvantage. She could touch the globe with the tips of her fingers, and it swayed. It didn't fall into her hands.

What do you seek to do?

She lowered her hands. "I don't understand why it's trapped here, but I want to take it with me."

The silence was longer and deeper. *Do you understand what it is?*

"It's life," Kaylin replied. And to her eyes, for a moment, it was. It suggested movement and fragility and energy and bursting pride; it suggested quick wit and quick temper. Eyes narrowed, she stared as it revolved; it stopped struggling against its confinement, as if it were suddenly aware of her.

As if it were holding its breath.

What you desire has been tried.

"Not by me." She turned her arms; the marks were glowing. They were the same color as the name that floated above her fingertips, but flat, confined in a different way.

Can you speak the name?

"That's not the way it works." But looking at it, she thought it might if she stared for long enough. "Can you?"

No, Chosen.

She blinked. "Why is it here?"

It is safe here. It is safe only here. Too much has been changed.

She bit her lip. Teela hated it when she did that, but Teela wasn't here.

She is.

Kaylin froze. She looked at the name, but the name—it wasn't Teela's. It couldn't be.

No. You are harmoniste. Take the name, but understand that it is one of the words that you must examine, one of the many, many choices you must make. The Teller will speak, harmoniste; but you will take the words that he speaks and you will choose a path that touches those words you feel must be touched. It is almost time.

"It's *so* not time." She lowered her hands. "When you say Teela is here, is she here the same way Serian is?"

She is here as you are here. She speaks, Chosen. Can you not hear her?

"No. No, I can't."

And you cannot hear him, either.

She looked at the name he referred to; as she did, the globe began to descend, floating as if almost weightless until it rested in her cupped palms. The glass was not glass; it was warm, and it felt almost like skin, but it dissolved as it met hers; the name did not. She shifted the position of her hands, cupping the name, enclosing it.

It bit her.

She didn't even curse. She'd taken two words from the Lake of Life—not that it had looked at all like a lake to her at the time—but neither of those had felt like this one, and in theory, one of the two was hers.

She knew, then. She knew what she carried. "He's not dead yet."

Silence.

She looked down, at the ground, at the darkness. It seeped into the sand, avoiding her boots. Avoiding her shadow, as if it were a danger. It made no protest, threatened no attack. She watched it go.

"Are there others?"

Yes.

"Where?"

It is time for you to join Gaedin and Serian.

"Wait!"

I am not constrained, as you are, by time. What do you require?

"The injury—the names—"

Yes. They are connected. They are the same. Taking the names, however, does not heal the wound. Do you understand?

No, of course she didn't.

"Can you take me to—take me to Teela?"

No, but I will send you to Teela, Chosen.

The dragon folded his wing and squawked. Loudly. Kaylin, hands still cupped with care around a name, felt the hair on the back of her neck stand suddenly, sharply, on end.

Light cut the shadows, shattering them; it was bright enough to blind. And blind, given the way her marks were physically burning, was going to be bad. Vision returned with tears; her eyes were burning.

Smoke did that.

"Kitling!"

She could see the blackened, charred ruin of what she assumed had once been wall. Standing beside it was Teela. She was armed; she carried a Barrani war sword. In her hands it looked wrong—Kaylin was used to seeing the long club there. She preferred it.

"What are you *doing,* you idiot! Don't just stand there!"

Kaylin blinked tears out of her eyes; she was afraid to move her hands. Teela cursed in rousing Leontine, her voice hitting a pitch of growl that only the Barrani Hawks could. She leaped over the two feet of burning wall and grabbed Kaylin's left arm.

Kaylin cried out; Teela yanked her arm, dragging her off her feet. Her carefully cupped hands flew apart as she stumbled. Teela's grip would leave bruises. Her eyes were so blue they looked black in the smoky hall.

Kaylin looked at her empty hands in a panic.

Against the palm of her left, flattened as all of the marks on her body were, was a word. A new mark. It wasn't gold, the way the rest of her marks now were; it wasn't the blue they sometimes became. It was red. But it was there. For now, that was all she needed to know.

She drew her daggers as she found her footing. The small dragon squawked. "Don't you start," she told him. "Be useful or be quiet. Teela—where in the hells is everyone else?"

"With luck, they've evacuated. The Lord's hall was attacked at several points."

"Why are you here alone?"

Teela glanced over her shoulder. "I wasn't," was her grim reply. Kaylin followed the direction of Teela's brief glance.

Kaylin! Three voices spoke at once. Only one of them twisted at her; only one caused pain because only one of them knew *her* name. She shuddered at the force of it, at what it contained, at the visceral fear; it was so strong, so raw, it almost overwhelmed her. She reached up to cover her ears. She only had one free hand, but tried anyway.

Severn! Severn—stop—I'm fine—I'm alive. I'm with Teela. I'm alive, *Severn.* She inhaled, inhaled, inhaled; exhalation was too short, too shallow.

Teela was cursing up a storm. Kaylin found it calming. Given the color of her eyes, that said something.

Severn—I'm alive. Please—think of kittens or bunnies or something normal. Think of Mallory.

He laughed. It was a wild laugh; she felt it; she was shaking. "This name thing," she told Teela. "I think I'm beginning to understand *why* the Barrani fear it so much."

"I am *not* going to ask."

"Let go of my arm. I'm not going to run off into the Ferals—or the fire. Let me check the guards—"

"They're dead. We were three," she added, "when the portal opened. We contained five of our enemies in the hall."

Kaylin looked pointedly at the wall.

Teela nodded; she ran a hand across her eyes. "You are the *last* person I wanted to see. And—don't take this the wrong way—but *what did you do to the dress?*"

Kaylin opened her mouth to answer and Teela caught her by the arm again. "Never mind—it'll have to wait. The halls aren't clear, and we cannot stand here talking."

"Teela—the Consort—"

"I didn't see her. I'm sorry."

Nightshade—the Consort?

Tell An'Teela to go west. Cut through the dining hall, avoid its center.

The Consort?

We don't know.

Lirienne? Where is the Lady?

She is not with us; her chambers were empty.

Did she go to the tunnels? Did she ask for the judgment of the green? Kaylin felt her internal voice rising; if thoughts could squeak, hers would be.

Her chambers were empty. If she is in the heart of the green, we will know, soon. He shut her out then. She began to widen her stride, to pace Teela. The small dragon dug claws into her shoulder and stared straight ahead.

The geography of the Lord's hall had changed. It wasn't the walls, although many of them sported new holes, or rather, it wasn't the destruction of the walls. It was the patches of floor, wall, and ceiling that looked melted and deformed. "Tell me again why this isn't shadow?"

"If you have enough breath to ask stupid questions, you have enough breath to run faster," Teela snapped, and picked up the pace. She paused twice, threading her way back through halls that still had visibly normal—if scarred and scorched— floors. "Where are your servants?"

Kaylin considered bouncing Teela's previous answer back at the Barrani Hawk, but decided against it—Teela could probably run faster; Kaylin wasn't so certain she could. She was already short of breath, given the length of the run, and it wasn't over yet.

But when they reached the dining hall, Kaylin froze in the ruins of the doorway. "Teela!"

Teela could stop on a pin. She did, and pivoted. "What do you see?"

Kaylin was staring at the center of the room that Nightshade had told them to avoid. "It's a portal," she said, voice flat.

"Then don't step in it."

"It's anchored in the center, Teela—but it's not contained there. Can you see the signature of its caster?"

Teela exhaled. Kaylin's arms were too numb to feel what she assumed they otherwise would; Teela was casting. "I can see one," Teela said.

"There are two. I recognize them both."

Kaylin didn't take her eyes off the sigil. The first time she had seen it, she had been suspended in the wreckage of her home. The second time, she'd been in the fiefs. This sigil mirrored the second sighting: it was strong, bold—and not small. But it was shadowed by a second signature.

The first time she'd seen the effect, she'd assumed the hand of two mages.

But she'd seen the inverse in the outlands, and she knew that the second sigil was barely visible because it so closely mirrored the first. The color was faint, the signature so weak it was barely visible. But she thought it faintly green—green smoke. Green shadow.

The small dragon sighed—audibly—and lifted a wing; it drooped. Clearly they weren't the only ones who were tired.

"Lift both." Teela came to stand on the dragon side of Kaylin. When the dragon failed to obey, she grimaced and added, "Please."

He hissed at her, but condescended to lift his second wing.

"Honestly, kitling, I'm thinking of removing them and making them something more dependably wearable."

The dragon batted Teela's face. Kaylin felt she deserved this and said nothing. But she looked, as Teela looked. Through the wing, the sigils were clear, and they were both distinct.

"There are two," Teela said. Kaylin glanced at her; in profile, she could see pursed lips. "I concur."

"With what?"

"The portal is active."

"Can you contain it, or should we try to find another way—" A thunderous roar ate the rest of the sentence.

"Teela—are they here to find you?"

Teela stiffened. "Why," she said, in the conversational tone she used on drug dealers who thought the Barrani Hawks were bribable, "would you ask that question?"

"Because you're not dead, and the guards are."

"They—and who exactly do you mean by that amorphous 'they'?—didn't stop to ask questions. The guards," she added, "are dead because they were not powerful enough. I am. How did you *get* here?"

"Gaedin and Serian dropped us through the floor."

Teela's eyes widened slightly. They couldn't get any bluer. "They risked the judgment of the green?"

"Yes. We were kind of hemmed in by the equivalent of an Arcane bomb and a looming shadow portal; there wasn't a lot of out left."

"And the green accepted you."

"More or less. Look—could we just do it again?"

Teela's eyes widened for real this time. "Only *you* could say something that careless. Kitling, there's a reason that men are now dead throughout this hall."

Kaylin had been wondering.

"It is the same reason that many of my kin choose to avoid the wakened Hallionne where they have any reasonable choice."

"This wasn't reasonable," Kaylin pointed out.

"No. Understand, Kaylin, that not all of the men who serve the Lord of the West March are native to the West March. They have all witnessed the recitation, and they are all Lords— but they are Lords of the High Court."

"Could you enter the tunnels?"

Teela said nothing. Kaylin thought that was the whole of the answer. The roaring—and the sound of cracking wood— continued at their back. "No. If I enter the tunnels, I will never leave them."

The small dragon lowered both of his wings. Before either Teela or Kaylin could complain, he pushed himself off Kaylin's shoulder, squawking in a way that suggested frustration and anger. It was almost comical to watch his chest swell in outrage.

Almost.

"If you surrendered to the judgment of the green, why are you here, kitling?"

"Where should I be?"

"In the heart of the green, of course. The Lord of the West March rules the green, but his power is political; it is not of the green, and his hall is in no way at its heart."

Great. "Teela—"

"Stay away from the green."

"I can't exactly fly. This entire place is the green, as far as I can tell."

One black brow rose. "You are meddling in things you don't understand."

"So what else is new? Believe that I wouldn't be meddling if anyone actually took the time to—oh—explain things first!"

The roaring banked sharply. Kaylin wilted. "…Sorry."

Teela shook her head. She nudged Kaylin out of line of sight of the door's damaged frame. The doors were present, but they were off their hinges. Nothing short of a small work-force could close them. "You watch your familiar." Sword held loosely in hand, she turned her back on Kaylin; Kaylin held her daggers.

Kaylin—it is not safe to remain in the hall.

Yes, we're aware of that. The center of the dining hall is a portal and we'd like not to accidentally walk back into the outlands.

You are certain? Nightshade's voice was sharper.

Yes. It's Iberrienne's work, or I'm Barrani.

The frame of the door cracked; it made the sound best associated with lightning, except up close and personal. Kaylin turned to see something the size of a large horse. It looked like a forest Feral—but larger, clearer, more distinct. Teela spit out three harsh syllables as the Feral roared.

Purple flame—at least judging by the sudden heat of it—flew from its mouth. Teela raised sword and split the stream; it passed to either side of her without singing her hair. Kaylin, standing behind Teela, felt the heat; she held her ground, raising her daggers. There was no way to close with a creature like this; she could throw.

She wouldn't, unless Teela moved.

The small dragon turned. But he did inhale in that long, slow way that dragons sometimes did. When he exhaled, he exhaled a stream that was gray and white to the Feral's purple. It didn't reach the Feral because it wasn't aimed there. His target was the sigil, the signature that any significant use of magic left in its wake. Signatures weren't the magic itself; they were the traces it left behind.

She opened her mouth to tell him that this was a waste of breath—literally—but considered the waste of her own breath and shut up. The magic that Iberrienne used wasn't a magic that the Hawks studied—and generally loathed. It wasn't the typical Arcanist fare. The clouds that the small dragon breathed were unique, and what the small dragon saw—or knew—he couldn't communicate.

But he'd saved her life a handful of times, and she chose to trust him now. She didn't pause to see the effect of his breath, because big, huge, and ugly had pretty much crushed the obstructing remnants of the doors, and he was way too close for comfort.

She turned back to Teela, and Teela—without warning—sent her flying into the nearest wall. Since it wasn't *that* near, Kaylin bruised her shoulder before finding her feet; she dropped one knife and retrieved it in a running roll that brought her back to her feet again.

Teela was already on the move. She carried the sword as if it weighed nothing—as if it were just an extension of her arm. Purple fire hit the floor in a splash; Kaylin expected said floor to darken and scorch. It didn't. As long as she dodged breath—and jaws, and claws—she'd survive.

Given the presence of a Feral that really didn't look all that Ferallike up close, she considered a portal to elsewhere to be less of a risk than it had seemed a few minutes ago. Teela, however, didn't. Kaylin saw sparks fly as her sword scraped the lower edge of creature jaws. It did about as much damage as it would against flat stone.

The creature roared.

Kaylin leaped out of the direct path of its open mouth, narrowly avoiding flame. The creature appeared to be herding Teela toward the center of the room; Teela was having none of it. If the creature were larger, it wasn't faster. It was *as* fast, but the momentum gained when rushing made it harder for the creature to maneuver.

Teela didn't have that problem.

Light was reflected off the whole of the creature's face. Kaylin guessed that the only damage done in this melee would be to the edge of the sword, and she grimaced when Teela struck again; she hated the sound of metal against stone.

The creature's eyes were small and inset into the black bulk of a face that was mostly jaw; it moved fast enough Kaylin couldn't get a direct shot at them—but she tried anyway. When Teela's sword bounced for a third time, the creature's neck elongated, its jaws snapping instantly, and loudly, shut at the spot where Teela had been standing. Teela slid sideways and they closed on empty air; the Barrani Hawk brought her weapon down across a momentarily closed jaw, with enough force to drive its head into the ground.

Kaylin threw her second dagger at the creature's exposed neck.

It stuck its landing.

"Teela!"

Teela didn't answer, but she'd seen. As the creature raised its head again, its neck retracted; the dagger Kaylin had thrown was dislodged, and clattered to the ground. Kaylin watched it fall; it wasn't in the best position for retrieval.

She cursed; if she'd been Barrani, she'd have a sword, and the next time it extended itself she could attempt to remove head from neck.

If the creature hadn't been so adept at fighting on two fronts—when, admittedly, the second front was Kaylin and *almost* insignificant—Kaylin would have taken the time to watch Teela in action, because Teela in action had some of the deadly, beautiful grace of—of Dragons. She couldn't. If she wasn't causing damage, she was drawing fire, and if she wanted to continue to do so, she had to make sure none of it caught her.

She ducked and rolled when something flew at her face, and realized only when it landed that it was the small dragon.

"Wing!" she told him, leaping. He dug claws into her shoulder, which was fair—she wasn't certain he'd still be attached otherwise. His squawking was lost to the fury of bestial roar. She didn't need to hear his complaint; clinging to a shoulder while balancing one open wing was difficult.

He pretty much plastered said wing to her face when she flattened herself against the wall, facing the creature's side. He was a good fifteen feet away, but she'd had experience fighting shadow one-offs, and knew the flank was no guarantee of safety; he could sprout an extra head with no warning. But she took the moment to look.

She froze, but the creature's lunge at Teela carried him farther away; he didn't take advantage of her momentary stillness.

He had a name.

She could *see* it as clearly as she had seen Ynpharion's, in his altered form. This creature's physical shape was larger; fur had been supplanted by obsidian, but it preserved a lot of the same characteristics; four legs, huge jaws. It also sported a tail that was split, and terminated in at least three strands. They etched grooves in stone when the creature had tried to cut Kaylin into several pieces with it.

"All is forgiven," Kaylin said, still staring.

The dragon said nothing.

"I don't think I can grab this one."

The nothing was somehow louder and frostier.

She hadn't lied. The name that she could see was twisting and shifting in place. It was golden, as most words were—but its light was uneven, brighter in some of the components, and so weak it could barely be seen in others. All around its shape and form was shadow; the shadow, however, was green. As green, seen through the mask of dragon wing, as the creatures eyes now were.

Iberrienne.

It was, she was suddenly certain, Iberrienne.

And his name, like Ynpharion's, was shadowed, twisted. The transformation went deeper; the name was larger. A thought occurred to her then: Ynpharion, drawn back by the use of his name into his Barrani life and Barrani self, had *loathed* Iberrienne.

But what if Iberrienne himself were corrupted in exactly the same way? What if he, too, had been changed? He wasn't so changed that he hadn't attempted to kill Bellusdeo, the only known, living, female dragon. Nor so changed that he couldn't move among the Lords of the High Court and the Arcanists.

Whatever the transformation's power, it had to work on what it had. She highly doubted she'd care for an uncorrupted Iberrienne.

The small dragon bit her ear, hard.

Teela hadn't slowed; neither had the creature. Kaylin *had* a weapon she could use against him. She just preferred him to be dead. But it wasn't going to happen soon, and soon was necessary. No one knew where the Consort was.

And so she began to gather what she thought of loosely as syllables. Ynpharion's name had *been* a name. Iberrienne's was only barely that. She could make out what she thought its shape had once been, but she couldn't be certain—and lack of certainty would get her nothing, in the end. Nothing but his rage if she came just close enough.

Teela could keep this up for another hour, in Kaylin's opinion; possibly longer if she pushed.

Just how long had Iberrienne been compromised? What had he been promised, and what, before he had listened to some unknown tale of ancient malice, had he hoped to achieve?

He wasn't as young as Kaylin had assumed—but she realized she'd made the assumption because he seemed so impulsive. He had the visceral hatred of Dragons that only the older Lords of the High Court held.

That melting part of his name was a stroke, not a squiggle; it was meant to tuck in, turn up in a slight slope at the end farthest from Kaylin. The center of the word was unbalanced, as words often were, but the light there was the most familiar. She started there.

Syllables gathered, but she realized, as she amassed them, that they weren't, in any real sense, syllables at all. She heard them as syllables. She heard them as Barrani words. But Nightshade was called Calarnenne by any member of the Court who didn't wish to offend the Consort. What she said, when she spoke his name, was not what they heard. What they said was too thin; it was flat.

Kaylin spoke something that had dimension and strength; it had shape, it had depth, it had structure. The syllables weren't sounds; they were blocks or bricks. If they interlocked in the right way with her intent and her will, they had form.

And that form was a cage.

The marks on her arms were glowing; she felt the mark on her forehead join them. Only the mark on her hand remained as it looked: red, wet with sweat, untouched by light. The small dragon crooned and nudged the side of her face with his head; she felt it at a great remove.

She hated the green wisps of smoke. She hated the purple flame. She hated the vulnerability that ownership introduced—

because, damn it, it *did*. But Ynpharion had remembered. Iberrienne would remember.

And she needed to know what had happened to the Consort.

The syllables snapped into place; she opened her mouth and as she spoke them and they sounded, to her ears, like thunder.

Iberrienne.

CHAPTER 15

He roared. She felt it as a physical sensation, like an earthquake. The ground beneath her feet broke, cracks appearing in flat stone as the creature turned. His eyes were glowing green—as they had the last time she'd encountered him.

"Kitling!"

Iberrienne turned the whole of his attention toward where Kaylin stood. To her surprise, she saw that the folds of her dress were glowing—and they were almost the same color as Iberrienne's eyes. It was the most disturbing thing about him now.

What was the blood of the green?

Iberrienne.

His hind-legs hunched; he intended to leap.

"Kaylin, *move!*"

She held her ground; every instinct screamed against it— but no. It wasn't her instinct; it was his. He fought her. She was surprised when her arm developed sudden gashes, because Iberrienne hadn't *reached* her. She cried out and raised her arms because she was wearing the damn dress and bleeding on it was bad.

It was unspecified bad. Iberrienne wasn't. He'd coiled to spring; he even attempted to do it. But she held him—barely—in place; he staggered. The stagger brought his impressive jaws closer to her face.

The small dragon reared; he didn't breathe and he didn't leap free of her shoulder.

"Kaylin!"

She heard Teela's sword strike the Feral. She heard it bounce, heard Teela's angry Leontine fury. If she survived this, Teela would shake her until her teeth rattled.

But she pushed, and she pushed hard, and it hurt. It burned. Her thoughts spiraled out of her grasp, returning in shreds— she let them go. She held one thing at the center of her thoughts: a name. His name.

She met and held his gaze. The green of his eyes lost illumination, shifting as they drained of light, into blue. Barrani blue. He staggered, dropped belly to floor; his growls became whines. Beyond the fire and fury and killing rage, there was—emptiness.

She thought then that had she tried this on the uncorrupted Lord Iberrienne of the High Court, she would have died. "Teela, don't! We need him!"

The Barrani Hawk lowered her sword; it appeared to take effort, as if gravity was pulling in the wrong direction. She didn't sheathe it. She didn't move. She stood to one side of the shrinking, black creature that was slowly dwindling, the strength of its external shape giving way to the more familiar form and figure of a Barrani man.

He was, unfortunately, naked. Kaylin couldn't remember Ynpharion being naked.

"What," Teela said, in a voice that made ice seem warm, "did you do?"

"I took his name," Kaylin replied evenly. There was blood in her mouth. It was, of course, her own. "Can you do something about my arms?"

Teela's eyes widened before they narrowed.

"I didn't cut *myself,* Teela. And so far no blood on the dress."

The Leontine curse was a comfort. "I do not know how you lived to be twenty."

"Twenty-one. And I'm not certain mortal blood will count—do you think it will?"

Teela glared her into silence. She didn't have random bandages on her person; the dining hall had tablecloths. She cut a chunk off one of them, and then tore it into strips.

"Is it clean?" Kaylin asked, looking dubious.

"It's clean *enough.*"

Kaylin considering reminding Teela that bandages that were too tight were a problem, and decided against it because Iberrienne was stirring. "Grab the other tablecloth," she said, wincing.

"Why?"

"He's *naked,* Teela."

"Yes, I'd noticed. I prefer it to what he was wearing."

Kaylin flushed.

"You've seen far worse in the morgue."

"None of those were alive."

"True—but you won't have to look at his internal organs unless he attempts to do something foolish. I trust a disembowled, dead man who happens to be naked will be less upsetting?" She prodded Iberrienne with her very booted foot.

Kaylin retrieved her daggers. "Are we out of danger?"

"If this creature was responsible for the fires, yes."

"Lord Iberrienne," Kaylin said.

He lifted his head. His eyes were blue; they were not, however, the shade she associated with Ynpharion's eyes whenever they happened to meet hers. He blinked and looked around the dining hall as if seeing it for the first time; had he been human, she would have said he was suffering from shock.

Teela grimaced and sheathed her sword. Bending, she caught him by the upper left arm and yanked him more or less to his feet. He stumbled. "I do not *believe* this. If I have to carry you—"

The words penetrated the fog of his blank expression. "An'Teela?" There was an open expression of confusion on his face. She had never seen a similar one on a Barrani before.

Apparently, neither had Teela. "Kitling, what did you do to him?"

"I told you—I used his name."

"How much resistance did he put up?"

She held up her cloth-covered arms, and then lowered them. "I don't think it was resistance that caused this. I mean—I don't think *I* did it."

Iberrienne shook himself. Kaylin made her way to a table and pulled off a cloth, which she handed to him while Teela looked—for the first time this evening—faintly amused. Iberrienne took the cloth and draped it around his body. If he looked completely out of it, he was still Barrani; he looked better in a tablecloth than Kaylin looked in anything.

She tried not to resent it.

He wasn't fighting her. Ynpharion, for the moment, was silent, as well. But he hadn't been when she'd taken the name, pulling him back to himself. Iberrienne appeared to have no fight in him. Not yet.

"Iberrienne," she said, her voice gentling for no reason she could put a finger on.

He nodded.

"Lord Iberrienne."

"Lord...Kaylin."

"We can't find the Consort. Do you know where she is?"

He was silent. Kaylin wondered if she'd somehow bungled the naming. The small dragon bit her ear. She glared at him. He glared back.

"Kaylin."

Kaylin began to lead Iberrienne in the direction Teela was walking. He offered no resistance—and no answers. She listened as she walked. Ynpharion put up a barrier of rage and humiliation every time her thoughts strayed close to his. She could crash through it—she knew that now—but she felt the pain she caused every time she did. He had never, on the other hand, caused physical wounds to appear anywhere on her body.

She wondered if he could.

"You're Outcaste," she told him quietly.

He nodded. She might as well have said, "Nice weather we're having."

"Teela?"

Teela glanced over her shoulder. "We have two halls. If the instructions you were given are valid, we should clear the halls and reach the courtyard in minutes."

"I'm not sure the Lord of the West March is in the courtyard."

Teela exhaled. In Elantran, she said, "As long as we're not in a building that's magically trapped and on fire, I'll consider it a win." She glanced at Iberrienne and then continued to lead.

"Teela?"

"*What,* kitling? I have had a very long week, and I'm not at my most patient."

"Is he going to get better?"

Teela's eyes rounded. "I swear, if you weren't wearing that damn dress—"

The small dragon hissed.

"Do not even *imagine* that I'm afraid of you."

The courtyard was empty; the fountain, however, continued to trickle water into its basin, as if nothing untoward had happened. Since Kaylin could see that doors on either side of the courtyard were off their hinges, she knew that the attackers had passed through the courtyard; they hadn't chosen to linger.

Reaction had set in; Iberrienne wasn't the only one who was in shock. Kaylin's arms felt cold as the heat of the marks deserted them; she felt exhausted. She plunked herself down beside the fountain, her back pressed into the lip of the basin. To her surprise, Iberrienne followed, and sat as she sat.

This was so not what she had expected. "Lord Iberrienne."

He nodded.

"When did you last see the Consort?" She exhaled, and trailed a hand in the water. It was cool, but it didn't deepen the chill she felt. After a long pause, she tried again. "Do you know where you are?" She hated to feel anything but resentment and fury toward this man: he'd kidnapped and killed dozens of people. He'd destroyed her home.

She couldn't find her anger. She couldn't even find the terrible fear that had kept her moving since she'd heard that the Consort couldn't be found.

"Kitling."

"Have you seen anything like this before? It's like—it's like lethe."

"I assure you Lord Iberrienne was unlikely to imbibe lethe."

"But—it's like that, isn't it? Doesn't it look like that to you?" Lethe was one of the few drugs prized by a small portion of the Barrani populace. It was—to Barrani—highly addictive, and it destroyed their perfect, immortal memory in bits and pieces.

"His eyes are wrong for it," Teela finally said. "Tell me what you did. Tell me exactly what you did."

Kaylin told her. "But—his name was malformed. It was—it was melty. Do you think I said it wrong?"

Teela gave her the same scornful look the small dragon had. "You can't mispronounce a syllable; if you got it wrong, he wouldn't be Barrani—at least in form. Honestly, kitling, it's like giving torches to infants. I can't snap him out of this—I'm tempted to try, but given your current mood, it'll only upset you.

"If he's in there, there's only one person who can find him."

"No," a new voice said. "There are two."

It was the water's voice. Teela leaped backward, landing—like a cat—on her feet. Her sword was free of its scabbard.

Kaylin, however, rotated on the bench, tilting her chin toward the column of rippling water that had risen out of the basin when she wasn't looking. It had the form of a person, but not the features that it sometimes took.

One water arm rose slightly, as if to touch Kaylin's face. *You are far from home. You are far from kin.*

Kaylin nodded. "You are, too."

I am not confined. I am not contained. And, Kaylin, I am not all one thing or all the other. Things move within me, currents carry experience from one part of me to the other. I change, and I do not change. I grieve, and I do not grieve.

You should not be here, Chosen. But you are here.

The small dragon rose on Kaylin's shoulder. He squawked, spreading his wings as he leaped into the air. He circled the pillar of water, making as much noise as he'd made all evening.

Kaylin felt the water turn away from her, although nothing had moved. The water suddenly ran cold, numbing her skin after the first shock of contact. She couldn't hear what the water said, but there were breaks in the small dragon's noise that might—just might—mean she was replying.

"Are you—are you part of the green?"

I am. I have always been part of the green. When it was a seed, Kaylin, I was the water that contained it.

Most people grew things in the earth. Kaylin kept this to herself.

I protect the green. To reach its heart, you must pass me. Did you not see the divide?

She'd seen a small stream become a torrential river.

Teela's eyes widened. "Are you responsible for this, kitling?"

"No. She's the water, Teela."

"*The* water?"

"The elemental water."

"An'Teela."

Teela's eyes shed a bit of their paleness. "Eldest."

"The story is not yet told, daughter. And because it is not, the green suffers."

Teela was silent.

"And you suffer, as well. It is time." To Kaylin she said, "Find the Lady."

"Where is she?"

"Find the Lady," the water repeated, "if you wish to wake Lord Iberrienne."

"I brought him because I thought *he'd* know where the Lady is."

"He does," the water replied. "If you wish to know what he knows, you might find the information—but you might break him in the process."

"He's already broken," Teela reasonably pointed out.

"As are you," the water replied; Teela's eyes looked black in the dim light. "And because you have been, he is part of your story now."

"She's not broken," Kaylin said, because Teela said nothing.

"The Lady is not yet dead." The water warmed in her hand, and for a moment, Kaylin could see a young girl with bruised eyes in the lines the water took as it coalesced and solidified. She lifted Kaylin's hand, the movement like the strong pull of undercurrent. Her lips folded in a sad smile. "I see you have already begun." She was looking at Kaylin's palm.

"Lady—what is the heart of the green?"

"What," she replied, "is the heart of a Hallionne? You've been invited to two such places."

Kaylin was silent.

"You understand, even if you cannot communicate it. The green is like the water, and unlike the water; it is like the Hallionne and unlike the Hallionne. It is a dream, Kaylin. And a nightmare. I am part of it, and separate from it. The Tha'alaan sleeps; I will not wake it unless you ask."

Kaylin swallowed and retrieved her hand. She looked at the bloodred mark on her palm. "I don't understand," she finally said.

"No. Find the Consort."

"She was with the dreams of Alsanis."

The water began to fall, returning to the basin that contained it.

"Teela?"

Teela was rigid with anger. "Do not get involved in this."

"If I don't, the Consort will die."

"The Consort who censured you and publicly humiliated you." She frowned. "What are you looking at?"

Kaylin almost shoved her hand behind her back, but that would have been as effective as breaking her own arm. In fact, given Teela's mood, it might be exactly that. She held out her hand, palm up.

Teela glanced at the palm of Kaylin's hand for a long, long

moment. When she spoke her voice was soft. It was the wrong kind of soft. "Where did you get that mark?"

"In the tunnels."

"No, you did not."

"In the cavern that the tunnels lead to, if you're lucky."

Teela's eyes had narrowed. She dropped Kaylin's hand. "If you asked for the judgment of the green, and you are not still trapped in its maze, how exactly did you end up here? You didn't come from the heart of the green; there's no way Lord Lirienne would have allowed you to run back into the halls. Kitling, look at me."

Long years of habit came to her rescue; she met Teela's extremely dark eyes. "I asked the green if it could send me to where you were."

Teela's eyes rounded in outrage. "I swear, when we get you back to Elantra, I will go straight to the Emperor himself and demand that you *never* leave the city again."

"Teela—no one knew where you were."

"So?"

"Severn was with Nightshade. Whatever attacked them took Evarrim down—I don't know if he survived or not. Lirienne was with Barian, everyone was frantic for the Consort—and no one knew where you were."

"So you came back *into* the heart of the fighting?"

"I didn't *know* where you were, Teela. And frankly, I was helpful. I know how you fight. I know how to stay out of your way, and I know when to cut in. I didn't get in your way—I'm not a kid anymore."

Teela, however, was frowning. "Did Gaedin teach you the greetings and the obeisances? Did he teach you the blessings?"

"No."

"Then how, exactly, did you ask the heart of the green to send you anywhere?"

"Because the green can speak."

Teela stilled. Kaylin had thought her motionless before; now, even breath appeared to have deserted her. "The green spoke to you."

"Yes. Like the water usually does."

"Did you find this new mark before the green spoke to you?"

"No, it was after."

Teela closed her eyes for one long moment. When she opened them, she glanced at Iberrienne. "We will find the Consort," she said, sounding—for Teela—defeated. "And then, dress or no dress, I am packing you up and sending you straight home."

"You can't—I'm the harmoniste."

"Do you want to bet?"

She really, really didn't. She rose, and when Iberrienne failed to follow suit, gently took his arm and pulled him to his feet. He frowned and shook his arm free, which caused the tablecloth to slip.

Kaylin had a strong desire to go back into one of the guest rooms—any room—and find clothing. Even a dress was better than this. Sadly, Teela headed straight out, walking briskly but not so fast that she left Kaylin and Iberrienne behind.

The Barrani were gathered like a war band. They were armed that way, too. The subtle—and not so subtle—politics of the first dinner had evaporated. They were angry, no surprise there.

Lirienne was enraged. None of it showed, except in the color of his eyes, and even then, it was dark enough that someone might mistake in their color. That someone was not, unfortunately, Kaylin Neya. She could feel his fury like a blow. It wasn't that she was attempting to touch it; it radiated out with such force it made a week of Ynpharion look like child's play.

She was almost afraid to approach him.

"Lord Kaylin." He knew, of course. "Lord An'Teela." His eyes widened slightly as he saw who trailed after them. "You have the Outcaste."

"We do. I thought he might be able to tell us where the Consort is."

Kaylin knew Lirienne could utter a single word, and what was left of Iberrienne would die here. She was no longer certain that would be a bad thing. She held his name, yes—but it felt incredibly fragile, a blown glass object meant to contain small, still things that wouldn't break it. There were fleeting images that she could almost touch, but they never coalesced into the solidity of voice or emotion that she could feel from Lirienne or Nightshade.

Hells, she wasn't even trying to contact Lirienne and he was almost overwhelming.

"An'Teela, what did you do to subdue him?" the Lord of the West March asked. He came to stand in front of Iberrienne. Iberrienne pulled the edges of the tablecloth more tightly around his shoulders before he met the Lord of the West March's gaze. His eyes widened. "Lirienne."

If the sight of a Lord of the Court dressed in nothing but a tablecloth hadn't already commanded the attention of all Barrani present, the tone of Iberrienne's voice did. He didn't use the unadorned name to signal public lack of respect, or to imply an inferiority of power or position on the Lord of the West March's part. His voice was neither neutral nor chilly.

It was said, Kaylin thought, with shy delight. She had never heard a Barrani speak this way, and she'd been forced for any number of reasons to listen to a lot of Barrani.

To her surprise—and relief—Severn appeared, stepping

around the Barrani who were content to let him pass. "Lord Iberrienne was injured in the outlands; it is possible that he had not fully recovered."

"He was not so badly injured that he could not field a size-able force with which to attack the hall." The Lord of the March paused.

An'Teela did not subdue him. It wasn't a question.

No.

What did you do?

She swallowed. *I could see his name.*

Silence.

I used it.

He fought you, then.

She exhaled. *Yes and no. I think—in the end—he wanted me to grab it. I have some experience with people who don't.*

Ah. You do not refer to me?

No. You don't care.

She felt his brief amusement. *That is entirely incorrect. I care. But not so much that I wished to die.*

You're not afraid of me.

No. What you could *do is theoretical. You have my name—but your hold over it has never been tested. Nor will it be, while you live. Teela does not wish your intervention to be known—and that is wise. No one of my people will assume that Iberrienne was brought low by you.*

Gee, thanks.

Do you wish it known, kyuthe?

Did she? She glanced at the assembled Barrani, Lords of the High Court, Lords of the lesser court of the West March. *No.* She hesitated.

Of course he knew. *You are concerned.*

Why did—why is he—looking at you like that?

Silence. He didn't want to answer. And she didn't want to

demand what he wouldn't willingly give, although in theory she could.

"Lirienne," Iberrienne said, when the Lord of the West March failed to answer. "Where is Eddorian? Is he not here?"

The Lord of the West March closed his eyes. And so, Kaylin saw, did Teela.

She was surprised when Nightshade also walked through the grim and silent crowd. The name, Eddorian, had dropped like a very large anvil into a very still pond. The Lord of the West March glanced at him, and Teela glared. Neither, however, spoke to stop him, and because they didn't, the Barrani Lords let him pass.

Iberrienne smiled. It looked *so wrong* on a Barrani face, Kaylin found it inexplicably painful to watch; it was far more personal than his unplanned nudity had been. "Calarnenne!"

"Iberrienne," Nightshade replied, smiling in turn. His smile was different, but to Kaylin, no less jarring. It walked the edge between pity and compassion—neither of which she had ever associated with the fieflord. He held out both of his hands, and Iberrienne placed his over them.

"Where is Eddorian?"

"He is not yet here."

Iberrienne's eyes rounded. "If he is absent, it will ruin us. My Lord was so proud that he had been chosen." He rose. "But—why are we here? It is not the hour of the green. Calarnenne—why are you wearing the Teller's crown? Where is Annarion?"

"Annarion is preparing for his first recitation, as Eddorian must be."

Kaylin looked at Teela as Iberrienne spoke. Her eyes were a shade that Kaylin couldn't remember seeing before—not blue, not precisely, although there was a lot of blue in it. She thought it amethyst, a deep purple.

Do not ask her, Lirienne said.

I've never seen that color before—I mean, not in Barrani eyes. What does it mean?

Grief, Kaylin. A deep, abiding, encompassing grief. It is not a color that you are taught, because it is seen so very, very seldom. Grief generally makes my kin angry—and the color of our anger reveals nothing that we do not wish to be seen. An'Teela...

Eddorian was one of the children, the lost children, wasn't he?

You already know the answer to that question. I will not insult your perception.

"I am the Teller," Nightshade told Iberrienne. "But come, you are not properly clothed, and when we gather for the recitation, you will be far more of an embarrassment to your father than a late Eddorian."

Iberrienne looked down at his tablecloth; as he had both hands in Nightshade's, it had slipped from his shoulders. "I don't—I don't understand. Why am I wearing nothing?"

"That is no doubt a story for a long, slow evening; it will keep boredom at bay. Come, Iberrienne." He looked to Barian. Of course he did.

Lord Barian, however, looked to—of all people—Kaylin. As if he knew, or as if he suspected. "He is as you see him," she replied, as softly as she could.

"Will you grant us the hospitality of the West March, Warden?" Nightshade asked. It sounded very formal.

The Warden, Lord Barian, nodded.

To Kaylin, Nightshade said, *Find the Consort, Kaylin. Find her and summon me if necessary.*

What will you do with Iberrienne?

I will see him clothed.

Why is he—why is he like this?

Nightshade didn't answer. Instead, with ineffable gentleness, he led Iberrienne away.

Silence reigned in the large clearing.

It was Kaylin who broke it. "Did the eagles remain with the Consort?"

Her question caused a ripple to pass through the Barrani; whatever disturbance Iberrienne had caused—and he had, there was no doubting it—passed.

"To the best of our knowledge, yes. The dreams of Alsanis were not seen by anyone else during the battle," Lirienne said.

It was to Barian she looked. "They remained with her. We took our leave—at her request. Two of Lord Lirienne's lieges remained with her, on the far side of her doors; she wished no company." Before Kaylin could ask, he said, "They are dead."

"And her chambers—"

"Her chambers are empty."

"Were they—"

"They were half-destroyed, yes. The eagles, when we arrived, were gone."

Barian glanced at Lord Lirienne, and then gave a brief shake of the head. "Preparations have been made, Lord of the West March. If you will countenance it, we will repair to the heart of the green."

She heard the *No* that he didn't speak, it was so visceral. "Lord Avonelle has agreed?"

Barian's lips tightened; it was brief. "She has."

Kaylin started to speak.

Do not interfere, Kaylin. It was Nightshade.

You're not even here.

No. The attack on the Lord's hall is unprecedented. Inasmuch as Barrani are safe anywhere, they have always been safe here; not even the three flights could breach the defenses of the green. In such a situation, there is no safer place.

Given the green and the Hallionne and the lost children, I'd consider that dubious safety.

Yes. You would. But if the Consort can be found, it will be by the will of the heart of the green. The politics of the green and its Wardens require caution—but caution takes time. Lirienne will accept the debt.

What debt? She's the Lady—she's the only one who can wake the newborns!

Yes. But he is from the East, not the Vale. Do not interfere.

This isn't the time for politics!

He laughed. He was genuinely amused. Politics among my kin end when life does. Go. You have touched the nightmares of Alsanis. It is possible that the heart of the green will answer Lord Lirienne— but he will be unable to go to where she is. You, however, might.

CHAPTER 16

Lord Avonelle was wearing armor. Gone was the very fine, very flattering dress she had worn with such cold grace at dinner. At a dinner that felt like it had happened last week. Kaylin looked up to see the two moons; she had no idea how much time had passed. It was still dark, but the edge of the visible horizon implied it wouldn't remain that way.

"Lord of the West March."

He inclined his head. "Lord Avonelle."

"Accept my apologies; the Warden informed me of the urgency of the situation with all speed. We were ill-prepared for an emergency of this nature. We have bespoken the runes, and we wait."

"I ask your leave to enter the heart of the green."

"The green will judge."

Kaylin didn't like the sound of that reply, but it was said without inflection. Clearly, even in emergencies, form was more important than function.

Avonelle stood aside. "Tenebriel will serve as guide."

Barian, however, stepped forward. He bowed to his mother, Lord Avonelle; her eyes were very blue. "I will serve as guide, Lord Avonelle."

She looked as if she wanted to argue.

"I am Warden." He turned to the Lord of the West March, his back taking the brunt of Lord Avonelle's silent anger. "The green will judge. Within the green's heart, the Lords of the High Court—and the Lords of the Vale—are responsible for their own choices and their own decisions." He raised his voice as he turned to the Barrani gathered behind the Lord of the West March. "Will you enter the heart of the green?"

Kaylin said, "I will."

Lord Avonelle said, in the least friendly tone she'd used yet, "You will leave your companion behind."

The small dragon turned his head toward Lord Avonelle. He met her gaze and then—very deliberately, in Kaylin's opinion—yawned. "My apologies, Lord Avonelle," she said, forcing herself to sound as arrogant as Teela in a mood. "But he goes where I go."

"Then you will not walk the green."

Lord Barian said, "Lord Avonelle, you are Guardian; your duties are clear. But I am Warden. Lord Kaylin has touched the dreams of Alsanis; she has drawn them into the Vale, where they have not flown for centuries. On both occasions—"

"Both?" The word was sharp.

"On both occasions, her companion occupied the position he now occupies. I do not believe that anyone who can touch the dreams of Alsanis means harm to the green. Had she woken only nightmares, I would abide by your decision. She did not." Lord Avonelle was silent.

Barian now resumed his formal conversation with Kaylin,

his expression grave. "You do not understand what the heart of the green is, but I perceive your determination. Will you accept my guidance, Lord Kaylin?"

"I will." She paused; a path appeared beneath the feet of the Warden. It led away from him. She started toward it, and was pulled up short by Lirienne's silent command.

You will wait, Kaylin; it is not safe to walk these paths without a guide.

Is it less safe than the maze?

Yes.

Great.

Teela stepped forward. "I will enter the heart of the green," she said.

It was Barian's turn to be silent.

Lord Avonelle moved. Before she could speak, Teela said, in a drawl that the Barrani Hawks would have recognized, "The green will judge." It was a challenge.

"I am the Guardian of the green."

"You are. You are not, however, the green." To Barian, she added, "Warden, I am of the High Court. I have worn the blood of the green. Lord Kaylin is *kyuthe* to me. I will go where she goes; I will accept the judgment of the green. Will you deny me?"

"An'Teela," the Lord of the West March said, "perhaps it would be best if you withdraw."

She ignored him. She ignored everyone except Lord Barian.

For one long moment he met and held her gaze; their eyes were pretty much the same color. "The green," he said softly, "will judge. Will you take that risk, cousin?"

Teela nodded.

The path just beyond Barian's feet began to glow.

No one spoke a word. It occurred to Kaylin only then that they were afraid to enter the heart of the green if that heart contained Teela. Barrani never acknowledged fear; they acknowledged danger. She waited to see how it would fall out. The Lord of the West March was already committed.

She was surprised when Ynpharion stepped forward. She had avoided the touch of his thoughts as if they were plague; his anger and his contempt—for both her and himself—was almost crushing if she spent too much time listening. Because of this, she avoided asking him anything, and avoided any attempt to command him; she had only set her will above his in the heart of the Hallionne Orbaranne.

It was therefore his choice, inasmuch as he had a choice. "I will enter the heart of the green and abide by its judgment."

He was not a senior Lord of the High Court. And what he did, she realized, the others must also be seen to be willing to do. The fact that he felt he had very little to lose was immaterial; the other Lords were not aware of it.

His statement had no effect on the Warden's people, but oddly, it was not the Warden's people that he resented.

"The green will judge."

He joined Kaylin on the path. He did not, in any way, acknowledge her, but he glanced with genuine concern at her arms—her bare arms, the marks on them visible. It wasn't the marks that concerned him. It was the dress. Kaylin guessed that the dress didn't normally rearrange itself and lose its sleeves in the process.

To her surprise, he said, *I do not know. I have never seen the blood of the green before you.*

"Close your mouth, kitling," Teela said, in quiet Elantran. "Or an insect will fly into it and we'll be subject to your whining for what remains of the evening." Kaylin closed her mouth and opened it again. "I am *so* not in the mood to hear whining."

"I don't understand why they're worried about you."

"No, you don't."

"Can you explain it?"

"No. I understand it, but I am done with explanations for the evening."

No one else would explain it, either.

Severn stepped forward. "I ask leave to enter the heart of the green."

Barian's jaw set for a moment. He had accepted Teela's request with obvious hesitation, but little surprise; he accepted Severn's the same way—but more.

Lord Avonelle lifted a hand. "You are mortal," she said.

"So is the harmoniste. It will not be the first time that I have entered the heart of the green."

And clearly Lord Avonelle remembered the last time without any fondness.

Barian closed his eyes for a long moment; when he opened them, he said a very cold, "The green will judge." Kaylin could practically hear what Barian hoped the judgment would be.

"Your corporal has courage," Teela murmured.

"He's not lying."

"No. I guessed that. He is wearing the blades."

Kaylin nodded.

"They were forged—if such a word can be used—in the heart of the green."

Kaylin's eyes widened.

"When the wielder dies, kitling, the blades fall silent. They wake in the heart of the green, if they wake at all. Many have lifted their dull, lifeless chains and many have carried them into the heart of the green. Very, very few have emerged."

"You mean, the blades remain sleeping?"

"No."

"Wait—wait—you're saying Severn took them—"

"Yes. He challenged the family who held the nascent blades in their keeping. He defeated—barely—the man who had not been willing to risk his own life to the judgment."

"Does the green kill a lot of you?"

Teela actually chuckled. "No. But the green is not fond of weapons, or rather, not the iron we wield. One takes a risk when one carries those blades into the green's heart. The judgment of the green cannot be bought; it can only barely be understood."

"The blades—I think the blades were damaged."

"Yes. In the outlands. He has not used them since."

"He did."

"Oh?"

"During the attack on the Lord's hall, he did."

"Did you happen to notice, since you weren't actually there, whether or not they were as effective as they normally are?"

She hadn't, and Teela knew it.

"The Warden risks much, this eve," Teela said quietly. Ynpharion did not appear to be listening, but he was.

"With you or with Severn?"

Teela's eyes were almost—almost—green. "With all of us, kitling. Lord Lirienne is not a risk, but you? Your corporal? Me?"

"Nightshade's not here," Kaylin offered.

"The risk Nightshade poses in the minds of all present is purely political. The risks we present are not. Avonelle is enraged." The thought amused Teela. It shouldn't, Kaylin thought. If she understood things correctly, Lord Avonelle was her aunt, her mother's older sister.

"Barian will survive it."

"Her rage, yes. But he will be guide. It is not without risk to him, either. There is a reason," she added softly, "that permission to enter the heart of the green must be given. Only during the recitation is it entirely safe to walk here. The guardians choose those they feel present the least risk; they will not allow them to enter the green this way if they fear to anger the green."

"But—but—"

"Yes?" She spoke the word as if it had two syllables.

"The tunnels. We can enter the heart any time we want. I mean, you can."

Teela did laugh, then. It drew a lot of attention, and the attention bounced to Kaylin when it became clear that Kaylin was the cause of her mirth. "Is that what they told you?"

But Ynpharion was staring at them both. The thunderous beat of his rage had dimmed. "You walked beneath the green?"

"Yes."

"When?"

"When the Lord's hall was attacked."

"And you are here? Should you not be in the heart of the green?"

"She should," Teela said, her amusement ebbing. "That, however, is not a subject to be discussed here; it is neither wise nor safe."

Severn joined them. Teela glanced at him. "You risk too much, Corporal."

"Kaylin wanted me here," he replied.

Kaylin met his gaze and then found her feet very interesting. It was true. She thought he even knew why.

Iberrienne.

Closing her eyes, she said, *I'm not a Wolf, Severn. I'm a Hawk. We both served the Emperor in our own ways. But—but—*

Yes. You consider Iberrienne so damaged you now see him as a helpless child. You understand that that doesn't change my duty?

She swallowed. *Yes. Look, I know, believe I know what he did. I know how many people he killed. He didn't consider their lives worth anything. If the fiefs were in our jurisdiction, he'd hang.* He wouldn't, but the Barrani would kill him. They didn't suffer their own to be judged in the Imperial Court—and as Iberrienne's victims were not Barrani, the Barrani High Court could not claim caste exemption and therefore caste justice. *I know he deserves to be executed. I know.*

Severn smiled; it was a shadowed smile. He was standing much closer to her than he normally did. *Could you kill him?*

I've killed, Severn. I've killed people who didn't deserve to die. I worked as an enforcer for Barren. If every murderer deserves death— I deserve it, as well. Me. She could still see Iberrienne's painfully open expression. *Whoever he thinks he is now is not the man who did those things. He looks—helpless. Young.* She swallowed. *No. No, I couldn't. I could have killed him—if I had the power— at any other time.*

He exhaled, lifted a hand, touched her shoulder. *The Consort is more important, for the moment.*

I'm not sure the Emperor would agree with that.

The Emperor's not here, and I have reasons of my own for entering the green's heart.

It was another long half hour before those who were willing to follow the Lord of the West March were gathered. Not all of the Barrani gathered here were willing to take that risk; everyone who had come from the High Court, however, was.

None of those men was Nightshade.

No, he replied. *I will stay with Iberrienne.*

I won't be able to—to call you.

He said nothing. She felt, of all things, anger. He was angry— but not with Kaylin. Not, she sensed, with Iberrienne, either.

"Warden," the Lord of the West March said.

"Lord of the West March." He frowned, and then his eyes narrowed. When he lifted them, he lifted them to sky. Kaylin, whose vision was nowhere equal to that of the Barrani, nonetheless saw what he saw. An eagle.

No, not one. Two. They circled, descending. Barian lifted an arm. Just one. He turned to Kaylin. "Lord Kaylin."

But Kaylin shook her head. "It's not me."

Barian frowned.

Lirienne—lift an arm. Umm, please.

He was surprised, but did as she had asked. He raised an arm, bent at the elbow as Barian's was. The two eagles landed then, one on each man's arm.

"Warden," one said. "Lord of the West March. Why have you come to the green?"

"I am guide," the Warden said. "The Lord of the West March seeks to reach the Lady."

The two eagles glanced at each other; they spoke. They didn't speak in High Barrani. They didn't speak in a language the Lord of the West March understood, either. She couldn't tell, from Barian's expression, whether he could.

But before they had finished their discussion, the small dragon squawked.

They turned their heads—only their heads, which looked so unnatural—toward Kaylin's shoulder. The small dragon squawked again. He squawked loudly.

"Chosen," the eagle on Barian's arm said, "show me your hand."

Kaylin blinked. She glanced at her hands. Clearly, she was tired; it took her a moment to understand why he'd asked. She lifted her left hand, palm out, toward the eagles. The eagle on Lirienne's arm squawked. He then spoke to his companion.

"Warden," one of the two finally said. "We are come to tell you that the wards will not wake."

Barian froze. One or two of the men who served him froze, as well. "None of them?"

"There are two; green will hear you if you speak the words of waking and invocation while in their presence. You will lose much time if you walk the longest path; the two are the only wards that will now respond, although the propiciants bespeak the others now."

"Which wards, eldest?"

"The seat," the eagle replied. "The oldest seat."

The answer meant nothing to Kaylin. She was clearly the only person here to whom it meant nothing.

It's not a chair, Severn told her. *It's considered the center of both the West March and the green. It's where the recitation takes place.*

When you came here the first time—did you see the other runes the dreams are talking about?

Yes. He withdrew.

Severn—don't. I can't make you tell me anything—but don't shut me out.

I won't. But, Kaylin, there are things I don't want to talk about. There are things I don't want to think about. This was part of my life as a Wolf; it has nothing to do with your life as a Hawk. I saw the runes. I passed them. But I didn't come here with a guide, or with the blessing—however reluctant—of the guardian.

Who did you come here with?

He was silent. She retreated; she felt irrationally stung, but couldn't deny the truth of what he'd said. She had never, for instance, talked much about Barren with Severn. There was a lot he didn't know. A lot she didn't want him to know, when it came right down to it. And why? Because if he did, he'd stop caring?

Maybe. Maybe that was part of it.

The small dragon bit her ear. She cursed at him in Leontine. In quiet Leontine, which didn't work so well.

Everyone was staring at her.

"Lord Kaylin?" Lord Barian said, as if prompting her for a reply.

Damn it. What did I miss?

The eagles have offered to lead us to the seat of life. Or rather, they've offered to lead you to the seat; they've agreed that we will accompany you if you decide to accept their offer.

And if I don't?

The implication is that we won't reach the seat. At all.

That's going to make the recitation difficult.

No, it won't. But if the Consort is trapped elsewhere, we'll have wasted days. The Barrani don't require sleep.

But they did require food. "Yes," she told the eagles, who were staring at her as if they could hear every word she hadn't said out loud. She watched as the path beneath their collective feet began to move.

At this point in a long evening that was, as the minutes passed, giving way to dawn, it shouldn't have been surprising. It was.

"What's happening?" Kaylin asked, forgetting everything she'd learned about the proper political address extended to powerful men. "Why is the ground doing this?"

"This may come as surprise," the Lord of the West March said, "but this is not generally the way we approach the heart of the green." They started to move. Either that or every other part of the landscape did.

"Look," she said to the eagles, dropping into Elantran. "Can we just, oh, *walk?*"

She felt Lirienne's amusement—and a hint of his approval. She did not understand the Barrani.

You ask the questions none of my kin will ask; they tolerate it because you are mortal, and mortal ignorance is expected. The Warden will answer the question you have chosen to ask, without insulting the High Court.

Why in the hells would an answer be insulting?

It would imply ignorance.

But you just said you are—

Indeed.

The eagles looked at each other. "The wards cannot hear," they said—in unison.

Lord Barian cleared his throat. "The path that winds its way through the heart of the green is not, in any sense of the word, a physical path. Only during the recitation is it laid bare; at that time, the whole of the green is turned toward one purpose, and one alone. At other times, the path opens as the propiciants speak the words of greeting; they open again when they speak the words of benediction. Each section of what you perceive as path is governed by the wards.

"Only in the presence of those who can speak the necessary words is the path revealed, and it is revealed almost step by step."

"You wished to travel quickly," the eagles added—again in unison, and again, to Kaylin. "This is the safest mode of travel for your companions."

That, however, was less well-done.

You'll note it's not me who said it.

"An'Teela. Teela," the eagles said.

Teela said nothing.

"The green is waiting. The wait has been long."

Motion didn't usually make Kaylin nauseous. The motion of the path did. It was like a gut punch accompanied by the sharp, stinging pain of her exposed marks. The hidden ones hurt, as well.

Lirienne, would you know if—if something had happened to the Consort?

Would I know if she were dead?

That was what she meant. She couldn't bring herself to use the word.

Not here. I find it odd, he said. Barrani could find things intellectually interesting at the worst of times. *You are mortal. You will die. You walk to death from the moment of your birth. Why, then, is death such a difficult concept?*

Because we can't avoid it.

But that wasn't the truth. Human death, Leontine death, Aerian death—and Barrani death—were all the same, in the end. It wasn't her own death she feared, although she went out of her way to avoid it where possible. It was what death meant. It meant absence. Permanent absence. It meant abandonment. The fact that it wasn't chosen by the person who left didn't change the fact of its effect.

Time didn't change it. Nothing could. You could learn to accept it—hells, you had no choice. But the loss? She bit her lip and glanced at Teela, hoping Teela wouldn't notice. Teela remembered everything. Teela remembered it as clearly as if it were stored in Imperial Records. Teela knew now and for as long as she lived, every single thing that was gone. All the details. All the details of how she had lost it.

Kaylin had never known her father. Teela had known hers—and she had both loved him and killed him.

Did that make it better, in the end? Could memories of her father's death somehow ease the cost of the memories of her mother's?

No, Lirienne said, his voice soft. *But that is always the hope. Teela is* kyuthe *to you.*

Kaylin said nothing.

Do you understand why, Kaylin? When she failed to answer, he said, *you have always seen her as invulnerable. Immortal. Nothing the Imperial Hawks face will kill her. She is safe, for you, because she is not mortal. She is the family that you cannot lose. She will not die. She will not change. Time will take nothing from her, and when it takes your competence from you, you will know that she is there.*

Why are you telling me this?

It is truth. But it is your truth. Hers is different. You are, to the surprise of the Barrani of both the High Court and the Vale, kyuthe *in her eyes. We understood why she chose to join the Hawks; she was...*

Bored?

Yes. You do not understand what boredom means to the Immortal. We understood. With her went a handful of Barrani who had neither the courage nor the desperation to take the test of name. That was unusual, but not unheard of. We did not know—until you— how attached she had become to your ephemeral world.

Me?

She faced the Dragon Court, for your sake. She returned to the High Halls, she donned both her title and the grandeur of her line, and she walked into the Imperial Palace. She did not claim her rank as an Imperial Hawk; before the Dragon Court, she claimed her ties to the High Court, and her rank as a warrior in the Dragon wars.

When? When did she do this?

You were younger, Kaylin. You were considered, I believe, a child by everyone but yourself. And the Emperor understood the danger of the marks you bear. He wished to see you destroyed. She wished to see you preserved. Her presence as a warrior, her title as a senior member of the High Court, and the weapon she bore, all made a threat she herself would never utter. She was willing to go to war—for you. If he desired your death, he would have had to kill her first. And, Kaylin—you did not see her.

You didn't, either.

He chuckled. *No. But my brother did. My sister did. The Consort attempted to reason with her. She listened. She listened with the respect due the Lady. She agreed with every argument the Lady made. She would not, however, be swayed. She was unconcerned with the loss of face.*

Let me guess. Attachment to mortals is right up there with dying for your cats.

It is exactly like that; I am informed that it nonetheless happens among mortals. It does not happen among my kin. She strode into the Palace to make her argument to the Eternal Emperor. She did not threaten him, as was expected. Her accoutrements were all the threat she allowed herself to make.

Kaylin looked at Teela; Teela was staring into the distance in a "don't talk to me" way.

She pleaded, Kaylin. She told the Emperor that your life was measured in decades—mortal decades; that it would end soon enough on its own. Lord Tiamaris argued against those years; he pointed out that if decades were so insignificant—in a city in which the majority of the occupants faced exactly that fate—what difference did they make? The harm you might do in those decades, the possibility of destruction, and at that, unpredictable destruction, warranted your death. It was prudent.

That, I knew.

Oh?

Marcus—my Sergeant—still hates him for it. She frowned. She *had* heard that Teela had gone to Court on her behalf. She hadn't questioned it; she barely remembered because she hadn't been asked to attend. She'd been told after the fact.

You think that Barrani do not love. I love my brother and my sister.

I know. That's what makes you—

Unusual? Or weak?

Unusual, she said, firmly.

It is a weakness, he said. *No, Kaylin. For you it is not. But the survival of your kind depends on numbers. You do not survive in isolation. It is not the same for my kin or the Emperor's. You think of love—when you think of it—as a strength, as a binding. And for you, it is.*

But bindings break when they are tested for eternity. Nothing, not even mountains, last forever. What has been a strength can shatter—with a single death, in a single moment. You call it a risk, he added softly. *But it is not a risk, for us; it is a certainty. But we live, Kaylin. We live. Love is not therefore unknown to us; it is sharpest when we are young.*

But I believe you understand. And if you do not, it is both my fear and my hope that you will.

"An'Teela."

Teela met the eyes of the Lord of the West March. He said nothing further; she said nothing. To him. To Kaylin, in Elantran, she said, "If the Exchequer doesn't hang for this, I will hunt him down and kill him myself."

Kaylin said nothing because the nausea was increasing. The passing trees and grass spun in circles; she closed her eyes, which helped—but not enough. She could still feel the ground vibrating beneath her feet; had she not been surrounded by Barrani, she would have dropped to her knees.

Hells with it. She dropped to the ground anyway. She was never going to gain Barrani approval; she could spend her whole life being as perfectly mannered and viciously political as they were, and she might get a pat on the head. At the moment, it wasn't incentive enough; she sat, crossing her legs beneath the flowing folds of her skirt. Having more ground beneath her—and a shorter distance to hit it if the dizziness overwhelmed her—helped.

She was momentarily grateful when the world stopped moving and very carefully opened her eyes.

She wasn't certain what she had expected of a place called the heart of the green. Mostly, a lot of well-tended grass—the kind that only rich people had—and trees. Maybe a fountain, or a small pond.

There was no grass here. There were two trees—two leafless, winter trees. There was what might once have been a fountain; the stone was preserved, but the basin was dry and empty. Kaylin approached the fountain, pausing once to ask silent permission of Barian, who frowned but nodded. If there were wards here, she couldn't see them. She glanced at the small dragon, who'd folded himself into the shawl position; he could only barely be bothered to lift his head. He sighed and lowered it again, without doing anything helpful first.

Fine.

She touched the fount's rim. It was warm; the clearing was warm. Not hot, not arid, but warm; it suggested sunlight on a day that the sun didn't choose to be punishing. But nothing grew here that she could see.

"I don't understand," she said.

CHAPTER 17

The small dragon whiffled.

"I wasn't talking to you."

"You were, of course, talking to yourself again. What have I told you about that?" Teela came to stand by her side; she didn't touch the stone. Her hands were loosely clasped behind her back.

"People will doubt my sanity."

Teela nodded. "Unless you happen to be the Arkon."

"In which case it's irrelevant."

Teela's smile was stiff, but genuine. "Yes. What, specifically, don't you understand?"

"This is the heart of the green. But—it's not very green."

"No."

"Was it always like this?"

"It has been like this for a long time."

"Which is a no."

"Kitling, honestly, if I could pack you up and send you

home—with any hope that you'd arrive in more or less one piece—I would. No. In my childhood, it was not."

"What did it look like then?"

"The trees bore leaves. The fountain was active; it was similar to the fountain in the courtyard of the Lord's hall—but it was, in all ways, more impressive." Her lips curved in a strange smile as she lifted her face. "The water spoke. Not often, not reliably, and not always in a language that the pilgrims could understand—but its voice..."

Kaylin thought of the Tha'alaan.

"Sometimes, the water offered glimpses of past history—again, it was not reliable; one could not simply ask. But on quiet days, the waters in the basin grew still, no matter how strong the breeze in the greenheart, and images would form; they were like—and unlike—our Records in the Halls of Law. We could not ask."

"Why is the water gone? If the fountain in the Lord's hall—"

"A question you should never ask in Lord Avonelle's hearing."

"That is a question that An'Teela has asked before," Lord Barian said. He joined them, his arm bent and lifted, the eagle upon it.

Neither Teela's expression, nor her posture, changed—but she wasn't happy to be standing so close to the Warden. "I was a child," she replied.

"Yes. Too young to be tested, and yet, An'Teela, you were."

"And did I pass the test?" Her smile was bitter.

"You are here. Your enemies are not. You survived the test of the High Halls. You are a Lord of the High Court, and a Lord of the Vale; you are the head of your line. In any way that success is defined by most of our kin, you are successful."

Funny. To Kaylin, it sounded like a no.

"Will you answer your *kyuthe*'s question?"

"I have no doubt," the Barrani Hawk said, in a familiar drawl, "that she will plague me until she gets her answers, one way or another. I am honestly surprised that I have not yet strangled her."

Barian surprised Kaylin. He laughed. Given the slight lift of Teela's brows, she wasn't the only one. "And I am not *kyuthe,* although we are cousins. I will not depend upon your obvious affection to preserve my life."

"My apologies, cousin." Teela's voice was soft. "You are your mother's son."

"Ah, yes. A plague upon ambitious parents, then?"

Teela closed her eyes. "And a plague, of a different kind, upon their children." She shook herself. "You will bespeak the wards, Warden?"

Barian nodded, withdrawing—as Teela had done—while standing in place. "Will you remain with us?" He spoke, of course, to the eagle.

"We must," he replied. "For now."

Kaylin frowned. "You said two of the wards would hear us."

"Yes."

"And there are two of you. Is that a coincidence?"

"No, Chosen."

"Why are the wards inactive?"

"The green is wounded," the eagles replied.

"The green has been wounded since—" She bit her lip and managed to stop the rest of the words from falling out. She couldn't stop the pit of her stomach from dropping to somewhere around her knees.

"The wound is bleeding now," the eagles said. They didn't mention how or why, for which Kaylin was grateful. "But wounds must bleed if they are to heal; they must be acknowledged."

"The green isn't a body."

"Is it not?" The eagles conferred briefly, and then said, "It loves, Chosen, and it grieves; it breathes and it knows the passage of seasons; it sleeps and it dreams; it bleeds. In its fashion, it knows time, and you have invited time to return."

"I didn't—" So much for grateful. Every eye—*every* eye—was now turned toward her.

The eagles tilted their heads. "Is it not true that there is no change without time?"

"I don't—"

"And there is no healing without time?"

"Yes, but—"

"Time is therefore essential."

"Can I finish a sentence?"

"It is time," they said, ignoring the question. "Time, at last. An'Teela has returned, Chosen, and the blood of the green flows."

Kaylin turned to the Warden; the Warden was pale, even for a Barrani. He stared—at her. "What have you done?" His voice was a whisper.

Teela, however, laughed. It was a wild, low sound. "This is *not* the first time I have come to the heart of the green. I have come as harmoniste; I have worn the blood of the green. I have survived—and my presence changed *nothing*."

"No, An'Teela. It is neither the first nor the second time. It is, at last, the third. Warden, we will hold the wards. You must ask Lord Kaylin to bespeak the water."

Kaylin's eyes widened; she was certain her brows had disappeared permanently into her hairline. "There's no water here."

The eagle said, "No. That is why you must bespeak it, Chosen."

Teela lifted a hand to the bridge of her nose.

Kaylin exhaled and—as quietly as she could—said, "At least you're not bored."

"You have almost singlehandedly convinced me that boredom is not the worst of all possible fates."

"Why is the water necessary? It wasn't before. If I understand what's happened here, you've held the recitations for, oh, *centuries* without water."

They waited for her to make her point. As she felt she'd pretty much made it, she surrendered. "I have no idea how to, as you put it, bespeak the water."

"You have spoken to the water."

"I've spoken to the water in the courtyard because it happened to *be there*." She dropped her hand into the curved, smooth stone basin. "You'll notice the big difference?"

"If you wish to locate the Lady, you will not hear the answer if it is given. You must wake the water, Chosen."

The Lord of the West March met Lord Barian's gaze. When he turned to Kaylin, she saw no rescue from either quarter; she saw hope, and it was painful. "If the dreams of Alsanis believe you are capable of this, there must be a reason for it."

"I'm only barely able to light a candle. I— If I could summon water, I might—*might*—be able to do as they ask, but I won't be able to do that for years. If ever." She exhaled. "If Evarrim summons water, I might be able to speak with the elemental. It happened with the fire he summoned."

"Lord Evarrim is gravely injured." Lirienne had quietly joined them. "Before you ask, there was only one other who could do what you require."

"Iberrienne."

"Indeed."

For obvious reasons, that wasn't going to cut it. Kaylin turned to the dreams of Alsanis, who were watching her with unflagging intensity. She wondered if they ever blinked. "Activate the wards." She frowned, and added, "You *can* activate the wards without the waters, right?"

"Yes, Chosen."

"Then activate them, and we'll see where we go from there."

Teela's arms were tightly folded across her chest, a posture she almost never adopted, at least at work. Her eyes were—no surprise—blue. She stood at Kaylin's side, although she watched as the eagles finally left their Barrani perches. They headed toward the two trees that Kaylin privately thought of as firewood. They landed on the dry, leafless branches and looked down at the gathered Barrani.

And then, of course, they began to sing.

The small dragon perked up, sat up, and opened his mouth as if to join them; he was far too close to Kaylin's ear. "If you want to sing, do it in the sky. I apparently need my hearing. It's a job requirement."

He bit her ear, but surprised her by pushing off her shoulder; he took to the air above the empty basin, and hovered there. The basin was between the two trees. It was, she thought, exactly in the center.

She watched, glancing between the two eagles and their respective perches. She couldn't see wards or runes, but none of the Barrani appeared too concerned with their absence. As she continued to wait, she discovered why: the trees themselves began to glow. The light was a faint gray—at least to start—and it spread from the eagles to the branches they inhabited. But as it spread from the first branch to the trunk, it grew in brilliance and in color, until the whole of the tree was glowing.

It was a golden glow that was familiar to Kaylin; it was one of the colors her marks took on at unpredictable times.

She glanced at Teela; Teela didn't look even vaguely surprised; nor did she look worried. "Are all of the wards trees?"

"No, but many of them are. Would I be wasting breath if I counseled caution?"

Kaylin nodded absently as she walked toward a tree. The Barrani made way for her, which was unusual enough that she should have been surprised. But she was focused on the problem at hand. She saw no runes and no writing anywhere around the trunk of the tree; nor did they become visible when she craned her head up.

She examined the second tree in the same way, with the same results. The small dragon squawked at her from above, which was a small improvement over the ear-biting, if she ignored the large Barrani audience.

"Lord Barian, are these wards now considered active?"

"They are not wards in the modern sense of the word," he replied.

"Meaning?"

"They allow the green to exist in a stable state. Without the wards, crossing the green is a difficult task; it is like—and unlike—the journey through the portal paths."

"But we were here."

"The dreams of Alsanis led us here."

"So—they're not like door wards in any way?"

"No."

"Good." Kaylin reached out her left arm and placed her left palm very firmly on the nearest section of trunk.

Nothing happened. Her palm felt warm—not hot, and not itchy—but warm. She looked up, peering into the crowd, and met Teela's steady, blue gaze. It got bluer. In Aerian, Kaylin said, "I don't think we'll find the Consort in time, Teela. I don't understand the green. I don't understand the *regalia*. I don't understand what happened the day you were brought here with eleven other children.

"But I get that they mean for you to be involved, even if you're not the Teller or the harmoniste. We don't figure this out, we don't find her. I know you can survive a lot longer than I can without food—and without heat or air, as well—but a lot longer is not all that significant."

In Aerian, Teela replied. "The green doesn't react to me the way it reacts to anyone else here."

"Join the club."

Teela's lips twitched. "If you have cause to regret this, you're not blaming me."

"Not for that, no." Kaylin's frown was a very familiar expression in the office. "But I have to ask you: Are you getting paid for this leave of absence?"

Teela headed toward the far tree without answering the question.

That was well-done, kyuthe.

What was?

Not one man here—or woman—could achieve what you have just achieved. Please tell me that it was not done in ignorance.

Kaylin said nothing. She felt Lord Lirienne's amusement, but it was slight; beneath it, worry, anger, and very real fear made ready to swallow it whole. He didn't attempt to hide these things from her; he hid them from his kin because he was Lord of the West March.

Kaylin placed her palm against the tree bark for a second time. She did so while facing the other tree. Teela approached it without obvious hesitation, and when she was standing in pretty much the same position that Kaylin was, she nodded. Lifting her arm—her right arm—she placed her palm firmly against the tree's trunk, as well.

Nothing happened.

Nothing happened until the small dragon suddenly shrieked, folded his wings, and dropped in a dead man's dive toward the center of a solid stone basin. Kaylin froze, her eyes rounding, her jaw dropping; she forgot to breathe.

"Kitling!"

Kaylin looked up; she saw Teela's eyes; the color unmistakable even at this distance: they were gold.

The small dragon didn't strike the stone basin and splat against it. He passed *through* it. He passed through it as if it were liquid. She pulled her hand from the tree and ran for the basin, lifting the skirts of her dress, although the dress had never impeded movement.

She stopped herself by running into the basin's lip.

"Kaylin."

She looked up. She looked up to see Teela—and only Teela. Every other person in the clearing had disappeared. Teela casually detached herself from the tree and headed toward Kaylin.

"Can you see anyone else?" Kaylin asked her as she drew close.

"Besides you?" Teela spoke Elantran.

"Besides me."

"No."

"Well, at least we're on the same page."

"We probably won't be if you aren't more careful. Are you trying to bash your face in?"

"What? No. I'm trying to see where the dragon went."

"I'm sure he'll find us."

"Oh? How?"

"He's enough of a pain it might be convenient if he stayed away. It's the way my luck has generally worked."

Kaylin snorted. She looked at the clearing. The heart of the green hadn't appreciably changed; it was still definitively not-green. The trees, however, were no longer glowing.

Lirienne? Nightshade?

Silence.

"I don't suppose there are any convenient doors?"

"Not that I can see," Teela replied. She stretched her arms and yawned; she looked incredibly feline. "But we might as well start looking. My guess is that this is as much of an invitation as we're going to get. You are going to explain what the dreams said, right?"

"Which part?"

"The part about bleeding. Or rather, the 'bleeding now.'"

"Oh, that part." Kaylin winced. "When we hit the tunnels to escape the attackers, we came to a giant, underground trunk. I mean, tree trunk. With roots the size of a small building. Did you see that when you were there?"

Teela was dead silent. It was the wrong silence, but with Teela, it often was. "What makes you think that I've been in those tunnels?"

"Well, Serian said...something. I don't know. I got the impression that everyone in the West March had seen them."

"The inferences you draw from a few words would cause most people to shut up forever. Not every citizen of the West March has had cause to seek the judgment of the green. It is not a guarantee of survival, and only when they face certain death—or worse—will they surrender to it."

"And you—"

"No. I have—I had—my own reasons. This is the first time since the end of my childhood that I have willingly surrendered anything to the green."

"Why?"

"Because you're an idiot," she replied. "I should have

known. The moment Nightshade attempted to make his deal, I should have known."

"I don't think Nightshade—"

"Don't think he what? You don't think he planned this? You don't think he manipulated you into the position you now hold?"

"Teela—how could he? The green chooses. He couldn't have known that the green would choose me. He couldn't have known that you'd be here. He certainly couldn't have guessed that the Consort would choose *this* bloody recitation to visit."

"He knew some part of what Iberrienne intended."

"I don't think *Iberrienne* understood what Iberrienne intended." Kaylin bit her lip. "But it's all tied up in the past, isn't it? Iberrienne lost someone here. I thought—I thought Iberrienne was younger. He's not, is he? He lost someone. Nightshade lost someone. You lost—"

"Yes." Teela started to pace. She disguised this by pacing in a straight line; Kaylin fell in beside her. Their stride and the even, slow fall of their steps were pure groundhawk.

"How long were you with them?"

"Pardon?"

"I thought—I thought you were all chosen and brought here together."

"We were."

"But you weren't just thrown together before you came."

"No." Teela exhaled. "Kitling, you don't like to talk about your past much. You spent years of your life not talking about it."

Kaylin nodded.

"We knew that your mother had died, that you had grown up in Nightshade. We didn't know every detail of your life between the time your mother died to the time you became our mascot."

"No."

"We don't know it all now."

"Teela—"

"And we don't ask, because it doesn't matter to us. Can you not do the same?"

They walked what would have been a city block before Kaylin replied. "I would—"

"That's not a yes."

"I would, Teela—but I think it does matter. It doesn't matter to *me*. You're Teela. You're always going to be the person who broke my first chair—"

"It was a shoddy piece of furniture."

"You broke my first lock, too."

"I replaced that."

"And the bed?"

"I only broke the slats." Teela glanced at Kaylin, and added, "But I take your point."

"I think the green is worried about you."

Teela said nothing.

"The Hallionne, too. At least the ones who talked to me." She hesitated. She thought, now, that part of the reason she'd been given the role of harmoniste—and the dress that went with it—was not her role as Chosen, but her friendship with Teela. "I don't know what you understand. If you told me that you understood what the green intended—and why— I'd leave it alone. I would."

Teela gave her a look that defined the word *skeptical*. "I'll allow that you'd *try*." She stopped walking. "And to be fair, I don't understand it myself."

"Do you want to?"

"You're remarkably perceptive today." Teela exhaled sharply. "I don't spend a lot of time thinking about the past—because for me, the minute I start, it's *not* the past. It's the disadvantage of immortal memory. None of the edges are dulled—and none of the pain. We hold long grudges," she added. "Your kin can't. What you think of as a grudge might last a year. Or six months. Or even a decade. That is not a long grudge for the Barrani.

"It takes effort to be here, kitling. It takes effort to see the West March as it is now, and not to walk it as it was then. Every memory of then leads to one place." She smiled. It was not a happy expression. "We spent more than a decade together. We lived and trained together. We were young. Even the Barrani are young at one point—but youth is such a tiny fraction of our lives. We dreamed," she added. "We dreamed of being heroes. Of saving our people. Of defeating the Dragon flights. We dreamed that we would one day be called upon to wield our people's legendary weapons.

"And we knew that we had been chosen. Each and every one of us. We fancied ourselves the best and the brightest of our kind. We were meant to be powers, Kaylin."

Kaylin understood what power meant to the Barrani. She said nothing.

"I could tell you their names. I can remember what they looked like, and when. We were…more open. Less cautious. Youth often is." Her smile deepened. "My childhood was not like yours. I understand that in many ways, I lacked the fears that drove your mother, and you, in the fiefs. I had food. I had shelter. I had the relative safety of my lineage. We all did.

"Perhaps because of that, we could dream in ways you didn't. I don't know. But we promised that we would thrive, Kaylin. That we would survive. That we would hold true to our beginnings when the wars were at last ended—we would not fall upon each other. We would not war against each other, not even in the name of our kin." She shook her head. "Such are the follies of childhood. I do not know if we would have held true to those vows.

"I was not the leader of our group. That was Sedarias. She was everything that neither I nor the Consort can be—even when young. She was cool, collected, perfect; her poise was terrifying. She could, with very little effort, pass for adult; of the twelve of us, she garnered the most praise. She understood politics, and the undercurrents of both power and weakness; she understood desire and how to manipulate it. She understood standing, status. I would say that compared to most of the mortals I've met, any Barrani child would be considered sophisticated—but even among our kin, there are standouts.

"But it was Sedarias who suggested the vow; Sedarias who first made it. Perhaps she meant to bind us to her; perhaps it would have worked over the centuries. I don't know. But she made the vow, and then asked that we respond in kind. She told us that she believed holding true to that vow was simply a matter of will, of power, of intent.

"We were, of course, the children of the powerful. We understood what was intended for us. But Sedarias—and Eddorian—were suspicious."

"Not you?"

Teela laughed. Or tried. "No. I told you—I wanted it. I wanted to be worthy of my father's regard and respect. I wanted to be what he wanted. But—I was young. I *liked* the vow, kitling. I liked the idea of forging unbreakable bonds with the only peers, the only friends, I had."

Kaylin missed a step. Given that the ground was totally flat, and mostly dirt, she had no excuse, and Teela noticed immediately.

"What connection have you just made?"

"It's just…I can't imagine even Barrani children thinking that promises could be unbreakable."

"No."

"Teela—"

There was so much pain beneath the surface of Teela's oddly gentle smile. "No, kitling. Not even the children we were could believe in a simple, spoken vow."

"Teela—what did you do?"

"Show me your hand."

Kaylin lifted her left hand and opened it for Teela's inspection.

Teela said, "Mandoran. We called him Manny; he mostly hated it."

"You can...read...the name."

"Yes, kitling."

"But—but—"

"Yes. In theory, it means they could read mine." She lifted her face to the skies, to the sunlight that fell from no sun. "But only if it had meaning to them. They are not what they were. I call them, Kaylin. I called them then. They did not hear me. They can't speak the name I gave them." She reached out and touched Kaylin's open palm. "And now, I think I understand why." She exhaled again and looked at the landscape. There was a lot of dirt, and very, very little in the way of foliage; even the dead, standing trees were absent. "This is not getting us anywhere."

"What happened when you were chosen as harmoniste?"

Teela stared into the vast and empty nothing for a long moment. She turned back in the direction they'd come from—if it was the same direction. They'd walked some distance, but even so, the trees should have been visible. They weren't, of course. At this particular moment, Kaylin didn't care.

"I had avoided the West March; I had avoided the green. It was the locus of so many of my losses. I lost my childhood, my friends, and the mother whose love I had always trusted.

I lost my father in a different way. We are not—any of us—adept at facing the first loss.

"My father did not trust me—but that is as it should be, in the end. Most of the Lords you will meet who are the heads of their lines became so only after the deaths of their parents. Many of those deaths occurred during the Dragon wars—but some were suspicious, regardless. And that, too, is an accepted part of succession.

"It is not accepted among your kind; when it is done, it is hidden, kitling. It is considered both shameful and a crime. But you have that luxury—your parents *will* die. They will age into their dotage. They will loosen their grip on the reins of power because they have no choice. Were you all to live forever? I do not believe that you would be so very different from my people."

"Less beautiful, less strong, and less graceful."

"Of course. I did not care that my father did not trust me," she added. "I considered it wisdom. But I could not afford the suspicion of the other Lords. And so, in time, I took the risk of returning to the West March, to face the past and all its barbs and losses, and to prove that I was stronger than my pain." She walked more quickly, and Kaylin had to work to keep up.

"And I did."

"What was the story?"

"The story?"

"You were harmoniste."

Teela nodded.

"You were—I'm—supposed to take the strands of story from the Teller."

"Yes."

"There was a Teller."

"Yes. You don't get *a* story, kitling. You get disparate parts of a thousand stories. You get fragments, you get names and places and small items—it's like having a hail of rocks thrown in your direction. You have to survive the hits; you have to catch *enough* of the rocks that you can build something from them. While being hit. It's not trivial. I was arrogant," she added. "I was full of defiance, rage, loss. I don't know if that affected what I could hear or see; I don't know if that affected the pieces I chose, the direction I took.

"But I survived, kitling. I was not transformed; nor, to my eye, were any of the very few participants that year." This was said with a much sharper smile.

"Teela—what did you do?"

"I listened. I listened, I watched. I wanted to hear their names again. Their names were lost here. Everything about them was. I wanted to hear them call mine again. Just that."

"But Terrano recognized you."

"Yes."

"He was on the road. He was with the Ferals."

"Yes, Kaylin. Yes. He was there, and he was everything I remembered. Everything—but I could not reach him. And he couldn't reach me. He had memories. But not—not what we promised. Not what we gave each other." She frowned. "I think," she said softly, "that that's where we need to go." She pointed.

Kaylin's eyes were not Barrani eyes. She squinted. But she couldn't make out what Teela could. Not until they had walked at least another mile.

She did stop, then. It was, to her eye, a pit.

CHAPTER 18

"What," Teela said, when Kaylin began to move again, "do you recognize?"

"It's probably nothing," Kaylin replied.

"I cannot believe that you expect *me* to bare my figurative soul when you cannot even bring yourself to answer the most obvious of questions. If you are going to demur, at least learn to lie with some competence; give me the option of feeling less insulted." She batted the top of Kaylin's head.

"Sorry. I don't want to think about it because I'm hoping I'm dead wrong."

"And what are the odds against that?"

"Generally pretty high. Just—not here."

"Exactly. What do you recognize?"

"When I woke the Consort the first time—after she absorbed the nightmares—I spent a lot of time floating around a sky full of stupid words. I mean, they were in theory my words because they're all over my skin—but you know, larger and floating in the sky. I knew I had to choose one mark."

"Knowing you, I'm surprised you managed to do it."

Kaylin reddened. "I took two."

"Ah. That sounds more realistic."

"When I had them, the small dragon kind of dived. Toward a pit. It looked small. It wasn't. It was huge. It was—" She frowned. "I think, if you could take the sides of the pit and flatten them, they'd be much larger than Elantra."

"So you're saying this pit is a lot farther away than it looks."

"I'm saying I really, really, really don't want this pit and that one to be the same, because I don't have wings in reality, and I can't fly."

"This is not reality, in case you were wondering. It is— think of it as the inside of a Hallionne's heart. I believe you did spend some time at the heart of Bertolle. You will find, if it is necessary, that you will either be able to fly, or *I* will." She frowned. "What else are you not telling me?"

"The pit is where I saw them," Kaylin whispered.

Teela did not pretend to misunderstand her.

"I think—I'm *sure*—I know who Sedarias was. And this isn't really getting us to water—" Kaylin fell silent.

"Let me guess," Teela said. "There was a fountain there."

Kaylin nodded. "The Consort was by the fountain. She was—she was singing to it, the way she sang to Kariastos and Bertolle and Orbaranne." She bit her lip and stopped moving.

"Kitling—"

"I saw you there. You were there. But—you were made of ice, where they were made of glass—and Teela—"

"Don't feel compelled to share the rest; I no longer require it."

"What I don't understand is, what was Iberrienne trying to

do to Orbaranne? I don't think he meant to just destroy her— or rather, he wanted something from the process."

"That is not the only thing you don't understand."

"Well, no. But—if Iberrienne was somehow doing it because of Eddorian, he was doing what the lost children want. What do they want, Teela?"

"This may come as a surprise to you, but I don't know. They don't want what I want, because, Kaylin, I *have* the name I was born for."

"It's got to be something to do with names. With True Words. I don't get it." Kaylin ground her teeth.

"You are such a Hawk." It was said with amusement, affection, and a touch of frustration.

Teela slid an arm around Kaylin's shoulders and began to drag her toward the distant pit. It made Kaylin feel young again, but without the resentment and the insecurity. Her feet left a short trail in the dirt.

The pit was not a cavernous, flattened, cylindrical city— which was both a relief and a disappointment. It was much larger than it had looked at a distance, but it wasn't larger across than the city in which Kaylin made her living. It was, on the other hand, pretty bloody dark, and as it had no architectural enhancements that Kaylin could see; there weren't convenient stairs leading down.

"Is this where we're supposed to be, do you think?"

Teela gave her A Look.

"Sorry." She walked to the edge of the pit.

"You'll be careful, right?" Teela said, joining her. Neither of the two Hawks were particularly height sensitive; they could hug the edge of the pit in relative safety.

"I'm always careful."

"I cannot believe the things you can say with a perfectly straight face. That *was* serious, wasn't it?"

Short of jumping, there didn't seem to be a way down, and neither of the Hawks carried rope. "You know—if this is the green's attempt to have a conversation, I wish it'd just use words, like the rest of us."

"You really, really don't," was Teela's grim reply. "Think before you speak."

Kaylin glanced at the sky. "Please tell me those are not clouds."

"I could, but you frequently complain when you think I'm lying."

"Did they just roll in when I said—"

"You know, kitling, you've seen a lot of the noncorporeal world. You've walked the outlands. You've walked the between. You've seen the heart of the Hallionne. Given the number of years you can actually expect to live—on average, and ignoring your total lack of basic caution—you've seen more than many of the Barrani who call the Vale home.

"Why do you still *expect* things to make sense?"

The storm clouds did not shed rain. They did shed a lot of lightning, and the resultant thunder was almost a physical sensation, it was so damn loud.

Lightning struck the ground ten yards in front of Teela.

"Things are going to get ugly," Teela said without looking back at Kaylin, who came to stand beside her.

"Why?"

"Can you not see them?"

Kaylin squinted as lightning changed the color of the sky. "See what?"

"The nightmares," she replied. "The nightmares of Alsanis."

★ ★ ★

The thing Kaylin hated most about Hallionne space or Tower space was this: people saw different things. They walked in different versions of reality. What Teela saw, Kaylin couldn't see. Lightning, yes. Clouds. Thunder. But not the nightmares. She'd seen what the nightmares did to the Consort, and she had no doubt at all that they could do the same—or worse—to Teela.

"How many?"

"Maybe a dozen," Teela replied, her face still turned toward the sky. "They're moving so quickly it's hard to count them."

"Are they heading this way?"

The Barrani Hawk's smile was grim. Grim and resigned. "Yes."

Kaylin closed her eyes. She meant to open them, but the moment her eyes were closed, the lightning became insignificant, as did the pit; it was the thunder she heard. And the thunder had a voice. It spoke words. They weren't words that she understood, not immediately—but she could pick out the rumble of deeply roared syllables.

The dreams of Alsanis spoke what Kaylin heard as Elantran. Not that many of their words made solid sense—but they could speak. They had never spoken like this. The thunder's voice was a roar of pain. Of pain, of anger, of loss, of denial. It wasn't one voice; it was many.

Many, she thought. The nightmares of Alsanis had never spoken aloud, not in a way that Kaylin could hear. "Teela!"

"I'm here."

"Can you hear them? Can you hear what they're saying?"

Silence. Well, on Teela's part; the thunder didn't stop.

"Yes, kitling."

"Do you understand it?"

"Yes."

Kaylin's eyes flew open. Teela had lifted her hands to the sky. Kaylin grabbed the left one and yanked it down to her side, which took real effort; mortal strength was not a match for Barrani strength—not when the Barrani was determined. "What are you doing?"

Teela looked down at Kaylin, and Kaylin saw that her eyes were now a deep purple, tinged with the blue that spoke of either anger or fear. "What I should have done, kitling. What I should have done years ago."

"This is *not* what you should have done!"

"I tried. As harmoniste, I tried to call their names. I tried to insert them into the story I was given."

"What story?" Kaylin shouted. "What story were you given?"

"Does it matter? I couldn't hold the whole of it. I could only barely choose something that made sense. Some path out of the chaos. But what I *wanted* was to tell the story of the lost. To call them *back,* somehow."

Kaylin tried to yank Teela's right arm down. She was now afraid because she still couldn't see the nightmares. She could hear the thunder's voice, but she was no longer certain that the thunder and the nightmares were one.

"I tried, kitling. But the truth is, I never left this place."

"Yes, you *did*. You left it, you left it *whole,* you came back to Elantra. You came to the Hawks, Teela—you came—"

"To you?"

"To me."

Teela's eyes were still purple. She looked gaunt. And young, Kaylin thought. She looked young. Teela lifted her arms again. "What you did for the Consort, you cannot do for me. You cannot see what I see, not here."

"Let me try!"

Teela shook her head. "You will, kitling. You are harmoniste. Nightshade is Teller. Perhaps you will hear what I couldn't hear. Perhaps your mortality will allow you to see clearly what I could not see." She staggered; her hands clenched in fists.

Kaylin placed one hand on the back of Teela's neck. At any other time, she wouldn't have dared; Teela, like the rest of the Barrani, had a loathing of healers that skirted the edge of murderous rage. What she couldn't see, she couldn't feel—but she hadn't attempted to heal the Consort when the nightmares had landed.

Teela staggered again.

"Teela! *Teela!*"

"I wanted to give them peace. I wanted to save some part of them. I wanted—" Teela shook her head, staggering again, her arms falling slowly, as if she could no longer bear their weight. "Remember this, kitling: there is no way back. There is no way out but through."

"This isn't the time for stupid philosophy—Teela!"

Teela shuddered, and Kaylin knew that she would not stop. The nightmares that Kaylin couldn't see were the only thing that mattered here.

"No," Teela said, her voice a whisper. "But it's me, kitling, or it's you. The nightmares of the Hallionne visit someone when they choose to fly."

The marks on Kaylin's arms were gray and flat. Nothing about this storm brought them to life. Nothing about Kaylin's growing desperation did, either. When Teela fell to her knees, Kaylin dropped to the ground beside her, hand still attached to the back of her neck. But there was nothing physically wrong with Teela; nothing that could be healed.

Kaylin had always thought—had always believed—that if she had been there, if she had been at her home the night of the worst loss she had ever endured, she could have *done something*. Something. Anything. But there was nothing she could do here. Whatever it was that attacked Teela, she couldn't see it, couldn't fight it. She tried. She tried to place the backs of her hands over Teela's shuddering palms; she tried to catch the nightmares before they touched her.

But she couldn't. They didn't touch her. They didn't suddenly become visible, and they didn't become the eagles the Barrani called dreams. She saw Teela's face lose all color; only her eyes retained any—and it was purple, the color that Kaylin had almost never seen. There was no green in them; nothing that spoke of happiness or peace.

Kaylin opened her eyes. She opened her eyes to the gray-green sky and the pit, and she understood that the pit itself had taken the rough shape and outline of a word—a word whose elements had somehow been obliterated, but in which the ground had retained a sense of what had once occupied it.

She caught Teela in her arms, tightened them.

"What have I told you about crying?" Teela whispered.

Kaylin told her what she could, in Leontine. "I don't *care* about the green. I don't care about Alsanis, either. I don't care about the lost children—I'm sorry, I *don't*. I care about you." She sucked in air that felt heavy and electric—and dry. "We're somehow in Alsanis, aren't we? Somehow? We're attached to the Hallionne.

"And this is *not* where we belong."

"Kitling—"

Kaylin raised both her face and her voice, and she shouted into and above the thunder. "We ask for and accept the judgment of the green!"

The ground fell out from beneath her. She tightened her arms around Teela and held on for all she was worth.

Really, as drops went, it wasn't terrible. But holding on to someone who was, for all intents and purposes, deadweight made negotiating a safe landing impossible.

"You," Teela said—because she was still conscious, some-how, "are an idiot."

"Whatever." Kaylin was afraid, for one long moment, to let go.

"Oh, I'm here," Teela told her grimly. "I'm glad you think that breathing is optional."

Kaylin let go. Her arms, however, had stiffened, and her hands were shaking as she tried to pry her fingers off Teela.

"You cannot leave well enough alone, can you?"

"It wasn't bloody well enough, okay?" Kaylin got to her feet. She was shaking, and she thought she might never stop. Teela's color hadn't improved any. "How many?"

"Pardon?"

"How many did you absorb?"

"I wasn't counting."

"Don't give me that look. If you want to commit suicide, you're going to have to do it when I'm not standing right be-hind you. Here." She put an arm around Teela's back, shoving herself under the Barrani's left arm and levering them both off the ground. "I don't know how long the path from here is, but we need to walk it. If we have to walk it in the dark, fine. We'll do that."

"Remind me to strangle Nightshade if we somehow man-age to survive this." Light flared in the tunnel. It was a fa-miliar tunnel, of rough rock, low ceilings, and unpredictable widths. "You're certain that your presence here—so soon after you got ejected—is not going to anger the green?"

"No."

"Do you understand the reason such an escape is so sel-dom used?"

"Yes."

"Then—"

"Are we dead?"

"Kitling."

"Are you?"

"Demonstrably not."

"Then we'll deal. One step at a time." She wanted to scream at Teela. Or swear. She contented herself with a few Leontine phrases, but her heart wasn't in them and they sounded pathetic, even to her ears.

"You're shaking."

Kaylin said, "So are you."

Teela chuckled. "We make quite the pair, don't we?"

Kaylin didn't reply.

The tunnels were the tunnels that Kaylin remembered, which was good. The first branch, on the other hand, reminded her that this was like a coin toss on which your whole life depended—which was bad.

"No, I don't know which way to go," Kaylin said, before Teela could insert a sarcastic comment. "Save your breath." She meant it, too. Teela's breathing was labored. Teela, who could sprint across the damn city and back without breaking a sweat. "If you want a say, stay awake."

"You understand that we're judged in entirely different ways by the green, don't you?"

"Yes."

"You may accept the green's judgment. You may leave. What if the green doesn't choose to release me?"

"I'm not leaving without you."

Teela laughed. "I wish you could have met them," she whispered.

"Given Barrani attitudes toward mortals at the time, I'm not sure it would have worked out well—for me."

"There is that. But I think you would have liked them. Well, maybe not Sedarias, not immediately." She closed her eyes. Opened them, but not all the way. "Allaron would have liked you. He liked small, helpless creatures. Of all of the candidates, he was the most inexplicable."

"What do you mean?" She knew, in cases like this, it was important to keep a person talking.

"Most of my kin are of a height, as you've complained about on any number of occasions. We are of a height, of a general build, our weight is roughly the same. There is far less variance among my kin than there is among yours."

"He was really tall, right?"

"Yes."

Kaylin nodded. "I think he was the second statue. But the thing about the statues—to me—is that they all looked very individual. Most of the Barrani look the same, at least on the surface. It's like you're twins, except, you know, more numerous."

"Allaron was large. He was stronger than most of the children his age. He was capable of astonishing feats of strength—but he was often quiet. Of the twelve of us, he was the most reticent. He would have liked you. He wouldn't even have complained much. You don't see our young," she added. "The children are very seldom raised in the city; they are kept away from the High Court until they are of an age where they might survive it."

"You were—"

"Yes. I was raised at Court. My father was a very powerful man; not for my safety would he deny himself the strategic arrangement of his place at Court. I spent some time in the West March with my mother, and he allowed it—at the beginning.

"But not at the end. He distrusted the Vale; he found the people of the West March rustic. None of us, once the plans were set in motion, were allowed to spend our childhoods in the more traditional environments. We were meant to excel in all things. We began our training early, and we were kept at it.

"Allaron was, as I said, strong. But all of his ferocity was in appearance. My father despised him."

"His own father?"

"His own father hoped that exposure to the rest of us would toughen his son up. I believe that's how mortals would express it." Teela closed her eyes again, and this time, the light that made the path navigable faltered. "Which way?"

"Right."

"The other right?"

Kaylin cursed. "Fine, left, then."

"Terrano had a sense of humor that you might have appreciated. He was—what is the Elantran word again? *Clown?*"

"*A* clown, but yes."

"He laughed a lot. He found things constantly delightful or amusing. Sedarias found Terrano very difficult to deal with—she had less of a sense of humor than Tiamaris."

"Did he have the typical Barrani sense of humor?"

"He had not yet developed the more refined edges, but he was Barrani."

"What did Terrano say to you?"

"They regret leaving me behind. It confused them, I think. They were changed. I was not. They felt that they had betrayed me, in some fashion, by abandoning me." She grimaced. "And I felt that I had done the same."

"You didn't—"

"My mother died in the greenheart. My father and his kin killed so many there." She closed her eyes again, and this time, it took her a lot longer to open them. "Blood is forbidden in the heart of the green."

Kaylin nodded.

"Do you understand why?"

"No, but I can make an educated guess."

Teela had the strength to snort, although her breathing continued to be labored. "The reason it's forbidden is that the will of the dying, expressed through blood, has power in the green. It isn't about a random life—it's about your *own* life. People who are unwilling sacrifices don't generally have the welfare of the green or its people at heart."

"Do I want to know how that was learned?"

"Probably not."

"Your mother died—"

"Yes. My mother, who had the blood of the Wardens in her veins. My mother, who could speak with Alsanis, who was welcomed—always—into his heart. She bled to death on the green. She asked for only one thing, kitling. Only one. That I be preserved. That I be unchanged, untransformed; that I remained *myself*.

"She was not the only person who died that day. The will of the others was harder, harsher; they wanted to preserve the green against the depredations of outsiders and people who did not live in—and of—it."

"How do you know?"

"I heard their dying thoughts. I heard their dying wishes. I heard the fear they felt—for us—when we were taken to the greenheart. I heard the hope that the recitation would pass without altering us; we were too young, too unformed. The Vale had no ambitions for us.

"And I heard our parents. We all did. I heard what they wanted. I heard what they desired. I heard their contempt for everything in the green except its power.

"We knew, by that point," she added. Her eyes were closed. Kaylin was afraid she wouldn't open them again. "We knew what the Warden and the Guardian feared. We knew that we were an experiment. If it was successful, we would, of course, be coveted and valued. We were not, in any way, valuable in and of ourselves. They didn't see us; they saw their own desires."

"Had we been older," she continued, "had we been, in truth, adults, this would not have surprised us. It wouldn't have wounded in the way that it did. Even the Barrani have the naive hope that mortal children know. We do not know it in exactly the same way, but when young, we believe in the promise of…affection. We learn.

"Just as you learn. You don't have to live with the truth for as long."

"Did you know?" Kaylin asked, before she could shut her mouth.

"Did I know what?"

"Did you know that your friends would kill every member of the High Court they could get their hands on before the Hallionne shut them in?"

After a long, labored pause, Teela said, "Yes."

CHAPTER 19

Kaylin didn't ask if Teela had tried to stop them, because she knew, as the lights once again flickered and dimmed, what the answer was. She had come to a junction that was not like the rest, and she wanted to shake Teela awake; the Barrani Hawk was shivering. She was cold to the touch. Kaylin had never seen Teela sick before; she'd never seen her with an injury that slowed her down at all. But she knew, from her experience in both Moran's infirmary and Red's morgue, that things were bad.

Things were bad and there was no chance of better if they couldn't get out of these tunnels. She had nothing to give Teela that would add any warmth; she briefly considered the harmoniste dress, but decided against removing it. If the green wasn't pissed off yet, she didn't want to tip the balance. She had to keep Teela moving.

There were three paths. One to the right, one to the left, and one that lead up. Kaylin was not at all certain that up was the direction she wanted. It was, however, the first time she had seen such a path.

There were stairs. They were worn in the middle, and shallow. The walls were rough, but they were definitely walls. Teela's light was now sporadic. Kaylin stopped for a moment and drew a heavy, gold pendant from the folds of her dress.

"What are you doing?" Teela asked. She hadn't opened her eyes.

"I'm hoping for light," Kaylin replied.

"You're going to try to invoke a *Dragon's* pendant in the *green?*"

"Teela—I need some light. There are no windows here, and no torches or stones; if the stairs change, if the walls drop away, we're not going to make it." She lowered her voice; the echoes were rebounding off the walls. "You can't keep the light up. Not now. I probably shouldn't have asked." If she made it back to the city, she intended to dedicate herself to Sanabalis's lessons. Light wasn't a hard spell. Any mage of Kaylin's acquaintance could cast it.

And why couldn't she?

She could blame Sanabalis. The urge to do so was strong. But it wasn't the truth. She distrusted mages. Every Hawk did, even Teela, who pretty much was one. Kaylin was a Hawk. She was accepted as a Hawk—and that had taken years. She'd worked so hard to fit in. To be taken seriously. She didn't want to lose that. She didn't want to *be* a mage in the eyes of the Hawks. She didn't want to be an outsider.

In order to remain in the Hawks, she'd been ordered to take magic lessons. So she'd taken them. She'd worked hard to do what Sanabalis told her to do—but not more. She hadn't asked questions, except the ones wrapped in derision or frustration. She hadn't tried to learn *more*. She'd told herself that it was pointless, useless; if the Hawks needed a mage, it gave the Imperial Order something *useful* to do.

And of course, she needed one now, and the Imperial Order was barely on the same continent. The marks on her arms—the ones that sometimes gave her access to a visceral and almost uncontrolled magic—were flat, dark gray. She couldn't use them when they were like this, and she didn't know *how* to activate them.

Kaylin wasn't the best of students, but she wasn't the worst, either, and she could have done much better than she had. She knew it.

"The Hallionne knew I had the medallion," Kaylin told Teela. "They never made me leave it behind, and they did let me in."

"This isn't a Hallionne. This is the heart of the West March. These are the lands that have never fallen to Dragons—or any other enemies—for all of our long history."

"Yes, I understand that," Kaylin replied, because she did. "But I don't think the Hallionne or the green really care about the Dragons. Or the wars. Not the way the Barrani and the Dragons do. I don't think they care about *me,* and the mark of Dragon ownership—me being the owned—is probably irrelevant to both."

"You're betting on it."

"Yes. This one's a bet I'm willing to make. Now shut up, you're distracting me."

"That was the point." Teela fell silent as Kaylin took the medallion in her free hand. It was warm to the touch—but it would be, given that it had spent most of its time against her skin. She didn't know if there was a word for light, if light itself had a name. She'd learned only the name of fire. But the elemental fire—even Evarrim's—had failed to burn her.

Sanabalis's medallion amplified her own meager power. She

had used it only once before, in a much more obvious emergency. And a much less terrifying one, in the end. Monsters were simple: they either killed you or they didn't.

Loss? It lasted forever. She didn't intend to let go of Teela while Teela was still breathing, because this was all she had. She didn't have immortal, perfect memory. She couldn't go back.

She searched that imperfect memory for the name of fire, for the now of it, and it came to her in grudging syllables. They were figuratively oiled; they slid from her grasp before she could lock them in place, avoiding her mental touch, rearranging themselves as if to hide. All names were like this. All. Even Ynpharion's.

But if Kaylin had been a name, she'd've probably done the same thing. She didn't. She didn't have eternity, either—but right now, she didn't need it. What she needed was light. What Teela needed was warmth.

And fire answered her call.

It came not as a candle flame, nor as bonfire; it took, instead, the form and shape of a man. His features were chiseled in lambent, orange-gold, his hair was like Barrani hair, each strand a hazy glow. He wore robes of flame, although they were the color of his skin. But it was his eyes that caught and held her attention: they were black, but hints of opalescent color caught light, shimmering and winking out of existence as if they were faint stars.

Kaylin.

Teela pried her eyes open. She exhaled and said something in Leontine. It was quiet enough Kaylin only caught half of it.

Kaylin, however, sagged in relief.

Why are you here? You are not in the Keeper's garden.

"You knew that. I spoke to you in the outlands."

The fire regarded her for a long moment.

"Do you know where we are? We need to find a way out." She glanced at Teela, who'd managed to keep her eyes open, even if they were slits. "Do you know this place?"

Yes. He frowned. *It is dark.* He gestured and fire spread in a thin, thin sheet from his hands. It passed around them; it burned nothing, not even a strand of stray hair. In the folds of this translucent, burning blanket, darkness evaporated. Kaylin was surprised to see the color of the walls: almost white.

The fire looked at Teela, his expression shifting. *She is cold.*

"She's not dead."

No, Kaylin. Let me carry her.

Kaylin opened her mouth.

I have carried you, Chosen.

"Teela, he wants to carry you."

"Do you trust him?"

"Yes."

"Very well. Let him carry me for as long as you can sustain him."

The fire slid an arm around the back of Teela's neck and the backs of her legs. Kaylin hovered; in the narrow staircase, this took work.

Where do we go?

"Up," Kaylin said.

He said nothing else. She found the fire confusing at times. In the elemental garden, the fire didn't use words. He seemed, to her admittedly prejudiced mind, almost childlike; he asked for stories; she told them. His idea of stories tended to lack things like character or narrative; he wanted stories about fire. About lighting a fire. About what fire did, what it was used for, and even how it saved lives.

But outside of the garden, fire had a different voice.

It is a smaller voice, he said.

Kaylin didn't consider it all that small.

No, but you are very, very small, Chosen. In the garden, it is hard to hear your voice at all; everything makes too much noise. He paused. *It is hard here, as well. You should not be here.* It was said in a tone that implied concern, but Kaylin found it forbidding anyway.

Without Teela's weight, climbing was trivial; the stairs went up in a straight slope. After the first dozen stairs, Kaylin stopped worrying that the fire would accidentally char Barrani skin, and she looked straight ahead. There wasn't much else to look at; the walls failed to sprout windows, doors, or other hallways.

"Kitling?"

"I'm here. I'm here, Teela."

"We're almost out."

Since the stairs and the hall that contained them continued for as far as Kaylin could see, she frowned and briefly placed the back of her hand on clammy Barrani brow.

"Remind me not to break your arms when I have the strength to do so. You know how I feel about your worry."

"Why do you think we're almost out?"

"I can hear voices."

Kaylin could hear nothing. Even the fire was absent its usual crackle. "Do you recognize them?" she asked.

"Yes."

This didn't make Kaylin feel any safer. She could guess, from Teela's expression, who she thought she could hear, and the last time anyone else could hear them there'd been a whole mess of injured and near-dead in their wake.

Kaylin couldn't hear them—but Kaylin hadn't seen the nightmares, either. "Tell me if you see them?" she whispered.

Teela nodded and turned her face toward the fire's heart.

The stairs widened. The halls therefore opened up as well,

to accommodate the shift in width. It was easier to walk two abreast, and Kaylin waited. She didn't need to walk beside the fire, but she wanted to keep Teela in easy reach.

Her fear that Teela would see something she couldn't proved to be unfounded. The stairs came to an end. Beyond them, white stone continued in a flat, bright plane. At their height was a Barrani Kaylin recognized: Terrano. The Terrano of the forest.

But she'd seen the glass statues in the heart of Alsanis's nightmare—and this boy had not been among them. He was smiling as he watched the fire approach; he appeared to have eyes for Teela. They were not, sadly, Barrani eyes.

"Teela! We're waiting!"

Teela struggled to stand; if she'd had the strength, she would have insisted on walking. She didn't, and if she was ferociously proud—and she was, being Barrani—she nonetheless had a strong streak of pragmatism.

It was Kaylin who spoke. "Who are you?"

He frowned, the exuberance draining from his face.

"Teela thinks you're Terrano—but you're not."

"Kitling—"

Kaylin shook her head. "I saw them, Teela. I saw them— they were like ghosts, but I'd remember them anywhere. This man wasn't one of the eleven."

"I recognize him," was the gentle reply.

"Yes—but you shouldn't. This isn't even what your Terrano looked like."

"The nightmares of the Hallionne are not considered a strict guide to reality. They are replete with symbols, with suggestions. What you saw was the Hallionne's interpretation."

"Yes," Kaylin said. "And no. I would bet anything I owned that what I saw is what they actually looked like. Except for the being made of glass part. How do you recognize him, Teela? How, when your memories are perfect? Does he really look like Terrano?"

"She doesn't see what I *look like,*" the young man said, his frown growing edges. "She sees who I am."

"Really? Why exactly are you trying to present *as* Barrani, then? Why don't you shed that and look like what you think you actually are? Because if you are Terrano, why can't you remember your *own* face?"

"Kitling—"

Terrano now looked confused. It was the type of confusion that could spill into anger, and from there, all-out tantrum; Kaylin recognized it although she usually only saw it in the faces of foundlings.

"Teela—"

"She's wrong," Teela said, leaning against Kaylin. "I did recognize you. I still do."

"You look the same," Terrano said, sounding more hesitant. Teela nodded.

"But you aren't here to join us."

"I don't know how," Teela replied. "I'm still what I was. I didn't mean to stay behind."

"No. The *green* kept you. The *green.* But Teela—we can *fix* it, now!" He paused. "Well…almost."

Kaylin felt cold. The fire wrapped an arm around her shoulder. It didn't help. "It's not that kind of cold," she whispered.

He said nothing. His black eyes were all but glued to Terrano, and she felt, as he watched, his growing sense of revulsion. It wasn't what he felt for the water, the earth, or the air; there was no respect in it.

"Terrano," Teela said, her voice much stronger than she was. "Where is the Lady?"

"Oh, she's with everyone else. I came to find you."

"Why you?"

"It's easiest for me," he replied, frowning. "Why have you summoned *him?*"

"It wasn't me."

"The mortal summoned him?"

"She is Chosen."

Terrano frowned. "She's the harmoniste."

"Yes, she is that, too. She is Chosen, Terrano." Teela frowned. After a longer pause, she said, "We were not taught about the Chosen. Not then."

"What is a Chosen? Is it a mortal thing?"

"The Chosen are almost never mortal. There have been Barrani who have been Chosen; there have been Dragons."

He spit. Clearly, Dragons were not high on his list of happy things. "But what is a Chosen, Teela?"

"Look at her arms. At her forehead. Do you recognize the marks?"

Terrano did as bid. He looked like a Barrani, but nothing about his posture or expression suggested the elder race. His eyes, however, widened. They were the same color as the eyes of the fire's Avatar.

The marks on Kaylin's arms began, at last, to glow. The glow was golden. Terrano's brows disappeared into the perfect line of his hair. It was comical, or would have been in any other circumstance. Kaylin saw much more of his eyes; they had no whites, no iris, no pupil. They were the eyes of the small dragon, the eyes of the fire, the eyes of things ancient and wild.

"She has *words*. She has *words* on her skin." He took two steps toward them; Teela stiffened. The fire stepped in front of them both, and to Kaylin's eye, his flames grew almost white.

"Teela."

"I can't leave the way you can," Teela told Terrano. "And I can't give the Chosen to you, I'm sorry; she is *kyuthe* to me.

One of the only friends I've found in centuries who is almost what you were."

"Does she know your name? Does she hold it?"

Teela shook her head. "I would never risk the pain of that loss again."

Loss, Kaylin thought. Not vulnerability. Not weakness. Loss. "Do you know hers?" Kaylin asked.

The silence was profound. After a pause in which the fire began to crackle, Terrano said, "We don't *need* names anymore. Teela, come with me."

"I cannot. I have absorbed the nightmares of Alsanis, and I have accepted the judgment of the green. There is only one way I can leave this place, if I am to leave at all."

"Try," Terrano said. He held out a hand.

The fire reached out and pushed it away. Terrano's eyes widened; his skin blistered.

Teela whispered a single, Barrani word. "Kaylin—the fire—"

"I'm not telling the fire what to do," Kaylin replied, with more heat than necessary. She didn't want Terrano touching Teela. She just…didn't.

"You can't let fire do whatever it wants!"

"You can't let Terrano do whatever he wants, either!" Kaylin struggled to lower her voice. "We're going up the stairs." She offered Teela a shoulder; Teela stiffened, but accepted it because she had no alternative.

Terrano backed away from the fire as the fire advanced. He backed into a hall. This hall reminded Kaylin of the High Halls in Elantra; the ceiling was so far above the ground she could kink her neck looking up at it. She didn't try. She could see that the walls were no longer roughly worked; they were smooth, and they were pillared. The pillars were carved in likenesses of Barrani, in alabaster, or something that looked like alabaster at this distance; they weren't close.

"Don't come here," Terrano shouted. Kaylin couldn't be certain who he was shouting at until Teela stiffened. "It's not the right place, it's not the right time—you're not ready yet!" He shrieked in outrage as the fire struck again. *"Teela!"*

"Kaylin—stop it. Stop the fire!"

Kaylin heard the pain and fear in Teela's voice as if it were a mirror of her own. She closed her eyes, and she called the fire.

He does not belong here.

No. But neither do I.

It is not the same, Chosen. He must be destroyed.

She thought he was right. But Teela's expression cut her. *Yes, but not now. Not right now. Come back to me. Carry Teela again. Please.* Please.

The fire hesitated. In the hesitation, Terrano saw an opening; he ran toward one of the pillars, leaped at the feet of the sculpture carved into alabaster, and vanished. Kaylin looked at the statue. She wasn't surprised to recognize it.

"I don't know if this leads us out," Kaylin said. "Or in."

Teela, however, was looking at the pillar. She mouthed a name.

"There are twelve," Kaylin told her.

"Of course there are." Teela glanced up at the fire as he lifted her.

"Does the green have nightmares?"

"You ask the oddest questions."

"It keeps my mind busy. What did he mean, Teela? Did you understand him? What was he hoping to fix?"

Teela laughed softly. "They left me behind. My mother's life blood was meant to buy my safety—and it did. It did that. But my friends don't see it as safety. They see it as abandonment. They left me. They went where I could not follow. Had I stayed in the Hallionne, had I stayed with them, they might have been able to do for me what was done to them.

"But my father escaped, and took me with him."

"Would you have stayed with them?"

"Does it matter? I'm here. I can't enter the Hallionne. If the green considers me unworthy, I will never leave the green. I am *tired,* kitling. You were right," she added.

"About what?"

"That is not what Terrano looked like. The statue, though, is."

"How did you recognize him?"

"I knew his name. I *knew* him. I don't know why he looks different, now; I imagine he—like most of us in our distant youth—had insecurities about his physical presence. He is no longer confined to that form; he has choice."

"Does he?"

"Demonstrably."

Kaylin frowned. "I'm not so certain about that. Iberrienne didn't, in the end. Ynpharion didn't. Whatever they absorbed, whatever they agreed to, it changed them in some fundamental way."

"It would have had to—they could transform."

"It changed what they *wanted,* Teela."

"And are our desires so fundamental? Is that what defines us?" She shook her head. "You will have to lead, kitling. I will have to trust you." Teela smiled at Kaylin's expression. "I don't think doubt will serve you well in the green. It slows you down, it teaches you not to trust yourself. I understand my own doubts and my own weaknesses, in this. They are constraining, but they have claws here; I cannot escape them."

"Except through me."

"Yes."

Kaylin exhaled. "Let's go."

She had to stop at the twelfth pillar, and she was relieved to find that it, unlike the other eleven, was one great column that seemed to almost hold up the sky. There was no likeness of Teela here.

"No," Teela said, as if reading her mind. "But there are twelve."

"I just think it's weird that they're pillars. I don't understand the symbolism. I think I understand why they were made of glass in the nightmare—it makes more sense to me."

"Why?"

"Because they're empty. They're vessels. Whatever made them real, for want of a better word, is all but gone."

"But not gone."

Kaylin lifted her left hand, exposing the mark; it was the only one that hadn't changed color. "But these pillars kind of hold up the roof."

"You are looking for too much logic."

"There's nothing wrong with logic."

"No—but you're trying to understand a book when half of it's written in a language you've never heard, let alone read. You're missing half of the story because it's not a story you can inhabit in any way. The Hallionne are not mortal. The green is not mortal. You are."

"You're immortal—do you understand it any better than I do?"

Teela shook her head. "The green and the Hallionne don't differentiate between your kin and mine. Oh, they understand there is a difference—but to them, we are locked into our shapes and we exist in an entirely superficial way. We live in the world. We are of it."

"And they're not."

"No. They exist in a space of their own. They overlap many roads. I think that visitors sometimes came to the Hallionne from the outlands."

"We did."

"Yes—but in an emergency. We don't, and can't, live there. If not for Bertolle's…brothers…most of us would never have arrived at Orbaranne. You would. Nightshade. I'm tempted to say the Consort."

"And you?"

She didn't answer, but turned her face up toward the light because there was light now. It was sunlight. It was the type of sunlight that artists painted, the type that fell through branches into the quiet of forest floor. The forests without insects and burrs and things that were all thorn with a tiny bit of root beneath. An arch opened up in the wall at the end of this gigantic hall, and it framed—at last—green.

Kaylin could see trees; she could see grass, or at least wildflowers. She could hear the trickle of water in the distance, which implied either river, brook, or possibly fountain. She could see sky, and the sky was the normal azure.

"I think we're almost there," she told Teela.

Teela nodded and closed her eyes.

There was no sun in the sky, which was the first oddity. Kaylin was so grateful to see life—or at least its imitation—that it took her some time to realize what was missing. There were no insects or birds. In all, this should have been idyllic.

It wasn't. It was giving her hives. The marks on her arms were glowing brightly. Of course. When they could have been useful, they'd been flat, gray, and lifeless.

She viewed the garden from a terrace. The terrace, like the hall itself, suggested Barrani architecture, and a path led from both the height and the base of its steps. Kaylin hesitated. She looked to Teela for an opinion; Teela was utterly silent.

The fire set her—carefully—down. *I will leave you now, Chosen.*

"I'm not—"

You are. I have been in this place before; it is peaceful, but it is not mine. Go. My part of this story is told.

"I can't carry her."

You can, if you must. Come back to the Keeper's garden when you are done. There are stories to be told.

The fire took warmth with him. Kaylin didn't need it, not here—but Teela did. She knelt beside the Barrani Hawk she'd known and envied and—yes—loved for so much of her life. And she was afraid—that was the truth. She hadn't understood, at her mother's deathbed, what death *meant*. Severn had.

But she'd learned. It was endless. It was loss. It was loss every day. It was an emptiness and a permanent lack of warmth.

Teela had been nothing like her mother. Teela was Barrani. Teela was *immortal*. Teela had taken her places her mother would never have taken her; had forgiven things her mother would never have forgiven. She wasn't always kind. No, scratch that, she was almost never kind. It wasn't her way. But she was solid. She was—mostly—safe.

And she wouldn't wake up.

Kaylin shook her. She shouted. She whispered. She even pleaded—because Teela couldn't hear her. That was the point, wasn't it? Teela couldn't hear her. God, Tain was going to kill her. Tain would be so upset.

They'd *all* be upset. This wasn't supposed to happen—if anyone was in danger, it was supposed to be Kaylin. Kaylin, who was going to die sometime anyway. She was crying, now. She was crying, and she had to stop because tears were useless. They'd get them nowhere, and they had to move.

But she hadn't lied to the fire: Teela was heavy. She was wearing too much armor. The armor could be mostly removed—and Kaylin did remove it. The sword, she kept; she attached it to her own waist, where it dragged across the ground. She would have tried to sling it across her back—half the Barrani war band did that—but if she had any hope of moving Teela at all, it was going to be by taking the brunt of her unconscious weight across that back.

Kaylin caught Teela by the arms, inserting her back between them; she bent at the knees and used momentum to propel herself to her feet. Teela came with her—but only barely, and her feet dragged across the ground. It was, short of just dragging her by the arms, the best Kaylin could manage—and she couldn't manage it for long.

No, she thought, clenching her jaws. She *could*. She could manage for as long as it took because she wasn't going to leave Teela behind. The path that led from the terrace was wide enough, flat enough, and solid enough. Kaylin followed it, letting it lead.

CHAPTER 20

The sun was high, even if it didn't exist; the day grew hotter as she followed the path. The grass that bounded the path on either side gave way to trees with silver bark; they provided no shade—only the disappointed hope of it. Kaylin had to stop several times, partly because her legs were shaking, and partly because she needed to check Teela's pulse. She couldn't hear Teela's breathing, even though Teela's head was more or less tucked beside her left ear.

She could hear water. It sounded too loud to be a fountain, but it didn't matter. The dreams of Alsanis had told them to find water. If she found water, she might find a way back. If she found a way back, if she was in the actual world, and not the dreams of perverse pocket realities, she might—just might—be able to help Teela.

She had woken the Consort, after all.

But she couldn't do that for Teela, not here. She'd tried. Kaylin frowned. The words on her arms were bright and golden, but they lay still. They didn't prompt her, and they didn't offer assistance on their own.

The sound of water grew closer, but Kaylin was practically crawling. She couldn't move quickly; desperation gave her enough strength to carry both of their weights, no more. Not until she heard the roaring.

She was immobile for one minute, glancing wildly at the trees she'd barely registered. She wasn't Teela. She couldn't fight Ferals on her own. But the roaring didn't disturb Teela at all, and Kaylin lowered her, roughly, to the ground. She drew the sword because it had the greater reach—and then set it down. Greater reach, or no, she wasn't competent enough to wield it against a truly dangerous opponent. She drew daggers instead.

But the roaring, when it came again, made her look up. Squinting against a daylight shed by no sun, she thought she could see a familiar winged shape. It was small—it was slight; translucence made it hard to be certain she wasn't mistaken. She stood in front of Teela as the winged creature flapped closer. Even when she was certain that it was the small dragon, she didn't move. She felt relief at the sight of him, but the hair on the back of her neck started to stand on end, and her skin— where the marks weren't—began to goose bump.

She had never been afraid of the small dragon. He had saved her life at least twice. Yes, he criticized her, and yes, he smacked her face—but so did the Hawks, or at least Teela on an annoying day. He had also killed Ferals, simply by breathing into their faces. She *knew* he was deadly, or could be deadly. The Barrani treated him with healthy respect.

Until this moment, she hadn't.

Then again, until this moment, his voice had never been a Dragon's voice. It was, now. As he approached, it shook the earth she was standing on. Yet when he did descend, hovering, he was still tiny. His neck was delicate, his wings wider and broader than they had been in any place but the dream of Alsanis. She could see, briefly, through their membranes—and the sky was violet and black.

He roared. It was like listening to Bellusdeo and Diarmat; Kaylin had two hands full of daggers or she would have covered her ears.

He snorted smoke. It looked like steam, not the usual clouds. He then landed—on the ground a yard away from Kaylin's feet. He looked up at her face, his eyes dark, the colors that skirted their surface bolder.

"I don't even know what you are," Kaylin told him, as he lifted his face and opened his small jaws. "I don't know where we are. But the whole dive into the stone basin, nose first? Don't do that again."

The small dragon cocked his head. He squawked. Except, of course, it was a roar of sound.

When Kaylin failed to answer, he snorted again; she knew, if he were on her shoulder, he would either smack her face or bite her ear. Instead, he stalked—which, given his feet, looked funny—toward Teela. Kaylin stiffened, shifting both position and daggers; the small dragon looked at the knives and hissed.

It was the hissing she associated with amusement.

She didn't sheathe her weapons. She watched him as he headed toward Teela, and she stiffened again. "Don't breathe on her. Don't even think it."

His eyes widened, and then he shook his head, looking for all the world like a child's version of a dragon baby. He did, however, nudge Teela's hand with the tip of his nose. He even bit her fingers, but gently, as if she were a dead bird and he were her mother.

Then he turned to Kaylin again.

And she understood what he was offering. He was tiny,

yes—but his voice implied that size wasn't necessarily an issue. He could, if she asked it, carry Teela. He could, if she agreed, carry her.

And if he did, she thought, as her throat went dry, he wouldn't *be* a small dragon anymore. He would be a large dragon, as much hers as Tiamaris was when he went Dragon. She couldn't own Tiamaris—or any member of the Dragon Court. She relied on their sense of humor, their indulgence, and her own relative insignificance in order to survive her mistakes and the many, many social gaffes she was learning to obliterate.

Except that he wasn't a Dragon. His eyes—his eyes were like Terrano's, like the fire's. They always had been. They were shadow eyes. Did she trust him?

She wasn't certain. Trust hadn't really been an issue before. He was like a cat. You could love them, and you could trust them to *be* cats. But you couldn't trust them not to wreck your furniture or your carpets, and you couldn't trust them to stay out of your food; you couldn't trust them not to kill helpless mice and leave parts of their corpses scattered around your home. It just didn't matter because cats couldn't kill you. They couldn't kill your neighbors or your friends.

Why was life like this? Why was she asked, so often, to choose between two different fears?

Because, she thought, that was mostly what life was: choosing between two different fears.

"Yes," she told him, before doubt and uncertainty made her change her mind. "Please. Carry her. Carry us."

He stepped back. Actually, that was the wrong word—he launched himself into the air, and flew ahead down the path. Kaylin returned her daggers to their sheaths as she knelt beside Teela. Teela was still breathing, or at least, she still had a pulse. She didn't wake.

Kaylin watched the small dragon.

His wings expanded first. She'd seen that, before; they'd become the size of Aerian wings in the dreaming world of Alsanis. They weren't Aerian wings. They were more membrane, less feather; they seemed less substantial only because they were translucent. They spread. They spread, and as they did, Kaylin could see a purple sky unfold in the azure that could be seen at any spot his wings didn't touch.

She vastly preferred the azure.

His neck elongated, thickening; it was still much longer than normal Dragon neck, and seemed flexible in the fluid way snakes were. His jaws grew, his face thickening and stretching; his legs developed a heft and musculature she wasn't sure she cared for. She couldn't see his tail; it was lost to the bulk of his growing body.

But he didn't seem to have scales; his body seemed smoother, more glasslike. And he wasn't actually all that far away from them when his transformation had been completed.

He roared. She could swear it sent her hair flying. Then, before she could say anything else, he pushed himself off the ground. His shadow covered both of the Hawks. Kaylin discovered that he could hover in pretty much the same way he had at a more compact size; his claws, however were not the pointers he used to get her attention; they were thicker and attached to feet that couldn't actually grip her shoulder; they were too large.

They could, however, surround her entire body, and one of them did. The other clasped Teela firmly. He rose.

"Can you carry us to the end of the path?"

He roared.

She needed a different method of communication; her own

voice hadn't changed, but she'd be deaf by the end of the day if his continued like this. She reached out to grab Teela's hand, although she was fairly certain the small—the nonsmall— dragon wouldn't drop her.

They began to move.

She didn't know what a familiar was. Truth? She'd been uncomfortable with the idea. Anything that made Barrani Arcanists covetous was never going to work out well for a mortal. She already had the marks of the Chosen, and she'd more or less made peace with those, in part because she was certain it was the marks that allowed her to work with the midwives. They saved lives.

No, *she* saved lives, using their power. It didn't make up for the lives she'd taken. Nothing would. There was no going back. But going forward, she could prevent deaths that would happen without her intervention. She could make a differ- ence in the lives of strangers—and this time, it would be a positive difference.

The small dragon—she really had to stop thinking about him that way—wasn't like the marks. He clearly had a mind of his own, and he could make it known, even if he couldn't speak. And he could speak—she just didn't hear his squawking as language. The Hallionne did. Hallionne Bertolle's brothers had. The fire had.

If he was something as ancient, as wild, as they were— why would be live as a *pet?* A pet owned by a mortal Hawk? How could she bind him and command him when she could barely keep Ynpharion from scorching what little self-esteem she managed to maintain? She'd relied on what she assumed was his interest or affection; she did treat him like other peo- ple treated their cats.

And she was beginning to realize that she couldn't keep

doing that. She had no idea how to change that. What had the Hallionne said?

She had to name him. The thought was terrifying; the only thing that calmed her was the fact that she *had* named the fire. She could. But she'd learned the fire's name; she hadn't had to come up with something that meant fire—because what would that be? Hot? Pretty? Deadly?

Did the dragon even have a name?

Terrano didn't now.

She froze, considering that. Iberrienne only barely had a name. His memories were not Barrani memories; they were broken and confused. She didn't understand why, but then again, Barrani birth was pretty much mystical; it made no logical sense. Work with the midwives had made it seem far less sensible than it had to start, and it hadn't made much sense when she'd first heard it, either.

She also understood that the Consort, the giver of names—and therefore the Mother of the Race—might be able to help Iberrienne. She doubted very much that she could help the lost children; what they wanted from her wasn't what Iberrienne required.

Kaylin closed her eyes; wind swept her hair out of her face. Water. Consort. Teela. Everything else could wait, unless it tried to kill her first. Opening her eyes, she looked down at the path. It was a slender, gray-white line in a field of green and silver that continued on, to the horizon—like a road might. She attempted to look behind, but the dragon's leg was in the way, and maybe, given the geography in places like this, that was for the best.

Forward, she thought. You had to keep moving because if you stopped you might never start again. Who'd said that to her? Oh, right. Teela.

She wasn't surprised when what was sort of road through

picturesque wilderness ended in a large, large circle. At the center of that circle, seen from this height, was, at last, a fountain.

"Is this where you were?" Kaylin shouted.

The dragon roared.

"Take us down. Do *not* drop us!"

He laughed. It wasn't the normal hiss, either; it was full-throated laughter; even his legs shook with it.

He did set them down before he landed, but he didn't land on them, which Kaylin had been half-afraid he'd do. He set them down a yard or two away from the fountain itself. This fountain was very much like the fountains in the grounds of the Imperial Palace. Water didn't trickle from thin air; it poured from the stone structure that stood in its center. It was not a small statue; the basin itself was almost a pool, it was so large; it was set into the ground, not over it.

Sprays of water caught light and made small rainbows of it. It was quiet here. There were no obvious shadows, no obvious threats. She felt the ground shake as the dragon landed.

Kaylin found her feet and immediately turned to Teela, supine on the ground. She then caught Teela's arms and draped the bulk of her body across her back, as she'd done once before. "I think we're here, Teela."

The statue at the center of the fountain was familiar, but until Kaylin was almost in the water—she stopped at its edge— she wasn't certain why. It was a figure—and it seemed to Kaylin's eye to be a human figure. A woman, or a girl on the edge of adulthood. Water spilled from her open palms—palms that were held in front of her chest, upturned as if in offering or supplication. Water trailed from strands of her hair.

Blood trailed from her eyes.

At this distance, it shouldn't have been obvious, but it was, and Kaylin didn't doubt what she saw. It was red. It was the only color in an otherwise white-gray.

Kaylin recognized the girl: it was the Avatar of the water. Here, in the heart of the green. If Kaylin had wondered how much of the landscape was drawn from her memories, she had her answer. This was Kaylin's version of the water. This was how her mind had seen the element the first time she'd encountered it.

There was no Consort by this giant fountain, but the eagles had said the water would tell them where the Consort was. First things first, then. She knelt by the edge of the basin, and she lowered her palm into the water. It was surprisingly cold—but the cold was bracing, and therefore welcome.

She should have been surprised when the statue moved; the water didn't usually take the form and shape of stone—and given the way the stone grated as it moved against itself, she knew it couldn't be liquid. Water splashed as the figure moved slowly toward Kaylin, lowering its hands to its sides and lifting its chin as it did.

The dragon roared.

Kaylin froze as the statue frowned and looked beyond her to what she presumed was the dragon itself. She was unprepared for the dragon's sudden leap. He landed in the water and sent it flying in a large spray which left every part of Kaylin that wasn't covered in emerald dress soaked. It soaked Teela, as well. It didn't wake her up.

The statue lifted its hands; the water that had been streaming from its palms froze instantly. Kaylin recognized the shape the ice took: it was a sword.

She almost called the dragon back—but she didn't. Because she understood that whatever this statue was, it *wasn't* the water she knew; it was some other thing. If it animated the statue, it wasn't bent on the protection of the memories of a mortal race; it was bent on something entirely other.

At the moment, that was the destruction of the dragon.

The dragon wasn't having any of it. Kaylin moved as his tail swung, gripping Teela's arms tightly enough she'd probably cut off circulation. The sword of ice glanced off the side of dragon jaw—but its blade didn't shatter. Neither did the dragon's jaw. It sounded like steel hitting stone.

The dragon reared up as the blade bounced; it inhaled. Kaylin knew what had to follow; she opened her mouth to tell the dragon to stop, but no words fell out. It was too late for them. Either that or they were the wrong words.

Breath, a stream of silver mist, engulfed the statue and its weapon. For one long second, Kaylin thought the mist would dissipate with little effect. The statue brought its sword down—but it hit water. Water froze in a circle that spread across the surface of the shallow pool. It spread everywhere that Kaylin's hand didn't touch.

She waited, her own breath held, and for far less reason.

The statue began to crack, as if it were made of ice, not stone. The dragon roared. The statue, lips crumbling, roared back. Its voice was not a dragon's voice—but it might as well have been. The statue didn't exhale breath the way dragons normally did when they were fighting.

No, it exhaled words, a dark cloud of lines and dots and hatches, a cloud of letter forms. Or at least they looked like letter forms to Kaylin. Not, of course, Barrani forms—although there was similarity in the components—and certainly not Elantran. But they were dark, like the smoke from burning flesh; they didn't attain the solidity of form that Kaylin's words could and sometimes did. They didn't look like True Words.

They looked like the shadows those words might cast, distorted by the landscape that underlay them. She watched as they coalesced; the dragon fell silent.

"Fly!" Kaylin shouted. "Get *out of there!*"

The dragon gave her a side-glance that, in any other immortal face, would have been dismissive.

"*I mean it!* Get out of there *right bloody now!*"

He pushed himself, slowly, out of the ice; it clung to his feet. Kaylin swore a lot. The statue cracked as the ice did. If the surface of the stone was a white-gray, the interior wasn't; it was dark, and it glittered.

Kaylin hadn't been worried about the stone; she'd been worried about the words. They looked familiar to her, and not in a good way; they reminded her of the words that Iberrienne had attempted to draw from the citizens of the fief. They reminded her of the words that Iberrienne had attempted to say in the heart of Hallionne Orbaranne.

Kaylin stopped breathing for one long minute. And then, in a desperate, almost unreasoning frenzy, she began to call the water she knew. She didn't use words; words would take too long. She was never good with words when she was terrified. She was afraid of what the words would do to the water—if the water was actually really here at all.

She almost cried when she heard a single word.

Kaylin.

Come to me, she thought. *Come to me right now. Come to where I am.*

I am here.

"Come here, come away from the—"

The water rose in a pillar; it was the shape of a woman, and it held Kaylin's hand. You couldn't hold water in your hands; it always slid through, dripping between your fingers. Kaylin tried anyway—but at least this time she had the water's cooperation. She pulled the water out of the shallow pool that was otherwise now ice.

You should not be here.

The water looked down at Teela, and Kaylin realized that while she'd been almost shocked to see fire take a human form, she expected the water to do so. The form wasn't natural to either.

The dragon roared. The ice—which Kaylin now understood was not, in any way, actual water—shattered. Gravity in the environs of the shallow pool broke. Hand still encased in water, Kaylin watched as the shards flew away to reveal the dark, roiling mass of words that remained.

"Can you read them?" she asked the water.

The water shuddered.

Kaylin glanced at her; her eyes—if *eyes* was really the right word for something that shouldn't actually have any—were closed. *Do you understand what has happened, Kaylin?*

"No."

A pity. You are Chosen; if you cannot understand, you will tell no story that the green can hear, and you will offer no healing to the wounds that now bleed freely.

Kaylin hesitated. "Can you carry Teela?"

I can. It will not help her now. You intend to return to the greenheart.

"Yes, I think so. But we need you there."

She lifted her face. *There is a risk.*

There was always a risk. "What risk?"

Watch, Chosen. Watch and understand.

Kaylin turned to the cloud. It was dense now, and it sparkled as if it had developed a surface that was hard and reflective. The density apparently made it heavier, because it began to sink. It touched the pool bed and it continued to sink, eating away at the stone beneath it; eating away at the earth beneath that stone. Kaylin watched as it slowly submerged.

The water rippled, but said nothing. Kaylin started to move; the water held her back, in the way undercurrents could. *Wait.*

"For what?"

There was no further answer. She looked up to see the dragon—the huge dragon—hovering above the sinking mass. Only when he landed did the water let her go. She walked to the edge of what was now a pit. The water lifted Teela and followed.

The blood of the green is rooted in me.

Kaylin looked down at her dress; she felt the water's amusement—and she felt, as well, its sorrow.

It is like, and unlike, the dress you wear. The green is injured; the blood from that wound runs through my veins in this place. I cannot stop it, and I cannot contain it; it becomes part of me, while remaining other.

Kaylin had reached the pit's edge. This was not the first time today she would stand at the edge of a pit. It wasn't, she realized, the first time that she'd stand at the edge of a pit that had this shape. It wasn't round. It wasn't oval. Its edge implied shape—the outline of a word.

It was, in miniature, the same pit that she and Teela had seen.

"Was this—was this caused by the blood of the green?"

No.

"Then—then what?"

The blood of the dying, the water replied. *Mortality is anathema to the green. Understand, if you can, that the green is not of you or your kin. It has an interest in what you do, but it can touch you only in one place—it is bound in all other ways. Or it was.*

Kaylin turned to face the water. "What does this word mean?"

The water was silent. But the dragon roared. The water spoke—to the dragon. The dragon, at far greater volume, replied.

You should not be here, Kaylin.

"No. Can you take us back?"

Yes. But I will not remain for long. I cannot now.

"Why?"

The water pointed at the pit.

There was no instant shift of scenery. The water, carrying Teela, began to walk away from what had been a fountain. A path opened on the other side of the pool, and she led them toward it. Kaylin was hungry. She was tired. She was aware that the dragon now flew in lazy circles above them.

She didn't ask him to carry her. She was almost afraid to do so.

"Will he—will he shrink again?"

The water was confused. She glanced at the dragon, and then glanced at Kaylin. *I do not understand the question.*

"He was smaller before. About this size." The explanation didn't appear to make the question any clearer.

I do not understand. Kaylin, when you light a candle you summon fire. You speak its name in a whisper; it is almost inaudible. When you summoned fire here, you spoke its name, and it was louder. But in both cases, you called fire, and fire came.

It was Kaylin's turn to be confused.

The nature of fire is fire. The nature of the—dragon?—is dragon. But I do not think the Tha'alaan would recognize this creature as Dragon. I do not understand your question.

"I didn't summon him. I didn't learn and speak his name. I didn't call him into being. He just—he arrived on his own. And he was a lot smaller when he did."

For one long minute the water ceased to move at all. Above

her head, the dragon's shadow covered them. *You do not know him. You do not know his name. You* must *know his name, Kaylin. You* must *name him.*

"But—"

It is only by naming that he can exist in your small life at all. She spoke to the dragon. The dragon replied. The earth trembled. *He cannot long remain what he has been, now. There is too much of him here.*

Understand what the water wants. It is complex, as you know. You have seen the tidal wave; you have seen the drowning. You have seen the infants. I am not all of one thing, or all of the other. But, Kaylin, it is only by the grace of the Tha'alani that I can speak with you as you see me now; it is by the grace of their constant experience and thought that I have some small control—and it is small—over my nature.

I am storm. I am death. I am life. I am all of these things—but at times, with will and effort, I can choose. I cannot always choose.

Nor, in the end, can he.

CHAPTER 21

The path ended abruptly, giving way to tall, dry grass. The water didn't pause; she continued. Because she was carrying Teela, so did Kaylin. Watching the water walk over the dry grass was a revelation. In the water's wake, the grass became the color of Kaylin's dress, and small flowers began to push themselves out of the dirt, budding and blossoming as if seasons existed beneath her feet.

It was striking; it was even beautiful.

"Look, can you tell me something? I don't understand how the green and the Hallionne are connected. I'd swear when we activated the wards we entered Hallionne Alsanis—but the wards exist in the heart of the green. To reach you at all we had to drop through Alsanis and into the tunnels."

You think of the green as a place. You think of the Hallionne as places. They are not that. They are, in a much larger way, like your cities and your citizens. They are not all one thing, not all the other; the Hallionne are bound by the words that form the reason for their existence, but they are not fixed as you are. And yet, Kaylin, some part of them once was.

The green, never.

They are part of the green. The green is part of what they have become.

"And the lost children?"

They are also part of the green. They are part of Hallionne Alsanis.

"But…they're trying to destroy the Hallionne."

Yes. They understand, in part, the nature of words. But they do not understand in full. The pit that you see as an outline of a word is their attempt to tell a tale. We are almost there.

But Kaylin knew, because in the distance, she could hear singing.

This was like, and unlike, her first trip through the nightmare of Alsanis. The Consort's voice was unmistakable; the song, however, was different. It took Kaylin one long minute to understand why, and when she did, it confused her. The Consort was singing in High Barrani. Given the extension of syllables and vowels, it wasn't immediately clear, because the songs the Consort sang to the Hallionne also contained similar vocal sounds.

But the sounds were words that Kaylin could actually understand. She saw a ring of standing trees—or of things that looked, at a distance, like trees. They weren't. They were stone structures, but branched, rooted. Something about them made Kaylin very uncomfortable.

Above these nontrees, the dragon roared. Kaylin was afraid that he would breathe; before she could shout at him, he did.

She shouted something different instead, and the singing banked sharply. Clearly this song was not like the songs of awakening.

Grey mist hit the strange stone grove, billowing at the

edges like cloud, not fire. Where it touched stone branches, the branches melted, running like molten rock toward the ground. But they burned nothing they hit; instead, they shimmered, like silver liquid. The water passed over them without concern. Kaylin wasn't as brave; she leaped over the small rivulets that seemed to flow, like giant, exposed veins, into one small pool.

The Consort stood on the other side of this network of tiny streams, but as the cloud spread, they surrounded her. She didn't touch them, either. Instead, she looked at the water. No, Kaylin thought, at what the water held.

The Consort's eyes darkened as she finally met Kaylin's gaze. She was either angry or afraid, and opened her mouth; she shut it before she spoke.

"Lady." Kaylin fell to one knee.

But the Consort shook her head with obvious impatience. "Not here. At Court, yes. But not here. Do you know what you've done?"

"We came to find you."

"And you could not come here with any other Lord?"

"Teela wouldn't stay."

The Consort's expression softened. "No," she said at last. "She wouldn't, would she? And no one of us, not even the High Lord himself, could command her when she did not wish to obey. It was never wise to make the attempt." She watched as the trees finished melting.

"How did you get here?"

"The dreams of Alsanis."

Kaylin blinked. "I don't understand."

The Consort's smile was bitter. "No. No more do I."

"I doubt that."

"Do you imply that I lie, Lord Kaylin?"

"Clumsy of me. I'm not usually that subtle."

To her surprise, the Consort laughed. Kaylin thought she would never understand the Barrani. "Great harm was done here when An'Teela was a child. You know of it."

"I know what's said."

"Teela is of the Warden's bloodline."

Kaylin nodded.

"As was her mother. The Warden's bloodline is dear to the green; it is gifted. Its gift does not extend beyond the green and the Hallionne; it does not touch the High Court in any significant way. But the green hears the Wardens and Alsanis speaks with them."

"He doesn't anymore."

"Ah, but he does. The nightmares come to the Warden."

"Unless you're here?"

"It is my privilege," the Consort replied. Kaylin privately thought it wasn't much of a privilege. "While I am in the West March, I can ease the Warden's burden. The nightmares of Alsanis are strong, and they are painful. The Warden can bespeak them, at times, and he can calm them, when they can be calmed at all.

"Of late, that has been seldom. Yet without the Warden, the whole of the West March would suffer their pain. Very, very few would survive it."

"You—"

"Yes. I am aware that I had some difficulty. It was perhaps hubris on my part. I believe Lord Barian would have endured in a way I could not without your aid. It is for this reason there has always been a Warden. There will always *be* a Warden. No politics of the High Court can alter that.

"The nightmares and the dreams are entwined. You think of them as shadow and light, but they are perspectives, Kaylin. They come from the same place. The dreams of Alsanis brought me here."

"To save you?"

"No. In the end, no. It is to save them." She turned, then, and gestured at the rivulets that once had been trees. "And you have brought Teela. The green has been waiting. Alsanis has been waiting, as well. Understand that the green is wounded. It is not dying, Kaylin; that is not the nature of its existence; it will not die. Nor is it injured in the way you and I might be injured."

"Why did they bring you here?"

The Consort, however, frowned. "What," she asked, her voice chillier by several degrees, "is on your left palm?"

Kaylin held out her hand.

The Consort caught it, pulled Kaylin almost off her feet, and examined it; she did not touch the mark. But her eyes, when Kaylin looked at her face, were gold; gold with a heart of pure green. She let Kaylin's hand go. "Do you understand what you've done?" she asked, voice soft.

Kaylin hesitated, and then said, "No. No, and maybe yes. I saw the word. I knew it was a name. And it seemed—fragile. If words can be fragile." She thought of Iberrienne. "I was afraid to leave it where I found it, so I gathered it up and took it with me when I left. I didn't—I didn't leave myself room for doubt. I thought I was helping, somehow."

"You have seen the Lake of Life," the Consort replied.

Kaylin nodded.

"But you have also touched it, Kaylin. You have touched it, and you have taken words from its depths. You carry one within you; you carried part of one to my brother. What you see is not what the rest of my people will see, not even here. I think Teela might have, but she could not have done what you have done." There was a brief hesitation, and then the Consort said, "No more could I. I am not Chosen. I am Consort; I am guardian of the names by which my kin know life.

"But you are a vessel. A container. You are the parchment on which the words might be both written and preserved. What will you do with the name?"

"I don't know. It's not—it's not like the other words. It's not like the other name." Kaylin tapped her forehead. "It doesn't react the way the marks I carry react."

"No. It wouldn't."

"Because they're not dead?"

"Because they are not dead. They are not of their name, but they cannot fully escape it. Not while Teela lives."

"They don't want to kill her."

"No. No, they do not. They want to save her. Teela doesn't wish to be saved. But she doesn't wish to be free, either. And so, she is here. And you are here. And I, in the end, am here with both of you."

"Did you expect this?"

The Consort shook her head, her eyes shading to the green-blue that was normal for Barrani. "When I chose to accompany you I was angry with you, yes. But I was also concerned. Calarnenne has history with the green. I believe you now understand what it is."

"I don't. I know it has something to do with the lost children." She hesitated. "But—so did Iberrienne."

"There is much loss, yes. Do you understand Barrani youth? It is—like mortal youth—a time of optimism and idealism. It is a time when we do not believe in caution, but choose instead a hope that is not leavened by bitter experience. That follows, with the passage of time. The things we love—and hate—in our youth, the losses we take, the deaths we endure—they scar us in ways that later loves and later losses do not. Those, we expect.

"I cannot judge, Kaylin. Were either of my brothers lost to such a gamble as the High Court chose to take, I do not think I would ever have recovered. I would function, yes. I would go on. But the rage and the hatred I felt for that High Court would never dim. Mortals forget, and that is a kindness, although it does not seem so to you, and perhaps never will. We do not. We remember whenever we choose to think about the past at all. We can almost walk in it, it is so real.

"I do not know what occurred between the twelve; I know only that were Teela to die, they might at last be free. Free to be or do what, I cannot say. They are not Barrani now—but they are not entirely other."

It struck Kaylin then that the Consort suspected the link between the twelve. She suspected that Teela knew the true names of the eleven; that the eleven, in turn, knew hers. She almost asked, but couldn't. It wasn't her secret to tell.

"If Teela died, and the eleven were freed, what would happen to their names?"

"Do you not know? No, perhaps you don't. You have seen the Lake, and you have touched it, and it has left you marked or changed—but you are not Barrani, and will never be Barrani. There are things you cannot understand. Their names will be lost to us. They will not return to the Lake."

Even hearing it felt like a blow to Kaylin. "Can you—"

"Can I preserve them?" The Consort closed her eyes. "I cannot do what you have done, no. But yes, in some fashion, were I to see what you have seen, I might strengthen them in a different way. I see the Lake, Kaylin. I see it all the time. It exists in the High Halls, and I may approach it physically— as you did. But it exists, for me, wherever my people exist." She took both of Kaylin's hands in hers.

"Is that why they want you?"

"Yes. They feel that they might approach that Lake through me. They cannot," she added. "Not even changed as they are. I will not survive the attempt, but they cannot succeed."

"They don't believe that."

"No."

"They're trying to take the words and remake them."

"Yes. They are like your infants; they are trying to speak as gods. They are trying to use the words in a way that the words cannot be used. They are trying," she said, voice soft and sad, "to lie in a language in which lies cannot be spoken."

"Why are they even—" Kaylin stopped. "Do they understand that that's what they're trying to do?"

The Consort's smile was deeper; it was tinged with an approval that Kaylin shouldn't have wanted, but did anyway. "You understand. No. They believe that any thought that can be expressed—no, any *desire*—is true in and of itself. You see the words that they attempt to speak. What do they look like to you?"

"Like the shadows of words, but—worse."

"Yes. All desires exist; there are words that speak of those desires, those words are true. But not all desire is reality. They believe that what the Ancients desired, they could bring into being by simply…speaking. Writing."

"Bleeding," Kaylin said, automatically.

The Consort said a long nothing.

"Lady, what is it that you think they want?"

"I would guess, if I could, that they wish to transform Teela as they themselves were transformed. I do not know. I do not understand the whole of their spoken tongue—they have created a language, the way the young sometimes do. I understand only parts of it, and not with clarity."

"And your song, the song you were singing when we found you?"

She glanced at the edge of what was no longer stone grove. "A lullaby. They do not hate me," she said. "Nothing they now attempt is personal."

"Would you kill them if you could?"

"Yes. But not with joy, Kaylin, and with no sense of triumph. I understand what Teela's mother asked of the green. But in the end, this is the result. The green is scarred, Teela is scarred, and the lost children exist in a state that is neither life nor death. But I think this time, we will have an ending, one way or the other." She looked up as the water drew close, carrying Teela, cradling her as the fire had done.

"What happened to her?"

"She did what you did—she absorbed the nightmares of Alsanis. I couldn't do what I did for you because I couldn't see them. At all."

"How many?"

"I don't know. I told you—I couldn't see them. There doesn't seem to be anything wrong with her physically, and I can't—I can't touch *her*."

"I would think it suicidal to try."

"She's unconscious. She can only kill me if she wakes up."

The Consort touched Teela's brow.

"Can you see her name?"

The Consort said, "Never ask that question of me. Never ask it again. It is not safe."

"For me, or for you?"

"For either of us, Kaylin. Do you understand the position of Consort is not hereditary?"

"It was—"

"No. I am offered the opportunity to take the test first; it is a courtesy. I could have refused, without dishonor; I did not. Had I failed, I would have died, and a search for a suitable candidate would have begun. My bloodline gives me no affinity; it gives me nothing special. The test that we face— a test you did not—is not short. It is not a decision made in a moment. There are spaces in which Barrani might live that are nonetheless not the world to which we were born. In those spaces, time has less meaning—but no Barrani, no Dragon, no mortal, can undo the past. We move forward. The testing that I underwent began before you were born. Were I to undergo such a test now, it would end long after you died—of the old age that takes all mortals, sooner or later.

"Some fail the test almost immediately. Some take decades to make the first, false step. There is no going back. No one of us understands what the test entails, Kaylin, until it is far too late. My mother passed. I passed." She smiled. "I passed in—how do you say it? Record time?"

"That's how we say it."

"My father, of course, was proud. Proud. I was his daughter."

"Your mother?"

"She grieved."

"I…don't understand."

"She had undergone the same testing, Kaylin. She knew what both passing—and surviving—in such a short time meant. The Lake chooses; it is not kind in its choice. I am not…the daughter my mother hoped for. I am not harsh enough, not strong enough. But I am not so weak that I could fail. I am not so weak that I could not sacrifice almost everything I loved in order to safeguard the source of all life. But I am weak *enough* that such sacrifice would never be made for any other reason." Her smile was both fragile and self-conscious, yet it looked strangely at home on a Barrani face. "I am not even determined enough to hate you for what you were willing to risk."

"She thought you'd be hurt. By your life."

"No. She knew I would be. She was Barrani, and Consort—but she was my mother. Even among my kin, the relationship is not without significance." She looked up at the sky, where the dragon hovered. "Do you know what you're doing?" she asked, voice soft. "Is this like your refugees, somehow?"

Kaylin very much wanted to say yes. She chose to say nothing instead.

"What has your familiar done to the trees?"

"They weren't really trees."

"That is not an answer."

"No." Kaylin hesitated, and then said, "I don't know."

The Consort's smile was rueful. "Perhaps I should have accepted the nonanswer. Come. Whatever he has done, he has done; the binding that kept me here has faded." Before Kaylin could speak, she added, "They were here, but they were not here. They are children, Barrani children, at heart."

"They're not Barrani."

"No, Kaylin—they are not. But they are not entirely other. They cannot be both—and they have tried. They do not think they are different; they think they are more powerful, less limited, but still essentially what they were." She closed her eyes. "You must leave Teela here."

Kaylin's jaw dropped. She didn't bother to close it without letting words fall out. "I am *not* leaving Teela here."

"Yes, Kaylin, you will. She is here, in the end, because of you—but this is where she must be. I am sorry. You anger me so often, I am surprised that I am able to feel compassion for you at all—but I do. Teela came here as harmoniste, once. She came, and she survived. But she failed. She failed and the dreams of Alsanis were dark for a century.

"What you feel for Teela, we do not feel; not in the same way. It is closest to what the lost feel. You wear the blood of the green, although you are like the youngest and least controlled of our children. But you are Chosen. You have drawn me from the nightmares of Alsanis when none of my kin could. You have come to me in the scar of the green, and because you have, we will be able to leave."

"I couldn't have come here without Teela."

"No."

"I *won't leave her.*"

"Then we will never leave." The Consort slid her hands behind her back. "And I admit that I am…weary. I am weary of the grief of both the green and Alsanis. I am weary of the loss and the fear of loss. I am not in pain. If I cannot leave, the failure, in the end, will not be not my fault. That is a terrible thing to confess, is it not? As long as it is not my fault, I can be at peace with failure."

Kaylin stared at her.

"You have felt it yourself."

And she had. "Why can't you leave without me?"

"Because without you, Chosen, we will fail."

"Fail *what?*"

The telling, the water said, unexpectedly joining a conversation Kaylin hadn't even been certain she could hear. *You are harmoniste. The Lord of the West March will speak, Kaylin; the Teller will expand upon every possible strand of the story he chooses to begin. No story has only one beginning, and no story has only one end. No story has only one strand; it involves the lives and the possibilities of so many that you will never even meet. Understand your audience when you begin to choose. Understand who the story must reach, and why. You have seen the wound at the heart of the green. You do not fully understand what it is or why it has waited; you must.*

The green cannot wait forever; the lost speak sorrow and grief and untruth in their rage and their pain. The joy they know is too fixed and too slight; it feeds nothing but despair.

You are Chosen. You have told stories before. It is your nature.

The dragon roared. Kaylin looked up; he spun around in

a large circle, and then, slowly and deliberately, landed. He was not small. He would never, she was afraid, be small again.

Teela is part of this place. She is part of its wound. She is loved by the green, and the green grieves for her. She has given it no cause for joy and none for hope—but the green hopes. I will guard your Teela, as I have guarded the blood of her kin for so many of your centuries.

"And if I fail? If I fail, will you give her back?"

The water did not reply.

"Eldest," the Consort said. She tendered the water a flawless Barrani obeisance. She caught Kaylin's arm. "Understand your own question, Lord Kaylin."

Kaylin said nothing.

"Success is not yours alone; nor is failure. But if you fail, the green will succumb. The names of the lost will *be* lost. Teela's name will be lost in a like fashion. But perhaps, in the end, she will be at peace. This is where she must be if there is any hope of success. And you, Chosen, must be at the heart of the green—in our world. The story you tell, the story you hear, the truth and the lies—they will be evident nowhere else. Do you understand?"

"No."

"The heart of the green exists in our world. It is not easily reached because it is a window into the worlds that exist beyond our reach. We cannot see as the green sees. We cannot feel as it feels. We cannot speak as it speaks; that was never to be our gift. But we can touch the green, and the green can—in that moment, at that time, touch us in a fashion. It listens, Kaylin.

"Our names were created *for* our world. True Words were created for our world. While we bear them, we might traverse the wilderness, but they cannot exist without flesh; we keep them safe. We are their roots and their connection to their origins."

The dragon *roared*.

Kaylin said, without thought, "He has no name."

"No. And I cannot understand him. But the eldest does. The green does. He is not *of* our world. Nor can he be, as he is. I do not know if he will be able to leave the green, but if he can, I am not certain he will not be more of a threat, in the end, than your Devourer." She sounded oddly unconcerned as she held out both of her hands and took Kaylin's. "I am sorry, Lord Kaylin. We cannot wait. They know what has happened, and they come now."

"How—how do you know that?"

"I hear the green." She lifted her face, raised her perfectly, clear voice, and spoke three words.

The world hardened instantly around them; the ground cracked and dried beneath their feet. They stood by the small basin of an empty fountain.

Except the fountain wasn't empty; the basin was full, the water rippling as water from above trickled into it.

"Lady!"

Kaylin turned, her hands numb the Consort was holding them so tightly. The Lord of the West March practically knocked Kaylin over in his rush to his sister's side. He felt her outrage, and ignored it, the rage and the worry and the fear of hope overwhelming anything as small as her offense. He caught his sister in his arms, lifted her off her feet, and half dragged Kaylin with her, because the Consort still had a death grip on the Hawk's hands.

He saw the color of the Consort's eyes, and the sharp pitch of relief banked. He glanced at the water, at the miracle of water in this place, and then, as the Consort did, he raised his eyes to the sky.

Hovering above them and casting the outline of shadow

over the whole of the clearing was the small dragon. Except, of course, he wasn't small now.

It was Severn who said, *Where is Teela?* He was the only one who asked, and he didn't ask out loud.

Kaylin yanked her hands free of the Consort's, and the Consort allowed it. She turned, almost blindly, toward Severn because she knew where he was: by her side. As close to her as the Lord of the West March was. He didn't hug her; he didn't pull her off her feet. She wasn't the Consort, in the end.

But when she met his expression, he did lift an arm, and she tucked herself beneath it, turning her face toward his chest. He said nothing. He asked no further questions. Not about the dragon that had captured the attention of every Barrani present; not about the Consort, whose rescue was the one thing that brought joy and relief to them all, no matter their rank or political affiliations; not about the water.

The eagles of Alsanis were sitting on their dead-tree perches.

"It is not the time," they said in unison. "Lord of the West March, Warden, we will lead your people out of the green. We will return three days hence; the Teller and the harmoniste must come to the green."

"And the rest of us?" the Lord of the West March all but demanded.

"Those who will take the risk, bear witness. Understand that the risk is as great as it has ever been for your kind. Only four must venture into the greenheart at the appointed hour: the Teller, the harmoniste, the Lord of the West March, and the Warden."

The dragon roared, and the eagles cocked their heads toward the sky. Birds couldn't frown; their beaks were fixed and hard. But the eagle on Kaylin's right said, "You should not be here."

The dragon roared again; Kaylin lifted a free hand to cover

her ear. The other, she pressed farther into Severn's chest. She didn't close her eyes, and because she didn't, she saw the heads of the eagles swivel in her direction.

"So be it," they said. They didn't sound happy. "Three days, Chosen."

CHAPTER 22

It was well past dawn when the eagles and their nausea-inducing method of travel deposited the pilgrims at the edge of the green, where a thunderous, midnight-blue-eyed Lord Avonelle waited. She wore the armor of the war band; she wore the sword. She had no less than a dozen similarly armed attendants.

The color of her eyes lightened when she caught sight of Barian; they did not, however, shade to green. "Where is Lord An'Teela?"

Lord Barian glanced, not at Kaylin, but at the Consort.

The Consort said, in a clear, resonant voice, "Lord Teela chose to remain in the green as the price of my release." Her eyes were a lighter blue, but they were tinged with a hint of purple.

Lord Avonelle was not satisfied with the answer, but she couldn't accuse the Consort of lying without offending the rest of the Court.

"We have been commanded by the dreams of Alsanis,"

the Lord of the West March now added, "to return at the appointed hour of the recitation. It was suggested that we number only four."

The lightening of Lord Avonelle's eyes reversed in a spectacular dive back into the near-black range. She was bristling with rage.

"Guardian," Lord Barian said, stepping directly in front of the Lord of the West March and the Consort whose weight he now supported. "It was suggested by the dreams of Alsanis. They feel that it is more of a risk than even the tale told to the lost. The Lord of the West March offers no disrespect to our line or your guardianship. The wards could not be activated. The propicients could not invoke them. Were it not for the dreams of Alsanis, we would never have reached the heart of the green."

She said a very tight-lipped nothing. Kaylin wondered, not for the first time, what the relationship between this Barrani mother and her son was like. Teela's mother was dead. Kaylin's mother, dead. Maybe the Consort's mother was right: those who survived had to be harsh and cold.

Lord Barian now turned to the Lord of the West March. "My domicile is not as fine as the Lord's hall, but the Lord's hall is compromised. It would be my honor to offer you, and your people, the hospitality of the Warden's perch."

The Lord of the West March bowed. It was not a perfunctory gesture. "It would be my honor to accept your generous offer." He glanced at his sister. She was, to Kaylin's eye, much paler than usual.

She offered the Warden a smile, but no other courtesy; judging from the color of his eyes, the smile was enough. He bowed to her and rose.

To Kaylin's surprise, the eagles landed on his shoulders. They were broad, Barrani shoulders, but the eagles were not small, and the Warden raised both of his arms, elbows bent, to offer them a less crowded perch.

Kaylin said nothing. She hid behind Severn. She didn't want to speak with Avonelle. She didn't want to speak with anyone. She couldn't. What she wanted to do was to go back to the heart of the green, throw herself into the water in the fountain, and swim all the way back to wherever Teela was.

She wasn't certain—couldn't be certain—that the Consort *was* lying to Avonelle. That was the worst of it. Everything she'd said in the heart of the green—every *single* word—could have been a lie, a way of leaving the green. And she'd do it, too, not because she valued Teela's life so little, but because she was the conduit to life for the rest of her people. No one would think what she'd done was wrong; no one but Kaylin.

Kaylin.

I don't want to talk to you right now, she told Nightshade.

Then perhaps it would be best if you were not shouting. I am not the only one who will hear your thoughts and your grief. I will not use them against you; can you be so certain that no others will?

She couldn't, and he knew it.

You must *learn to hide this, Kaylin.*

I am hiding it. It's on the inside of me.

You have learned how to hide thought, Kaylin; you have learned how to shield what must be shielded. You are mortal; you are exhausted. Even exhausted, you must not forget. You found the Lady.

Yes.

Understand that the High Court is, once again, in your debt.

Kaylin said nothing.

Yes. You understand what that means. You are not wrong. Given a choice between her own life and the life of any other member of our race, she is duty bound—honor bound—to save herself. If you think this does not grieve her, you fail to understand her.

It's easy for you to say. You want what she wants.

Ah. No, you misunderstand the Lady. But yes, Kaylin. What Iberrienne wanted—before he lost so much of himself—I want. I did not understand what had happened to Iberrienne; I understood only that he had seen his brother. The brother he thought lost. He has spent centuries attempting to do just that—only that—in secret. I knew.

Why did you turn him in?

Silence. It didn't last. *Do you not understand?*

No. I don't ask questions to make conversation.

It was the only thing I could offer that would bring you here.

You knew. That I would be harmoniste.

No. It was, from the beginning, a gamble. You are Chosen. You do not understand your power; no more do the Barrani. But I have seen what you have done with it. You stumble. You fail to plan. But you free the trapped. You tell stories that I cannot hear, but cannot doubt.

Kaylin stumbled; Severn caught her, sliding an arm around her waist. She was too tired and too dispirited to care when her stomach growled, but she did watch—a little vindictively—as a large shadow crossed the green, catching Avonelle's attention. The dragon had followed the eagles at a discreet distance— but something the size the dragon now was would never, ever be stealthy.

Avonelle's eyes did not take on the gold of surprise, which was a pity. They didn't really shift at all; the color of fear— which the Barrani never acknowledged—was pretty much the color of their more socially acceptable rage.

She did, on the other hand, feel Nightshade's surprise. *Kaylin, what is this?*

Small dragon. Well, not so small dragon.

He didn't appreciate her humor. This made her feel a little bit better.

What happened to it?

I needed him to carry Teela. Which guttered the little bit better entirely.

Can you control him? The question was sharp, insistent.

She glanced up at the sky and the underside of translucent belly. At this distance, he looked almost like himself. If he squawked instead of roaring, it would almost be a comfort. He predictably roared.

No.

You allowed him to...grow...without being certain of your control? Since the answer was pretty self-evident, she didn't bother with one. Instead, she said, *Which one of the lost was yours?* Because she wanted him to leave her alone, and she was pretty certain the question would shut him down.

It did.

Kaylin had only seen a small portion of the Warden's perch; her visit to Lord Barian's ancestral home had been cut short by the presence—and demands—of the dreams of Alsanis. She was exhausted by the time she reached the Warden's halls; she was dragging her feet in a kind of stupor that meant morning would start sometime around late afternoon. Given that it was pretty much full-on daylight, it might start later than that.

Severn walked by her side, and to Kaylin's surprise, the Consort joined them; her brother walked by her side and the Barrani High Court, disheveled, bruised, and otherwise less perfect than normal walked both in front and behind. Avonelle didn't live in the Warden's perch; it was a small mercy on a day when mercy was in short supply. Kaylin took it.

The eagles stayed with Barian; he led the High Court into his halls. Kaylin, by this point, was tired enough that taking a seat with her back to the nearest wall seemed like a better option than tripping over her own feet. Severn glanced at her. A minute later, maybe less, he stepped in front of her and crouched. "Climb on."

She hesitated for less than ten seconds. Yes, being a Lord

of the High Court made demands on dignity. No, at the moment, she didn't care. She let herself be piggybacked down the tall, wide, light-filled halls, and surprised herself by drifting off.

Lord Kaylin. Lord Kaylin—wake.

The voice was unfamiliar for one long moment; Kaylin snapped out of sleep, and the shattered edge of dreams, when she recognized it. It was Ynpharion's. She recognized the background blend of bitter humiliation and rage. Both were muted. His concern—his fear—was not.

She rolled out of bed, which was her first mistake; the beds in the perch were obviously meant for people at least six feet in height who nonetheless always landed on their feet. They were much higher off the ground than the rickety bed she'd once owned.

She landed on her knees, shook herself, and gained her feet as smoothly as she could.

Ynpharion?

She felt his impatience at her obvious ignorance, but he answered. *Yes.*

What's happened? Are we under attack? What time is it?

It is almost midnight, he replied, with just a hint of condescension. *Both the Lord of the West March and the Warden gave orders that you were not to be disturbed. I believe they have changed their minds. We are wakeful; the Lady herself has been roused, and she is…concerned.*

Great. Kaylin made sure she had her daggers, although they didn't provide much comfort; too many Barrani, too many swords, and too much shadow magic. She longed for Elani street with a passion usually reserved for hating it.

Severn was at her door before she'd opened it; he was armed with the two blades of his weapon chain. She stared at them.

Ynpharion, is Iberrienne still alive?

The question confused him, which Kaylin took as a yes. "What's happened?" she asked as she exited a room that did not—at first glance—appear to have a door ward.

"Your dragon is breathing on select buildings in the West March."

Kaylin wanted to turn back to her room and crawl under the bed. "Any particular buildings?"

"You're not going to like the answer." He began to walk down the hall; she followed at a jog, to make up for the difference in their stride. She recognized where he was leading her, although it was a lot more crowded than the last time she'd seen it—he headed straight for the giant trunk around which stairs were wound. He took them two at a time; the lack of rails on the side that faced an increasingly grim drop didn't bother him at all.

"Did they have their council meeting?"

"No. The Consort called a recess, given the current situation. Lord Avonelle might have argued, but she's now occupied with the wards in the green."

"The ones that don't work?"

"Yes."

Two small mercies.

Sleep had done Kaylin good. Lack of food hadn't. She reached the top of the viewing platform thinking about bread. And cheese. And meat. They were petty concerns, given Severn's news, which is probably why she clung to them. Ynpharion was on the viewing platform.

So was a very pale Evarrim.

Severn—why is he even standing?

The Consort asked for his presence; he acquiesced. You are not, of course, to notice any weakness or injury he doesn't speak of himself.

He looks like crap.

Yes. Iberrienne is, however, not in a state to provide information at this point in time. Nightshade spent hours closeted with Iberrienne. The Consort joined Nightshade when she returned.

What happened?

I don't know. Iberrienne is not considered well enough to attend, and Evarrim is considered the only other High Court expert in residence. He is therefore here.

So was the Lord of the West March and the Warden; both men were blue-eyed and grim. The eagles sat on the railing, facing outward; they might have been carved of stone. Beyond them, in the clear, midnight sky, Kaylin saw a cloud that was moving at great speed in an otherwise still sky.

"Chosen," the eagles said, although neither moved.

She glanced at her arms; the marks were glowing a pale, faint blue. She was surprised when the Lord of the West March handed her a large drape of cloth. It was a jacket, sort of. It had sleeves very similar to the sleeves that had once been part of the dress she wore, but it was heavier and warmer. She doubted it was immune to water, fire, or dirt, but was grateful to have it anyway; she was cold.

"How long has he been out there?"

"He has been in our skies since you returned." It was Lord Barian who answered. "What is he doing?"

Since that was more or less her next question, she swallowed it. She had no idea, but felt bald acceptance of her own ignorance was a career-limiting move. She walked over to the rails and took up a position between the two eagles. They both turned their heads—only their heads—to face her.

The not-so-small dragon was circling, in a desultory way. His flight path at this distance seemed very constricted; she squinted, cursing her vision.

Ynpharion—what's in the sky beside the dragon?

The nightmares, Ynpharion replied, *of Alsanis.*

Are they flying in a pattern around him?

Yes.

Are they...attacking him?

"They are, Chosen," the eagles said in unison.

She watched as the dragon roared; his voice probably blanketed the entire West March. It wasn't as bad as the breath that followed. It clipped one small shadow. She watched as the shadow's gliding path faltered. The shadows looked exactly like that, to Kaylin—they implied eagle.

What had she done? She'd caught the shadows, intercepted their flight, and pulled the eagles out of their insubstantial darkness. The dragon's breath didn't have the same effect— and why would it? The shadows gained weight, plummeting from the sky. They did not—at this distance—change shape; no birds emerged, and nothing less threatening took to the sky in their place.

Kaylin drew the jacket more tightly around her shoulders.

"Can you command your familiar?" Evarrim said. Kaylin had come, grudgingly, to understand that among the Barrani, Evarrim was considered blunt and to the point. And he was. His machinations, his desires, and his power, were always on display; it was hard to assume that he was in any way friendly.

Kaylin was silent for a long moment. "I've never tried," she finally said.

Evarrim's brow furrowed. Kaylin decided, at this point, that ignorance was less useful than dignity.

"What do you think he is trying to do?"

She was watching the nightmares as they fell from the sky. The dragon's breath seemed almost silver at this distance, seen in moonlight and night sky. "I'm not certain. The building he's flying around—it *is* a building, isn't it?" It was, to Kaylin's eye, a shadowy apparition.

Silence. Barian finally said, "Yes."

"I don't remember seeing it before."

"No, Chosen. It is the Hallionne Alsanis. It has lain under protective wards for centuries. No visitors to the West March have seen it as you see it now."

"Have you?"

"No. I remember Alsanis. I remember the form Alsanis chose to take."

"Let me guess. It wasn't an edifice of crystal shadow."

"You are correct."

"Did the dragon—"

"The wards are down. Lord Avonelle has ordered an evacuation of the buildings closest to the Hallionne."

Kaylin watched for a few more minutes because the building was taking shape with the passage of time. It was not—yet—the height of the Warden's perch; it was, however, taller than the towers of the Lord's hall. Nor did it seem to be shrinking.

"Lord Barian, with your permission, I would like to approach the Hallionne."

She felt Lirienne's surprise; it was colored with strong disapproval. He did not, however, say no. He observed correct form.

"The recitation will take place in two days," Lord Barian replied. As replies went, it seemed to have missed the question. Kaylin waited.

"It will take place," the eagles said, "sooner."

There was a lot of silence then. Kaylin, who was aware that the Warden was in theory responsible for the recitation, looked at the eagles. "How much sooner?"

"Can you not hear it begin, Chosen? Can you not hear the words?"

"Most of the words I can hear come from me, and I'm having a hard time keeping them on the inside of my mouth." She said this in sharp Elantran.

"The Teller is leaving the domicile," the eagle to the right said.

"He has the Consort and Lord Iberrienne with him," the eagle to the left said.

"I'd like about two days more sleep before I do the job the dress chose me for."

The eagles craned forward so they could look at each other. They then turned their heads toward the Lord of the West March, who was now standing rigidly near the exit. "Lord of the West March. Warden. You cannot reach the greenheart now."

"It is not the appointed time," Barian said.

"There is now only one path to the greenheart," they replied. "And time does not pass predictably. If you can walk the path at all, you will need Teller and harmoniste."

Silence.

"And Lord of the West March, you must choose. The Lady will travel with you."

"I will not take that risk."

"She is the Consort, Lord of the West March. Her duties are not to you; they are not even to the High Lord."

Nightshade, what in the hells are you doing?

We approach the Hallionne, Kaylin. Can you not hear it?

No.

You asked me which of the lost was mine.

She wasn't particularly proud of the question.

You will have your answer. Come. I understand the shape of the story I am meant to tell, but it does not begin here, and if it ends here, it will end in one of two ways. I cannot do what you must do, although I would have taken the blood of the green over the Teller's crown.

It didn't do Teela any good, was Kaylin's surprisingly bitter reply.

No. And in the end, it is unlikely that I would have succeeded where she failed.

Kaylin closed her eyes. She opened them, squaring her shoulders, and turned to face the Lord of the West March. "Will you order your people to remain behind?"

"It is not our way to strip ourselves of strength when we walk into the unknown."

"Lord Barian?"

"The Court of the Vale has far less to prove than the Lords of the High Court—but no, Lord Kaylin. I will order none to remain behind who wish to accompany us."

"And you'll go?"

His smile was very odd. "It has been centuries since I have entered Alsanis. My childhood and all of the duties of my line lie there. I am not Teller, I am Warden, but if the doors open, I will enter them. We had intended to let you sleep; you are mortal. But the green has its own seasons, and the Hallionne, their own rules.

"If I understand the eagles, you are summoned, Lord Kaylin."

The Lord of the West March took his leave almost before they'd finished speaking; Evarrim lingered. It was to Evarrim that Kaylin went. She offered him a stiff, formal bow. He lifted a black brow in response.

"I will not venture into Alsanis," Evarrim said.

She thought it a small wonder that he had remained on his feet, but kept this to herself. "What do familiars want?" she asked, voice soft. Since she was among Barrani, soft words would carry almost as far as louder ones.

"There are very few extant records of such creatures. They are legend. It is hard to abstract history from legend, and it is my suspicion that it would be irrelevant."

"Why?"

"Because no two of our legendary sorcerers were alike, Lord

Kaylin. They amassed power in different ways, and used it to different purposes. We make assumptions based on our own observations of those who have power, but they are not sound assumptions. Power affects the powerful in different ways."

"But the familiars—"

"They are not creatures of this world. Even you must understand that. In legend, they were able to shape the world. The creature as he appeared for most of the journey was not significant, but he was not insignificant; his abilities belied his size. You think of him as a mortal pet."

She didn't deny it.

"He is not. But even you must realize this now."

Kaylin nodded. "He's like an elemental. A summoned elemental. Except I didn't summon him."

"No. That may tell in your favor; I cannot say. In the three stories of which I am personally aware, the familiars were sought. They were not stumbled over as a byproduct of a world-threatening event; the world-threatening event was created to draw them into the world. In that way, they are unlike elementals. We know the name of the fire," he said, his gaze intent, his eyes narrowed. "And perhaps, if we knew the name of the wilderness from which the familiars are drawn and of which they are part, we would be able to summon them in the way we call fire, water, earth, and air. Such studies have been made; none have been successful.

"The fire spoke to you in the outlands. I summoned it; it was my power that kept it leashed and present. But it spoke to you, Lord Kaylin, and without considerable expenditure of power on my part, it was you to whom it answered. I do not know what power summoned the familiar; nor do I know what its intent is. But, Lord Kaylin, absent your presence or my control, I know what fire wants."

So did Kaylin. "The will of the fire," she said quietly, "isn't all one thing or the other. It's complicated."

"So, too, the familiar. But there are currents in the fire's will. Were I at the peak of my power, I might contest your claim; I admit that it has been much in my mind. But I would not do it at this recitation, and I believe if you cannot control what you have been all but guardian to, there will be no recitation. The Teller, the Lord of the West March, and you yourself, will be lost. If we are very lucky, we will not face a similar fate."

"How lucky do you think you'll be?"

"The Barrani seldom believe in luck that we do not make with our own hands." He turned to the Warden. "She must join the Teller."

"Understood."

The Lord of the West March spoke with the gathered members of the High Court; the conversation—if there was one—was short. They had come to hear the recitation, setting out—in some cases—after news of the presence of a harmoniste reached the High Halls. But they understood what had occurred when Teela was a child, and they saw, as they filed out of the Warden's Perch, what remained in the wake of that disaster.

Lirienne did not demand that they accompany him; he made clear that the Consort intended to enter Alsanis, but he also made clear that the gathered might of High Court and Vale had done nothing to retrieve her on either of the two occasions she had almost been lost. Lord Kaylin, he reminded them, had been solely responsible for her survival on both occasions.

"Lord Kaylin," Ynpharion said, "did not preserve her life on the forest paths."

"No," was the grave reply. "And Lord Kaylin did not protect her when the Lord's hall was attacked. But Lord Ynpharion, neither did we. I will not command. I will not demand.
Lord Iberrienne will accompany us, at the Lady's request."

Kaylin didn't understand Ynpharion. He had, over the
course of a day—or two, depending—accepted what he had
spent weeks raging against: she held his name. She had a power
over him that even the High Lord didn't have. His anger, his
sense of self-loathing, was still present, but so vastly diminished Kaylin thought there was an actual chance she might be
able to ignore it one day.

*You saved the Lady, not once, but twice. She was angry, Lord
Kaylin. She was angry with you; she is not angered now. I do not
understand mortals, and I have lived far longer than you have within
the confines of Elantra. But I understand my people.*

You hold my name. But mine is not the only name you hold.

She said nothing, aware that her own ability to hide her
thoughts was going to cause so much trouble in the future.

*You do not command the dragon because you do not understand
the truth of command. You only barely commanded me, and in so
doing, returned me to myself. So I will tell you what I know of the
transformed: they are not Barrani. They remember; in that, they are
Immortal. But how they respond to what they remember, what they
desire because of it—it is not what we desire.*

*And my desires changed, Lord Kaylin. I would call it subtle—
but it was not. When you spoke my name, when you burned away
the taint that it fed, I was instantly awake, and instantly what I had
been before I acceded to Iberrienne's offer. Yes,* he added, before she
could ask. *I wanted power. You already understand why.*

She did.

*But the power he gave was not the power I wanted. I understood
only yesterday that Iberrienne himself faced the same change, and I
have seen what it has done to him. You hold his name, and you are*

afraid to even speak to him because you are afraid he will shatter. There was contempt in this last thought—for her—but also a very strong confusion.

I serve you because I have no choice.

Kaylin said nothing.

But I now understand that in serving you, I serve the Lady. I serve the Lord of the West March. I serve a sorcerer. I see legends walking—and flying. I see the twisted ruins of a Hallionne long lost to my distant kin. If disaster follows in your wake, it is not unmitigated. He hesitated, and then added, *I remember what the transformed remember. Iberrienne would have drained the name that was released upon the death of my companion.*

You preserved it.

You preserved it, and you wear it, but you do not destroy it in the wearing. The Consort believes that you will return that life to the Lake. And if you can, it means you have seen what she has seen, and you have survived. I know what she hopes to achieve. We all know. But if she fails, she believes that you might succeed. It is her highest duty. I will serve with what small grace I can muster. You live such a short time.

CHAPTER 23

What do you remember? Kaylin asked Ynpharion. *What did you think you were fighting* for?

Freedom.

From the tyranny of name?

You understand.

No, I don't. You still have a name or you wouldn't be here. Was the name supposed to be transformed, somehow?

If we understood the form of our hidden selves, we could, with will and careful intent, revise it. If it became known, we could change it enough that knowledge was not a weapon that could be wielded against us. And we discovered that we could change more. The tyranny of form no longer bound us. We could walk the fixed lands—the world, as you call it. But we could walk the outlands, and we could walk the space between spaces. We could speak with the hidden and ancient things that live where the living cannot—creatures of which we had had no awareness before we were given the keys to unlock our cages.

He spit.

They were not cages. Had he been speaking out loud, his voice would have trembled with the intensity of his anger. *They were the essence of what we* are. *The shadows bled the strength from the words, but they could not completely change them; they could change their meaning in the gray spaces where names do not exist.*

Kaylin frowned. She turned to Barian, who walked by her side as they left his home. "When the Lords come to the West March to listen to the *regalia,* it is rumored that some are empowered by the experience." She spoke in careful High Barrani.

His nod was cautious; it didn't encourage discussion.

The advantage of belonging to a lesser race was the expectations it engendered; he had far fewer of her. "It is why the most promising of the young were chosen, was it not?"

"Yes."

"How were the Lords changed?"

His eyes widened. They were blue; she didn't expect their color to shift in any way. "I am not certain I understand the question."

"How was change measured?"

He frowned.

"Lord Lirienne? Does it still happen?"

"Yes. It is not predictable, Lord Kaylin. It is not a dependable change, and there are no indicators prior to the recitation; men and women with great power are changed; men and women with almost no discernible power are changed."

"Yes, but—how? The Barrani I know imply a lot of power but don't demonstrate much of it. I'm certain I haven't seen a tenth of what Evarrim can do."

"That is a question that Lord Evarrim would be able to answer."

"And not the Warden?"

"Very few of the Lords remain in the West March; it is rustic, and the Court of the Vale is less…active. Such changes would not necessarily be marked in a venue in which displays of power are less necessary."

She thought of Lord Avonelle, and Lord Lirienne graced her with the slightest of smiles.

"Does the change involve elemental powers?"

"Elemental powers?"

"Does it strengthen the ability to summon?"

The Lord of the West March was silent.

"Does it give more insight into the between, the gray spaces, the outlands? Does it change the ability to draw wards and runes, to imbue them with power?"

The silence grew. At length, he said, "Yes. There are other abilities which are also strengthened. What do you now suspect, Chosen?"

What did she think? That something, somehow, was altering the base structure of a name? Nudging it, tweaking it, somehow pushing it into a very slightly different shape? The changes that occurred—where they occurred at all—didn't destroy the person who received them. It didn't do what had been done to the lost children, and what had been done, in turn, to the Barrani who had become Ferals.

Why?

A name was a name. It was given at birth. Did the Barrani somehow grow into it? Was it more rooted, stronger somehow, with age and experience? Were the children susceptible because they had not yet grown into the word that would define them? Were they altered because they had no way of protecting what they didn't fully understand?

Or was Ynpharion altered not because of the shadows but because of the length and constancy of the exposure to the things that weren't meant to live here? Did the recitation give a glimpse of that world to those who could retain it? Did it sensitize them without altering the nature of what life meant?

Ynpharion—

Yes, I understand the question. I do not remember being told a story.

Did you understand what Iberrienne was attempting to do when we—when we first met?

No. He hadn't finished, but was silent for a long moment. *Yes. I think I believed that he was trying to change the world. To make it freer. To rid it of the constraints and the limits placed upon us by our creators.*

Was this his idea?

It was our *idea; we believed it. We could see the world that he could see. We did not have the power to change it, but the power exists in the words left us. We could use those words. We could use them to alter reality.*

The names.

She felt his revulsion. He didn't bother to mention the Lake of Life; even the thought of it in this context revolted him. Yet it was what he had believed.

Do you have any idea of how that was supposed to work?

No.

And Iberrienne seems to have only half a brain left. Did you ever see his brother?

Brother?

She took this as a no, but said, *Iberrienne lost his brother to the recitation. He was one of the twelve; I think his name was Eddorian.*

She felt Ynpharion almost freeze in place. He didn't answer, but he didn't need to answer.

Kaylin exhaled, turned, and caught Ynpharion's arm, dragging him out of his momentary paralysis.

They spoke very little as they walked toward the Hallionne Alsanis. The green of grass and trees gave way to something that might have been stone or ash; it was roughly circular in shape, and the Hallionne stood at its heart. Nightshade, Iberrienne, and the Consort stood at its edge, waiting; the shadow cast by the enormous dragon in the sky above darkened the ground as he flew.

The Consort looked back as her brother approached; they exchanged brief, almost silent words—or at least almost silent to Kaylin. She then turned to Kaylin. "Lord Kaylin."

Kaylin offered the Consort a perfect bow. She'd had enough sleep that she wasn't tripping over her own feet. When she rose, the Lord of the West March had stepped aside to make room for her; it was a less than subtle hint. Kaylin took the vacated position by the Consort's side.

"Can you hear him?"

"Yes." The Consort glanced at Ynpharion as she spoke. She did not otherwise acknowledge him.

"Can he hear you?"

"I do not know, Lord Kaylin. I have never spoken to Alsanis as Consort." She glanced at Iberrienne, and then said, her voice gentling, "Are you ready?" It occurred to Kaylin that Iberrienne was theoretically Outcaste, and unlike Nightshade, he didn't have the protection of the Teller's crown. Nor did it matter.

Iberrienne nodded. "Eddorian is calling."

The dragon roared. Kaylin wanted to roar back. Instead, she began to walk.

Ten yards from the edge of the gray circle, she found the first of the fallen nightmares. It retained its shape, but the darkness of shadow had left it; it now seemed like an artist's impression of a bird—a shape that implied flight, without any of its form. She glanced at the Consort for permission; the Consort nodded.

"None of us now understand what we will face. You are Chosen." Kaylin opened her mouth; the Consort held out one graceful—and imperious—hand. "What you choose to risk, risk. We will accept it."

Kaylin glanced at the Warden. Lord Barian's gaze was fixed on the fallen nightmare. Kaylin had no cause to love those nightmares—but the eagles had emerged from them. Then again, she had no reason to love the eagles, either; they spoke more clearly, but they had taken the Consort from the Lord's Hall into the heart of the green.

She felt the marks on her arm begin to warm. She touched the fallen nightmare; it felt like stone beneath her palm, rough and porous. At her back, Severn unwound his chain.

"Don't," she told him.

"It's still a weapon," he replied. "It doesn't break spells, but it's effective in every other way."

"You can't use it here—"

"But he can, Lord Kaylin," Barian said. "If it is to become what it was, he must."

Kaylin bit her lip as she attempted to lift what felt like stone. To her surprise, it was much lighter than it appeared. She turned to say something to Barian and stopped at the expression on the Warden's face.

The nightmare rose. Its solid wings labored in the air a yard above Kaylin's hands. The eagles that rested on Barian watched in silence. Kaylin held out both hands as the not-quite-stone, not-quite-bird failed to fly. It landed in her palms.

And then it spoke. Kaylin didn't understand a word.

The eagles, however, did; they replied, in the same tongue. The creature in her hands shook at the sound of their voices. It had no mouth; it had a crevice that implied beak and emitted syllables. After a sentence or two—judging only by intonation and pauses, it shivered again, and this time, it pulled a head out of the porous mass of its body. It was an eagle's head. Nothing about its body changed, but Kaylin's eyes rounded.

"Lord Kaylin?"

"This is—I think this is—"

The eagles leaped from Barian's arms to Kaylin's shoulders. Their claws didn't pierce skin, but it was close.

"What are you?" the creature transforming itself in her hands asked. He asked in Elantran, or what passed for Elantran; Kaylin's suspicions hardened.

"I'm mortal," she replied. "Human, even."

"What is that?"

"I'm not Barrani."

"You are not one of the children, then."

"No."

"Why are you here?"

"Apparently," she replied softly, "I'm here to wake you. You are Alasanis's brother, aren't you?"

"Alsanis is here? Where?"

The eagles answered, screeching. Kaylin couldn't understand a word they were saying. She glanced at the Consort, who was frowning.

"You could understand it?"

"It sounds like it's speaking Elantran to me," Kaylin replied. "And I guess that means it's not."

The gray eagle face was joined by wings, and legs. The legs were a little off, possibly because they were of uneven lengths. She watched as he adjusted them. "I don't like this shape. It is too small."

"If you're going to get bigger, don't do it in my hands."

"Oh?" He looked at her hands, and she noted, as he did, that his eyes were like black opals. "Will it harm them?"

She set him on the ground. "He's like Wilson," she told the

Consort. To the bird that was slowly changing and expanding his shape, she added, "How many of you are there?"

He blinked. It was disturbing because he had grown a third eye. "How many?" He turned to the eagles and asked them a question she couldn't understand; the eagles replied, and whatever they said caused the creature to laugh. "How *many* are you?"

Kaylin started to count, and one of the eagles tightened his claws. "There is only one of you."

"Don't tell me that—tell him."

"We have. He does not understand the concept. We will fly," the eagle added. "We will search."

The dragon roared, and the stone eagle, which was doing a good job of becoming a standing puddle, froze. It looked up—well, the head did; the wings had kind of dispersed into something disturbingly liquid—and its face changed shape. It roared back.

Kaylin was once again reminded of Bellusdeo and Diarmat, minus the outrage on either side. She covered her ears with her hands and rose. But she looked up at the dragon, and felt momentarily happy. Yes, he was larger, and yes, he had changed. But the gift he had given Bertolle, he had attempted to give to Alsanis.

"It is not safe," the stone said, its shape at last settling into an almost-familiar one. No, not almost. She heard Nightshade's breath stop—funny, that that was a sound. She recognized the Barrani who now stood before her with his opal eyes, although she had only seen him once. He was Allaron.

But the statue that now began to take on the texture—and color—of flesh shook his head; black hair gleamed in a drape down his back. "We are not. We are the brothers of Alsanis."

"Why do you look like Allaron?"

"Do I?" He frowned. "Is it upsetting?"

"No," Kaylin said quickly. "We're fine with it. You don't have to change your shape again."

"It is small and confining, but—small and confined as you are, it is appropriate." He frowned. "Alsanis is waking. The children are crying. Come." He paused, and then bowed to the Consort. He appeared content to ignore everyone else. "Lady."

The Consort inclined her head; her eyes were an odd shade of blue. "Will he hear me?"

"Yes, Lady—but they will hear you, as well. They are troublesome. They occupy us, they exhort us, they demand. Alsanis is..." He frowned. It was not a Barrani expression; it was too quick and too open. Turning, he lifted his arms; light bled from his fingertips like slow lightning. He chased it with the thunder of his voice.

The dragon roared.

The awakened brother roared back, and then turned, his eyes round with outrage. "You have not named him."

"No."

"Why? How can he be here without a name?"

"I don't know his name."

The brother—Kaylin considered calling him Roger— frowned. "Of course not. You could not contain his name; it would devour you. Did you not impress a name upon him when you summoned him?"

"No." She wasn't going to explain that she hadn't summoned him. On the other hand, it appeared that the dragon was, and loudly.

One of the Hallionne's distant walls cracked in response, the fault line spreading like fractures in glass.

The brother fell silent. "It is almost too late. Come, Lady. Come, Chosen. Alsanis waits." He turned to Nightshade and the Lord of the West March. "Be prepared. There are too many stories and too little time." He began to walk toward the shadowed, crystal building.

The eagles didn't return. There were no other fallen shadows on the straightest path between their current location and the cracked wall, and Kaylin hesitated. She remembered the brothers of Bertolle.

"We are awake now, and we are here. We are not Bertolle's kin, but Alsanis's. More forms are not necessary." He glanced at the Consort and shook his head. "Now is not the time. No song of awakening is necessary, Lady. He is awake. He does not sleep. He has not slept since the green was washed in the blood of the dying; he will not sleep until the tale is done. And until now, he could not speak with us *unless* he slept.

"But, Lady, when the time comes, if it does, you will know. Sing then." He fell silent, his dark eyes narrowing, his frown etching literal lines in his face, his hair spreading down his back and his legs to blanket the ground at his feet. She had seen Bertolle's brothers lose control of their shape, but still found the fluidity of something that looked *almost* natural disturbing.

"The children are awake. They are not happy."

"Have they *ever* been happy?" Kaylin asked; it was a rhetorical question.

The brothers of the Hallionne did not apparently do rhetorical. "Yes, once. They remember. But it is thin, Chosen. It is an echo. A shadow. They hear Alsanis. They hear what he does not say. They hear his sorrow and his rage and they hear the echoes of us. He has not slept," he repeated. "And he does not dream."

Kaylin didn't argue; they had reached the cracked wall. If she'd expected to see a door, or anything that implied door, she was doomed to disappointment. The brother placed one palm over the point from which the fractures had spread. "They mean to hold the door."

Kaylin didn't point out that there was no door.

"They speak to Alsanis now; they are loud." He drew his hand away from the wall. Kaylin had time to throw her arms over her eyes before he slammed a fist down. She heard the crack of crystal. She didn't, however, hear the tinkle of falling pieces that generally meant it had shattered.

He struck again, undeterred, with the same effect. Kaylin lowered her arms as he lowered his hand. He turned to face them, his brows a single line across a subtly changed face.

"Bearer," he said, his voice grave. It was to Severn he spoke. It was to Severn's blades that he looked.

Severn didn't hesitate. He stepped forward, one blade in either hand. "They were damaged in the outlands. I do not know if they will succeed where you have failed."

"You fail to understand the nature of the blades," the brother replied. "And yet, you wield them. They were not damaged; they served the purpose for which they were forged. They must serve again. I cannot command you, bearer, but we will find no purchase in Alsanis if you do not surrender them to the wall."

Severn nodded. He glanced, once, at Kaylin, and grinned. She felt what he didn't put into words, and shied away from it. This weapon was part of his identity; it was as much his as the Hawk's tabard was Kaylin's. But he didn't doubt Alsanis's brother, and he didn't argue or bargain. Instead, he pulled both blades back and thrust them into the wall, at the same spot it had been struck multiple times.

The brother spread his hands as the wall shattered, flesh becoming—in an instant—a thin, flexible shield. If the shards of former, crystalline wall were sharp, the brother didn't bleed;

he didn't seem to notice. But he didn't shed the bits and pieces, either; instead, the shield shrank, until it once again formed two separate, Barrani hands.

Beyond him, beyond them all, was a gaping, jagged hole. Kaylin was fairly certain that the edges were sharp enough to cut anything that wasn't a multidimensional Immortal.

The walls were not the only thing that had shattered, though.

The blades had done so, as well. She could see shards of metal among the crystalline pieces, and hilts in Severn's hands. They shook, briefly; he sheathed their remains in silence. He didn't hesitate, and he didn't mourn; he'd made the decision. He'd made the decision understanding exactly what Alsanis's brother had asked—and what the cost would be.

That much she felt before she tried to avert her mental gaze. She settled on Alsanis's brother as the safest because there was nothing mortal about him, and the building to which he was related didn't generally respond to normal grief, rage, or fear as if they were emotions relevant to, well, being a building.

"Do not bleed in the Hallionne," he helpfully told them. Lifting his face—or some of it, which was just as disturbing as it sounded—he roared to the sky; small pieces of wall shook loose as the sound reverberated.

The dragon descended.

It was a good damn thing the gap in the shattered wall was so large; descent didn't cause him to lose any of his impressive size. She thought his eyes were the size of her fists, and deliberately avoided looking at his jaws or the curve of claws that seemed to pass through the ground, rather than sinking into it.

But she reached out and touched the space between what would have been dragon nostrils, which would *also* have been courting dismemberment if this were any other dragon. He met her gaze and blinked.

"He ate one of my marks," she said, turning to the Consort. "When he first hatched. I don't think it counts as naming him, but I think—I think it must have provided some sort of anchor."

"That would explain much. It will not satisfy Lord Evarrim."

"Nothing satisfies Lord Evarrim."

"Do you remember what the word was?" the Consort asked. She hesitated for a long moment, and then lifted her hand and set it just below Kaylin's. "He is not warm."

"No. I don't remember what the mark was; if we were in the city, we could dig it out of Records by process of elimination." She didn't ask if it mattered; she now believed it did. "How long do you have?" she asked him.

He shook his head, dislodging their hands. Alsanis's brother approached. He didn't bow, as he had bowed to the Consort; he met—and held—the dragon's gaze. "Time," he finally said, "does not mean, for us, what it means for your kind."

"Mortals?"

"No. The living. He does not intend you harm; he very much wishes the opposite. But he chose to wear the jess of your mark, Chosen, and he has all but consumed it."

She didn't point out that *eaten* had a specific meaning, because she doubted, for the small dragon—or the large—it did. "Can I give him another one?"

"Yes."

But of course, no marks rose from her skin, and she really didn't think that biting off a chunk of her arm would have the same results.

Kaylin was accustomed to the interior of sentient buildings. Judging by the interior of this one, Alsanis was no longer sane. If the exterior wall had resembled shadow-imbued crystal—albeit somewhat malformed—the interior did not match. Here, the ground was uneven, and it was only barely ground. There were patches of what she would bet were sky to the left, shimmering slightly in the uneven light.

Nothing cast that light.

Interspersed with that sky was jagged rock, but the rock itself seemed to be composed of layers of detritus; Kaylin thought she could see a door jutting out from one large, flat curve. She definitely saw windows, and most of them weren't in walls. Then again, she couldn't actually see many walls.

The Consort linked arms with Kaylin, to Kaylin's surprise.

"You have a tendency to get lost," she said, smiling slightly. "And while it generally has interesting results, I would like to be lost with you should it happen."

"You don't—"

"Oh, not for your sake. The men worry; it is unpleasant. What do you see, Lord Kaylin?"

"Everything. I mean—a bit of everything. There's a pillar, there—it's broken. There's a half wall that melts into gray mud. There's an…arm, I think. I can't tell, it doesn't end in a hand. In the distance, I think there are mountains. There are windows in the ground to the far right—or holes that open into sky, because there *also* seems to be a lot of sky. That one's raining. I don't see much furniture, and I don't see any other people."

"No."

"Do you?"

"No; I hear them, though. Can you hear Alsanis?"

Kaylin shook her head. "You do?"

"I do. The lost are with him."

"All of them?"

The Consort frowned. "I cannot be certain; I cannot count voices."

"Do you hear—do you hear Teela?"

"No. But that is not a bad sign; were I to hear her from this remove it would mean that we are too late."

Alsanis's brother shook his head. "What you fear is impossible, Lady."

"Oh?"

"Every Barrani in the West March—every Barrani the green might touch—will be altered and lost to you first. Teela cannot be touched."

Kaylin frowned. After a long pause, spent picking her way over what looked like stone slats, she said, "Why?"

"The price was paid, Chosen. It was paid in life's blood—Teela is beloved by the green; it feels always, and only, the affection and the terrible fear of her mother, and it has accepted the geas that death placed upon it. No harm, no change, will come to Teela while she stands upon the green."

Kaylin almost missed a step. She said, quietly, "The children are trying to destroy the green."

"Yes. They themselves are confined by their attachment to Teela. If she cannot join them while the green exists, they will destroy the green. It will," he added softly, "destroy them; that is Alsanis's fear."

Kaylin didn't understand why he cared.

"No, you do not. He has labored here these many centuries, with no respite, to find some way of preserving them. They are his guests. He hears their voices. They are not what they were when they came to him; they are not what they might be were they free. But he cannot confine all of what they have become. He cannot speak in a way that moves them; they are too intent upon what they see and hear. They will not be moved.

"Can Teela talk to them?"

"She cannot speak—"

"I mean, can she change their mind? Can she convince them to—"

"To what?"

"To stop trying to destroy the green."

"An odd question."

"It's not—"

"Do you not think Teela desires what they desire?"

"No!"

The Consort's hand tightened. "Lord Kaylin. Kaylin. It is often more complicated than simply yes or no. Teela was raised with children who were lost to the recitation. They were not rivals. They were not from the same lines; they were not in competition with each other. Had they been blood kin, it is unlikely they would have become as close as they did."

"There is *no way* Teela wants the green to be destroyed!"

"No. But I am not so certain, were there not another way, she would not join them. Can you be?"

"Yes!" Kaylin pulled her arm free of the Consort—or she tried. The Consort was Barrani, and she didn't want to let go. There'd probably be bruises. Teela had certainly left similar ones in her time. And probably for the same reasons. Kaylin knew what she *wanted* the truth to be. But she'd known Teela for less than a decade. In Barrani time, she was just a passing acquaintance. She fell silent.

It didn't last. "Where are you taking us?"

"To the heart of Alsanis," Alsanis's brother replied.

Kaylin developed a healthy respect for the Tower of Tiamaris as she attempted to follow Alsanis's brother. Tara kept the halls wide, the ceilings tall, and the windows even and long. The floors were either stone or wood, and they didn't sag or change texture unexpectedly beneath passing feet. Chunks of roof did not suddenly liquefy and fall on the group like a wet, rotting corpse. Doors did not rear up like frothing, panicked horses and attempt to drop on her visitors, and the landscape wasn't filled with the sounds of screaming, weeping—or laughter that made screaming and weeping sound good in comparison.

There weren't any doors between the hole in the wall—a hole that pretty much vanished from sight when they'd walked what Kaylin estimated was ten yards—and their unseen destination.

But there were wards.

The first time they encountered one, the Consort froze. Kaylin could see her eyes darken to pure midnight. The Warden was likewise on alert—but Nightshade, Iberrienne, Lirienne, and Ynpharion didn't appear to be as upset.

"Lady," the Lord of the West March said. "What has happened?"

It was Kaylin who answered. "There's a ward here."

"I see no ward." Lirienne glanced at Barian, and Barian nodded grimly.

"Calarnenne?"

"I do not see it."

Severn?

I do.

Why?

He didn't answer. And she realized she couldn't force an answer from him because the ownership of the name went in the wrong direction. Not that she would ever have tried. She felt his amusement at both thoughts.

Kaylin really wanted a name to hang on Alsanis's brother. It was hard to say, "hey, you" more than once or twice; Kaylin wasn't always big on manners, but it seemed kind of rude even to her. Absent name, she turned to him. "Can you see the ward?"

He frowned. "This?" He asked her, pointing. "You call it a ward?"

"That's what it looks like, to me. What do you call it?"

"A place," he replied. "A belief. A statement of intent. It is meant to mark significance."

"And if I touch it?"

"Why would you touch it if you do not understand what it is meant to invoke?"

Since this was an intelligent question, Kaylin bit back the short string of Leontine trying to force its way out of her mouth. She turned to Barian, who had, if she understood his position as Warden, more experience with wards than anyone else in the building.

Barian said, "It is as you see it. It is a ward of the green."

"Do you know which one?"

He stared at the ward. "You do not understand," he finally said.

"No, clearly. This is the first time I've been to the West March. It's also hopefully—no offense intended—the *last* time I'll visit the West March."

"It is not a ward of Alsanis. It is, in structure, in form, and in content, a ward intended for the green. It should not be here."

Kaylin frowned. "The green and Alsanis are connected, though. When Teela and I activated the wards in the green, we were transported to Alsanis."

"Impossible."

"It can't be impossible. The wards are here."

"You were mistaken, Lord Kaylin. The green is not all of one thing or all of another. You misinterpreted what you saw."

She stopped herself from folding her arms across her chest. In Barian's position, she'd probably be dubious. Of course, if she were Barian, she wouldn't find his attitude irritating. "I don't know the green, and I don't know Alsanis. But the nightmares of Alsanis were there, and what I saw was an echo of what the Consort saw when she contained the nightmares themselves.

"We didn't get back to the green until I called for the judgment of the green. Which—and I may have misunderstood Serian—should have been impossible if I was already *in* the heart of the green.

"And," she continued, raising a third finger to accompany the two she'd lifted while enumerating the previous points, "the Consort was taken by the eagles of Alsanis *to* the green. We didn't find her in Alsanis. And given the shape of Alsanis at the moment, that's probably a blessing. We found her in the green. The eagles told us the wards were inactive—they couldn't be woken.

"I'm guessing," she finished, pointing at the ward that hovered in the air just beyond them, "that this is why. Somehow, they're here."

CHAPTER 24

The Warden was silent for a long moment. He looked, not to Alsanis's brother, but to the Consort. She inclined her head in silence. She did not, however, let go of Kaylin's left arm.

"I don't know the greetings and the blessings—or whatever they're called," Kaylin continued. "But you do. I don't recognize specific wards."

"Lady, with your permission?" Kaylin didn't understand why he'd asked the Consort; the Lord of the West March was in theory the highest ranking person here.

If he'd committed a subtle breach of etiquette, the Consort failed to correct him—and given the affection in which she held her brother, Kaylin assumed that he hadn't. "You are guide, Warden. You recognize the wards."

"Yes. These are meant to mark—and hold—the path to the greenheart. It is possible that they will lead us there, regardless of where we start; the green does not remain in a fixed, geographical state without the wards as anchors." The implication was clear: neither, at the moment, did Alsanis. "It is just as possible that they will lead us to the heart of Alsanis."

"Which is where his brother is leading us now," Kaylin said.

The brother nodded. "You cannot walk the roads I walk. There is nothing within Alsanis that can harm me."

"Not even Alsanis?"

"Not even Alsanis, although that is a matter of desire, not ability. I believe it is understood that you cannot walk as we walk." He hesitated, and then added, "You, Chosen, could. Until your familiar is too large, and the bindings break, he could carry you there."

Lord Barian bowed to the Consort; she stepped to one side of the ward, gently dragging Kaylin with her. The Warden then lifted his palm to the ward's center. He touched it. It had been blue, lines etched in midair with no wall or visible means of support, not that magic actually required any. When it came into contact with his hand, the light shifted, losing color until it was white, but gaining in brightness.

Kaylin narrowed her eyes against that light; it wasn't enough. She looked away, and saw, as she did, that the ground beneath her feet was, in fact, becoming solid and uniform. It didn't coalesce, though; the shifting images, the patches of nearby sky, the puddle of something that resembled green mud, began to fade. They lost color as the ward gained light; they lost substance, almost as if they were sinking through whatever it was that lay beneath them.

And that, to Kaylin's relief, was a path made of oddly shaped, interlocking stones. Clearly it didn't come as a relief to the Warden, but at this point, it didn't come as shock, either. "This is the path into the heart of the green?"

He nodded.

Kaylin had never understood the way the green was connected to the Hallionne; she now knew that the Barrani didn't, either. But it didn't matter; there really was only one way out, and it lay at the heart of Alsanis.

They followed the path until it began to fade. Every time it did, they encountered a ward, and Lord Barian both touched and invoked it, strengthening the fading path as he did. It wasn't fast, but it didn't induce overwhelming nausea. It did induce stress; she could feel time falling, as if it were sand in an hourglass that couldn't be turned over again.

But she counted the wards, because other than walking, there wasn't much else she could do. Oh, she could look at the no longer small dragon, but he was like that sand. She felt his presence like storm clouds. She was the small fishing vessel too far from port to be guaranteed any safety.

In some storms, there was no guarantee.

When they reached the eleventh ward, the Warden said, "This is the last one."

"You're certain."

"In the green—in the green that I know—it wouldn't be. But this character means the end of the journey. The end of the path." He turned to the Lord of the West March and bowed. "I have served as guide, but the arrival is in your hands, Lord Lirienne. Lord Calarnenne, Teller, Lord Kaylin, harmoniste, be prepared; the rest of us are now simply audience."

The Lord of the West March bowed in turn. He took a step forward on this last leg of the path and paused there. To the left and the right, in the distance, there was horizon; the land—such as it was—was not flat; it was broken in places by things that reminded Kaylin very much of the art that escaped the Oracular Halls. Had it been simple paint or clay, it would have been interesting; it wasn't.

She was certain she would have found it less disturbing if she had seen any signs of life in that landscape. She hadn't.

The only living things that appeared to inhabit the Hallionne were the people who walked a path that belonged in the green.

The path continued forward. Nightshade fell in to the left of the Lord of the West March, matching his stride. Kaylin understood that she was meant to occupy the position to his right, and found she didn't want it. The Consort, however, said, "It is not simple ceremony; it is not a matter of etiquette. Nothing in the green is. Come, Lord Kaylin." And she pretty much dragged Kaylin along with her; she walked to Kaylin's left.

Kaylin was reminded, then, of Teela. She wanted the reminder, even as she found it painful. "We will find her," the Consort whispered. As if she could read minds.

As if it were necessary.

What if she doesn't want to leave? What if she wants to stay with them? They were the wrong questions, and Kaylin managed not to ask them. It wasn't what Kaylin wanted—but what Kaylin wanted never made a difference, in the end. What was, was. She couldn't change it; she could only endure.

The dragon roared. He didn't land, but at the moment, the path didn't have a roof; it had a lot of ugly sky. A bit of what might have been lightning, and distant rain. A bit of green sunlight.

No eagles, she thought. No nightmares. None but the ones she carried within her.

She was surprised when the tree came into view, because it looked exactly like a tree. So much of the interior of the Hallionne had no solid features; you couldn't call it a building because *building* implied deliberate construction, architecture, things like walls, floors, and ceilings. The tree however had brown bark. It had a trunk. It had roots, or at least the top part of roots, and branches that filled the sky above.

Only as they walked toward it did Kaylin realize it was not a *small* tree, and when they failed to reach it after twenty minutes, she revised that to *huge,* and then *bloody gigantic.* And she knew, then, which tree this was; she knew where the roots rested. She knew that it was the heart of the green.

Then again, Hallionne Sylvanne had been a tree, too.

The path came to an end. Which is to say, it passed beneath the rounded surface of exposed root. It might have continued beyond it, but the Lord of the West March called a halt. There was no ward here that Kaylin could see.

But she recalled that she had only seen the ward when she'd looked through the wings of a small dragon. She heard his magnified voice; felt it in the interlocking stones beneath her feet. He couldn't fly easily above the tree; he could circumnavigate it, but instead, chose—for the first time—to land.

Every breath she could hear momentarily banked as he did.

"You cannot see him," Alsanis's brother said, unexpectedly. "But, Chosen, he sees you. He sees what you cannot see."

Which was about as helpful as most of the words that fell out of ancient, immortal mouths. "This is where we're supposed to be?" she asked.

He failed to answer. It was the Consort who said, "No, Lord Kaylin. It is the outer edge of the heart of Alsanis, and it is closed to us."

"Clever," Nightshade said.

"What's clever?"

"They expect us to destroy the tree."

"We can't."

"It would not be wise, no. But it serves as barrier here. If we breach that barrier, we will find them."

"I don't think they care."

"No. They expect to be found; if we destroy the tree—"

"They'll be able to do what they've been waiting to do."

"That is my guess, yes. You understand what this tree is?"

"Yes. It's the heart of the green. The living heart of the green."

The dragon roared.

Kaylin said, "I know how to enter it."

The Warden said, "This tree is not like the Hallionne Sylvanne, Lord Kaylin. It is like a body; you do not enter it by asking permission."

She nodded, and then said, "But there's a way in, now."

The Lord of the West March frowned. She felt his surprise, his consternation, and his slow sense of something that felt like approval. *We cannot ask for the judgment of the green here.*

No. But I'm certain that if we can approach the base of the roots of the tree, we can find what I found. A wound. An entry.

He looked at her, waiting. And she looked up at the dragon. "Move back along the path," she told her companions without looking back. The dragon's eyes were wide, round, dark; the flashes of color across their surface seemed to have slowed. She could almost see an image in them, but only out of the corner of her eyes; it was like the faintest of stars. She couldn't see it if she examined it directly.

"I need your help."

He roared. She was almost certain all of her hair was now standing on end.

"We need a way down. You know where we have to go. You probably know it better than I do."

The familiar sibilants of his laughter made her smile. Somehow, causing amusement in a creature this size just felt less humiliating.

"Can you do it?"

He folded his wings, lifted his great, long neck, and looked down at her from an almost-regal height. He spoiled the effect by scratching his nose. She thought about the egg hatching, and about the permanent shoulder ornament that had crawled out of it. She'd mostly complained about him.

To be fair, she mostly complained about Teela, too. But Teela hated sentiment. It put her off her lunch, as she so often said. The small dragon couldn't give her the same warning, and maybe he didn't care. But she thought she would miss him if he were gone.

She missed so many things once they were gone.

"Help us," she whispered.

The dragon inhaled. Kaylin inhaled, as well. She dropped her arms, let her shoulders slide down her back. She felt wind; it was cold. But the dress itself was warm. It was, she thought, as she glanced at the folds of its skirt, glowing faintly with a familiar green light. In Iberrienne's eyes, she had thought it repulsive. On its own, it wasn't. It was the color of Barrani eyes at their happiest, lit from within.

The dragon exhaled. Kaylin was the terminating point for the stream of silver cloud that left his open jaws. She flinched, but didn't move.

Kaylin!

But she shook her head at the Barrani voices inside her mind. Ynpharion was silent.

I asked, she told Nightshade and Lirienne. *I asked for this.*

Her eyes teared. She let them. She felt tears warm her cheeks as they fell. She didn't take her eyes off the dragon until the cloud had cleared. She'd seen his breath melt steel, changing it into a liquid that she could cup in her hands. She'd seen it kill Ferals. She'd certainly seen its effects on the High Court; they feared it.

There were so many things she feared more at the moment, she had no room for more fear.

Have room for caution, Lirienne said, with some anger.

She almost laughed. She understood when the time for caution had passed—and it had passed the moment she had left Teela in the heart of the green. She wondered, idly, what the dragon's breath would do to her; it did nothing, at least at first.

But the marks on her arms began to glow silver. And the dress she wore began to shift color, as well, taking on a sheen that implied iridescence when the cloth rippled. It didn't seem to change shape, though. She blinked away the last of the tears; to her surprise, the dragon appeared less translucent in her vision.

She turned to her companions. If the dragon looked different, they didn't, although the Barrani, with the single exception of Nightshade, looked almost shocked, their eyes midnight-blue. It was the dress. Of course it was the dress.

I am not entirely certain, Lord Lirienne said, *how you survived An'Teela's temper all these years.*

She couldn't strangle me; she's a Hawk. Kaylin was surprised to find herself smiling at the thought. *If it helps, I'm most of the reason she learned to curse in Leontine. Look,* she added, although it wasn't necessary. The stones of the path began to sink. They didn't dissolve, and they didn't sink in concert; they sank in recessed steps.

"We have to go down," Kaylin told everyone. The dragon roared; the stairs—the oddly shaped, uneven stairs—shook. "I think we also have to hurry."

The Lord of the West March took the lead, almost shoving Kaylin off the path in order to do so. Kaylin was willing—barely—to give it to him. Taking risks—as she had—was one thing; exposing other people to them first, quite another.

"He is Lord of the West March," the Consort said with a soft smile. "He has his duties and his responsibilities. Even if he did not, it is not his way to throw a stray mortal into the path of the unknown within his own domain."

Kaylin nodded, but scurried immediately after him. The Consort was forced to let Nightshade follow, which at least two people disliked, Ynpharion being one. This surprised her.

If he kills me, she told him, *doesn't that work to your advantage?*

The Barrani Lord failed to answer. He couldn't cut the Consort off, as Nightshade had; he didn't wear the Teller's crown. But he followed the Lady stiffly. He could feel Kaylin's confusion and her amusement, and the last was definitely not to his liking.

"What will you do with the dragon?" the Consort asked as they descended.

"I'm not certain. I don't think his part in this is done yet."

"No. Do you understand what his part in this is?"

Kaylin shook her head. "I would have said it was impossible that he have one—this story started long before either of us were born."

"You don't believe that." She spoke in Elantran.

"I did. But...no. He doesn't really have an age. I, on the other hand, do."

Nightshade said a word, and the stairs were flooded with light. Kaylin blinked different tears out of her eyes. *Was that necessary?*

Yes, Kaylin. It was dark.

But it hadn't been, to Kaylin, which was a first. If the Barrani found it too dark for vision, Kaylin was usually bumping into walls, or anything else that stuck out.

What did you see?

Stairs, mostly.

Ah.

She still saw stairs. She realized, with a start, that there were no walls; the stairs descended in a winding, tight trail, toward the distant earth. They were narrow stairs, without rails, and without an obvious central pillar. But they felt familiar. She could have been running up—or down—the stairs that lead to the Hawklord's tower.

She couldn't run down these ones without knocking Lirienne out of the way, which seemed the very definition of career-limiting. He reached ground as she did, and he approached roots that looked very familiar.

"You must lead," he began. But he looked up, over the rounded surface of root.

Kaylin, however, looked down. "Can you see the river here?"

Lirienne frowned. "No, Lord Kaylin."

The Consort caught her arm. She could tell, from the expression on the Consort's face, that she could. It was not a comforting expression.

Kaylin turned to the Lord of the West March; he was climbing. He was climbing with confidence and grace, and he stopped only when he had reached the height of a root that was very close to trunk. Kaylin could see shards of wood and something darker in the air. "Don't touch those," she told him.

He maneuvered carefully around them, heading to the gap in the trunk that Kaylin had caused by touching a lone ward. Nightshade passed Kaylin.

"Lord Kaylin," the Consort said quietly.

Kaylin nodded and followed. She followed with vastly less grace, and had to accept help from both Severn and the Consort to find enough purchase to climb. Climbing was one of her strengths, but she didn't do it with grace—which, come to think, was an apt description of the way she lived the rest of her life, as well.

Lord Barian came up after Kaylin, and he stopped at the

gap in the trunk, staring. In the light cast by Nightshade, she could see his expression; she could also see his pallor.

"It was like this when I found it," Kaylin said. She felt compelled to add, "but the damage was concealed by a ward."

"You invoked the ward."

She nodded. "I walked into the gap, and I heard the green."

"You are certain that it was the voice of the green speaking?"

"Yes."

Lord Barian turned to the Consort. "I spent so little time in your city," he told her. "Are all mortals this…surprising?"

"In my limited experience, no."

"That is some small relief. The mortals outnumber us; they always have."

"Kaylin?" the Consort said.

Kaylin nodded and once again entered the breach.

She stepped into sunshine, and lifted her hands to shade her eyes. The Consort followed; Kaylin could see debris in the folds of the Barrani woman's dress. Ynpharion entered behind them, Iberrienne in tow. The enmity he felt for Iberrienne was gone; it had been replaced by a wordless, nameless pity. Kaylin couldn't blame him; she felt it herself.

Severn pulled up the rear, but she found herself waiting for him, as if afraid he would be sent back, somehow. His eyes widened slightly as they adjusted to sunlight. There was sun here. And there were trees, grass, even the sound of running water. In the distance, trees formed horizon, or as much of it as could be seen.

"It wasn't like this," Kaylin said quietly. "Not the last time. This is what the heart of the green looked like, isn't it?"

He nodded.

But the Consort said softly, "There are shadows, Warden. Can you not hear them? Stay on the path."

The Warden's smile was soft. "It is a gift, Lady. I will gladly walk this path again."

"Even if you understand what occurs at its end?"

"Even then. I can hear the green. Lord Kaylin?"

"I can't hear them," she confessed. "And I'm happy with that."

The Lord of the West March continued—once he had ascertained that no one had been lost in the passage—to lead. The Consort released Kaylin's arm, and to Kaylin's surprise, scurried ahead to catch up with her brother. He bent his head to listen to whatever she had to say, and to Kaylin's greater surprise, laughed. His laughter was deep and almost musical, and it reminded her that he was capable of mirth.

He has long been a Barrani Lord of whom you might otherwise approve, Nightshade said.

Unlike you?

Very, very unlike me. He is Barrani, of course; he is a significant Lord of the High Court. He is impressive enough that he can display sentiment and its weakness without falling prey to the weakness itself. She felt Nightshade's quiet excitement. He, too, was caught by the familiarity of a green that hadn't been seen for centuries. Maybe it reminded him of youth.

Not of mine, he replied. *But yes, Kaylin. You asked me a question I did not choose to answer.*

Did you understand what had happened to Iberrienne?

No.

Would you have taken the risks you took if you had?

I fail to understand, he said, after a long pause, *why you waste time and effort asking questions to which you know the answer.*

I don't know, or I wouldn't ask.

You don't wish to know, Kaylin. You assume the Barrani are all alike—why, given the variance in human behavior, I do not know. We are not mortal. It is immortality that defines us when we leave our youth. Mortality defines you. You never leave your youth.

We do.

No, Kaylin, you do not. You have decades in which to live with the decisions you have made; decades in which to work to keep love and loyalty alive. You change because you age; you choose different lives. You are not bound, in all ways, by the past; you come from it, it informs you, but it does not imprison you.

You do not understand the ways in which we are always caged. It is not just the matter of a name—although you have seen the extents to which some of my people will attempt to escape even that weakness.

She had.

This was not an example of that, not directly. The twelve had barely discovered the joy of the bonds one can make with true names.

Those aren't generally considered joyful, Kaylin replied.

Not by the wise, no. But the wise do not consider love or sentiment a joy, either. They are weary, Kaylin. They have seen the failure of too much.

She frowned. *If you're unchanging—if we're defined by change, and you're not...*

Yes?

...isn't your love unchanging? Doesn't it last longer?

He offered her an arm, and after a moment's hesitation, she accepted it. *It is a weakness,* he said. *You have heard that; it is true. What we love, we love forever; what we love we fear to lose. We are held hostage by affection. No; affection is too slight a word, although it is the one most commonly offered, where love exists. The joy, we remember, but the pain of loss lasts as long, and, as with mortals, as with all who feel emotion, we come to doubt that the joy was worth the pain.*

We do not always love our kin. It is not wise. We are often placed in situations in which we must disavow—or kill—them. You despise this.

She often did.

But it is irrelevant. You define us by the politics. If we had that strength, we would define ourselves the same way.

You do.

No, Kaylin, we do not. It is the politics we are willing to share. Come; we are almost there.

Where?

The heart of the green. The true heart. I do not know what you will see. I do not know what is waiting. I have hope, he added softly.

And is that hope worth it?

I do not know. Ask me in a century. Or two.

She glared at the side of his face, and he surprised her. He laughed out loud, the sound just as rich, just as deep, as Lirienne's.

Judging from the expression on Ynpharion's face, it had surprised him, too—but Iberrienne's smile was just as wide as Nightshade's, and just as excited. He wasn't skipping—that would have been enough to assure Kaylin she was dreaming—but he was practically beaming. She'd worked alongside the Barrani for almost eight years, and she'd never seen anything like it.

It broke her heart.

Don't see them as children, Severn warned her.

I don't.

But...she almost did. She could see the youth in them; it seemed so fragile, it made her want to hold her breath. Hope was pain. She knew that. But for moments at a time, before it broke, it was joy.

And it was with joy that they walked this path, in something that seemed almost like a city garden, and came, at last, to the heart of the green.

★ ★ ★

Kaylin recognized the two trees that stood there, although they had almost nothing in common with the two husks she'd seen; they were taller, fuller; they were in blossom, and in this case, blossom meant flowers. The flowers were a delicate shade of pink at the edge; the hearts implied something darker and brighter. Petals were strewn, almost artistically, across the grass in the shade beneath their bowers.

But she was certain they were the trees she and Teela had touched when they'd arrived in a barren, desert version of this place.

It was the fountain that caught her attention; there was— no surprise—water in its basin. The water, however, was not clear. She almost stumbled, but Severn slid an arm around her shoulders, because—of course—he'd seen what she'd seen, and seen it first.

The basin was full of not water, but blood.

CHAPTER 25

The blood set a different tone. The Lord of the West March lifted a hand in warning, and they stopped; only the Warden ignored his subvocal command. Only the Warden had that right. He walked to the fountain's basin and stopped there; he didn't touch the water. Kaylin thought he was making certain that nothing from the fountain reached the ground itself, and given the various warnings she'd been given, that made sense.

But she approached the fountain, as well, once Lirienne had lowered his hand. So did the Consort. "Be cautious," the Consort said quietly.

Kaylin nodded. She didn't attempt to touch the liquid in the basin, but she examined it more closely. At length, she turned to the Barrani. "It's not blood," she told them. "I mean, there's blood *in* it, but the water is here."

"You are certain?"

"You can hear the green. You," she said softly to the Consort, "can hear the shadows. I can hear the water." She could.

Its voice was so quiet it might have been easy to miss it, but it was here.

The only thing missing was Teela.

No, she thought. Not the only thing. She turned to look down the path that had led them here, but wasn't surprised when she couldn't find it. Sometimes, there was no way back. She couldn't see the dragon. She couldn't hear him.

She started to ask, but stopped when the Lord of the West March came to stand beside her. He didn't look at the fountain. He didn't look at Kaylin. Instead, he began to speak. She glanced at his face, and saw his eyes: they were midnight-blue. Which made sense because she didn't recognize the voice he spoke with, and she didn't recognize the words he spoke, either.

No, Nightshade said. He didn't approach Lirienne; instead, he walked to the base of one of the trees, just as Teela had done only the day before. *It is time, Kaylin.*

But—but nothing's been said, there's been no…

It is time. Can you not hear him?

She could. She couldn't understand a word. She glanced at the Consort; the Consort's eyes were now the color of her brother's, although she spared Kaylin one sharp glance which clearly said "Move your butt." But minus the vulgarity.

Kaylin made her way to the same tree she'd stood beside. Or at least a tree that stood in the same relative position. She lifted a hand to touch its bark, but noticed that Nightshade hadn't.

She'd never been clear on the role the Lord of the West March was supposed to play. She didn't understand the difference between his role and the role of the Teller; couldn't understand why the green needed two. Until she heard Lirienne's voice.

It was not, in any way, his voice. It wasn't Barrani. It was storm's voice. It was, she thought, the voice of the green—but channeled into sound by the form that momentarily contained it. She couldn't understand a single word of it. She wondered if it always came through like this.

She had expected that the *regalia* would be like the stories told by Sanabalis and the Arkon in the tongue of the Ancients. She'd secretly expected to see words form, the way they had when she'd first heard the story of the birth of the Leontines. But Lirienne's voice was not Sanabalis's.

It was storm without form, without cloud, without lightning or rain.

Yes, Nightshade said.

Can you understand a single word he's saying?

He didn't answer. She looked across the red, red water of the fountain, and met his gaze; above his eyes, the gem in the center of the Teller's crown was radiating light. She hoped it wasn't radiating heat in equal measure.

Her own dress—the magical, revered blood of the green—was glowing with iridescent light; she wasn't even surprised when the light separated from the cloth and grew. It reminded her of night sky on very rare evenings. But it changed the shape of the circle built around the fountain; it changed the color of a landscape that was, finally, green.

She heard Lirienne's voice. She touched his thoughts briefly and shied away; they were so discordant, they clashed with the syllables leaving his mouth in a steady stream of thunder. Nightshade's were less chaotic, but no easier to untangle; she stopped trying when he, too, began to speak.

She understood what Nightshade was saying, or rather, she understood the words: he was speaking in Elantran. It was just Elantran that made no sense. Individual words were clear as a bell, but they didn't seem to go anywhere; they weren't grouped in a way that implied sentences, or even muddled thoughts. He could have read a dictionary with just as much effect, except there at least the words would have *some* hierarchical order.

She listened. She listened, trying to pick out individual words, aware that her role as harmoniste was, in theory, to shape story, to build a coherent narrative from the strands offered her by the Teller. She didn't even recognize the words as strands of different stories; perhaps they were. Perhaps they were coming in all at once and Nightshade was able to parse single words as they passed by; perhaps he could see sequences and had no other way of containing them.

It wasn't going to help her. She wore a funny dress. She had thought the dress would give her some sort of power, some built-in influence, that would at least make the job possible. At the moment, it wasn't. Her visible marks, however, were glowing a bright, bright silver. Without thought, she removed the jacket Lirienne had given her, and dropped it by her feet.

She was surprised when the jacket touched the stone at her feet and disappeared, fading from view as if being worn had provided the only anchor for its substance. She looked away from Nightshade, and saw that Lirienne still occupied the space directly between them. She couldn't see anyone else.

We're here, Severn said. It was the first time she'd been able to hear anyone when the green had decided to relocate her. *We can see you.* He paused, and then added, *Don't forget to breathe.*

She closed her eyes. Nightshade's voice became clearer, but the mishmash of random words didn't make more sense. *Think. Think, Kaylin.* She didn't worry about Lirienne; he was Nightshade's problem. Nightshade was somehow pulling strands of related story from the flow of the green's words. She wanted to know how, but knew it didn't matter.

She was supposed to make sense of what Nightshade *said.* To somehow choose the words that would give form and shape to the green's story. To scratch the surface of it, somehow, while still presenting as much of it as humanly possible. She blinked. She let go of Nightshade's voice for a moment as she considered this.

The transformed, the lost, the elementals—they existed in spaces that the living couldn't. They probably had stories of their own—stories that made no sense to anyone else. Certainly not Kaylin or the Barrani. Their worlds overlapped, but a person who could live in ten places simultaneously was not telling a story that someone who could live only in one could understand.

But the people gathered here, in the heart of the green, were living. They were solid. They had forms that didn't change at whim. They needed food, air, water; some of them needed sleep. They could see the world they lived in; they couldn't simultaneously see the outlands and whatever else existed for the Hallionne.

The recitation was a story—a communication from something that was not living, not in the way people lived. It encompassed what the green knew. She thought that what Nightshade was drawing from it was what the living *could* know. She heard it in Elantran because it was her mother tongue.

She understood, as Nightshade continued to speak, that she was the end-point. What she said, what she managed to capture, what she managed to convey, was meant to be heard by those who bore witness. She didn't understand how that was meant to change people, to nudge their names, to shift their perceptions. And it didn't matter.

The marks on her arm, silver and bright, began to pulse.

She listened. She listened as if her life depended on it. She tried to pull sense from words, tried to find sentences, bits of thought, even of intent, as Nightshade spoke. He wasn't shouting, but his tone wasn't measured; the beats of the same words differed, sometimes in emphasis, sometimes in intensity.

The light from the dress slowly spread. The light from the gem in the Teller's tiara spread, as well. Nightshade and Kaylin stood beneath the bowers of two trees, at the center of a growing radiance. The two spheres—for it seemed to Kaylin that the light now traveled in spheres—met at the Lord of the West March.

It was light, multihued, and bright; it wasn't solid.

But where it touched, it shattered.

She felt the impact and staggered; shards and splinters flew out from the point of collision, and she lifted her arms to protect her eyes. They struck those arms, and she felt a visceral panic as they pierced skin; they hurt. She was not allowed to bleed on the green.

But when she lowered her stinging arms, she saw that they hadn't been cut. Her marks, the marks that defined her as Chosen, were glowing more brightly—but there were no wounds. She looked across to Nightshade, but her eyes didn't make it that far.

She could see the Lord of the West March, but there were now three of him; they stood in the same spot, almost in the same pose, but they overlapped. And at their back, the fountain had shifted, as well. At its center, suspended above the basin as if she were essential sculpture, was Teela.

Her eyes were closed. Her skin was paler than usual. Her arms were raised, palms splayed flat above her head, as if she were holding up the sky. Her mouth was moving, but at this distance, Kaylin couldn't hear her words; they were drowned out by Lirienne's and Nightshade's. Nightshade's had shifted;

she could now hear streams of sentences, overlapping each other, as if he spoke simultaneously from several mouths.

She tried to listen; she had eyes for Teela, and only Teela. She wanted to know what Teela was trying to say. She wanted to run from the lee of the tree and climb up the basin to get the Barrani Hawk down. She didn't. She started to move and she heard—to her surprise—the rumbling roar of angry dragon.

His voice overwhelmed all other voices. Even her own.

Teela's eyes snapped open, her lips still moving, her arms bending slightly as if the sky had gained weight.

Kaylin left the tree. Her dress did not stop glowing; neither did her marks. She headed straight for Teela and stopped only when the dragon roared again. She could see his shadow across the whole of the fountain and the trees; she looked up as he descended.

The descent was lazy, desultory; his wings were spread in a glide. But she could no longer see sky through them. She couldn't, she realized, see them as wings at all; their edges were fraying, like the edges of old pants.

His voice, she recognized; it shook the earth beneath her feet.

Teela's eyes widened; she lifted her face to look up at the underside of the dragon. She lowered her face, her eyes rounder; they narrowed as if she had only now become aware of where she was.

Of, Kaylin realized, *one* of the places in which she was standing. "Teela!"

Teela's head snapped around so quickly, she'd have whiplash. Her eyes widened. Predictably enough, she looked unhappy to see Kaylin. "What are you *doing here?*"

There was only one answer to that question; the problem was that Kaylin *wasn't* doing the job. She was here as harmoniste. She was here to untangle the bits and pieces of story that

Nightshade was now throwing, in discordant harmony with himself, in her direction.

And she knew, looking at the Barrani Hawk she thought of as family—privately, where it wouldn't offend Teela with sentimentality—that Teela was at the heart of the story, some-how. But...it began before her birth. It began before the birth of the Hallionne. It began when the Ancients walked, and possibly before they did; it began with silence.

She could hear that silence now, although words were wound around it. Nightshade's voice became clearer, stron-ger; she couldn't sense him in any other way.

"Kitling, go *back*."

Kaylin shook her head and lifted a hand to stall Teela's lec-ture. Teela was afraid—for her. The fear felt like a little bit of home. And that was the point, wasn't it? Kaylin built as much of a home as she could for herself, time and again, and los-ing any part of it was like losing peace and the hope of safety. What Teela wanted didn't—hadn't—mattered. Kaylin had al-ways assumed that they wanted the same things. They were both Hawks. They were both *good* at their jobs.

But they weren't the same people; they weren't even the same race. There were things Kaylin had done that she'd never shared with Teela; she'd never shared them with anyone, ex-cept perhaps Tara, and that, by accident. And there were things that Teela had done that she'd never shared, either, and maybe for the same reason.

"Teela," Kaylin said, distinctly, "I love you."

Teela looked as though she was about to hurl a volley of angry Leontine, and Kaylin turned as the dragon finally landed.

He was not a dragon now. He was not small. She couldn't even understand *how* he'd landed, because there wasn't enough room in this small, fountain-dominated clearing to support him. He didn't crush the Lord of the West March; nor did he crush Nightshade. Kaylin, however, found the lack of light and air problematic.

He had, she thought, no face. But he had eyes, and they were the same as they'd always been, writ large. Writ impressively large. Large enough that she should have been able to see her reflection in them. What she saw, instead, was something that looked like words.

He turned his gaze on Nightshade; Nightshade didn't seem to be aware of his presence, but Teela was. Kaylin didn't understand what the creature who was no longer dragon wanted from Nightshade until she realized that she could no longer hear all of the threads of the story he'd been speaking.

Her eyes rounded. "No!"

She heard his voice, his rumbling response; it was no longer a roar. She thought it almost—almost—contained words, but they weren't words she would ever be able to understand. In a panic she shoved her arms in front of his eyes, which now seemed to exist without sockets. If he understood what she was offering—if she did—he paid no attention, and none of the marks—not a single damn one—rose to feed itself to him.

He was going to eat the stories.

He was going to devour them, and leave her with no way of telling what needed to be told. And she knew that if he did, she would never save Teela. She understood that the green was in danger, that Alsanis was all but exhausted, that the lost children were a threat to their former people—and she didn't care.

What she cared about was Teela.

Think, Kaylin. She reached past the creature, although it was difficult as he appeared to be wrapped around her like a gigantic, uncomfortably heavy blanket with eyes. She reached and she began to choose. Not the silence, although that was a story of its own. That one, she could give to the creature.

Not the Ancients. No, wait—one small strand of their story was sharper and heavier than any other strand appeared to be. She drew it into her hands and wrapped it around her arms, as if the spoken word and the marks could be held in the exact same way. But the rest, she fed to the creature.

It was hard. She didn't know what would happen to the pieces of history that she rejected—for she understood them as history now; they were the foundations upon which Teela stood, at least figuratively. She heard Alsanis's name. She missed some of its beginning, but she understood enough to know that he was built by the Ancients. By two. She couldn't hear their names, but understood that an echo of them existed in the history itself.

And she heard grief, she heard farewells. She heard the promise of eternity, and the threat of it. She caught those almost reflexively. To the dragon, she fed the story of the forests and the insects and the brooks and streams, shielding Alsanis from his hunger. Shielding the story of his grief. She couldn't save the story of his brothers; she had no sense of what they had been before Alsanis became Hallionne, because the creature devoured it.

He devoured, as well, the story of the Dragons. The real Dragons. Sanabalis's people. She panicked and shouted at him, and lost more words; she couldn't afford it. She knew it. But she felt that she couldn't move as fast as the creature now could; she couldn't *see* whether or not something was important. She couldn't assess it in time.

But she caught bits and pieces of the war. Of the Hallionne at war. Of the green at war. Of the Dragons and the Barrani and the weapons forged in the green. She let the weapons go. She let the wars go. She kept only the bare essentials because the stories of the wars were so long and complicated. She thought maybe they would feed the creature *enough* that he would stop.

Instead, he seemed to grow.

"Kitling—"

"I *know*, Teela!" But not, apparently, enough not to *shut the hells up* and ignore all other distractions.

She looked into the creature's eyes. She could almost step *into* them, they'd grown so large. She didn't. She could see the words they contained, now. The words were harder and more angular than the letter shapes she thought of as True Words; they were not golden, not blue. Silver, she thought, or gray, but strangely insubstantial. They looked like—like smoke.

They looked very much like the words that she had seen in the outlands when Iberrienne had attacked Hallionne Orbaranne. The words were not True Words, not in any sense that she understood them. But they weren't the words that Iberrienne had tried to use at the heart of the Hallionne Orbaranne, either.

She thought she understood.

When she heard Nightshade begin to speak of words, of language, of a language of power and birth, she caught the threads of the story without conscious thought, folding them around herself as if they were now a part of her. Her arms burned, and her eyes teared, and she looked at herself in the creature's eyes, and saw that the marks on her arms were as insubstantial and smoky in reflection as the words that existed at the heart of what she'd thought were simple, if gigantic, eyes.

And she heard about the blood of the Ancients; she heard about the words around which they'd carved and created the world in which Kaylin now lived. It was one of many such worlds, all contained, all built, on similar words, each of which told a story. They were, Nightshade told her, words meant for these worlds. They existed only here, were meant to exist only here. They defined and created solid spaces—the spaces between two people, the spaces between birth and death, between seed and sapling and tree.

They defined time. They defined its passage.

The creature spoke.

He spoke as Kaylin caught this one thread, and buried it; he pulled at it. She could feel him as if he were a giant, intelligent vortex into which all meaning must vanish.

She didn't understand his purpose. She didn't understand why *anyone* would want to summon something that ate words, that consumed meaning. He was here, yes. But this was not where he belonged.

She understood why fire was summoned; she understood water. Even earth and air made sense to her—but they were inextricably linked to this world. Fire, water, earth, and air existed without will in everyday life. There was no echo of the small dragon, the large dragon, or the creature it had become, in Kaylin's world. What ate words? What devoured meaning?

And yet, somehow, this creature or one part of it, had been summoned before.

Why?

What did it mean?

"Kaylin!"

She didn't shout. She had, she realized, been gathering strands of history as if they were objects. Those that spoke to her in some way, she kept. She didn't question why; it was entirely instinctive, but at this moment, she had nothing but instinct to guide her. She wasn't surprised to discover that the stories about words and language had drifted into stories about life. About birth. About the first rough attempts to create something small and contained that was nonetheless independent enough that it could live and grow and create in a diminished fashion.

There were rules, she thought. Life had rules. Not the ones parents handed down; not even the ones the Emperor did, although flouting those generally ended the life they were meant to govern. The words that gave life—the names—*were* True Words. But they were more. She couldn't quite figure out how; they didn't *change*. But they grew, nonetheless. It was the act of living that altered them, in subtle ways strengthening some part of their essential meaning.

It was why the loss of the word—not the life that contained it—was so *wrong*.

And those words had been given to the lost children, not when they'd been chosen to enter the green, but when they had been presented to the Consort. At that point, no knowledge of what awaited them in future guided her choice. Kaylin wasn't certain what did, in the end. Nor was she certain the Consort could explain it, if asked.

Something had happened to the children, here. But…their names hadn't been changed.

Kaylin glanced at her palm; the mark that lay against it was the color of new blood, which was not a color she associated with True Words. It was the color she associated with life, with birth, and with pain. She had kept it, and knew now that it was one of eleven such names. It existed in the green, and only in the green—but it didn't belong here.

Why had it been protected all this time?

The stories about life drifted into stories about being, becoming, and ending. She didn't understand that endings meant death until she found the story trapped at the heart of the green, and she lost so much of it to the creature that had ridden on her shoulder for most of his existence.

There were no stories about him that she could hear or

touch; she kind of wanted him to choke on them, at the moment. But she concentrated on the stories about death at the heart of the green; death at its edges were part of war, and although they might have hinted at something important, she couldn't afford to hang on to them. She could keep hold of so little, between the creature and the speed at which the information was offered.

She held on to the deaths at its heart; she did more. She spoke of them. Aside from shouting at Teela in frustration—and in fear—they were the first words she had deliberately spoken out loud.

The green was alive in some sense; it was sentient. It spoke. It felt—as ages passed—sorrow and inexplicable grief, and it felt joy in equal measure. But it was not alive in the way the Hallionne were; it was not alive in the way the Barrani were. It existed where worlds existed, but it existed apart from them. She didn't speak of its birth because if its birth was part of the multitude of histories that left Nightshade's lips, she hadn't rescued it in time.

It was like—and unlike—the True Names that gave the Barrani life. The words at the heart of the green were not words meant for the living; they could not exist in Kaylin's world. The words that gave life to the Barrani were words it could read; it could see them so clearly, it defined life *by* words. Mortals made distant sense to the Hallionne; they made sense to the green only the way cockroaches, mosquitos, and plants did.

Blood was not forbidden the green: death was.

And death was forbidden the green because the words of the dying could not escape its grasp. They weren't meant to be part of the green; the green was *not* of this world. And yet, not of it, it was part of it. It touched and spoke with the Hallionne, who were altered in just such a way that they could hear its ancient, endless voice, its plethora of voices. It heard the Hallionne's voice, its many voices. It heard the Hallionne's dreams.

And it heard the voices of the Barrani during the recitation. A window was open, then; a moment permitted in which the two—the lesser, fragile, fixed children of the Ancients, and the greater and eldest—might communicate. It might tell the Barrani their history. With will, and the right combination of Barrani, it might speak to the Barrani of its *own* history; it might give them a glimpse of the things that did not naturally walk the world. It might speak of its desires and its dreams and—last—its fears.

Kaylin understood these things only as a mortal might, although Nightshade spoke of dreams and desires and fears, and she fed those, her hands shaking, to the creature.

When the Barrani died in the heart of the green, when they shed their blood upon it, they surrendered the thing that gave them life: their name. Kaylin felt horror at this—it was a profound, an endless, loss. Mortals believed in souls. The Barrani believed in names. Teela often equated the two—souls and True Names.

The Barrani lost their souls here. They weren't trapped, as they were in the High Halls; they were drained of the very thing that made them *names*. She closed her eyes. Opened them again. She couldn't see the Consort's face, and for once, she was grateful. She knew what she'd see in the Lady's expression.

But the power that the name gave the Barrani conferred the ability to speak directly to the green. It made their desires—their final desires—as clear to the green as the green's own desires were, because for a moment, before they were extinguished, they *were* part of the green.

Those wishes, those desires—they couldn't be coerced; they couldn't be changed.

The people of the Vale had died in the green. They'd died by order of Teela's father. His name flitted past, and she let it go with vindictive fury, hating him for just this minute. They didn't understand what their lost thoughts would do. They didn't understand what their hatred and, yes, fear, would cost the green.

No, that wasn't true. One woman did. One woman. Teela's mother. She was Vivienne, of the line of Wardens and Guardians. She knew. She emptied her thoughts of rage and fury and bitter betrayal. The only thing she wanted, the only thing, was the safety of her daughter. The fact that her daughter bore the blood of the man who commanded the killings meant nothing to her.

She regretted only the fact that she had repaired to the High Court, away from kin and home and green; that her daughter, Teela, had not been raised to hear the distant voice of the green and to understand its ancient and abiding will.

Maybe Kaylin told this story first because it was about Teela. Maybe she told it because she, too, had lost her mother, and she wanted to believe—oh, all children wanted to believe— that *if* she were to be abandoned, it would be for reasons as perfect and clear as this one.

And maybe she told it because, as she began to speak, she could *see* Vivienne in the heart of the green.

CHAPTER 26

Kaylin wasn't Teela. Vivienne was not her mother. But she was certain that she would have known this woman anywhere. She looked like Teela. Not in the way that all Barrani women, except the Consort, did, although she had all the racial characteristics of her race: the long, dark hair, the slender build, the high cheekbones, and, at this moment, eyes of midnight-blue. No, it was in the shape of her face, the length of earlobes, the way her chin tapered to a sharper point.

If Teela had been run through by multiple blades, she would have looked like this.

Her eyes were on her daughter's face.

Teela had climbed down from the fountain, somehow. Whatever she'd been holding at bay was forgotten. Her mother knelt by the fountain, and in the distance, Kaylin could hear the shouts and the cries of fighting; she could hear swords against swords, and harsh Barrani orders.

She could hear the prayers of the Warden. She hadn't expected that; she couldn't see him. Nor could she see the other combatants; not until they fell. Their dying bodies came into view as they did; they were close, so close, to Vivienne.

Kaylin reached for Teela, and then let her hand fall. She couldn't call her back; she couldn't stem the flow of words because she understood that it was her words that had built this image, that had made this history real.

And as Teela walked onto the green—a green that contained no Warden, no Ynpharion, no Severn—they joined her. Kaylin watched as they appeared, translucent at first, but gaining in solidity as she spoke. The eleven children. Some of their names, she knew. Some, she hadn't heard until this moment.

Sedarias came first. She looked so proud, so aloof, so arrogant. She glanced at the bodies of the dead and the dying without so much as blinking; she stood above them all. But when she looked at Teela, she froze for one arrested moment, her eyes—her blue, cold eyes, shifting in that second to a very rare amethyst. Like Kaylin, she lifted a hand; like Kaylin, she let it drop.

But she turned to Kaylin, her eyes wide, her lips parted as if to speak. Then she smiled and turned away. It was a very Barrani smile.

Annarion came next, seconds behind. He was much like Sedarias—cold and proud of bearing. But what she would not do, he did; he saw the dying Vivienne, and his gaze went immediately to her daughter. He walked over the fallen, pausing only once to touch the side of a man's neck before he rose again and made his way to Teela's side.

Eddorian followed. His eyes were almost instantly the same shade of purple that Sedarias's had taken, but on his face, with his drawn expression, it looked natural. He didn't approach Teela; to Kaylin's surprise, he offered Sedarias—a woman who almost certainly would take insult at the implication that she needed support—an arm. And she *took* it.

Allaron followed. He was, as she remembered him, a giant of a Barrani, and although he had the natural grace of his kin, he seemed to slouch a bit more; he had always been self-conscious about his size; he had always been pushed to excel in acts of physical prowess.

And he had. But significantly, it was Allaron who cried. He didn't weep; Kaylin had never seen Barrani weep. His eyes were an open amethyst. A Barrani man put a hand on Allaron's shoulder, and Allaron turned, looking down; he met the eyes of Valliant—who, like any mortal child of Kaylin's acquaintance, loathed his name. Allaron was one of the few, even among the twelve, who failed to tease him for it.

Terrano, however, had teased him without hesitation. He was mischievous, but he could laugh at himself—which was unusual for a child, and even more unusual for Barrani. He came to Allaron's left. There was no sparkle, no joke, no witticism; he was drawn and pale. He wanted to go to Teela. He couldn't.

Not counting Teela, six of the lost had arrived. The seventh was a woman, called Serralyn. She wore her hair in unusual braids that framed her face and made her look older. Had she been motionless, her expression would have matched Sedarias's; she wasn't. Even standing, her hands moved; her feet tapped the ground. She looked as if she could burst into motion at any moment.

At this one, she was looking at Teela's profile, at Teela's dying mother, and hugging her arms to herself; she opened her mouth to speak, closed it, took two steps forward, and then a step back. Kaylin felt a pang of sympathy: no one who wanted all their teeth offered Teela open sympathy. Ever.

But…Serralyn had known Teela before she'd become a

Hawk. Maybe, in the old days, she'd been different. Judging from Serralyn's growing distress, probably not.

Torrisant appeared—and the first thing he did was straighten his clothing, which, to Kaylin's eye, was already perfect. He lifted a hand, raising two flat fingers, and a bird—a bird that had been no part of Kaylin's conscious telling—landed on them, warbling.

Fallessian appeared just in time to kick him; the bird squawked in outrage and flew, tiny claws extended, toward Fallessian's perfect face. He laughed and fended it off with his hand—taking care not to actually connect with the little ball of fury. He didn't speak—none of them had—but the look he turned on Torrisant clearly said, "Now is not the time."

The tenth of the children appeared then, eleven if one included Teela. He looked no younger than any of the rest; to Kaylin, even now, *children* was the wrong word to describe them. But Karian was grimmer and more controlled than any of the others except Sedarias; he didn't have the obvious arrogance of the young Annarion, but there was something about him that suggested, strongly, that his arrogance was a wall that couldn't be breached, climbed, or otherwise opened.

He walked, with purpose, toward Teela.

No, Kaylin thought, toward her mother. But he paused, a frown creasing his forehead, not his lips. He turned to Sedarias and Annarion, and then, when they failed to give him the answers he had pretty clearly demanded, turned to the green, to the clearing, and...to Kaylin.

To the harmoniste.

There were eleven children; Teela was at the center. Kaylin knew their names. She knew their personalities. She knew some of their history, although the creature had devoured their edges because she wasn't quick enough or strong enough to see the whole of their shape and importance before they had passed her by.

She knew that the twelfth had not yet arrived. Some part of her knew that this was history, and some part of her knew that it was more. Regardless, Mandoran had failed to arrive in the heart of the green—and they were waiting for him. Just as, she realized, they had waited so many centuries for Teela.

Her arms were shaking; she felt, as she lifted them, that she'd spent the afternoon doing nothing but heavy lifting with no breaks, although she didn't realize it until she lifted her left hand. She opened her palm. The rune in its center was Mandoran's name. Teela had said as much in some other country, at some other time.

Bloodred, wet, it had the shape and the texture of a True Word. She held it now. She had taken it to protect it. She had taken it to preserve it. But while she held it, Mandoran couldn't join the rest. She looked at the name. Mandoran's thread, Mandoran's history, was part of the tapestry three people were weaving, and if she couldn't find his thread, her part would falter. She wasn't certain what would happen then.

Maybe nothing. Maybe the eleven would vanish and the telling would end and Teela would be Teela and safe. She could stay away from the West March. She could refuse to come back here. She could remain in Elantra, with the Hawks, in the shadow of the High Halls.

But she'd done all that. She'd done all that, and in the end, this is where she was trapped. Nothing had changed, for Teela. Maybe nothing could.

Teela said that she had tried, when she had been chosen as harmoniste. She hadn't told Kaylin *what* she'd attempted. But Kaylin was certain that the lost were involved, somehow. Teela had known that they weren't dead because she knew their names; they were part of her. She was part of them.

She had never offered Kaylin the same friendship or the same opportunity.

The creature roared. His eyes were now half the size of Kaylin's body, and it took her a moment to realize that while he wasn't translucent she was seeing past him anyway, which should have been impossible. Just what was she seeing?

She lifted her hand, opened her palm; she turned it out, toward the eleven who now waited. The only person present who didn't turn to look at her was Teela. Teela had eyes only for her mother. She knelt in front of the dying woman. Even as a child, she'd known death when confronted with it.

So had Kaylin.

But this death was eternal, it was endless. This was the death that Teela saw every time she thought about her mother. It was this clear for her, this real, this solid. Everything else that had happened surrounding the death was part of it, wed to it, tied to it.

But...Mandoran's name was *not* a name, not quite. It was the slender remnant of something that seemed so thin it would no longer support life. It held form, but not a substance that could return to, or come from, the Lake of Life. The marks on Kaylin's arms were a brilliant, brilliant white; they burned.

She was used to this. It was a familiar enough pain that it was almost a comfort. It didn't involve helplessness; it didn't involve cowardice. It wasn't about death and the endless silence that followed it. It was just—heat. A little like burning. But it was a pain that sometimes conferred power.

Today, she took it in both hands. She understood what the name she had saved lacked, even if she could never put it into words. The thought made her smile because putting power into words was exactly what she intended to do. It was, she realized, like healing. Very like healing. The name knew its exact form and shape; it was injured, yes, but it retained enough of itself that she could press it between her palms and feel what it now lacked.

She began to heal it, palms pressed flat against each other. As she did, her palms warmed; the heat from the name was entirely unlike the heat that permeated the rest of her skin. The creature's great eyes—and it seemed to be *all* eyes, now—looked at her hands with interest. She tightened her grip. *No. This is* not *for you.*

He roared, but she'd pretty much had enough; she roared *back*.

Around them, history passed in streams; he had momentarily forgotten to, oh, eat them. Kaylin, on the other hand, had forgotten to catch them and bind them. But this was what her life was like: moments of intense focus, and moments of reaction. It had a beat and a rhythm that she both despised and accepted.

Hands cupped around Mandoran's name, she released it. And it hung in the air, emerging from the flat of her palm in a pale, pale gold that had dimension. It wasn't large, or at least it didn't start out that way; it couldn't have, confined to her palm. But she held the creature back, somehow, and she watched as it drifted, at last, into the green.

The other ten had appeared on their own, first as ghostly images of themselves—as real as the glass statues in the Hallionne's nightmares. But they had taken on form and substance and color, becoming as real as Teela while Kaylin watched. Mandoran did not do that. The name, his name, drifted toward them, as if it were part of an ancient tale, rendered in dragon voice.

They saw his name. Their eyes took on the gold of the name itself. They were silent, arrested; even Teela turned her head to see what had caught their attention, although no one even attempted to speak. Her eyes widened, as well, becoming, in that instant, as gold as the eyes of the people she had trusted and loved so much she had gifted them with knowledge of her name.

Mandoran coalesced *around* his name as Teela rose. She *stumbled*. She stumbled and she opened her lips on a name that Kaylin couldn't hear, but nonetheless knew. And then she looked at Kaylin.

At Kaylin, who was standing beneath a tree, the long skirts of the dress she'd worn for weeks now seeping—literally seeping—into the ground beneath her feet. Teela's eyes went from gold to green to blue in such rapid succession they seemed to be all of these colors, and none of them. And then she turned back to her mother, but this time, she ran. The stiff distance, the immobility of grief and knowledge, seemed to have deserted her entirely.

Or maybe, Kaylin thought, it was Mandoran's presence. He was the twelfth, here. They were complete. She could *be* the Teela she'd been the day her mother had tried to rescue her daughter. She could leave centuries of experience and wariness behind. She caught her mother in her arms.

And this time, Kaylin thought, there was no father, no High Court. Maybe this was a better story.

The creature's eyes were now as tall as Kaylin, and in them, she could see a stream of words, of language, that was in all ways too complicated, too big, too *other* for her. True Words sometimes made her feel small and insignificant, but not in the same way. She heard Nightshade's words, and she gathered them, but even as she did, she looked at the stories held in the eyes of something so large it might have devoured whole worlds—for she couldn't see a body at all; she might have been an insect standing on the bridge of a nose so vast she couldn't conceive of it as anything but land and sky.

On the day the twelve had come to the green it had been

sunny. Clear. The trees had whispered and the Barrani had heard their ancient voices and considered themselves blessed. But it wasn't a blessing; it was a warning. Not a threat—there was no menace in it, but there was sorrow. Grief. Loss.

On the day that the green had chosen to speak to the gathered and expectant members of the High Court, it had not spoken of power. She understood that it had *never* knowingly spoken of power. Instead, it spoke of loss. It spoke with the voice of Alsanis because it heard what Alsanis did not say; it struggled to understand what it heard. It spoke with the voice of Orbaranne, and the voice of Bertolle; it spoke with the voice of Kariastos. These were part of the green and yet separate from it; they heard the thoughts and the will of green and they interpreted it for those who came to seek their shelter.

It spoke of their weeping. It spoke of their pain. It spoke of the need they denied. They had made their choice. They had chosen one desire over another. They had locked themselves into the existence of the Hallionne, and they had done so *gladly*. But the sorrow had grown in their voices, and the joy of making the right decision—if there was ever any such thing—was only barely enough to sustain them. They chose to sleep.

Sleeping, they controlled far less of their voices; when they dreamed, they were closest to the green. And so the green heard. It heard, but it didn't understand.

On that single day, when all such speech, no matter how difficult, was allowed, the green spoke to the Barrani of the West March because the Barrani might understand what the green itself did not: loneliness. Abandonment. Grief. Love.

On the day Teela and her companions had come to the green, these were the heart of its story. And on that day, Teela's mother had died. The lost, the other eleven, then understood that they faced danger, death—or worse—and that they were *meant* to face it. They had been given to the High Court to be forged, as all significant weapons were, in the heart of the green; if, like poorly tempered blades, they shattered, it signified *only* failure.

They were children, at heart.

Maybe, Kaylin thought, as tears fell unhindered down her cheeks, people were *always* children at heart. What the green asked, they *heard*. They felt it *all*. It was so much in tune with who and what they were, they had nothing to temper it with. They had no way of resisting. The green, for that moment, was *of* them, *like* them. There was no home and no safety for them in any other place…so they clung to the green, and when the story was done, they held on as tightly as the living possibly could.

Kaylin doubted a mortal could have done it; there was nothing with which to anchor themselves to the green.

They found freedom in Alsanis. They found freedom in the green. But not love, not from the green; it wasn't living. It wasn't a person. If it moved, it moved slowly; if it changed, if it gathered knowledge, it was slow, as well.

Only Teela had been left behind. Teela had heard the green's story, and she had felt its resonance as strongly as her kin. She felt the loss, the shock of it, and the echoes, and the certain sense of its eternity, more strongly. She understood—she'd understood it then—what it meant for the people whose lives and names she had shared.

Only Teela was left behind.

Only Teela.

The green had devoted the whole of its power to protecting Teela from itself. In exchange for the life, for the *word,* at the heart of her mother. But Teela's name was connected to the names of the other eleven. They formed a bond, yes; they also formed a chain.

If they had not trusted each other with so much hope, and so much youthful optimism, the eleven would have vanished into the green and the things that lay beyond it. They couldn't. Because they lived and the words lived, and the bindings, so tenuous, held them. They were aware of Teela. And Teela? Was aware of them.

And they had waited. They had searched. They had troubled the green and the Hallionne. They understood that the world was made of words. That the living were. That everything that they had ever touched or shaken or destroyed had come from the words of the Ancients. But in all those words, in the ones they could touch and the ones they only barely infer, they couldn't find the words they needed to free Teela. To bring her...home.

They never stopped trying.

It was Eddorian who suggested their final solution. It was Eddorian who pointed out that entire *worlds* had been created from nothing, as laboratories for the Ancients, those absent creators who, like any neglectful parents, had spawned and moved on. If worlds could be created, if words that distilled the essence of love and hate, war and peace, birth and death, could define the fates of whole races, the words themselves had power.

They only needed to *find* the words that would allow them to re-create one small, isolated event in the past. They needed to save Teela's mother's life. The rest were inconsequential. If Teela's mother did not die in the green, Teela would not now be trapped and unreachable. Teela would, as the rest of them, finally be allowed to leave. She would be with them.

But...they had a Barrani understanding of power. They understood that the Hallionne had almost unlimited power within a small, focal point, and they had attempted to unmake Orbaranne in order to gain that for themselves. They wanted to change *one* small event. One small event, one minute, one hour in *one life.*

The green did not want Orbaranne's death. No more did it wish to lose Alsanis, and strangely enough, the eleven didn't wish to lose him, either. He was their cage, yes, but he was also the only home they had. They had grown into their confinement; they had played in the limitless possibilities of the space he governed; they had rested at his heart.

And yet, without power, they would never have Teela back.

They needed new words. They needed new possibilities. They needed, they realized, to destroy the green. It was the only other option available.

Kaylin shook her head. She walked away from the tree, the eyes of the creature following her. They were larger now; they were taller than Kaylin. They no longer looked like eyes to her, they were so large.

"Yes," Mandoran said, which surprised her. "We tried. We tried to summon a familiar. We failed. We tried again, and we failed."

Kaylin blinked. She felt—she heard—history continuing to unfold around her and she let it go now. She heard the green's voice, the green's incomprehensible voice, and she knew that today, the story the green told was the continuation of that earlier story. But now, the green understood a little bit more.

"And now, you have brought yours. Teela knows you," he continued, looking slightly surprised.

"What—what is a familiar?"

He smiled. It wasn't a friendly expression; it was full of the usual Barrani condescension. "Do you not understand, yet? Look at him, Chosen. He shows you *all* that he is now."

She'd been looking; it was hard not to. She could see the words coiled in him, and they were words without end. They *weren't* True Words. But they were words that had movement and strength and depth; they had shape and form. They were made of shadow and smoke and the type of light that strikes from a distance, like the light on forest floor.

"Do you understand?"

And the sad thing was, she did. In the familiar, in the small dragon, in whatever the small dragon was part of, she saw the words he contained. Some of them were words that felt familiar, shadows of True Words. Shadows of names. Some were words she was certain she would never see in life. And all of them were waiting.

All of them. If she spoke these words, if she asked the familiar to speak them, they would be *almost* true. Even thinking it, she saw the light ripple and change; she saw iridescence give way, at last, to gold.

And she understood *why* sorcerers of legend had risked entire worlds to summon such a creature. Because those sorcerers could speak the emerging words. They could, for a moment, be gods, be Ancients. They could change the course of history. They could remake a world. Nothing was beyond them because in the space the familiar occupied, that he was part of, all things were possible. All words were true.

All words could be true.

She lost the thread of the story then.

Because *all things were possible.* Because *history could be changed.* Because if she had the familiar and his power, Jade and Steffi would never need to die. They would never *have to* die. She could rewrite it all: her mother's death. Or Steffi's and Jade's. Severn's choice. Everything. She could remake the fief of Nightshade. She could remake the fiefs entirely. She could change the world so that the pain she'd suffered need never be suffered again.

And even thinking it, words emerged, as strong, as golden, as names in the Lake of Life.

She turned to Mandoran, and was surprised to get a face-ful of Teela instead.

That, and two hands, one on either shoulder, and a lot of teeth-rattling. Teela was blue-eyed and angry. She was not the child who had come to the green to be blessed and em-powered. She was the Hawk. She was the Hawk, except there were tears on her cheeks and her lips were trembling.

She had never come so close to striking Kaylin.

Kaylin didn't know Teela's name. Teela had never trusted her with it, not the way she'd trusted the eleven. But she knew that Teela wanted what they wanted: in the end, she wanted to be free. In the end, she wanted to join the only people she had truly loved.

Yet she was angry at Kaylin, right now, right here, for even thinking it—because she'd always known what Kaylin was thinking, from day one. She'd often belittled it because that was what Barrani did.

"Do not make me hit you," Teela said through clenched teeth. She threw one backward glance at her mother, now suspended, blood no longer running from multiple wounds. "Do *not* make me do this. I have seen this day every day of my life, kitling. Every. Single. Day. It drove me to kill my fa-ther, the single act I refuse to regret in a long history littered with regrets.

"Do you understand? This *made me*. It made me what I am now. Whatever you profess to love about me—it comes from this."

Mandoran came to stand beside Teela; he put a gentle hand on her arm. "Teela—" And then he stopped, his eyes wid-ening.

Teela's eyes widened, as well.

Mandoran turned to the others, who stood frozen as if hold-ing breath. "I can—I can *hear* her. I can hear Teela!"

"What. Did. You. Do." Teela grabbed Kaylin's left hand; there was no longer a mark on her palm. She froze, looking into the eyes of the familiar; eyes that now seemed to stretch halfway up to the sky, the words there multiple and endless.

"I—"

"Kaylin."

"I healed it, Teela. The name. I—I healed it."

Teela let go of her hand. She closed her eyes. Then she turned and threw her arms around Mandoran's neck; he laughed, although he was clearly surprised. Kaylin would have spoken, but there was something in the hug that made her feel like a voyeur. She wasn't part of Teela's life; not the way these people were.

But she understood what Teela's anger meant, what Teela was trying, around the shape of her own pain, her past, and her grief and loneliness, to tell her.

And Kaylin turned, at last, to the words.

CHAPTER 27

"I know," Kaylin said to a creature that was no longer small, no longer a dragon, no longer simply an annoying but unique pet. "I know what you are, now."

She felt the rumble of his voice; she felt the voice of the green. She understood that the moment was almost done, and she understood what she had to do, because she understood that it was all she *could* safely do.

She approached Terrano first; he frowned, the way any Barrani with little experience of mortals would. She tried not to hold it against him. She wasn't surprised to find that he wasn't solid; he had no flesh, nothing to impede the progress of her palm as she pressed it against, and then through, the center of his chest.

He frowned and stepped back. *No.* His lips moved; nothing else did.

Kaylin closed her eyes. "We don't have time for this. You can stay, Terrano, or you can go. But you can't live between, like this. The word at the heart of your existence here, the word the green has tried to somehow preserve, belongs here. Leave it, and go, or stay with it and become it."

"Terrano," Mandoran said.

But Terrano shook his head, his lips quirking up in an odd smile. "I can't go back. There's nothing for me. My family is dead now. I didn't even kill them," he added, without a care in the world, and without any sign of grief. "I waited for Teela. But I waited so we could *leave* together. There are worlds out there," he added. "Not like this one. Different. Better. We can be anything. We can be *nothing*. I won't. I won't do it. I *don't want it*." Terrano was part of Teela. Teela was part of Terrano. "Save her mother. Save her, and she won't lay her curse on Teela."

"It wasn't a curse."

"It *was*. Save her."

And at this moment, it didn't matter. "I can't do what you ask."

He laughed. "You are the *only* one who can."

And she wanted to. She wanted to do it because if she could, she could save all her own dead. There would be no ghosts to lay to rest. There would be no paralyzing, self-destructive guilt, no self-loathing, no *loss*.

"This is the lie," she told Terrano softly. "I didn't understand how lies could be told with True Words. And they can't. Everything you can say with a True Word *is* itself. But we don't speak True Words. We don't speak true language; we speak its echoes. We dimly understand the shape of the words—but they don't mean the same thing to two different people. They can't.

"This is the lie," she continued. She turned to the giant eye of the familiar. "I can see what you want. Can you see it? It's there. And beside it, the heart of what *I* want. The only thing I've truly, desperately wanted in my life; the only thing I would die for.

"And they're the same, Terrano. They're the same. There are some words that *can't exist* here, not in the real world. Not in our lives. We can daydream them. We can pray for them. We can hope, and plead, and grieve. But we can't make them real—because they *aren't*. There's no way back. And the lie is that there *is*.

"Maybe familiars can grant that. Maybe they have the power to make the lie real. I have to guess that's exactly what they can do. But—it's still a lie. Because it's not part of the real world. It's part of our dreams. It's part of our nightmares. It's part of the us that we carry around inside of our heads. But that's all it can ever be."

He stared at her for one long, frozen moment. "No," he said. "It's not. It's *not*."

And Teela said clearly, "Vote."

Her voice carried; it rippled through the green. It was, in all ways, a Sergeant's voice. Marcus would have been proud.

But Kaylin said, "It's not a matter for vote. Mandoran didn't have a choice. I'm sorry for that. But you've lived centuries since the day your mother died. So have *they*. If you can't go back, if you can't deny what those centuries of living mean to you, they shouldn't have to do it, either." She turned to Mandoran and said, simply, "I'm sorry. I can't undo it."

"I won't force that change upon anyone else. I can't. But I won't let you run wild. Hundreds of people have died because of you. I won't let you kill the Hallionne or destroy the green."

"If we die here, the names will be lost—"

Kaylin shook her head. "Chosen, remember? I won't let the words be lost to the green. I'll return them, in the end, to the Lake."

"Terrano," Mandoran said again.

But Terrano shook his head. "I can't. I can't do it. I love you. I love you all as if you're part of me. But I'd lose all my limbs first. I'd go blind, deaf. I can't do it."

Kaylin closed her palm into a fist and withdrew it. Terrano's eyes widened. They seemed, for a moment, to sparkle. His face lit up with an incandescent smile; it took her breath away. It took all of their breaths away. He began to fade. Even before he was no longer visible, he was no longer Barrani in appearance, but the warmth of his unfettered delight lingered like a pall.

When Kaylin opened her hand again, she wasn't surprised to see a mark there. A red mark, much like Mandoran's had been. It was a less complicated letter form, but it was thinner and paler.

She approached Sedarias next, because Sedarias was the de facto leader of this group, inasmuch as it could be led. As she'd done for Terrano, she pressed her palm against, and then into, her heart.

"And so, all our years of waiting and planning have come, in the end, to this? We are to be diminished and returned as a curiosity to the Courts that were willing to sacrifice us?"

The familiar roared.

She raised both brows in a look of autocratic outrage that was nonetheless cool and contained. "Oh?"

"He speaks only the truth," a familiar voice said.

Kaylin was surprised, because it belonged to the brother of Alsanis. She couldn't remember the moment at which he'd disappeared; maybe he hadn't.

"You have been part of Alsanis for a long time, even in the reckoning of your kind. You might remain as guest. Or as ward. He has heard your voices when ours were lost to him. If you make this choice, he cannot compel. He will not be your cage, Sedarias. But if you allow it, he will be...your brother."

"My brother," Sedarias said grimly, "attempted to kill me four times in my childhood." But even saying it, she smiled. "Yes, Lord Kaylin. Terrano found ways to leave us. It was not Eddorian who approached Iberrienne, but Terrano. He was always ambitious, always precocious.

"I will accept what you offer."

Where Terrano had faded, Sedarias grew more solid. Kaylin's hand was pushed out; she didn't withdraw it. She saw the faint tinge of purple to eyes that then shaded green as they widened; she smiled. She didn't speak. But she looked at Teela and Mandoran, and then turned back to Kaylin. "Will I remember everything?"

Kaylin was surprised. "Yes. At least—I'd bet money on it. Mine, even."

Sedarias looked confused, and then looked up at Teela. Kaylin left them and moved on. She offered them all the choice, and they accepted what Terrano had rejected. But when she approached Annarion, he frowned. "The mark you bear—"

She had forgotten about the mark. These days, she almost always did. It was now just part of her face. The High Court more or less accepted it. The Vale? Maybe that was part of the reason they had been so unfriendly—but maybe not. They were Immortal; she wasn't.

"Yes," she said tersely. "It's your brother's." To her great surprise, he looked concerned, not disgusted.

"You must be mistaken—"

"Believe that I know where it came from. It's on my skin, remember?"

He glanced at the *rest* of the marks on her skin, and she grimaced. "It is not like those."

"No, it's not. Maybe. Umm, I should tell you two things. Nightshade is Outcaste."

Annarion's eyes shaded to indigo.

"And he's the fieflord of, well, Nightshade. He owns the Castle there. Oh, and—"

"That is three things."

"Numbers are not my strong suit. He's here. He's the Teller."

"I see." He turned, then, to Sedarias, and offered her the slightest of bows. "It appears the world has changed since our incarceration."

"Oh, undoubtedly. Did you have some concerns?"

"Not until this mortal brought them to my attention." He left Kaylin and moved to join the group, and it was a group now; they were standing in the shadow of one gigantic eye; it was the whole of the sky in Kaylin's view, at least on one side of the world.

And the words—the words she'd wanted, the words that had taken the sheen of gold and truth, filled that sky. And she did want them. If Jade and Steffi had never died, she could live with Severn. She would probably be living with him. It hadn't been much of a life, compared to the one she'd built in Elantra with the Hawks—but she'd been happy then.

It was just *one* thing. It was just so *small*. If she could arrive *in time*. Just that. Just that one thing. She would save Severn, too. She would save him from the torture of guilt and the absolute knowledge that he was—that he could be—a cold-blooded killer.

"Kitling."

"Don't you have somewhere else you need to be?" Kaylin didn't take her eyes from the sky; she couldn't.

"Yes."

"Then go there. I'm fine, Teela. I've got this."

Teela slid an arm around her shoulder. "Yes. You do. You won't mind if I stay here anyway, just to be as annoying as you generally are when you worry at me?"

"I think the others are waiting for you."

"Oh, not me," Eddorian said, joining Teela. "I've seen a lot, but to be honest—and if I know Teela, you know how rare that is among our kin—I've seen nothing like this. Are you going to destroy the world?"

"I think I understand why Teela likes you," Valliant added. "Mortals are so unpredictable. You haven't come all this way to end the world, have you? It would seem a waste of effort. You could have just left this corner of it to us."

"Oh, leave the poor mortal alone," Serralyn told him. But they all came to stand beside her, watching, their eyes bright with genuine curiosity. Yes, they were as old as Teela—but they hadn't spent their life in *this* world. She couldn't tell who she felt more sorry for—the children or the rest of the Barrani.

She had a suspicion it was the rest of the Barrani, and that didn't bother her at all.

She turned back to the giant eye. "No," she told them all. Looking up at the creature, or across at it, she said softly, "Yes, it's what I want. But I also want wings. I want to be beautiful. I want to be strong. I want to be perfect.

"If every wish I ever had, if every *fear,* could become real, instantly, I would destroy the world. I didn't understand how it could happen, before. The stories about familiars—the ones we have—never make it clear. But I—I understand it now. What I don't understand is how any sorcerers survived summoning familiars. I'm not even a sorcerer. I can barely light a candle. I still can't do it reliably on command." She lifted her arms; her marks were now gray and flat. "You might recognize them. You might even be able to read them. I don't, and can't. But it's—it's a borrowed power. It's not mine. I don't control it. If you came to me because of the marks, I'm sorry.

"Close your eyes. Go back to sleep. We'll try not to wake you again."

The eye did not, predictably, close. Instead, the creature inhaled; the words that had filled the whole of a night sky were sucked into a maelstrom of other words, of different light, until they were lost. She reached out instinctively to try to... do what? She forced her hand back to her side.

She'd had the chance. She knew. She would have died for them. If it would end there, she thought, even now, she could do it. If there was some way to trade her life for theirs, with nothing else lost in the balance, she thought she could die. She was grateful that she didn't believe in ghosts, because she couldn't imagine facing the two girls to tell them that she couldn't take the risk. How would they ever believe that they had been important to her?

They would know you.

She frowned. "Who said that?"

"Who said what, kitling?"

They would know you, Kaylin.

"Never mind." The eyes were closing. Or at least, to Kaylin, it looked as if they were; it took her a few seconds to understand that they were actually shrinking.

You will do.

"Do for *what*?"

Worlds have been destroyed before. Not one. Many. And it starts, as it almost started for you, with one *moment.*

"And you couldn't *stop* it?"

All possibilities exist in me, some darker and some brighter than others. All words, all languages, all silences, all emptiness, all isolation. I am not the containment. You are. You are what stands between me and the world in which you live. Some of the words are *your words. You would recognize them. Many are not.*

"But I didn't summon you."

No more did you summon the water, Chosen. But she hears you when you call. The fire speaks your name. I did not come to you. You found me. You came to me.

The eyes were now the size of Kaylin, although they existed in the air without a face as a frame.

"Kitling—"

"I'm doing what I can, Teela," Kaylin said—in brusque Elantran.

She was surprised by the sound of Teela's laughter. Teela tightened the arm she'd draped around Kaylin's shoulder. "Yes. You always did. I remember the day you ended up in the lethe dealer's den—you'd run yourself practically to exhaustion. You didn't lose them," she added, fondly. "You were fourteen. I thought it extremely unlikely, with your sense of caution, you'd survive to see fifteen.

"But you did. And sixteen, beyond it."

"Teela—what did sorcerers do with familiars?"

Teela shook her head. "I didn't lie; I have no idea. I would have bet against their being real."

"With your own money?"

"Yes. And I actually have some, unlike some people."

I contain all words, the creature said. *But not all words can contain me. What would you have of me now?*

"Go to sleep. Go back to wherever it is the water and the fire go when they're dismissed."

I cannot return, Kaylin.

"You can't stay here," was her flat reply. She felt Teela's arm tighten. "You can't hear him, can you?"

"No. Probably for the best."

"Why can't you go back?"

Ask Teela to explain.

Kaylin did. She asked while she watched the eyes grow smaller still; they were now the size of her head.

"You can't summon elementals without understanding—fully—the name of the element. But the name is not the whole of the thing; you wouldn't survive the attempt to summon all of fire."

"How do you know?"

"It's been tried, historically. You spoke with the elemental Evarrim summoned."

Kaylin nodded.

"Could you dismiss it?"

"No."

"Why?"

"Because I didn't summon it. I wasn't its anchor."

"Exactly."

"I didn't exactly summon the small dragon, either, Teela."

"No."

"If the summoner dies, the fire can be contained—"

"In theory, yes. Sometimes the death of the summoner frees the fire; it returns to the plane from which it emerged. Sometimes the death of the summoner simply allows fire to burn. It cannot be extinguished by natural water. It cannot be extinguished at all if there is not another adept who can speak its name and forcibly contain it. Dismissing the element requires the name."

"I know fire's name."

"Good. What is the name of the small dragon? If you can't figure it out, one of us will—and if we do, and we survive the attempt to contain—and control—the familiar, it is us, not you, who will make the decisions."

Allaron approached. "Teela has always been like this," he said, his voice soft. "She makes threats that we all know are empty." He was, to Kaylin's discomfort, speaking in Elantran. Elantra hadn't existed when he had entered Hallionne Alsanis. "She's angry," he added, which was kind of like saying fire was hot. "But she hasn't lived the lives we lived. When the Lady was trapped in the nightmares of Alsanis, how did you reach him?"

Kaylin frowned. "I touched the Consort."

Allaron shook his head.

"What he *means* to say," Mandoran cut in, "is how did you catch Alsanis's attention? How did you speak to him without entering his domain? You did," he added. "We heard it."

"What did you hear?"

Mandoran frowned. He fell silent; Kaylin could almost hear them conferring in the privacy and intimacy granted by True Names.

Teela said, "They can't describe it."

"You've heard the ancient tongue—"

"Yes, but perhaps the particulars are not *appropriate* for the venue." She frowned and added, "They didn't hear it the way you heard it. They didn't have to. It was not something that could be contained in *our* words. I don't know what you did— but I think it's what you must do here."

"Alsanis heard you…speak. He knew, because you did, that you understood," Mandoran added.

Kaylin wanted to beat her head against something. She lifted her arms. The marks were gray, flat marks; they didn't glow.

"And we heard you, as well," he added quietly. "We heard, and we almost remembered. Speak to him as you spoke to us."

The eyes were smaller now. Smaller than her fists.

"I can't," she said softly. "I'm not where I was." She looked around the heart of the green; there were no corpses here. Vivienne was no longer bleeding to death. Teela was Teela, but the ten who stood gathered around her looked far more solid, far more real, than they had. The fountain's water was no longer red with ancient blood.

But the ground was not barren stone and dirt, and the trees— Ah, the trees. "It's almost over."

Teela nodded.

It is, the small dragon said. *It is almost over, and when it is done, I will be uncontained. I have done what I can to limit the damage I will do.* His eyes were the size of large cat eyes, and they were once again nested in the translucent face of a delicate, glass dragon.

But Kaylin shook her head. She raised an arm, mimicking Barian, and the small dragon alighted as if he were an eagle, a dream. She put him, gently, on her shoulder.

That is unwise, Kaylin.

She nodded. She heard Nightshade's voice; it was hoarse. She could no longer hear Lirienne. The blood of the green had billowed; the skirts possessed a very, very long train. They had no sleeves, but the fall of fabric had shifted; the silk was both heavier and warmer, the style of dress distinctly different. Only an idiot would attempt to run in skirts like these; Kaylin privately doubted that walking was a possibility.

But she gathered the endless yards of fabric over her left arm, and she made her way to the fountain; the basin was full and clear.

The sky was now a clear azure—and it had a sun. It was a familiar sun. Nightshade's voice was an echo. She turned, small dragon on her shoulder, to see Teela and ten of the lost children gathered around the fountain. They were talking, but half their sentences trailed off abruptly into either nothing or open laughter. It was as shocking in its way as anything that had happened in the West March.

Allaron lifted Sedarias off her feet and spun her around. Kaylin's jaw almost hit the floor; nothing about Sedarias implied indulgence or affection. Her expression was fixed, frozen, as Allaron lowered her to the ground—but her eyes were a deep, emerald-green.

They were facing out, away from the fountain's water. Kaylin saw the water rise; if they did, they didn't acknowledge it; they were thrumming with excitement, expectation, nervousness, as the green returned—Kaylin understood this now—to the world. Or rather, as the green left it. But this time, it left the Barrani in its wake, its story told.

"You said I found you."

Yes. He lowered his head, and spread himself more or less comfortably across her shoulders. *What am I, Kaylin?* The small dragon bit her earlobe. She cursed him in quiet Leontine, which, given the audience was mostly Barrani, didn't make much of a difference.

What am I?

"Kitling." Teela's eyes had lost some of their green.

Kaylin knew why; the small dragon's wings had grown. And grown. He was still mostly draped across her shoulders, but the wings now covered her like a cape. They were translucent, but caught sunlight in a way that suggested color. She felt them tighten, but they were warm, like the palm of a hand.

She was, she realized, both cold and tired. The sun didn't feel warm. Nothing did, except dragon wings—and they weren't wings now; they were too soft, too pliant, too shapeless.

She turned toward the water. It rose in a familiar column, a familiar shape. When it lifted an arm, extending a hand, Kaylin made her way across the very mundane, very solid, heart of the green. She lifted a hand in turn and placed it across a liquid palm.

He is not as we are, a familiar voice said. Her eyes were the color of every patch of water Kaylin had ever seen, simultaneously. They were open, rounded slightly in a way that suggested concern. Concern and stillness.

"I know."

You must answer his question, Kaylin. The form and the shape he takes now has no mooring. It will be all things at once. All things, and nothing.

"What kind of nothing?"

The water failed to answer. *Tell him,* she said instead, *the stories you tell us in the Keeper's garden. Tell him what he is to your kind.*

Kaylin exhaled. One hand in the water, she lifted the other; folds of translucent warmth rose and fell as she shifted position. Teela was standing apart from her cohort, watching as Kaylin was slowly engulfed in a cocoon that could be more felt than seen. She'd had whole days like this, when bed and sleep and silence were the only options that offered any comfort at all. She didn't think often of Steffi and Jade; she shied away from it now because it always cut. It always would.

But thinking of them left the same, invisible bruises. Because she knew she'd made the right choice and it didn't *feel* right. It felt wrong. All the if-only, all the what-if in her life had come back to this: it was done, and nothing she could do could change it. But…she could have. Because she had him and *he* could. And she couldn't grasp the words. No—that wasn't true. It was a lie. She could have. She could have taken that risk, could have spoken the lie in a way that made some sort of truth of it.

And she hadn't.

And she wouldn't.

How did you live with that? How did you look yourself in the mirror without seeing the face of a coward and a liar?

The small dragon bit her ear.

She inhaled. Exhaled. You lived with it the same damn way you'd lived with the deaths and the failure the first time. Badly. Badly, at first. But it was just another thing to hate. Just another thing to survive. She'd done it before, but honestly?

She'd been so certain that she couldn't. She'd been waiting for life to end, too afraid to end it on her own.

And she wasn't that child anymore.

"I can't give you words that won't come," she told the small dragon, looking up at the face of the water as she spoke. "But I'm not sure they would bind you anyway. I'm not sure they would give you form or shape or whatever it is you need. I'm not a sorcerer. I'm not immortal. I'm nowhere near ancient— although I'm going to feel like I am tomorrow. If I wake up.

"I understand how you relate to my life—my small, tiny life. You're my dreams. You're my daydreams. You're my what-if's. You're the way I torture myself at night, when sleep won't come, or sleep won't stay."

The small dragon was utterly still; he might, for a moment, have been made entirely of glass.

"But without some of those dreams, without the pain and the what-if, without the guilt, I wouldn't be a Hawk. When I was five I couldn't even imagine crossing the bridge. I stood on the outside of a life I thought I wanted, but I couldn't make myself walk over the river. I don't *know* what's possible, most of the time. Hells, on a bad day? I feel like walking across the street safely is impossible.

"You're not hope," she continued. "Because when I think of Steffi and Jade, I have *none*. I have the dreams of who they might have been if they were still alive. I have dreams about arriving in time to save them. You know what those dreams are. You saw them. You heard them.

"But you're the place hope comes from, and sometimes, that's the only thing that keeps me moving. So. I need you in my life. I need you like fire or water or air or earth. Without what you are, I'd be dead a dozen times over. More."

The small dragon tilted his head to one side. His eyes were now the size they'd been for almost all of his short life, or at least the part of it that overlapped with Kaylin's; his wings were not. But they thinned as she watched; she saw them as gauze now, but they were as long as the skirts of the reformed dress.

"I don't want to live without you, because I don't think I can. I don't think anyone can, not even Teela."

"I heard that."

Of course she had.

"But I don't know how to chain you. I don't know how to cage you. I don't know how to control you or keep you—"

He bit her ear again.

She briefly considered strangling him. His wings tightened, but they were so thin now, they had no strength. Yet they were warm. She let the water go, and gathered an increasingly tattered cape around her shoulders and her arms, hugging it as if it were fabric and she were a child again.

But she wasn't a child. She wasn't surprised to see the wings slowly vanish, but their warmth remained as the small dragon sat up on her shoulder and yawned.

"Kitling."

She looked up at Teela, whose eyes were now blue. Happiness—no, joy—apparently didn't last long.

"What is he doing?"

Kaylin frowned. "What do you mean?"

"Can't you see them?" Teela said something about survival instincts in distinctly uncharitable Leontine. She marched over to Kaylin, her boots striking stone hard enough to break it. She caught both of Kaylin's wrists. "What are you holding in your hands?"

Kaylin started to say "wings," but fell silent; she was holding strands of multicolored light. They were becoming insubstantial, even as she tightened her grasp. "Mostly…nothing."

Teela shook her. "Look at your *marks*."

She did, and her eyes widened. The marks were no longer the dark, coal-gray they were when they were inactive. Nor were they gold or blue. They were multihued and scintillating; they looked very like black opals; like the eyes of the small dragon.

The small dragon hissed. It was the continuous exhalation that passed for laughter in winged lizards. And he was that now. He looked unchanged.

She poked him. He bit her finger, but not hard enough to break skin. He did hiss at Teela, in an entirely less amused way, when she failed to let go of Kaylin's wrists.

It was never about names, the water said, from a remove. *You are mortal, Kaylin; not even the Ancients could contain the whole of the elemental you hold in your hands. They did not try.*

"But what is he now?"

What was he when you found him? He is not less. He is, I think, more. But he has chosen. He has named you.

"But—"

It is not a name in the Barrani sense of the word, no. But the story you told him was the story he chose. He will not be what he almost became, she added softly. *His power is dependent upon yours, and you are...mortal. But while you allow it, he will remain with you.*

"If I ask him to leave, will he leave?" He bit her ear.

I have one task to perform for the green. There is one other mortal who waits in the greenheart; he waits for you. Tell him to come to the waters of my fountain.

"Why?"

He will understand. Or perhaps he will not; the greenheart is not what it was when last he ventured into it. She lifted a hand again. *Come home. Ybelline is concerned.*

"About me?"

No, Kaylin. But she will speak to you if you approach her. It is time.

Kaylin walked out of the heart of the green, and into the heart of the green, Teela by her side. "I'm fine," she told the

Barrani Hawk. She even gave her a shove in the direction of the rest of her kin. "I'm honestly fine. There's nothing that can hurt me here."

Teela snorted, but it was a halfhearted sound; she wanted to join the others. After a short while, she did.

Nightshade wore the crown of the Teller and the Teller's robes; they were unchanged. Kaylin's dress was not. It was still green, but the skirt hadn't shrunk any. She grabbed the train and bunched it in her arms.

The Lord of the West March stood by the side of his Consort, his eyes blue. The Warden stood between Nightshade and Lirienne, his eyes even darker. Ynpharion stood behind the Consort, his hand on the hilt of a sheathed sword. His eyes were the usual blue of caution. The Consort's eyes, however, were the color of Kaylin's dress.

Annarion was speaking with Nightshade. The others were loosely grouped around them. Kaylin glanced at Severn; Severn was watching, but he kept his distance from every other person in the clearing. He smiled as Kaylin stepped into view.

Where's Iberrienne?

I believe he chose to retreat.

To where?

The Hallionne Alsanis. It wasn't entirely his idea; the eagles came.

Kaylin swallowed, and Severn offered a wry grin. *He is invited to remain in Alsanis with his brother. I may visit if I so choose.*

You can't kill him in the Hallionne.

No, was the grave reply.

She shouldn't have been happy. She was. *Oh. You're to go to the fountain.*

She expected confusion; what she got instead was surprise. Surprise and hope. He kept them mostly to himself as he approached the basin into which clear water ran. Kaylin followed, dragging material. She could see nothing in the fountain itself but water.

Severn, however, didn't have that problem. He reached into those waters, and when he pulled his hands clear again, he was carrying two familiar blades.

"The green," Lord Barian said, "favors you, Lord Severn. I admit that I was ill-pleased when the blades chose their wielder the first time you made your way to the heart of the green."

"And now?"

The Warden's smile was soft; the blue faded from his eyes. He looked up at the bowers of ancient trees; he looked down at the waters of a fountain which was no longer dry. "The green works in mysterious ways. My blessing is not required, but if it brings a measure of peace, you have it; were it not for your willingness to surrender what you had once been given, we would not now be here."

He turned, then, to Kaylin. "Let the train down, Lord Kaylin. Let it be. It is the green's way of making clear that you have told the tale the green would tell if it could speak as we speak. The Vale will see. The Vale will know."

But Kaylin shook her head. She glanced over her shoulder at the sound of laughter—Barrani laughter. "I think the Vale would know anyway."

CHAPTER
28

Kaylin woke to snoring. This wasn't unusual, but usually, the snores were hers. Tonight, they belonged to a delicate, translucent dragon. He hadn't spoken a word since she'd left the green. She'd spoken several—to him, in Leontine, and they'd had the usual effect.

The room itself was large, but it was cool and quiet; it had windows—and these windows, at least, reminded her of home. Of her old home. They weren't glassed or barred; they opened to air and breeze. The fact that neither of these—air or breeze—appeared to come from the West March in which the building was situated no longer bothered her; she was in a Hallionne, after all, and the Hallionne had a very tenuous sense of place.

The Warden had repeated his offer of hospitality, of course, once they'd left the green. But even offering it, he gazed—with green-eyed longing—at the facade of the Hallionne Alsanis. The Hallionne itself no longer appeared to be made of shadow-mired crystal; nor did it look like a tree, a cliff, a river, or a patch of random, grass-covered dirt. It was, it seemed, made of stone and glass, and its spire—for it had one—ascended to neck-cramping heights.

Which didn't stop Kaylin from looking.

The Guardian—Lord Avonelle—had been waiting for them. Her eyes were blue and her expression was as friendly as winter. The bitter, killing kind. But she'd offered the Teller and the harmoniste a perfect obeisance. Kaylin privately thought it almost killed her. She then offered them a phrase so archaic Kaylin only barely recognized it as High Barrani.

The Warden's eyes remained a cautious blue; they didn't verge into gold. But he was utterly still. Absence of movement often meant surprise, in the Barrani. Of course, it often meant "you're about to die if you don't move," as well.

Lord Avonelle's eyes were a shade darker when Teela joined the Teller and the harmoniste; they were a color that Kaylin couldn't describe when the rest of the lost children, save only Terrano, followed. She only barely offered the Consort a correct gesture of respect; Kaylin thought the snub to the Lord of the West March wasn't actually deliberate. He didn't seem to care.

He looked—as Barian did—to the south, where a spire Kaylin had never seen stretched toward the clear sky.

"Alsanis."

Kaylin couldn't think of the lost children *as* children; it was patently ridiculous. They were older than she was, at least chronologically; they were taller, stronger, and more confident. They smiled, yes, and sometimes they laughed outright; they were slightly more demonstrative than most Barrani—but then again, everyone was.

Regardless, they left the green. They offered the Consort

the obeisances that Lord Avonelle had given strictly for form's sake, and they held them—as Kaylin had once done—until she bid them rise. She took her time.

She is cautious, Lirienne said.

Kaylin understood why. She knew she should be as cautious, but it was much harder for her. Teela trusted these people.

We trust, when we are young, Lirienne replied. *And when trust is broken—and it is, Kaylin; that is the nature of our kind—we learn caution. We learn wisdom. The gaining is never pleasant. There is not the insignificant fact that they intended to destroy the Lake of Life.*

She started to argue, and stopped. It was true. *They wouldn't do it now.*

That is my suspicion. It is the Lady's suspicion, as well. If she is to trust the truth of your supposition, it will take time. The young, he added, *are infamously impatient—but these were considered our best and our brightest. They will wait.*

Lord Avonelle didn't bow to the cohort. Her expression made the Consort's long pause seem friendly and thoughtful in comparison. She did, however, say, "Alsanis offers his hospitality to all who return from the green."

Sedarias nodded stiffly, a regal, downward tilt of chin. "We have already been thus informed, Guardian, but we appreciate the courtesy you have shown us." She broke away from the group and approached Nightshade. "Lord Calarnenne."

"Sedarias."

"Escort us to Alsanis. If there are to be guests and the halls are to be open, we hope to be better prepared than you have found us." She held out one commanding arm.

Kaylin felt her jaw drop when he smiled ruefully and accepted what was only barely a request.

She does not do it for his sake, Lirienne said quietly, *but for Annarion's. There will be trouble there, I think, but not yet. Tonight, tomorrow, there will be only celebration, only joy. Joy comes seldom, kyuthe, and where it does, it must be savored.*

Kaylin glanced at Avonelle's shuttered face. She felt Lirienne's very real laugh in response. The laughter stopped abruptly as Severn stepped into Lord Avonelle's view. *If your Corporal is wise, he will avail himself of Alsanis's hospitality for the duration of his stay.*

He's been—

She is aware of what he now carries. She is aware that the green has granted him what her kin have been denied, time and again, when they abased themselves in the heart of the green. What she herself has been denied. It is only barely acceptable when she is passed over for a Lord of the Court.

Which, technically, he is.

Yes. Technically. He is not what you are.

No.

This is not the first time he has been granted such a gift; the first time, it was considered theft and trickery.

Because it's so easy to lie to the green.

He was amused. He kept it entirely off his face, although he spoke as he offered his sister an arm. *It is not difficult—at all—to lie to the green; it is difficult to make oneself understood at all.*

Kaylin waited for Severn as the Barrani began to drift toward the Hallionne. He shook his head, and carefully removed yards and yards of fabric from the crook of her elbow.

"It's going to get dirty—"

"It won't. Trust the green. Wear it, as it was meant to be worn."

She started to argue, but the small dragon sat up and squawked in her ear. "I swear, you bite me again and you'll be walking home."

She'd walked, as if she were part of a solemn procession. Her legs hurt, her arms felt so heavy she could barely lift them.

What she wanted at this very moment was to crawl into her bed—the bed that was splinters and feathers—and sleep for three days.

But the Barrani of the Vale came, standing to either side of the procession of which she was only part. They were silent. Only two of them detached themselves from the crowd, but she recognized them: Gaedin and Serian. They quietly saw to the fall of her train, and they took up positions of honor at her back.

She wanted to tell them that they'd been instrumental in saving them all, because the shortcut had given her the knowledge necessary to save Teela. She even opened her mouth. But Serian's warning glance caused her to shut it again. She wasn't used to being the center of attention; she tried to enjoy it, and failed. But Diarmat's many lectures served one useful purpose: they kept her moving. She held her head high. She didn't fumble or even speak.

Not until the gates of Alsanis rolled open to welcome them all, because waiting for them in the long, grand hall, with its many lights and its many, many arches, was a Barrani man who was not, she was certain, Barrani at all.

"No, Lord Kaylin," he said, and he bowed to her in full sight of the Vale. It was a low, graceful, *perfect* bow. "I am not. But the Barrani are my distant kin, and I have longed, for centuries, to speak with them again. I bid you welcome. I bid your Lord Severn welcome, as well. While you live, my doors will always open at your command, and you will always find sanctuary and welcome here.

"You will find welcome, should you return, in the green." He then turned and offered an equal bow—to the Consort. "Lady."

She offered the Avatar of Alsanis her hand; he accepted it, bowed over it, and then placed it on his arm. "Come. Food is waiting, and water, and wine." He turned, and then turned again. "Barian."

The Warden bowed.

"In the long years of my exile, I have heard your voice, and yours alone of all your kin. Join us."

Dinner was a loud and, for Barrani, raucous affair. Even Kaylin, sick to death of Barrani functions and politics, found herself laughing—in particular when Mandoran and Allaron decided to have an impromptu eating contest. A certain amount of decorum was present wherever the Consort generally was, but the cohort didn't seem to be aware of it, and if she was offended in any way, the Consort kept it to herself.

But Kaylin suspected, given the green of the Consort's eyes, that she wasn't.

She wasn't even upset when Kaylin, flagging to the point of nearly dropping her chin into dessert, excused herself from the table and the rest of the immortal merriment. Severn escorted her as far as her room—and in Hallionne parlance, it was a long walk. Nor did the Hallionne intend her to share, at least not with anyone who wasn't a small shoulder ornament.

The last thing she remembered clearly was getting out of the dress and hanging it in a closet. Well, draping it over a hanger in a closet. She left the green boots beneath it. She expected both the closet and its contents to be gone in the morning.

She didn't remember reaching the bed, but it was pretty hard to miss something this large. The small dragon sat up and warbled.

There was no noise in the room. But it wasn't anything in the room that had woken her.

In the distance, Nightshade was angry.

She rose and dressed, and this time, she took clothing from the pack leaning at a tilt against the far wall. The closet was, of course, a nonentity in the room. She made her way to the door, and from it, into the halls; her eyes adjusted to the light slowly, but it didn't matter. She had the strong feeling she could stumble through Alsanis wearing a blindfold and she'd fail to trip, fall, or injure herself in any way.

She made her way to Nightshade. Clearly, she was still half-asleep if an angry fieflord was an emergency to run toward and not away from.

"He is not angry with you," Alsanis said. His Avatar had appeared beside her between one step and the next.

"What is he angry about?"

"Annarion."

Which would make it the world's shortest happy reunion. "What has Annarion done?"

"Sedarias feels it best that she and her friends remain here for some time. She does not feel it is wise to leave the Hallionne in a state of ignorance. The world has changed since they first left it, and to maneuver in what remains, they must have knowledge."

Kaylin nodded because this made sense.

"Annarion will not be remaining."

"Wouldn't that make Sedarias angry?"

"Sedarias? Why would she be angered?"

"If she doesn't feel it's safe—"

"She understands Annarion's reasoning, and she accepts it."

"Nightshade doesn't."

"No. He wishes Annarion to remain here. He has... insisted? Commanded?"

And Annarion had refused. No wonder Nightshade was pissed.

"Calarnenne is Outcaste. It is not—or will not—be safe for him once he leaves the Hallionne. It would not, I think, be safe for Lord Iberrienne, either, but Lord Iberrienne will remain. The Consort has done what she can for him," he added, his voice softening. "But he was much damaged by his interactions in the outlands. Will you tend him?"

But Kaylin shook her head. "No. He is—he will—recover." She hoped. "But I don't want him to be what he was."

"You are afraid Lord Severn will kill him."

"It's not a fear—it's a certainty. He can't do it here; he won't try. But Iberrienne as he is now is not a danger to anyone."

"Eddorian will protect him."

She thought it should work the other way around.

"Why? Eddorian was the elder of the two. Eddorian understands some of what was done; he cannot, however, heal the damage. He will ask you, I think."

Kaylin said nothing. She approached an open door in a hallway full of closed ones.

"They are brothers," Alsanis said softly. Kaylin realized that the term, brother, meant something to Alsanis that it probably didn't mean to anyone else here. She didn't argue. Instead, she stepped into the room.

It wasn't a bedroom; it wasn't a sitting room, either. It was a Barrani courtyard, open to a cool, gray sky, and artfully dusted with fallen leaves. Both of the men in its center stiffened and turned as she entered. She recognized them. One was Annarion, and the other, the fieflord of her childhood. The Teller's tiara no longer graced his forehead.

Nightshade was not the only one who was angry; Annarion was pale with it, his hands in curved half fists by his side. The Barrani turned to face her.

"Leave," Nightshade said.

She ignored him. "Don't even think," she added, "of using your mark against me. Not here. The Hallionne won't allow it."

"Oh?"

"I'm betting my life on it. Are you willing to bet yours?"

His brows rose, and a very tight smile tugged at the corner of his lips. Turning to his brother, he said, "May I have the privilege of introducing Lord Kaylin?"

Annarion was not amused. Not even close. The mark on her cheek seemed to inflame, rather than quell, his fury. He was not, however, angry at her. "I am aware of who Lord Kaylin is." He bowed to her. He bowed stiffly and very formally, granting her a respect that she would never have gotten in the High Halls. "Private Neya," he added, accenting the name in Elantran.

"It's my preferred title, yes." She hesitated, and then said, "I heard you're leaving the West March."

He seemed unsurprised. "Yes. I have spoken with the Lady, and she has agreed to allow me to accompany her party back to the High Halls. I will present myself to the High Lord."

"You're not a Lord of the Court."

"Not yet."

Kaylin felt her stomach drop, the way it would have had she jumped off a cliff. Her brows rose, her eyes rounding; she couldn't stop them. "You can't seriously be thinking of taking the test of name?"

"Can I not? My brother has, and he has survived."

"I don't mean to insult you," she said, in even Elantran. "But you didn't do a *great* job of holding on to it the last time."

His brows rose, and color came to his cheeks. He didn't, however, argue.

"Look," she continued, when Nightshade failed to speak, "you can go to the High Halls. But the name—"

"I will have *no standing* in the High Court unless I take—and pass—that test. And I require standing. In the end, we all will."

"If you fail, your name will be lost!"

He stared at her. "Of course."

She stared right back.

"You cannot think that I would fail a test that even a mortal could pass?"

"Everyone else in the history of the High Halls who *has* failed hasn't been mortal."

"I am aware of that. My brother all but insisted you undergo that test."

She started to argue, and faltered. "I am not," she said, with greater dignity, "his brother or his kin. I'm—as you point out—merely mortal. One of the masses. If I failed, he lost nothing."

For some reason, this made Annarion more angry, not less. Kaylin was used to judging Barrani mood by eye color; in Annarion's case, it wasn't necessary. "Is this what he told you?"

"He didn't need to say it," she replied, gentling her voice. "I've worked with Barrani for almost half my life. I understand most of their attitudes."

"Marking someone was considered barbaric, even in our youth. Did you agree to this?"

"Why are you even asking the question when you already know the answer?"

His brows rose; his lips twitched. He looked very much like his brother then. "I wish to hear my brother's defense."

"He doesn't *have one.*"

"No. But even that admission would tell me something; it is why he refuses to speak. Can you bear that mark and not understand even this about him?" He looked at Nightshade. "Brother, what have you become in my absence?" His voice broke.

Kaylin felt it like a blow, and couldn't say why. She lifted a hand almost involuntarily. "He gave me his name. Annarion—he *gave me his name.*"

Nightshade's eyes darkened. He said, and did, nothing. Not even in a way that Annarion couldn't hear.

Annarion stared at his brother's graven face. "Teela asks me to tell you, Private Neya," he said, "that two wrongs don't make a right. She expects this to mean something to you."

Kaylin winced. Teela would be listening. Of course she would. And she'd probably have about a hundred things to say about it in the morning. She considered taking the portal paths and hoping that she landed someplace close to Elantra just to avoid them.

"But, Lord Kaylin, understand the difference: his name was his to offer, just as mine was mine to offer. What you did not offer, he should never have taken. And he would not have, when I knew him. He would not have." He turned to Nightshade then. "How can time change a man so?"

"I owe you no explanation," Nightshade said softly. "Nor do I owe the High Court one; I am Outcaste. The matters of the Court are not—"

"You can say that, even now, when you came as Teller?" Annarion demanded, his voice rising.

"The crown came to me."

"Will you play these games with *me?*"

Nightshade smiled. "All of the best games are for the highest stakes."

Kaylin thought Annarion would hit him. She stepped between them, facing the younger man and seeing, beneath his fury, his bewildered pain. "You were gone," she said. "You were lost. Do you think it meant nothing? Do you think it caused no pain?" She hesitated; he marked it.

"Teela's not happy."

"Teela is never happy. You'll have a few centuries to get acquainted with this fact." She caught his arm. "Come back to your room."

"Do you think to protect him?" Annarion demanded.

Kaylin shook her head.

"Do you think, then, to protect me?" He laughed. He laughed out loud; it was a bitter, but genuinely amused sound.

Kaylin tightened her grip on his arm; the small dragon hissed.

Annarion's brows rose. "I beg your pardon?"

The dragon squawked.

"If you do not watch your tongue—"

"Wait, wait—you can *understand* him?"

Annarion looked confused. "Yes."

She turned narrowed eyes on the dragon, who shrugged his wings and refused to meet her gaze.

"Lord Kaylin—he is yours and you can't understand him?"

She exhaled. She turned to Nightshade, whose eyes had lightened slightly. "Can you understand a word he's squawking?"

"No, Lord Kaylin." He met—and held—his brother's gaze. "I have given you what advice I can. If you will not consider it, if you will not accept its hard-won wisdom, I will leave you."

"I will return home."

"There *is no* home, Annarion."

"There must—"

"I am *Outcaste.* If you wish to earn the scorn of the Court, you may come to visit the fiefs—but you will find no home to your liking there."

"Our line—"

"You will recall our cousins? Their children hold the line."

Annarion's eyes darkened. "And you dare to tell me that I am not to take the test of name? You can stand there and talk to me of *unnecessary* risk? I am severely disappointed in you, Calarnenne. You have abandoned the responsibility of our family and our line; do not even dream of demanding that

I do the same." He turned, Kaylin still attached to his arm, and walked away.

Go with him. If I am not to strangle him with my own hands, I would not have him perish. I am, however, seriously tempted; I have not been this angry since...

Since you last saw him?

Or perhaps just after. You will find him a staunch ally in future—if he survives. He is young. He will not become someone you would approve of when he is reckoned adult by our people, but while your lives overlap, he will be someone that you can understand. And perhaps you will understand him better than I.

Teela is almost as old as you are, and I approve of her.

You do not know all of her history; no more do you know mine. Annarion's, however, is within the grasp of your brief life to date. Mortals have a saying: Be careful what you wish for. It is...vexing. I will not see you in the West March again.

Kaylin was halfway down the hall when Nightshade added, *I am in your debt, Chosen.*

When Kaylin returned to her room, Teela was in it.

"I assume Alsanis okayed this?"

Teela shrugged. Her arms were folded across her chest, and she stood—instead of lounging across a convenient flat surface. "I want to warn you not to interfere," she said. "But I hate to waste my breath. What are you going to do with him?"

"Annarion?"

"Of course."

"I'm not sure I'm going to tell you," Kaylin replied, removing clothing as she made ready for sleep, attempt two. "Especially if I don't want him to know."

"She has you there," another voice said. Mandoran appeared in the doorway, balancing a tray that had ten people's worth of food on it.

Kaylin's jaw dropped.

"What?" Teela said, slowly relaxing her arms. She glanced around the room and eventually ended up on the bed. Sideways.

"Nothing." Kaylin stopped undressing and felt, for a moment, at home. Mandoran wasn't Tain, but Teela was absolutely Teela. "Did you come to say goodbye?"

Mandoran laughed. Kaylin fell almost instantly in love with that laughter. It held affection, knowledge, and sheer delight.

Teela glared at him, which made him laugh louder.

"She's not staying," Mandoran said.

"If I weren't feeling lazy," Teela told him, "I'd leave. You could have my conversation for me and I'd be spared the effort."

"You're—you're not staying?"

"Don't make that face."

"Your eyes are closed, Teela. You can't see my face."

"I have the expression etched in memory. And I can see what Mandoran can see when he's not laughing so hard he's crying."

Which, of course, made him laugh more.

"I was going to stay. Not for long. But...I can hear them now. They can hear me. They can truly speak to each other. They don't need me here. Whereas you?"

"I'm not a child."

"No, of course not. If you were a mortal child you'd be under Marrin's wing, in the foundling hall; I actually pity the people who are stupid enough to try to hurt any of her orphans. But you're going to be living with a dragon. You have the Halls of Law. You're no doubt going to have an ambitious and disenfranchised Barrani Lord, and you have the world's most annoying pet."

The small dragon squawked.

Mandoran's eyes rounded just before he fell over laughing. "Don't ask," he said, holding up a hand. "I'm not going to tell you what he said; Teela would only kill him. Or try. Don't worry about Teela," he added. "She's not like Annarion; she's tough."

"Annarion—"

"He believes in people. Even when Teela was one of us, she believed in no one *but* us, and it took her some time to come around. Annarion's more optimistic." His smile faded. "He's very upset about his brother. We're worried that he'll do something stupid. So, Teela's going back to Elantra with you."

Kaylin was so grateful and so relieved she had no words. Which is why she didn't miss the next thing Mandoran said.

"And I'm coming with her, too."

"What?"

"Well, I thought I'd take a look at the High Halls, visit what's left of my family, and maybe join the Hawks."

"Do *not* make that face, kitling," said the Barrani Hawk whose eyes were still closed. She was massaging her forehead. "He can't possibly get into more hair-raising trouble than you did."

"But he's—"

"You were *thirteen* when you started tagging along with us. If you're telling me Mandoran can get into more trouble than a cocky thirteen-year-old mortal..."

"Yes?"

"You're wrong." She opened her eyes. "Mandoran is leaving now."

"Am I?"

"Yes. You can leave the easy way or the hard way."

He laughed. "If it makes you feel better, Lord Kaylin, she's not going back strictly because she's terrified of the new ways you'll attempt suicide."

"I have never attempted—"

"It's because of Eddorian. Iberrienne has not been declared Outcaste, yet. The Emperor—a *Dragon,*" he added, with genuine disgust, "has ordered his death. But the Barrani might be able to contest this; the execution is not a public matter. At least, if Teela's right. She's going to talk to the High Lord, the Hawklord, and possibly the Emperor. I think she thinks it would help you, as well, although we're not quite clear how."

Because Severn wouldn't be sent out again. Severn wouldn't have to kill Iberrienne.

Mandoran headed toward the door after Teela propped herself up on one elbow.

In the darkness of Alsanis's night, Kaylin heard singing in the distance. She glanced at Teela, or at what she could see of Barrani profile. "Can you hear the Consort?"

"Yes. She has always had a beautiful voice."

"Do you know the song?"

"Yes."

"Teela—"

"You saved them. You saved them when they didn't know they wanted to *be* saved. I didn't know it, either. They were only barely aware of their names; not aware enough to use them. They couldn't hear me—but they couldn't hear each other, either. Now we can. They're not what they were. But I'm not what I was.

"What we did was stupid. It was reckless. It was willful."

"You mean the names?"

"You see? You *have* been paying attention."

"Do you regret it?"

"No. I will. I'm certain I will. But, no." She fell silent for a long moment. "I had no idea, when I picked you up in the Halls, that this is where it would lead."

Kaylin closed her eyes.

"I think Nightshade had hopes—and that angers me."

"Teela—"

"If you're going to tell me that at least they were hopes you approved of, save your breath. Every criminal feels justified in his actions. Every single one. Are you going to keep interrupting me?"

"No."

"Hah. Where was I? Even if I had known, I wouldn't have risked you. If the choice had been mine, you would have been packed up and sent back to the Halls."

"I had the dress."

"Yes. Which is why the choice wasn't mine. It's odd. My life has revolved around the day my mother died. My life in the High Court has been tainted by it; my family has certainly changed because of it. Only when I was in the Halls of Law was it irrelevant. And I valued that. I valued it highly. You were part of that life, not this one. I was enraged when Nightshade marked you. I was even less happy when you got lost and wandered into the test of name. His hand was behind it. Don't bother denying it.

"But now, I'm wondering what he saw that I didn't—or couldn't. I wouldn't have risked you here. Yet without you, we would—all of us—still be trapped. You've freed them. You've freed Alsanis. You've freed Barian."

"His mother's not thrilled about that."

"Even better. I never liked my aunt. You're interrupting again."

"Sorry."

"You're interrupting an *apology*. From me."

"It's the shock."

Teela chuckled.

"You don't owe me an apology."

"Not yet. But I will. You've proved yourself here. But you're still a mortal. You're still our mascot. I don't think I can untangle that. I don't—truth be known—want to."

Kaylin relaxed into the pillow. She was surprised, because her throat tightened. She was, she realized, crying. But it was dark, and she was silent. Maybe Teela wouldn't notice.

"What have I told you about crying?"

"It makes me look weak and pathetic."

"Hasn't changed."

"I *am* weak and pathetic."

"You don't even understand what those words mean, kitling. You are, however, an idiot. But you're *my* idiot, and I don't intend to let go of you. Sedarias will keep court here for longer than your natural life. If I stay, you'll age and you'll die before we're done. I'll miss it all.

"I hate mortality."

"Not keen on it myself."

The dragon hissed.

"Oh, shut up, you," Teela told him.

★ ★ ★ ★ ★